THERE WERE SPARKS OF DESIRE IN HER EYES, MATCHING HIS OWN. . . .

Jonas laid his hand next to Kate's satin-smooth cheek, and she pressed her face against his palm. He lowered his head closer to hers, pausing just short of her lips as if to wait for the pull of gravity to close the maddening gap. When at last their lips finally touched, they were like two inventors about to embark on a tricky experiment—excited about what they were about to do, but cautious and careful, wanting to thoroughly test each new stage before proceeding to the next.

Kate stared up at him, her mind anticipating what it would feel like when they got past the experimental stage. "I have an idea," she whispered.

"Dammit, Kate! This is no time to be thinking up ideas." With that he crushed her mouth with his own, intent on clearing her mind of anything but the sensations of being kissed by him.

PETTICOATS AND PISTOLS

by

Margaret Brownley

A TOPAZ BOOK

TOPAZ
Published by the Penguin Group
Penguin Books USA Inc., 375 Hudson Street,
New York, New York 10014, U.S.A.
Penguin Books Ltd, 27 Wrights Lane,
London W8 5TZ, England
Penguin Books Australia Ltd, Ringwood,
Victoria, Australia
Penguin Books Canada Ltd, 10 Alcorn Avenue,
Toronto, Ontario, Canada M4V 3B2
Penguin Books (N.Z.) Ltd, 182–190 Wairau Road,
Auckland 10, New Zealand

Penguin Books Ltd, Registered Offices:
Harmondsworth, Middlesex, England

First published by Topaz, an imprint of Dutton Signet,
a division of Penguin Books USA Inc.

First Printing, July, 1995
10 9 8 7 6 5 4 3 2 1

 REGISTERED TRADEMARK—MARCA REGISTRADA

Printed in the United States of America

TO ROB COHEN
*Whose imagination and vision
makes her an inventor
in her own right. . . .*

Chapter 1

1896

An explosive boom ripped through the air that cold dismal day in January, rocking the little town of Hogs Head, Indiana, and sending its residents running for cover.

Corraled horses reared and galloped in circles, their high-pitched whinnies coupled with the frantic barks of dogs trying to escape. Hogs squealed, cows bellowed, and chickens flew across barnyards, scattering feathers as freely as outlaws spending counterfeit.

The fur of Mable Cummings's cat stood straight up as the terrified animal shot a black streak down Main Street. The cat barely made its escape before men and women, mostly farmers and their wives, began crawling out from beneath the various horse-drawn vehicles parked on the dirt-packed street. Brushing mud and half-melted snow off their clothes, they were joined by others who stormed out of the wooden frame buildings that lined both sides of the street.

"Kate Whittaker's gone too far this time!" someone snarled.

"I'll say she has. And if the sheriff won't do somethin' about her, then it's up to us!"

The crowd grew in size as it stomped down Main

Street, past the general store where Aunt Hattie, its hard-of-hearing owner, remained blissfully unaware that her niece had once again stirred the town into an uproar.

Sheriff Eugene Williams looked up from his desk and, seeing the angry mob sweep past his diamond-paned window, grabbed his hat and fur-lined coat and dashed out the door.

"Hold your horses—"

"Get out of the way, Sheriff."

"Yeah, you've had your chance. . . ."

The crowd forged down Main Street over the railroad tracks and past the wooded area to the road called Rocking Horse Lane. Kate lived with her aunt and uncle in the tall clapboard house that stood at the end of the road, amid a small grove of winter-bare cottonwoods.

It was the general consensus of the town that the four-story house, counting the cellar and attic, was an eyesore. Two front windows were boarded up from a previous explosion. A pile of rubble was all that remained of the chimney toppled two blasts prior. It was a tribute to its builder that the house still remained standing after so many years of mishaps caused by Kate's inventions gone amok.

The townspeople approached the house in wide-eyed silence, but only because it was difficult to be heard over the deafening roar that seemed to rise from the very foundation.

The grizzled sheriff raced ahead of the crowd and held up his hands. "Stay here!" he yelled, glaring at anyone who might possibly challenge his authority.

"What is that awful noise?" someone shouted back.

"That's what we're going to find out." It was so cold, his breath formed a white misty plume in front of him. "Now, stay!" The sheriff turned, tugged on the upturned brim of his hat, and walked with purposeful strides through the sagging gate and up the icy path leading to the front porch. His fervent hope was that the whole kit and kaboodle wasn't about to be shot to kingdom come. It sure in hell sounded like it.

Patches of snow still remained from the blizzard that had hit the area weeks earlier in December. From the looks of the dark ominous clouds overhead, more snow was on the way.

Shoving his hands in his coat pockets to protect them from the cold, the sheriff stepped over a piece of rusted iron half buried in a mound of snow and walked around a wooden barrel attached to a strange-looking contraption. This wasn't the first time he'd plowed a path through the cluttered yard of the Whittaker home. Not by any means.

Twice as many complaints were lodged against Kate Whittaker than were filed against all the saloons and whorehouses in town put together. His lack of success in dealing with the brash, impetuous young woman made him wonder if he was cut out for law enforcement.

He had inherited the job of sheriff from his father, who was still considered a hero for ridding the town of all nine of the troublesome Brannon brothers some thirty years ago.

Stepping over a heap of scrap wood, the sheriff almost slipped on a patch of ice. He grabbed hold of a wagon wheel and eased himself onto what was left of the front porch. Muttering beneath his breath, he gulped a bracing lungful of air before raising his fist to the door. His father had it easy; he never had to deal with the likes of Kate Whittaker.

* * *

Kate heard the urgent pounding on the door, but only because her latest invention had run out of fuel. The motor had sputtered and coughed, then stopped all together.

She examined the rag carpet stretching across the floor of her aunt's cluttered parlor and smiled to herself. Her newly invented carpet cleaner worked better than she could have imagined. Not so much as a speck of the powdery plaster that had fallen from the ceiling during the explosion moments earlier remained on the nap of the multicolored carpet.

Delighted with the performance of her carpet cleaner, she wished some of her other projects worked half as well. The fuel-driven buggy, for example, which had resulted in the loss of several perfectly good runabouts and had caused considerable property damage. Then there was the dynamo, which she had been trying to improve since installing it in the basement three years prior, and the boiler that was constantly overheating and was responsible for blowing out the windows.

If she didn't think of a way to keep the dynamo from backfiring soon, or the boiler from blowing up, there wasn't going to be any plaster left on the ceiling—or anyplace else, for that matter.

The banging on the door persisted and finally grew too loud to ignore. "Oh, what is it?" she muttered to herself.

Rushing to the door, she brushed aside the wisps of reddish blond hair that had escaped from the confines of her bun, straightened her soot-covered apron, and cracked the door open in a way she hoped would discourage her unwanted visitor.

"Why, Sheriff . . ." She swung the door open wide and glanced in surprise at the sea of angry faces staring at her from over the top of her leaning fence. "Is something wrong?" Her heart fluttered in alarm as she searched the sheriff's face. "Nothing's happened to Aunt Hattie or Uncle Barney, has it?"

"No, no, nothing like that."

"Then what is everyone doing here?"

Her question brought an angry response from the crowd.

"Quiet!" the sheriff yelled. He turned his attention back to Kate. "Miss Whittaker . . ." He cleared his voice. He'd known her since she'd first come to stay with her aunt and uncle twenty years ago at the age of five. "Kate . . . as you know, we've had many complaints about your d'turbin' the peace . . ."

"Disturbing the peace? Oh, you mean the little bang—"

"It was more like an explosion . . . a very loud explosion."

"Oh. I didn't think it was that loud." Kate gave the scowling mob an apologetic smile. "I have one little problem to work out with my dynamo—"

"There's always a problem with one of your machines!" cried Thelma Paine, the town seamstress. "Look what you made me do. You scared me so much, I stabbed myself with a needle." The dark-haired matron held up her thumb for all to see. A humorless woman, her tightly puckered face resembled a schoolgirl's first sampler.

Kate refused to feel sorry for the woman. If Thelma would use a proper sewing machine instead of doing everything by hand, she wouldn't have injured herself. Kate had little patience with people who refused to try new ways.

"That's nothing," shouted Wayne Jenkins, the town barber, who, out of respect for the fine head of hair that once donned his now shiny pate, answered to the name of Curly. "Look what the blast made me do to poor Narrowsmith."

All eyes swung to the tall skinny man who was minus one half of his drooping soup-strainer mustache. A sympathetic gasp rose from the crowd and Kate covered her mouth with the tips of her fingers. "Oh, dear. I really am sorry, Nicholas." She was the only one who called him by his given name. "I never meant—"

"You never meant ... that's all you ever say!" This sharp retort came from Smoky Joe, the owner of the Red Rooster Saloon. His thick smelly cigar clamped between his teeth, Smoky glowered at Kate. He never forgave her for the day her fuel-powered buggy ripped a hole in the side of his building. "I lost two bottles of my good whiskey—"

"I'll pay you for it," Kate promised. "I'll pay you all back as soon as the United States Patent office grants ..."

Her voice was drowned out by the loud groans rising from the crowd. She'd promised to pay back the town for years.

"You ain't gonna get no patent!" Curly spit out.

"You ain't gonna get no husband, either," scoffed Thelma, still nursing her sore finger. "No man worth his salt is gonna want a woman who's always covered in soot."

"Or one that goes around blowin' up the house," agreed Curly. "It gives a man hives just to think about it." He gave his bald head a vigorous scratch.

The sheriff replaced his hat. "This is your last warnin', Kate. One more problem and I'm gonna hafta lock you up in jail."

Kate's eyes widened. "Jail?" To her knowledge the jail had not been used for anything other than storage for the entire twenty years she'd lived in the town.

"D'turbin' the peace is a serious o-fense," the sheriff explained as if to justify his threat. Then, for the benefit of the still-angry crowd, he added, "And don't you forgit it."

Kate watched the sheriff maneuver back through the obstacle course that was her yard. When he reached the safety of the gate, she slammed the door shut. Disturbing the peace, indeed!

As she returned to the parlor, her frown turned to a smile upon noticing little Jimmy Moresall scooting down the stairs on his behind. Kate had rescued Jimmy from one of the orphan trains that stopped periodically in Hogs Head on the way to Colorado and other points west.

Jimmy's parents had been killed during a train derailment when he was only three. It was during this same accident that Jimmy lost the use of his right leg. He'd lived in various orphanages for the last four years, and when it appeared that no one was willing to take on the boy, he was put on the orphanage train, in Kate's estimation, like he was nothing more than a piece of damaged cargo. Even now, after six months, it made Kate furious to think about it.

Admittedly, she had grown quite fond of him, but she was concerned that Jimmy might have a more serious problem than she was equipped to handle. For one thing, he refused to use his crutches or be seen in public. She knew nothing about handling such emotional problems, and even less about raising children.

She did know, however, he should be in school with other children his age. He was quick to learn and had shown so much interest in taking things apart and putting them back together, Kate had given him his own workbench in the cellar, next to hers. When she had time, she taught him reading and arithmetic, but mostly they worked on motors together. It gave her great pride to think the boy could dismantle a motor faster than a hog could finish a crib full of corn.

But did that sharp-toothed, grating Mrs. Bagelbauer, director of the school board, care a fig about that? She did not! Instead, she kept pressuring Kate to put Jimmy in school. Kate was all in favor of school, of course. But it wasn't as if that was the only way to get an education.

In any case, how in heaven's name was she supposed to get Jimmy to go to school if he wouldn't even use his crutches? Or leave the house?

Besides, her first concern was to find Jimmy a permanent home. She grew more worried with each passing week. It was becoming increasingly evident that her chances of finding him a desirable family were slim if not altogether nonexistent.

During the six months that Jimmy had been living with her, Kate had personally contacted each suitable family in the county trying to talk the locals into taking him. None of these families wanted to be saddled with a child who couldn't walk, couldn't labor in the fields or otherwise pull his own weight. Kate couldn't blame the farmers, she supposed. Most were struggling to feed their own families and could ill afford to take on another child.

She only wished that that annoying Thelma Paine hadn't declared an interest in the boy. Lord forgive her for thinking it, but the woman was a fossil. She still lit her home with candles, for goodness' sakes, and didn't even own as much as a proper cookstove! Kate would no sooner allow Jimmy to live with the woman than she would allow him to live with Madam Miranda and her "working" girls.

Kate waited until Jimmy reached the bottom step

before picking him up and carrying him into the parlor. "Can you believe it, Jimmy? The sheriff accused me of disturbing the peace. What do you think? Did I disturb the peace?"

Jimmy giggled, his blue eyes shining with glee. "I think you made a lot of noise." Jimmy was seven years old, but Aunt Hattie said he was too smart to be only seven. So Jimmy told everyone he was sixteen. Kate didn't like the boy stretching the truth, but Aunt Hattie, who wasn't above doing a bit of age manipulating herself, said he was only exercising his right to be whatever age he darn well pleased.

Jimmy was small for his age, allowing Kate to carry him with relative ease to Uncle Barney's favorite chair. Returning to the carpet cleaner, she studied the motor attached to the round metal canister. The carpet was clean, but it had been difficult to work the cleaning wand across the floor. There was still too much suction.

She had only recently converted to an oil engine. Oil was considerably less expensive than gasoline, but it was more difficult to regulate the amount of explosive mixture flowing to the motor. The cleaner had previously sucked her aunt's good carpet off the dining room floor and when her uncle tried to save it, the machine gobbled the shirt off his back.

During the last week, she had installed a throttle valve to control the power of the engine. All that was needed was a little adjustment . . .

She dropped to her knees and fiddled with the valve. She then grabbed hold of the crank and gave it a vigorous turn. "Just a nice quiet start." She talked to her inventions like most people talked to their pets. She winked at Jimmy, bringing an even wider smile to his face. "Ready?"

Jimmy, who loved nothing better than to watch

Kate at work, covered his ears and held his eyes shut tight. "Ready!"

It wasn't a large blast by any means. Actually it was nothing compared to the noise the dynamo had made earlier.

If the sheriff hadn't been standing in front of the house talking to Curly, he probably wouldn't have even heard it.

Chapter 2

Word of Kate's arrest swept through the town like dust on a windy day. Upon hearing the disturbing news from one of her customers, Kate's Aunt Hattie immediately turned the CLOSED sign in the window of the general store she'd owned for more than a quarter of a century, and tore down the weathered boardwalk toward the jailhouse.

One arm raised high over her head, she shook her fist and shouted her objections for all to hear.

"How dare they put my dear sweet Kate in jail!" Her black silk skirts flapped around her thick legs and stout ankles. The rustling sound of silk against her lisle stockings made her sound like a braking steam engine. Her black woolen shawl completed the picture by billowing from her shoulders like thick black smoke.

She wore her faded orange-red hair parted in the middle and pulled into an untidy bun at the nape of her neck. The startling color of her hair did nothing to distract from her uncanny resemblance to an ironclad locomotive steaming through town. Anyone who saw her coming knew to quickly step aside.

Kate's Uncle Barney, having heard the news from Smoky Joe, who heard it from his aunt's friend's sister's daughter, left his harness shop to rush to the jailhouse. A tall man, with a walrus mustache and graying sideburns, his severely arched eyebrows had been carved high into his hairline after years of living with his unpredictable wife, giving him a look of perpetual surprise and confusion.

Today, his expression conveyed more perplexity than usual as he barreled down Main Street, reaching the sheriff's office at the same time as his indignant wife.

"How could you let them do this?" Aunt Hattie demanded.

"Oh, fine. Blame me, will you?" Uncle Barney tore open the door to the sheriff's office, practically ripping it off its rusty hinges, and held it ajar for his wife.

Upon seeing her niece behind bars, Aunt Hattie rushed inside the cramped office and burst into tears. "This is dreadful, dreadful, absolutely dreadful."

"Don't worry, Aunt Hattie. It's not really as bad as it may seem." Kate pushed against the bars of her jail cell and the door sprang open. Giving the sheriff an apologetic shrug, she ushered her aunt and uncle inside.

"Isn't it locked?" Uncle Barney asked in amazement.

"The sheriff said there was something wrong with the lock."

Uncle Barney looked aghast. "My word. Who ever heard of a jail without a proper lock?"

"Don't worry, Uncle Barney. I'm on my honor. Sit down." She pointed to the small sorrowful cot next to the back wall.

Her aunt took one look at the lumpy mass that passed as a mattress and shuddered.

"I hope you don't . . . catch anything. You never know who's been in here." She glanced around the tiny cell as if she expected to see the remains of a previous prisoner.

Kate didn't want her aunt to worry about her. "I don't believe anyone's been here. I had to wait for Sheriff Williams to empty the cell. He's been using it for storage for years. Now he has no place to store his Fourth of July decorations."

"It serves him right!" Aunt Hattie exclaimed. She ran a finger along an iron crossbar and stared with disapproval at the amount of dust she'd gathered. "This is an outrage. What is Eugene thinking?" She brushed her hands together. "All you did is make a little noise."

Uncle Barney shook his head with impatience. "There you go, Hattie. Talking about things you have no knowledge of—"

"What did you say? Speak up. Why are you always mumbling?"

"I said it was a loud noise!" he yelled, making Kate flinch.

"I hardly noticed it," Aunt Hattie protested. "I was sorting through my new shipment of calico," she explained to Kate, "and I heard this tiny little pop . . ." she glared at her husband.

"That's because you're deaf in one ear and can't hear out the other."

"What did you say?"

"I said—"

"Uncle Barney, please . . ." Kate's Aunt Hattie refused to admit she had a hearing problem and no matter how much anyone harped on the problem, no one was going to convince her otherwise.

Squeezing her uncle's arm meaningfully, Kate quickly changed the subject. "I think I know how to solve the problem with my carpet cleaner. It's the fuel regulator."

"What's wrong with the fool alligator?" Aunt

Hattie asked, glaring through the bars at the sheriff, who was sitting with both feet propped on his desk.

"Fuel regulator," Kate repeated, this time louder. "I turned it the wrong way and too much fuel was injected into the motor. All I have to do is turn it the other way and it will work perfectly." Thinking of how close she was to success made her heart pump with excitement. "This is it. I just know it is. I'm so close, I can taste success. We're going to be rich!"

"Rich?" Aunt Hattie repeated, her eyes bright with interest.

Uncle Barney winked at Kate. "Nothing wrong with your aunt's ears when it comes to finances."

Kate took her aunt and uncle by the hand. "My carpet cleaner works. Or at least it will work, once I regulate it."

Aunt Hattie beamed with maternal pride. "I always knew you were a genius." Her face grew serious. "But you promised to let me sell it in my store."

"I haven't forgotten," Kate said, releasing their hands.

"And you won't let those two awful men, Shears and Rhubarb, get their money-grabbing hands on it?"

"That's Sears and Roebuck . . . and no, I won't." Her aunt would never forgive the two men for starting a mail-order house and infringing, as she called it, on her business.

Her aunt sniffed in disdain. "You won't believe how many people order their goods from the Shears, Rhubarb catalogue."

Uncle Barney opened his mouth as if to correct his wife's mispronunciation, then apparently changed his mind. "It's a free country, Hattie. They can order their goods anywhere they damned well please."

"They can order the same merchandise at my store at a lower cost if you don't count postage, and they won't have to wait none, either. I've lost over half my customers."

Aunt Hattie had been so incensed when the catalogues first arrived in town, filling up the entire length of the train station, she conducted a one-woman crusade. For days, she marched up and down Main Street carrying a sign of protest. Uncle Barney was appalled, but Kate secretly considered it her aunt's finest hour.

The catalogues mysteriously disappeared and naturally everyone blamed Aunt Hattie, who, though she voiced her hearty approval, staunchly denied having anything to do with it. Secretly, Kate suspected that her Uncle Barney, tired of eating the miserably charred meals Kate had prepared for him in her aunt's absence, was the real culprit. But of course, she never voiced her suspicions.

Once the catalogues had disappeared, Aunt Hattie hung up her picket sign and returned home. Peace was once again restored to the Whittaker home, allowing Kate to hang up her apron, so to speak, and once again concentrate on her inventions.

Now Kate tried to appease her aunt. "Don't worry, Aunt Hattie. Your customers will be back. Just as soon as the novelty wears off."

"I don't care what they wear when they shop. They can shop in their undergarments for all I care."

Uncle Barney rolled his eyes to the ceiling and ignored Kate's silent plea for patience on her aunt's behalf.

"We'll get every last one of your customers

back," Kate promised. "Believe me, as soon as I get the patent for my carpet cleaner, we're in business. They'll flock to your store from miles around."

Aunt Hattie folded her arms across her chest. "That'll serve Shears and Rhubarb right."

"So when are you going to apply for the patent?" Uncle Barney asked.

"As soon as the sheriff lets me out of jail." Kate turned to her aunt beseechingly. "Maybe you should go home and check on Jimmy." Although she was standing directly next to her aunt, she lifted her voice so her aunt could hear every word. "Jimmy was upset when the sheriff took me away. Fortunately, Curly agreed to stay with him. I told Jimmy you and Uncle Barney would take care of him until I return."

"Well, of course we'll take care of him," her aunt declared, patting Kate on the arm. "Don't you worry about a thing."

The door of the office flew open and in walked Quincy Litton, the editor of the *Hogs Head Gazette*. He tipped his derby to Kate. "Good afternoon, Miz Whittaker. Barnard." He pointedly ignored Aunt Hattie, who glared at him. The two had feuded for years, ever since the day he had yanked an obituary for one of Aunt Hattie's friends to make room for a paid advertisement for Dr. Hammonds Brain Pills and Smelling Salts.

The feud turned into an all-out battle on the day he headlined the news on the front page that the first Sears, Roebuck Consumers Guides had come to town. The sheriff had been forced to post a watch in front of the newspaper office to keep Aunt Hattie from physically attacking the man.

Now Quincy pulled out his writing tablet and glanced around as if to decide who to interview first. "Howdy, Sheriff. Thought you might do me the honor of answering some questions." He was a short, hefty man whose ill-chosen plaid suit made him look as bulky as a whiskey barrel. His fleshy face was divided by a large bulbous nose anchored by a horseshoe mustache.

The sheriff lifted his feet off his desk and ran his palms along the side of his head to flatten his hair. He hadn't been interviewed by the editor of the newspaper since he rescued Mable Cummings's cat from atop the Haywards' silo. "Be happy to."

Quincy sat on a ladder-back chair and reached for the pencil tucked between his ear and hat. "How does it feel to have a live prisoner behind bars?"

Aunt Hattie leaned toward Kate. "What's he talking about? A wide lizard?"

Kate repeated what Quincy said, taking care to enunciate clearly. "A live prisoner. He wants to know how the sheriff feels about having me locked up."

Aunt Hattie's face grew red with rage. "Don't you dare answer that question, Eugene!"

"I have to answer it, Hattie," the sheriff said. "This is the editor himself."

"I don't care if he is a creditor. You can find another way to pay back what you owe."

Litton rose to his full four-foot-eight height. "Don't you start with me again, Hattie. I'm only doing my job. Folks expect me to report the news and you ain't got no right to tell me what I can and can't print in my own newspaper."

Hoping to avoid any further misunderstanding on her aunt's part, Kate repeated what the editor said, word for word.

"Report the news?" Aunt Hattie gasped incredulously. "Like you reported Ethel Hodgkin's death?"

"Dying ain't news. It's a fact of life."

Aunt Hattie sniffed in contempt. "You want news, Quincy, well I'll give you news. You print one unkind word about my niece and you'll never find another Pollocks Crown Stogie in my store!"

Litton snapped his writing tablet shut. "Then I'll order my stogies from Sears and Roebuck!"

"You'll what?"

"You heard me. Sears and Roebuck!"

Insults flew back and forth as Aunt Hattie and Quincy tried to outshout the other.

"Aunt Hattie, please stop," Kate begged. But the two ignored any attempts on her part to restore order. When the arguing duel showed no signs of restraint, Sheriff Williams pulled out his gun and fired a single bullet into the ceiling.

Aunt Hattie and the editor fell silent, but they continued their combat with visual stabs. Finally, the editor stuffed his writing tablet back into his pocket. "I'm not taking any more of this. I'll talk to you later, Sheriff." He stormed from the office, slamming the door shut behind him.

"Good riddance!" Aunt Hattie called after him. Clearly thinking herself the victor, she brushed her hands together and looked unbearably smug.

Uncle Barney, whose eyebrows had ridden a tad higher during the shouting match, shook his head.

The sheriff sighed and ran his fingers through his thinning hair. "Now look what you've gone and done, Hattie. How can I earn any respect in this town when I can't even get my name in the newspaper?"

"Don't you worry about a thing, Sheriff," Aunt Hattie said magnanimously. "I won't hold you to blame even if your name is in the newspaper. Now if you would be kind enough to let my niece out of this horrible place you call a jail, we will be on our way."

The sheriff folded his arms across his chest. "I'll let you out tomorrow, Kate."

Aunt Hattie gasped. "You're going to keep her in this awful cell all night?"

"I have no choice, Hattie. It's my job."

"Well, maybe it's my job to make sure that I no longer carry your favorite pickles and you can't get those through any ole catalogue!"

"Aunt Hattie!" Kate exclaimed. "You can't bribe the sheriff."

"I ain't bribing no one," Aunt Hattie insisted. "I'm just informing him of an inventory adjustment."

"Well your invent'ry a'justment just got you a free night in jail," Sheriff Williams growled.

"What?" Aunt Hattie glanced up at her husband as if to confirm what she thought she heard. "Did he say he was going to keep me here?"

Uncle Barney nodded his head and looked suspiciously unfazed by the sheriff's latest threat. "I'll be back to get you in the morning." He patted Kate on the shoulder. "Don't you worry your head none over Jimmy. I'll take good care of him. Have a good night, Hattie." With that he walked out of the cell and quickly left the office. Watching him, Kate could have sworn she heard him whistling softly to himself.

"Well, I never!" Aunt Hattie declared, her hands on her hips. "You just wait, Sheriff, come election time." The town hadn't held an election in years, but that didn't faze Aunt Hattie. "I take back what I said earlier. I *will* blame you for having your name in the paper and I'll make damned sure that everyone does likewise. And another thing . . ." On and on she went, reciting every real or imagined misdeed that could possibly be held against the sheriff.

Kate shook her head in amazement. Her aunt may have a hearing problem, but there was nothing wrong with her memory. Meanwhile, Aunt Hattie ignored Kate's attempts to calm her down, and barely paused for breath as she continued her diatribe.

The sheriff lifted his eyes to the small bullet hole in his otherwise pristine ceiling and muttered. "Lord, help us through the night."

Chapter 3

Spring had finally arrived in Waller Creek, Iowa. No one was happier to see the long dreary winter come to an end than Jonas Hunter. He rose early that morning in late April, long before dawn had broken or the roosters had begun to crow, threw on a pair of canvas overalls and, since it was still cool, a flannel shirt, and hurried outside to join his father and brothers in the barn.

All seven of the Hunter men were similar in stature. They stood lean and tall, with broad shoulders and sturdy muscular arms.

Though his physique marked Jonas as a Hunter, that's as far as the resemblance went. He was the only Hunter offspring to take after his mother's side in coloring and facial features. His dark wavy hair and soft brown eyes made the heart of every milk-maiden and farm girl for miles around flutter in anticipation.

Lately, though, he'd fallen into the annoying habit of thinking up ideas for his inventions at the most socially inept times. As much as he hated to admit it, the local girls seemed to have grown hopelessly dull in recent years. Not one had bothered to read a book or even a newspaper. It truly amazed him how many hours women were willing to while away with idle chatter and useless gossip. They never seemed to grow tired of ruminating over which farmer's son had taken a fancy to which farmer's daughter. A second, though no less passionately pursued, topic of discussion favored by the gentle sex was French fashions.

Who cared what they were wearing in Paris? Sometimes out of sheer boredom, he grabbed his companion and kissed her firmly on the lips just to keep her quiet.

While this method succeeded in keeping the young woman in question too occupied to speculate on which of their friends was nursing a broken heart or in romantic pursuit—or whether the Parisian designers were thinking to widen or narrow (or shorten or lengthen) skirts—it did little to combat the lack of intellectual stimulation he thrived on. For him, hours of mindless chatter were enough to extinguish even the most ardent desire.

As disconcerting as this was to a man of Jonas's passionate nature, nothing was quite as upsetting as what had occurred the night previous when Stephanie Schroeder had broken down sobbing during the Waller Creek Spring Barn Dance and declared for all the world to hear that he had no right to make a woman think he was interested in her when it was perfectly clear he was not.

Even the fiddlers had stopped playing at the height of her outburst. A hush had settled over the crowd as everyone turned to stare. "I am interested," he'd stammered.

"Oh, no you're not!" she'd stormed. "You stopped right in the middle of kissing me and jotted down notes for your inventions."

It was true, of course, but she neglected to mention how she had spent nearly the entire evening describing every last tedious ruffle and piece of lace she'd seen while on a recent trip to New York.

"Come on, Stephanie, you know how my being

with you makes my mind work in the most amazing ways. I can't help it if you make me think up so many wonderful inventions. You're truly an inspiring woman."

It was clear to him that Stephanie didn't want to be an inspiration. No woman did.

Just thinking of what had occurred last night at the barn dance made him shudder. He never meant to be insulting or in any way hurtful to her. Maybe he expected too much from a woman. Maybe men and women weren't meant to talk to one another. It was the only way he could think to explain the diversity of interests between the sexes. Certainly it would explain why Stephanie's eyes glazed over at the mere mention of one of his inventions.

Still, the other men didn't seem to have trouble. Never had his brothers complained about the local women being dull. Quite the contrary.

Maybe it was just him. This latest incident made him vow to try a bit harder to concern himself with local gossip and fashions. Maybe then his mind would be less inclined to wander.

He walked through the gate separating the main house from the vast vegetable garden, and followed a dirt path leading to the chicken yard. It wasn't the first time he'd tried to mend his ways. If it hadn't worked before, why would it work now? If only he could find a way to make a woman feel flattered rather than insulted when he thought up an idea in her presence.

It wasn't as if he failed to give credit where credit belonged. As a gesture of appreciation, he named his inventions after the woman who had done the inspiring. It seemed only fair. Among his achievements was a Betsy tin can opener and an Annie-Mae scale for weighing chickens. For his trouble, he got little in the way of gratitude and once got a black eye when Annie-Mae threw the scale, complete with one of those newly bred Rhode Island Reds, in his face.

The same hen was waiting for him now when he strolled into the chicken yard. Upon seeing him, she clucked furiously and flew to the roof of the coop. Ole Red didn't appreciate anyone messing around with her nest and she didn't care who knew it! Sighing, Jonas leaned over to turn off the machine that kept the coop a perfect seventy-two degrees year around, and provided four hours of extra light each day.

He reached into one of the nests and picked up a still-warm egg.

He held it up toward the rising sun and examined it; a smile crossing his face. The egg was considerably larger than a regular-sized egg, and there were twice as many of them. His little experiment worked!

He quickly gathered up the rest of the eggs and strolled back to the house. If his experiments continued to reap such rewards, chicken would no longer be a Sunday-only treat. Why, people could have chicken every day of the week if they wanted.

Who would have thought that kissing that nice, but ruefully passionless, Stephanie Schroeder would give him the idea of putting a light in the chicken coop to increase egg production? He would be eternally grateful to the woman, even if she did embarrass him in front of the whole town.

He finished the rest of his chores quickly. He was anxious to ride into Waller Creek. Maybe that letter from the United States Patent Office had finally arrived.

Just before noon, he rode into town and tied his horse to the weathered hitching post in front of the brick-faced post office. Mr. Evans, the postmaster, greeted him with a nod and gathered up his creaky bones from an even creakier chair.

"Anything for me?" Jonas asked. He'd made this trek nearly daily for three months now, except for when his trip had to be postponed due to the Sabbath or blizzard conditions. It had been a bitter cold winter, lasting weeks longer than usual.

The postmaster shuffled along the back wall and pulled a letter from the H slot. "Sure do look like it." He slid the letter across the rough-grained counter.

The envelope bore a return address from the United States Patent Office. Jonas picked up the letter and let out a yelp.

Mr. Evans grinned. "That the letter you been waiting fer, son?"

"You bet it is!" Jonas tucked the official-looking envelope into the pocket of his overalls. It was a day to celebrate. If things worked out as he hoped, he could probably afford to fly Stephanie and the others to Paris and let them ogle over French fashions to their hearts' content.

He hurried outside to his dapple-gray horse. He patted his pocket. A letter as important as this was best savored in private.

He mounted his horse and raced out of town, heading for his father's farm. "We're rich!" he shouted at the top of his lungs. His rawhide hat bopped against back; his tawny brown hair was ruffled by the wind. "Rich!" Just wait until his father heard about this!

He thundered past several farms on the way to his family's. He cast a covetous glance at the Morrises' steam-driven harvester that was too big to store in the barn. Jonas still thrilled at the memory of seeing that machine in action last fall. It cut a swath forty-five feet wide as it rumbled through the fields. It would take dozens of men days to do what that machine had accomplished in hours. If only he could talk his father into purchasing one. It would save so much time and energy, it would pay for itself in one harvest.

Jonas picked out his father's stooped figure in the distance and a surge of guilt put a damper on his jubilance.

Walt Hunter, owner of the largest farm in Waller Creek, suffered swelling in his joints that made movement slow and painful. This last winter had definitely taken its toll.

The five older Hunter boys blamed their youngest brother for their father's failing health, saying he spent too much time with his inventions and not enough time on chores. Jonas hated the farm; he had other plans for himself, other dreams, other worlds to conquer. He couldn't help it. For twenty-two out of his twenty-eight years he had tried to be the son his father wanted him to be, but he could no longer pretend to be something he wasn't. He was an inventor, not a farmer. Still, as necessary as it was to follow the dictates of his heart, it was hard to keep from thinking he'd let his father down.

Seeing his father's stooped figure behind a horse-drawn grain drill intensified the guilt. If only he could convince his father to buy one of those gas-driven tractors. So what if it meant mortgaging the farm or going deeper in debt? Why, they could seed the entire farm in less time than it took his father to seed a single acre. Jonas was convinced such a machine would pay for itself in a single year's time.

Jonas rode to the older man's side, waving the letter in one hand. Maybe now the sacrifices his

family had been forced to make on his behalf
would finally pay off. "We're rich!"

His father tugged on the heavy reins, bringing
the two sturdy draft horses to a halt. He turned
toward Jonas, his stained rawhide hat shading his
face against the dazzling noonday sun. The old
man's faded eyes were filled with doubt.

Walt Hunter considered Jonas the most unpro-
ductive of his offspring. He accused his youngest
son of always coming up with harebrained ideas for
the sole purpose of trying to get out of work.

"Is this another one of your get-rich-quick
ploys?"

"It's my fertilizer spreader, Pa. I've got a letter
here from the United States Patent Office."

Walt spit out a stream of brown tobacco juice.
"You and your fertilizing machine. How many
farmers do you think are going to plunk down their
hard-earned money for one of your machines?"

"Not everyone is as stubborn as you are, Pa,"
Jonas said. It hurt that his father held such a low
regard for the inventions he had worked so hard
to develop, but in some strange way, he understood
it. His father had started the farm over thirty-five
years ago, before the War Between the States and
before mechanized farm equipment was available.
He had turned over every square inch of his land
with his own two hands, using the simplest farm
tools imaginable, many of which he made himself.
But his father's old ways weren't Jonas's ways.

"Don't you see, Pa? If you would use my inventions, I guarantee your workload would be cut in
half."

"If my youngest son would assume his responsibilities, there would be no need for me to invest
money I can ill afford in mechanized equipment."

"I'm not asking for your money," Jonas protested. "What I want is for you to give me a chance to prove my ideas are sound."

"You ain't interested in farming, and I ain't interested in your ideas."

Biting back anger, Jonas pressed his knees into the sides of his horse and galloped away. What would he have to do to prove to his father that there was more to life than farming? That hard physical labor might have been a matter of honor in the past, but today such work was unnecessary as far as Jonas was concerned, and maybe even foolhardy.

It was true, of course, that some of his inventions had failed to live up to his expectations. . . .

The mechanical milking machine, for one. The cows were so spooked after that fiasco, it was weeks before they settled down enough to produce milk. Was his father furious over that one! Then there was the time Jonas blew the roof off the chicken coop. . . .

Still, it was Jonas's opinion that his father—indeed, the entire family, including his poor, overworked mother—showed a serious lack of imagination by not seeing the potential in his newest invention.

Jonas called it a fuel-powered fertilizer spreader. By attaching it to the back of a horse-drawn or gasoline tractor a farmer could cover acres of land in a few hours. It was so much more efficient than the hand-held sprayers presently available. Jonas was convinced it was about to revolutionize the entire farming community.

He dismounted upon reaching the farmhouse, and hurried inside. He could hear his mother in the kitchen preparing the noonday meal. The tantalizing smell of roast beef and fresh homemade pies greeted him as he took the stairs two at a time and dashed into the room he shared with two of his five brothers. Four of his seven sisters were married, leaving only three still living at home. He could hear the strident chords of the piano, indicating that his sister Becky Sue was giving a piano lesson to the offspring of a local farmer.

Imagining the feel of money running through his fingers, he pulled the envelope from his pocket and took a moment to savor it. Standing in the warming rays of the sun that filtered through the white lace curtains, he took a deep breath. Fresh air floated through the open window and Jonas likened it to the sweet smell of success.

No one in his family, not his father or mother, nor his brothers, their wives, his sisters, or their husbands, would ever again have to work as hard as they had in the past. He'd buy Becky Sue a new upright piano and his mother a reservoir cookstove, lined with porcelain and guaranteed to maintain "cold door knobs" at all times. And he would buy all the mechanized farm equipment available and insist his father use it!

At long last, Jonas would no longer have to feel guilty for shirking the duties around the farm that he so thoroughly despised.

Ah, success.

Unable to contain his impatience a moment longer, he ripped open the envelope and unfolded the letter. "Dear Mr. Hunter," he read aloud. "We regret to inform you . . ."

Jonas's jaw dropped open as he quickly scanned the remainder of the letter, unable to believe what he read. It appeared that someone else had applied for a patent on a machine identical to his.

"It's not possible!" he explained. He read the letter several times over, puzzled by the reference to a fuel-powered carpet cleaner. What was the matter with the patent office? He'd made it perfectly clear on his application that his invention was called a *fertilizer spreader*. A carpet cleaner, indeed!

It was a mistake. A government muddle.

And now the Patent Office required him to travel all the way to the Department of the Interior in Washington, D.C., to straighten out the mess. He couldn't believe it. It was an utter outrage!

"This is an outrage!" Kate wailed, waving the letter sent to her by the United States Patent Office.

Uncle Barney set aside the leather harness he'd been working on when Kate came charging into his shop to read him the letter. "Now, now, Kate. Calm down."

"How can I calm down? Didn't you hear what the letter said? Someone else has applied for a patent for an identical machine. How could this be?" She placed one hand on her waist and pursed her lips.

Watching his niece with her disheveled hair and the fine-boned face that was seldom seen without smudges of soot or grease, Barney shook his head with fond tolerance. In truth, he was often bewildered by the two strong-minded females in his life. If Kate wasn't on some crusade or other, her Aunt Hattie was. Why couldn't they be satisfied to accept life as it came without feeling obliged to be up in arms over the least little thing?

"Someone stole my idea!" Kate exclaimed. "It's the only thing that makes sense."

"It doesn't make sense at all. In order to steal your idea, the person would have to be able to get to your notes. Now, who do you know in this town who could do that?"

Kate thought for a moment. "I caught Smoky Joe skulking around not long ago." It was soon after finding Smoky Joe on her property that she'd installed a series of mechanized pistols aiming out of the windows, which she called her skulker's alarm. The pistols were aimed away from the tripping wire to give an ominous warning without bringing harm to the trespasser. If it turned out that it was, indeed, Smoky Joe who had stolen her notes, she would be tempted to reposition the aim of the pistols.

"It's got to be Smoky Joe!" she exclaimed. "Who else could it be?"

Uncle Barney shook his head. "Smoky Joe hasn't got enough up here." He pointed to his temple. "Besides, even if he did steal them, what good would it have done? I doubt he can even read."

Her uncle had a point. "What about Nicholas? He always has his nose in a book. Besides, he's still upset with me. He blames me for Curly shaving off his mustache."

"I've known Nicholas practically all his life. He would never stoop so low. I'm telling you, no one stole your idea. The Patent Office has made a mistake. And as soon as you appear before—what did they call it in the letter?—the board of reviewers, it'll all be cleared up."

"I hope you're right, Uncle Barney." Kate folded the letter and shoved it into the pocket of her pleated skirt. "Even so, it's an expense I'd not counted on." She had been able to save a modest amount of money by selling some of her labor-saving devices to farmers' wives, the most popular being a portable milking machine with a built-in lactometer for testing milk quality.

"What do you care about expenses? When you

start marketing your machine, you'll be a rich woman."

Kate's face softened. Despite all the trouble she'd caused them through the years with her inventions, her aunt and uncle never stopped believing in her. "And I will pay you back for everything. I promise."

"What nonsense you talk. Pay me back, indeed. Now run along with you, before you start getting sentimental on me."

Eager to begin making her travel plans, Kate decided to do as he said. She would pay back her aunt and uncle, no matter how much they protested. But first she must straighten out the mess in Washington. The sooner she could get her patent, the sooner she could start querying manufacturing companies. With a little luck, she could have her carpet-cleaning machines ready to sell in her aunt's shop by December. "If I find out someone has stolen my idea, I won't be responsible for my actions! I'll . . . I'll . . ."

"Do me a favor and spare me the details," Uncle Barney pleaded. "Besides, I've got work to do."

"Very well, Uncle Barney, but I'm telling you, if I ever get my hands on the man . . ."

The rest of her threat was lost as she shot outside in her usual unladylike haste, the door slamming shut behind her. The other pedestrians wisely stepped out of her way.

Watching her through the window, her uncle shook his head and went back to his workbench. Kate grew more like her aunt every day.

He picked up the harness he'd been working on before Kate had interrupted him and muttered to himself, "Heaven help the man if Kate ever gets her hands on him!"

Chapter 4

The clerk at the United States Patent Office peered at Jonas over the wire frame of his spectacles. He had a long narrow face, a wide flaring nose, and skin the color of day-old cream. "I can assure you, sir, there's no mistake."

Jonas took a deep breath and bit back his impatience. He'd stopped at the United States Patent Office on his way to the hotel from the train station. He'd been forced to draw money from his bank account to make the trip. It was money he'd earned from the maintenance work he'd done on the gas-driven tractors that were proving so popular in Waller Creek. The machines were still fairly new on the market and were unreliable. Jonas could have a full-time job repairing these tractors if he wanted, which, of course, he didn't.

His inventions and repair work allowed him to save enough money over a period of several years to market his fertilizer spreader, his latest and most promising machine to date. Once he had his patent, he intended to go into full production. It annoyed him no end to have to spend his savings on an unnecessary trip to the nation's capital.

He fully expected to arrive at the Patent Office and find the mistake had already been caught and corrected. Obviously, it was not going to be quite that easy.

He spread the creased letter on the desk in front of the clerk. "Perhaps you can explain to me how it was possible for someone else to apply for a patent on my fuel-powered fertilizer spreader?"

The clerk looked over the letter. "I think you are the one who's mistaken, sir. The letter makes no reference to a fertilizer spreader. Your application was for a carpet cleaner."

"I know nothing about a carpet cleaner. I invented a machine that allows a farmer to fertilize his property. Your office has made an error and this has caused me a great deal of inconvenience."

The clerk shuffled through a stack of papers. "Here we are," he said, apparently finding the appropriate document. After a moment, he looked up. "This explains everything."

Jonas sighed in relief. "I certainly hope so."

"Yes, it's all perfectly clear. You requested a patent on a fertilizer spreader . . ."

"That's what I've been trying to tell you."

"And another inventor requested a patent on a carpet cleaner."

"There you have it."

"The problem is . . . the two machines are identical."

Jonas placed both hands on the counter. "What do you mean, identical? What could a machine designed to spread fertilizer possibly have in common with a carpet cleaner?"

"I have no idea, sir. I'm just telling you what it says in the report."

"This is inconceivable. May I speak to your supervisor?"

"My supervisor has left for the day. You'll have to present your case to the board of examiners."

"My case? You make it sound like I'm on trial. All I want is a patent."

"That's all I can tell you. Of course, you're entitled to obtain legal representation."

"A lawyer?" Jonas was incredulous.

"It's quite proper," the clerk assured him. "There are many lawyers specializing in patents. If you would like a recommendation . . ."

"That won't be necessary," Jonas said. He had no intention of wasting money on a lawyer. Besides, he still clung to his earlier opinion: There had to be a perfectly reasonable explanation for the confusion. He was still convinced the mistake would be promptly resolved and he could go home. It made no sense to waste his hard-earned money on legal representation. "I don't want a lawyer," he said.

The clerk gave a disapproving sniff that did nothing for Jonas's peace of mind. "As you wish sir." The man's carefully composed face seemed to suggest Jonas would regret his decision. "You are scheduled to appear before the board of examiners at ten o'clock tomorrow morning."

Jonas thanked the clerk for his time and left the office, his hand wrapped tightly around the leather handle on his worn traveling bag. Not expecting to stay long, he brought but few belongings. Naturally this included his Sunday-best suit to wear in front of the examiners, along with the schematic sketches of his invention and his carefully documented notes.

A cold wind cut through his wool trousers and coat. The ground was still wet from an earlier rainstorm. Spring obviously arrived at the nation's capital even later than it did in Waller Creek. Folding up his collar, he hailed a hansom cab to take him to his hotel.

The horse's hooves clip-clopped along the cobblestone streets, down Pennsylvania Avenue and past the large white mansion known as the White House.

Jonas hardly noticed the building, nor did he give more than a cursory glance at the various historical monuments they passed. His thoughts kept him far too occupied to appreciate the sights.

Someone had stolen his idea. That was the only possible explanation he could think of to explain the mix-up at the Patent Office.

He couldn't wait to get his hands on the conniving no-good thief. By the time he finished with the scoundrel, the man would never steal again!

Kate arrived at the Patent Office fifteen minutes before she was scheduled to appear before the board of examiners, a portfolio containing sketches of her carpet cleaner beneath her arm.

She wore a silk taffeta dress the same blue color as her eyes. Her normally unruly reddish blond hair was tucked neatly beneath a felt hat, its single plume matching the color of her dress. The hat was too plain to be stylish, but its simplicity gave her a look of credibility, the long rigid quill an air of authority.

The dress was equally plain in design, with no ruffles or lace or other unnecessary trim. Her skirt didn't even have as much as the plait in back that was presently in vogue.

She purposely chose an outfit that would not call undue attention to her appearance. It was of utmost importance for the board of examiners to view her as a serious-minded inventor and she meticulously planned her clothes accordingly. No one could guess from looking at her that underneath the plain prim dress, she wore a brilliant red ruffled petticoat.

She was greeted by a clerk who directed her

down a long narrow corridor to a small conference room. Nine men whom Kate assumed were members of the board of examiners sat behind a long rectangular table facing several rows of empty chairs. The men were looking over their notes, and not one seemed to notice her arrival.

Only one other person was in the audience, a man whom she'd guessed was probably in his late twenties. She took her place in the front row across the aisle from him, and the man gave her a polite nod.

His thick wavy hair was tawny brown in color and framed an arresting square face. Brown eyes ringed with dark lashes were leveled beneath a brow shadowed with lines of impatience. Clearly, the man didn't want to be here, she thought. Well, make that two of them.

She returned the gesture with an uncertain smile and sat rigid in her chair, wondering how long it would take to straighten out the error and receive her patent. What a nuisance this was, having to leave Hogs Head to travel all this distance. She was worried about Jimmy. He had cried when she'd left, and she'd been unable to think of little else since boarding the train. The poor boy had been so upset, his tears had almost broken her heart.

She knew, of course, he was in good hands with her aunt and uncle. Still, she felt guilty. Although neither of them ever complained, it was physically tiring to carry a seven-year-old boy from room to room. Even more of an inconvenience was the fact that Jimmy refused to leave the house, which meant her aunt and uncle would have to take turns staying home with him or find someone willing to watch him during the day. She only hoped that someone wasn't that annoying woman Thelma Paine.

If only she could convince Jimmy to use his crutches.

At ten o'clock sharp, a short stocky man with a white square-cut beard banged a wooden gavel upon the table, calling the meeting to order. Since only two people, not counting the examiners, were in attendance, the gavel seemed to Kate a tad unnecessary.

She glanced once again at the man across from her. It was obvious he was waiting for someone. He kept looking over his shoulder at the open doorway behind them. Kate was curious about whom he was waiting for. A woman? Probably. His wife?

Keeping her lashes lowered, she cast a sideways glance at his hands. He held a silver pocket watch, but no rings were visible. So he wasn't waiting for his wife. Having determined that much at least, Kate gave the speaker her full attention.

Jonas glanced down at the Alaska silver-stem watch in his hand. It was the cheapest watch sold in the most recent Sears, Roebuck Consumers Guide, but it kept impeccable time. He pulled the thick silver fob to its full length and opened the hinged case cover with his thumb. It was fifteen minutes after the hour. Where was the scoundrel? And why hadn't he shown his thieving face?

The commissioner of patents introduced the other reviewers and then proceeded to read a list of complex and in some cases downright unfathomable procedures for handling patent disputes.

Jonas pocketed his watch and folded his arms across his chest. There was nothing to dispute, as far as he was concerned. Especially since the other—he tried to think of a word appropriately slanderous enough and couldn't—*party* had failed to make an appearance.

He glanced at the woman across from him, who appeared to be hanging on to every word the commissioner uttered. He wondered if perhaps she knew the thief. Almost as soon as the thought occurred to him, he dismissed it. Her plain dress and stern hairdo marked her as one of those self-styled righteous feminists who were making news all over the country, and which he had long vowed to avoid.

Today, however, he managed to push aside his own distaste long enough to let his gaze linger on the beguiling way the plain lines of her frock followed her womanly curves. She had full round breasts, a tiny waist, and not even the softly draped skirt could hide her shapely hips.

He found it interesting to note that she wore the fashionable side-buttoned boots that were introduced three years earlier at the Chicago World's Columbian Exposition, and had not yet become widely accepted. Even more interesting than her choice of footwear was the fact that she was tapping her foot with impatience matching his own. Odd as it seemed, he and this Miss Righteous had something in common, after all.

Intrigued now, he completely forgot his own impatience. It was while watching her foot that he spotted the startling flash of red beneath her hem. . . .

Chapter 5

"Excuse me, sir . . . sir."

Jonas was so engrossed with the tiny glimpse of a red petticoat, it took him a full minute to realize the commissioner of patents was addressing him.

Embarrassed to be caught remiss, he rose to his feet and cleared his voice. "Ah, I believe you were talking to me."

The man who had introduced himself at the start of the proceedings as Commissioner Hobbs gave Jonas a look of censure. "Are you Mr. Jonas Hunter?"

"I am."

"Are you the same Jonas Hunter who applied for a patent on the fuel-driven carpet cleaner?"

Jonas gritted his teeth, took a deep breath, and proceeded to correct the commissioner in a firm though polite manner. "I applied for a patent on a fertilizer spreader."

Commissioner Hobbs looked befuddled as he frantically flipped through the stack of reports in front of him, knocking over a glass of water in the process. This caused a moment of panic as the other examiners hastened to pull documents out of the way and mop up the water with their handkerchiefs.

As soon as order had once again been restored, the man sitting next to Commissioner Hobbs handed him a sheet of paper. The commissioner scrutinized the report. "Ah, yes, here we are. A fertilizer spreader."

Jonas's hopes soared. Maybe the mix-up would soon be cleared up and he could go home.

Commissioner Hobbs then turned his attention to the young woman. "Are you Miss Kate Whittaker?"

The woman rose to her feet, keeping herself as rigid as a telegraph pole. "I am."

"Are you the same Miss Kate Whittaker who applied for a patent on a fuel-driven carpet cleaner?"

Jonas almost choked. "You?" he cried in astonishment, waving his hand. "You stole my idea?"

The woman's eyes flashed with indignity, the plume on her hat seeming to soar another notch higher. "I most certainly did no such thing. If anyone stole anything, it's you. You ... you ..."

The pounding sound of the gavel drowned out her insults. "Miss Whittaker! Mr. Hunter!" The commissioner looked appalled. "If you don't mind, we will keep our tempers under control. Now, are you or are you not the Kate Whittaker who applied for the patent?"

"I am!" Kate said, glaring across the aisle at Jonas.

Unable to believe the turn of events, Jonas sat down and glared daggers back.

Commissioner Hobbs cleared his throat and proceeded to read the two applications. "It appears that you both complied fully with the rules of practice and I see here that you each signed an oath declaring yourselves the sole inventor." He sat back in his chair and regarded the two applicants as if they were wayward children who needed a good scolding. "Now, I ask you. How can two people both claim to be the sole inventor?"

Jonas folded his arms across his chest. In his mind, the answer was perfectly clear; Miss Whittaker had committed fraud.

Kate lifted her chin, confident that the commissioner knew the answer even as he asked it. Why, everyone could see through Mr. Hunter's polished facade. He might look like a respectable citizen, but beneath his admittedly attractive appearance, he was a liar and a cheat.

She turned her attention back to Commissioner Hobbs, who was holding up two sketches.

Jonas leaned forward in his chair upon recognizing one schematic drawing as his own. The other sketch resembled his enough to give him a cold chill.

"You can see our problem." The commissioner turned the drawings this way and that for all to see. "Both you, Miss Whittaker"—smiled for her benefit—"and you, Mr. Hunter . . . submitted identical designs."

"With one important exception," Jonas argued. He rose to his feet once again to better make his point. "Miss Whittaker's drawing shows the rubber hose attached to the wrong side of the canister. That would suck everything into the canister. That proves she doesn't know what she's doing."

The woman rose to her feet, her head held high, her eyes flashing with dangerous blue fire. "It is you who attached the hose wrong. Where else should the dirt go but into the canister? The way your hose is attached, it would fly across the room!"

"I won't have anyone put dirt into my fertilizer!"

"And I won't have anyone put fertilizer into my—"

"Mr. Hunter!" The commissioner mopped his damp forehead with a handkerchief and cleared his throat. "Miss Whittaker! Please, both of you, sit down." He waited for the two of them to comply with his wishes before he continued. "Now . . ." he focused his narrow gray eyes on Jonas, "would you be kind enough to make your presentation?"

"I would be delighted to." Jonas shot Kate a look of triumph before walking up to the front, where he could best be seen by the examiners. He was encouraged by the fact that the woman had not been allowed to speak first as good manners would customarily dictate. This indicated to him he was favored by the board of examiners. He had nothing to worry about. By letting him speak first, the board had clearly indicated whose side it was on.

Convinced the board of examiners had already made up its mind, he relaxed and took his own sweet time. He wanted to savor Miss Whittaker's reaction when she realized she didn't have a chance in blue heaven of getting away with her little scam.

Naturally, he would insist that she be punished to the full extent of the law. Naturally, she would plead for his forgiveness. However, at the moment he was finding it hard to imagine Miss Whittaker pleading for anything, given the bold way she was looking at him. *Oh, but you will plead for mercy, Miss Whittaker,* he thought. *Make no mistake about it.*

It annoyed him that she watched him with such a look of indignation on her pretty face. The way she carried on, one would think *she* was the injured party.

"Gentlemen of the board . . . and Miss Whittaker. I have spent the better part of the last five years developing this revolutionary machine."

Kate watched him like a hawk waiting to swoop in on its quarry. *In a hog's eye you have!* she mouthed silently, hoping he could read her lips. The nerve of the man!

"Excuse me, Miss Whittaker, did you wish to say something?" The thief looked directly at her, his handsome dark face plastered with arrogance.

Irritated that he had drawn her into the spotlight, she widened her eyes in what she hoped was a look of total innocence and virtue. It wouldn't do for the board of examiners to know—Lord forgive her—how tempted she was to murder the man. "Please continue, Mr. Hunter." Oh, she could be sweet when she wanted to be. But just wait.

He gave her a gentlemanly bow, which only increased her irritation. "I'm much obliged."

Commissioner Hobbs leaned toward Kate and gave her an encouraging smile. "You'll have ample opportunity to present your case, Miss Whittaker. Just as soon as Mr. Hunter has completed his."

Kate gave the commissioner an appreciative smile that made him turn red, then turned her attention back to her opponent. "That's comforting to know."

The thief's attention was diverted toward her feet. He appeared to be staring at the hem of her dress. A quick visual check revealed that the lower part of her skirt had risen slightly, allowing a glimpse of red petticoat to show. She quickly remedied the problem, but too late. The thief had discovered her secret love of bright-colored petticoats. The mocking look on his face as his eyes locked with hers was enough to tell her that he considered her choice of undergarments further proof she was incapable of defending her rights. She raised her chin in defiance. She would show him. Oh, yes, she most certainly would.

Clamping down on her jaw, she glared at him, determined to let him have his say. Let him tell the board of examiners how *he* invented *her* machine. Give him enough rope and he was bound to hang himself.

She concentrated on his every word and gesture, convinced that at any moment he would say something utterly preposterous and give his scam away.

"My machine works on the principle known as the vacuum," he explained. "Vacuum simply means any pressure lower than atmospheric pressure. See this . . ." He pointed to the motor-driven fan on the sketch. "The purpose of this fan is to create a suction that forces air into this opening. The air travels through the canister." He indicated each step as he spoke. "It goes through the bag that carries the fertilizer and then blows it out of the hose."

Kate leaned forward. He was good. Actually he was eloquent. He had taken her carpet cleaner and simply attached the hose to the exhaust, rather than the suction opening, thus creating a machine that served a different purpose. Obviously, he thought no one would notice his machine was identical to hers. Who knows? Had they both not applied for a patent at the same time, maybe no one *would* have noticed. This was no amateur con man, she was sure of that.

By the time he had finished his presentation, the members of the board of examiners looked ready to hand him the patent on the spot.

Mr. Hunter thanked the nine examiners, turned, and winked at her. Then, strutting like a rooster in a henhouse, he returned to his seat. Shocked and furious at his flagrant air, she glared at him, her eyes burning with indignation.

Commissioner Hobbs weaved his fingers together. "Are you ready to make your presentation, Miss Whittaker?"

"I most certainly—" She stopped herself in mid-sentence. The commissioner and the rest of the examiners were only doing their job. No sense venting her anger on them. Besides, it might only hurt her case. "I'm ready, sir." She smiled at each reviewer in turn.

Apparently thinking her pause meant she needed more time, one of the board members, a thin-skinned man whose short thick neck reminded Kate of a turtle, spoke up. "Would you care for some tea, Miss Whittaker, or some water?"

Jonas couldn't believe his ears. No one had thought to offer *him* refreshment.

"No, thank you," Miss Whittaker replied politely, looking extremely confident. Watching her like a farmer monitoring a storm, he sucked in his breath and clamped down on his jaw. What an actress!

Aware that Mr. Hunter was watching her every move, Kate took her place in the front of the room. Convinced the truth was about to become evident, she held up a sketch of her machine. "Mr. Hunter is correct in explaining how the principles of vacuum work. Obviously he reads the *Electric Age* magazine." She couldn't resist directing a quick glance at him. Cold dark eyes stared back at her from the granite mask on his face.

Undaunted, she continued, "The atmospheric air is forced through this hole in the side of the canister. Dust and other household lint is sucked into the hole and is trapped in this cloth bag. The air rushes through the porous material and escapes through this hole."

One examiner yawned, another glanced at his watch. Kate resented how the men seemed to think Mr. Hunter's explanations were more interesting or perhaps more credible than hers. Clearly, she needed to try another approach.

She set the drawings on the chair in front of her. "Gentlemen, I have worked on this invention for the last six years. I can produce witnesses who will attest to this." She glanced at Mr. Hunter, who acknowledged her claim of people willing to speak on her behalf with an obvious and calculated glance at the hem of her dress.

Kate's temper flared. He was purposely trying to intimidate her! Well, he wasn't going to succeed at his little game. Not if she had anything to say about the matter!

Refusing to look his way during the remainder of her presentation, she went into minute detail as to how she had invented her machine, stopping on occasion to answer a question put to her by one of the examiners, and trying not to show her annoyance that no one had queried Mr. Hunter.

"Isn't it rather odd for a woman to invent things?" she was asked by one rather pompous-looking examiner with a clipped British accent and a monocle.

"Odd?" Kate asked. "In what way?"

"It just seems highly . . . shall we say . . . unusual. It would seem to me that a woman of your considerable grace and beauty would be too busy managing her household to fuss with things so decidedly masculine in nature."

Kate opened her mouth to give the pompous fool a piece of her mind. Fortunately, Commissioner Hobbs spoke before she had a chance to ruin any likelihood of the board ruling in her favor. "I don't believe it's our duty or purpose to make a social commentary. Our job is to determine which of these two people is the sole inventor of this machine. If you would be so kind as to continue with your presentation, Miss Whittaker."

"Thank you, Commissioner." She proceeded to describe the many trials and errors that led to the invention of her machine. "I had great difficulty in finding a fabric that was thin enough to allow air to flow though, but heavy enough to contain the dirt," she explained. "The secret is in the weave."

When she had finished making her presentation, she glanced at her dark and brooding foe. A worried scowl had replaced his earlier arrogance and she was forced to remind herself that victory was best declared with quiet reserve. People disliked an ungracious winner almost as much as they disliked a poor loser. Ah, but once she was alone in her hotel room, she intended to kick up her heels and sing to high heaven.

Still, she couldn't resist giving the bold scoundrel a dose of his own medicine. Keeping her back toward the examiners, she looked Mr. Hunter square in the face and gave him a most unladylike wink. She sat down, not caring a fig if her red petticoat showed. She didn't care about anything at the moment but the look on his face.

His surprised expression was worth any lack of propriety on her part. Only one other thing would give her more pleasure, and that was a favorable ruling by the board of examiners.

The commissioner and the other examiners gathered in a huddle. The low drone of their voices made it impossible for Kate to hear what was being said. Their bland, rather bored expressions told her even less.

Kate felt the heat of Mr. Hunter's eyes on her, but she steadfastly refused to look his way. The thief! Her only hope was that he got what he deserved.

At last the examiners returned to their seats. Taking his place at the center of the table, Commissioner Hobbs remained standing. He gathered his notes and cleared his voice. "Miss Whittaker, Mr. Hunter. The board has requested more time to review all the material you've presented us with today. If you will return next Wednesday, we will inform you of our decision."

Kate couldn't believe her ears. How could the examiners not see through Mr. Hunter's ruse? Why, anyone with half a brain would know the man was a scoundrel of the first order!

Gathering up her portfolio, Kate left the conference room in haste and was greatly annoyed when Mr. Hunter charged after her.

Chapter 6

"Miss Whittaker!"

She gritted her teeth upon hearing the man call her name. She had nothing to say to him—or at least nothing she dare say in public. On the other hand, she didn't want him to think she was in any way afraid of him.

She whirled about, ready to give him a piece of her mind. Instead, her gaze froze on his long, lean form and the angry words that came to mind died before ever reaching her lips. Had the circumstances been different, she might have been flattered to be chased by a man as pleasing to the eye as Mr. Hunter. But though her heart thudded at the sight of him, she was neither flattered nor amused.

Despite his impressive height, he ran down the steps of the federal building with an easy grace that made the dark angry scowl on his face that much more incongruous.

He'd hardly made it to her side before he started with his accusations. "Suppose you tell me who put you up to this trickery of yours."

Kate tightened her fingers around her portfolio. So he was going to continue to play his little charade, was he? Even with no examiners in sight? "I have no idea what you're talking about."

"Oh, don't you, now? You expect me to believe you're an inventor?"

She clenched her jaw and fought for control. "And why is that so difficult for you to believe, Mr. Hunter? Because I'm a woman?"

"We're talking about motors, Miss Whittaker. Machines. You have to admit that most women have little if any knowledge about how such things operate."

"That's not what Mr. Edison believes."

At mention of Thomas Edison, he drew back and raised a dark brow. "Isn't it, now? I'd be most interested to hear what Mr. Edison has to say about women."

Kate lifted her chin in defiance and quoted from an interview she'd read in a recent magazine. "He said women have a special aptitude for invention."

Mr. Hunter rubbed his clean-shaven jaw, drawing attention to the intriguing indentation centered on his chin. "It would appear Mr. Edison has found a unique way to endear himself to you. I must admit, I'm a bit surprised you would fall for such an obvious attempt at flattery."

Shocked that he would turn a perfectly innocent statement into an insult, she stared at him in speechless disbelief.

He regarded her with narrowed eyes. "On the other hand, given your scheming nature, maybe you would. Tell me, how many ideas did you manage to steal from Mr. Edison?"

Kate was so incensed she found herself sputtering. "How . . . how dare you suggest such a thing. I've never even met Mr. Edison, but I'm sure if I did, he would show me the same respect he shows all his colleagues."

"You are the most shameless scamp I've ever encountered. I doubt there's another woman alive who would have the nerve to fob herself off as one of Edison's colleagues."

"You are a fine one to speak, Mr. Hunter. Few impostors would have the nerve to do what you did and do it so well. I must say, your presentation before the board was every bit as accurate and precise as my own."

"I can't argue with you on that account. Your own performance was flawless. Have you ever considered trying Shakespeare next? It seems a shame to waste such acting abilities on a handful of unappreciative patent examiners."

Kate's seething temper threatened to explode. "I can assure you, Mr. Hunter, that was no act. I'm an inventor and I intend to fight for what is mine."

"You're a cheat and a fraud, Miss Whittaker, and don't think for one moment that you're going to get away with this little scheme of yours."

"And you, Mr. Hunter, are despicable!" It wasn't bad enough that he made his accusations in private, but now he was announcing them from the steps of a federal building for all the world to hear.

She dropped her foot to the next step, but he prevented her from leaving with a quick grab of her arm. Not wanting to make any more of a scene than was necessary, she held her breath as she stared into his dark, menacing face.

His voice was hard, and held a threatening edge. "You're not going to get away with this. Not if I have anything to say about it."

Too angry to be intimidated by him, she stared him straight in the eye. "The board of examiners had no trouble believing I'm an inventor." She kept her voice low, hoping he would do likewise.

"They didn't rule for you."

She lifted her head haughtily, her eyes flashing dangerously. "Nor did they rule for you."

"But they will, Miss Whittaker. Make no mistake about it. It would be to your advantage to tell me who put you up to this. Give me the scoundrel's name, and I won't file criminal charges against you."

Having all she could take of his insults, she could no longer hold her anger in check. She pulled her arm away from his grasp, almost losing her balance in the process. He reached out to grab her, but she quickly recovered and moved up a step to avoid his touch.

"How dare you try to make *me* look like the culprit." Her voice rang out loud and clear. No longer caring who heard her, she ignored the curious stares from passersby. "We shall see which way the board rules. Now if you'll excuse me . . ."

"Wait!" he called, but she had already rushed down the remaining steps and climbed into a hansom cab. She doubled over to accommodate the ridiculously tall and rigid feather on her hat and in doing so afforded him the most charming view of swaying female posterior he'd ever encountered.

A flash of red showed beneath the hem of her dress just before she disappeared altogether. Staring after the horse-drawn cab, he let his breath out in one deep sigh, shaking his head with utmost regret. What a pity the woman with her flashing blue eyes and charming upturned nose had a heart of larceny. What a waste!

Kate left her hotel the following morning, hauling her carpet cleaner with her. Feeling tired and out of sorts—not at all like her usual sunny self— she was anxious to accomplish her business in Washington and return home.

Worry had kept her tossing and turning throughout the long, lonely night. She was worried about Jimmy, worried about her aunt and uncle, worried about finances. She told herself that once she had completed arrangements for the production of her machine, most of her financial problems would be resolved. She could start taking orders and as soon as the money began to pour in, as it was bound to do, she would then increase production.

If it wasn't for that fraudulent, scheming, unprincipled rogue, the patent would already be in her name, and she wouldn't be required to stay in Washington these extra days, wasting time and money. How dare the man try to benefit from *her* invention.

What if the board of examiners ruled in Mr. Hunter's favor? Not that it was likely, of course. Surely the examiners were experienced enough in such matters to see through Mr. Hunter's ruse.

But suppose they didn't. Suppose they decided that a woman could not possibly invent anything of value, and certainly nothing that required a motor or an understanding of vacuums. What possible defense would she have against such primitive thinking?

How could she ever afford to repair her aunt's and uncle's house or to take Jimmy to that Boston clinic that specializes in leg problems if the examiners ruled against her? Unless she found a way to help Jimmy, she had no chance of finding a permanent home for him.

Feeling more discouraged than hopeful, she nonetheless plodded along the boardwalk, ignoring the curious stares directed at her machine. The desk clerk had told her the manufacturing company was only three blocks away, but it seemed a lot farther, due in part to her depressing thoughts, but mostly because of the difficulty in keeping her carpet cleaner from rolling into the busy street.

The underside of the canister had been fitted with wheels, but it was difficult to maneuver it along the cobblestone street and the uneven boardwalk.

The wind had settled down sometime during the night. Patches of blue stretched between billowing clouds that skidded across the sky like fluffy white bunnies. The sun peered briefly through a break in the clouds, then disappeared.

Small puddles of water left from a recent rainstorm made it necessary to walk with care. Even so, her boots were thick with mud by the time she reached her destination.

She scraped the soles of her boots along the edge of the steps of a large brick building and rang the bell. The sign overhead read J. W. Matthews Manufacturers.

The door opened, revealing a man with graying sideburns and dressed in a dark suit and vest. "May I help you, miss?"

"Mr. Matthews is expecting me," she said. She had written the owner of the company a letter a month prior, and told him she was traveling to Washington. She had received a favorable response.

"Wait here." The man was only gone for a few minutes. "Mr. Matthews will see you now."

She picked up her carpet cleaner and followed the man down a dark narrow hall, past evenly spaced closed doors. The man stopped in front of the double doors at the end of the hall and tapped.

"Come in!" The voice was gruff, impatient, not the kind of voice to invite friendliness or confidence.

The man gave Kate an apologetic shrug and hurried away, leaving her to enter the office unescorted.

Mr. Matthews sat behind a large desk writing with one of the new Waterman fountain pens Kate had read about, with the improved constant ink flow. He neglected to afford her the courtesy of looking up. "What do you want?"

Swallowing her apprehension, Kate closed the

door behind her with more force than was warranted or intended. Mr. Matthews lifted his eyes, his pen held in midair.

"My name is Kate Whittaker. I received a letter from you. You said you would be interested in seeing a demonstration of my machine." Kate kept her voice firm but polite.

He grunted, his face offering little more warmth than his voice.

On the assumption the strange throaty sound was permission to proceed, Kate dragged her machine across the room to his desk, which she noted was cluttered with all manner of gadgets that appeared to be new inventions. Each was marked PATENT PENDING.

She had rehearsed this moment numerous times in her mind. More determined than nervous, she spoke in a strong clear voice. "As you may remember from my letter, the purpose of this machine is to rid households of unsightly dirt and unhealthy dust."

Mr. Matthews placed his pen behind his ear as if it were a pencil, and sat back in his chair. He had a narrow forehead, thick brows, and thick lips. He regarded Kate with curiosity, but gave no indication he knew who she was or even if he'd personally read her letter. "Your invention is called a . . ."

"Carpet cleaner." Confidence building, she rolled the machine to the middle of the room. "It sucks up dirt, dust, and lint without the drudgery of having to take carpets off the floor to beat them. I'm prepared to give you a demonstration."

Mr. Matthews rose and walked around his desk to take a closer look at the machine. He was a short man, barely taller than Kate. "It's rather a strange-looking machine, isn't it?"

Not sure if this was an insult or merely an observation, Kate continued her well-rehearsed spiel. "I guarantee that every household in America will be clamoring for this machine once it's patented—"

"It's not patented?"

"I expect to receive approval for a patent by next Wednesday," she assured him. "I'm looking for a manufacturing company to produce these machines at high quality and low cost. Your company came highly recommended." She had actually seen the company's name in the Sears, Roebuck Consumers Guide. Of course she would never let her aunt know she so much as owned a catalogue, let alone used it to try to market her own products.

She pulled out a small pouch filled with dirt and dumped it onto the carpet. She tilted the canister to show him it was empty and, with no further ado, cranked up the motor.

Mr. Matthews eyes widened. "What the . . ." His voice was drowned out by the roar of the carpet cleaner. He fell back against his desk and slapped his hands over his ears.

After the carpet had been cleaned to Kate's satisfaction, she switched off the machine. She lifted the lid to the canister and tipped the machine forward to allow him to see inside. "As you can see, the dirt has been completely removed and stored here for easy disposal."

Mr. Matthews drew his hands away from his ears. Much to Kate's disappointment, he appeared more bewildered than impressed.

What a pity she was forced to do business with men, she thought as she replaced the top of the canister. Most men failed to see value in making a woman's household chores easier. It was Kate's opinion that the Sears, Roebuck catalogue had far more labor-saving tools for men than for women. Kate vowed to change this.

"If you like, I'll clean the carpet behind your desk—"

"No, no! That . . . won't be necessary."

"Very well." She wrapped the rubber hose around the canister. "So when can you start manufacturing?"

"Not so fast, Miss Whittaker. There's a lot to be considered. How much capital are you willing to invest?"

Kate's mouth went dry. She had assumed that a manufacturer would, upon seeing the moneymaking potential of her machine, cover the initial start-up costs until such time as they could be recovered from orders. "Capital?"

"It costs money to produce a product. You don't even know if your product will sell."

"Of course it will sell. Why wouldn't it? Do you actually think women enjoy the drudgery of cleaning rugs?"

"That's what Mr. Sears said when he ordered those grapefruit shields that were guaranteed to make breakfast safe and squirt-free. He's now stuck with a warehouse full and it's his own fool fault, if you ask me. I told him that the housewife is a hard sell. She'd rather do things the way her grandmother did than put her trust in some newfangled invention."

"I don't agree with you, Mr. Matthews. I think with the right packaging and promotion, my carpet cleaner will sell like hotcakes."

"Like the grapefruit shields?" he mocked, stifling a yawn.

"With one big difference," Kate said, refusing to be discouraged. "My carpet cleaner is a necessity. Once it's properly introduced to the American housewife, I guarantee that not one woman would want to do without."

"How do you propose to introduce this to the American housewife?"

"My aunt can sell anything when she puts her mind to it."

"Your aunt?"

"She owns a general store in Hogs Head, Indiana."

Mr. Matthews frowned. "This kind of product requires wide distribution." He walked around the machine, scrutinizing it. He stared into the canister and rubbed his chin thoughtfully. "I'll tell you what. If you can get Mr. Sears to agree to carry it in his catalogue, perhaps we can arrange some sort of financial agreement."

"I can't do that, Mr. Matthews. I promised my aunt she would be the sole distributor. Besides, I'm not sure Mr. Sears is the right person to sell a household product such as this. A woman would have far more credibility."

"Credibility? A woman?" Mr. Matthews shook his head as if he couldn't imagine such a thing.

Not willing to give up so easily, Kate outlined her carefully thought-out business plan. "The best selling point of my machine is the performance. That's why I intend to hire a group of women drummers to travel around the country, visiting housewives in their homes and cleaning their rugs. A woman can much more easily develop rapport with a customer than a man."

"Rapport with the customers?" Mr. Matthews made it sound as if Kate had suggested something criminal.

"I can't think of a better way to convince housewives such a machine could save time and drudgery than to demonstrate it in their very own homes. A reasonably ambitious drummer could sell as many as eight, maybe even ten machines a day.

Multiply this by ..." Kate reeled off her carefully tabulated figures from memory. She was positive her approach had merit.

Mr. Matthews failed to look impressed. "This is all very interesting, Miss Whittaker ... but we have no way of knowing that your idea will work. Whereas Mr. Sears and Mr. Roebuck have a proven reputation and a capital of over a million dollars."

While Mr. Matthews was clearly impressed with such numbers, Kate was not. Mr. Sears wrote every word in his catalogue himself, taking great liberties in the number of supercilious adjectives and exaggerated claims he used in describing its contents. She wouldn't put it past the man to take a liberty or two in describing his wealth.

"If you refuse to put your machine in Mr. Sears's catalogue, I'm afraid we can't do business, after all, Miss Whittaker."

"You're quite right," Kate said. "I would require a man with vision and one who has enough business acumen to recognize a profitable opportunity when he sees it."

Mr. Matthews wagged a short stubby finger at her. "I'll have you know, Miss Whittaker, I am a *very* successful businessman."

"So was Mr. Contrell," she said, naming one of the many well-known businessmen who went bankrupt three years earlier, during the depression of '93. "Now, if you'll excuse me, Mr. Matthews, I won't take up any more of your time." Mustering as much dignity as was possible while dragging the unwieldy carpet cleaner behind her, Kate left his office. This time she slammed the door shut behind her deliberately.

Chapter 7

Kate refused to be discouraged, and not even the disappointing meeting she'd had with Mr. Matthews could dampen her hopes or enthusiasm. The J. W. Matthews Manufacturing Company was not the only one listed in the Sears, Roebuck catalogue, although, unfortunately, most of the others were located in New York City.

Perhaps one of the department stores in the area could tell her the names of some local companies. It would be a shame to waste the time she was forced to spend in Washington.

Energized by her plan of action, she hailed a cab and headed for the Evan and Swain Emporium next to her hotel. One of the clerks, a tall young man with sallow skin, was kind enough to copy the names and addresses of three local manufacturers on a piece of paper.

"I'm most obliged to you," Kate said, taking the neatly printed list from him. She turned to leave, thinking to stop by one of the companies before it grew too late.

Rolling her carpet cleaner by her side, she walked up and down the aisles of the store and looked at the amazing array of goods on display. Never had she seen such a wide variety of merchandise. An entire counter was devoted solely to watches. Never could she imagine such a large se-

lection existed—far more than was presented in the
Sears, Roebuck mail-order catalogue. Open-face
watches were displayed next to intricately engraved
railroad watches.

One watch made her stop dead in her tracks. It
was identical to the one belonging to Mr. Hunter.
Recalling with vivid detail the man's handsome
face, she heaved an impatient sigh and continued
to peruse the watch counter. "The man was despicable," she muttered beneath her breath. "A swindler, a liar and . . ."

A lovely enameled lady's chatelaine watch
caught her eye. She'd give anything to be able to
buy the watch for her aunt. But, unfortunately, it
would take the money she needed for train fare
home. She turned away with renewed determina-
tion. One day she would be able to afford fancy
watches and she would buy the very best for her
aunt and uncle. Of course, it wouldn't begin to
make up for all the trouble she'd caused the two
of them throughout the years, or for the damage
she'd done to their house. Nothing could do that.

In the aisle ahead, a small boy, not much older
than Jimmy, knocked over a pyramid-shaped display of Dr. Rose's Dyspepsia Powder. Several of
the cartons broke open upon impact. White powder
spilled across the floral carpet, settling beneath a
cloud of chalklike dust.

"Now look what you've done, Charlie!" the
boy's mother scolded.

A clerk brandishing a feather duster, descended
on the hapless boy and his mother like a black
hawk defending its territory. "Yes, look what
you've done, you spoiled little—"

The boy's mother gasped. "How dare you speak
to my son like that!"

"And how dare you bring that ill-mannered child

into this store!" A small crowd of shoppers, mostly matronly women dressed in fashionable suits and plush fur capes, gathered to watch the two shout insults back and forth.

Kate's heart went out to the forgotten boy, who looked close to tears.

"Excuse me," Kate said.

Both the furious clerk and the outraged mother turned to stare at Kate. Neither seemed to appreciate her intrusion. "If you would both be kind enough to step aside, I shall be happy to clean up the mess."

Without asking what authority Kate had, the two moved away to continue their shouting match next to the display of Dr. Auriclo's Australian Heart Cure.

The argument escalated and might have continued indefinitely had Kate not started up the carpet cleaner. The machine's deafening roar filled the store and both aggrieved parties fell into open-mouthed silence.

Onlookers slapped their hands over their ears and watched in astonishment as Kate's magic cleaner sucked every last speck of Dr. Rose's Dyspepsia Powder from the carpet.

Kate turned off the machine and smiled as the crowd broke into applause.

"That's amazing!" cried the boy's mother.

"Yes, yes!" agreed the clerk.

The boy gave Kate a look of gratitude as his mother grabbed his hand and yanked him out of the store with a promise never to return.

A portly woman dressed in a tailored black suit with a matching cape walked briskly toward Kate. "Excuse me, miss. My name is Mrs. Jenkins. I'm the head housekeeper for the White House."

Kate wasn't sure she'd heard right. "You mean the president's home?"

The woman dipped her head in a half nod. "The very same one."

Delighted and rather amazed to meet someone so close to the president of the United States, Kate extended her hand to the woman and smiled warmly. "This is, indeed, an honor. My name is Kate Whittaker."

"I'm delighted to make your acquaintance, Miss Whittaker. President Cleveland and his wife are throwing a large party next week for some important foreign dignitaries."

"How interesting," Kate said. "You must live a very exciting life. Do you attend many of Mrs. Cleveland's parties?" Newspapers had been filled with glowing accounts of Mrs. Cleveland's gala parties.

"Oh, my gracious, no. That wouldn't be proper. My job is to make certain that everything is ready in advance. Mrs. Cleveland is known for her housekeeping abilities, you know. She's very particular."

"I can see why she would be anxious to make a good impression." Mrs. Cleveland had married the president ten years prior, during Grover Cleveland's first term. It was the first time a president had taken a wife while in office and the public's interest in the beautiful and gracious woman was no less intense today than it had been when she was a bride.

"Yes, indeed, she is. She takes her duties as lady of the White House very seriously." Mrs. Jenkins looked proud as a prodigy's mother. "I'll have you know, she personally took it upon herself to shake the hands of all nine thousand guests attending a White House luncheon."

"That's amazing," Kate exclaimed, unable to imagine that many people in one place.

Mrs. Jenkins continued, "She inspects every square inch of the White House herself before each formal gathering. Why, once she made me polish the president's desk three times. You won't believe the uproar over that. The president has less regard for cleanliness than the missus, especially when it comes to his office."

"This is extremely interesting," Kate began politely, not wanting to offend. Somehow it didn't seem proper to stand around gossiping about people as important as the president and Mrs. Cleveland. "I'm afraid I'm in a bit of a hurry."

The woman's hand fluttered to her ample bosom. "Oh, dear, and here I am prattling on about nothing. What I meant to do is invite you to the White House."

Kate stared at the woman, incredulously. "Oh, I don't think I could possibly impose—"

"But you wouldn't be imposing. Mrs. Cleveland would love a demonstration of your machine. Perhaps you would be kind enough to clean the carpet in the downstairs reception hall. Mrs. Cleveland will be most grateful, I'm certain, as she's always reluctant to entertain in the room because the carpet is so difficult to clean."

"I shall be delighted to clean the carpet," Kate said, feeling somewhat overwhelmed by the prospect of meeting the president's wife. "Are you sure Mrs. Cleveland won't mind?"

"Mind? She loves visitors. She holds 'at-home' days so that women wishing to meet with her can do so." Mrs. Jenkins clasped her hands to her chest. "I can hardly wait to break the news to her. She loves modern conveniences. Why, when she found out that the Harrisons had been too afraid to use the electrical lights that had been installed during their term, she immediately walked up to the nearest light chain and tugged on it herself." Mrs. Jenkins looked almost as ardent as a zealot describing a holy apparition. "It was a beautiful moment, seeing electrical lights for the first time in the White House. A beautiful moment."

Kate remembered feeling much the same way when she first turned on the electrical lights in her own home. Not that she had time to enjoy the momentous occasion, since no sooner had she pulled the light chain than the attic had caught fire. "I'm sure it was."

"Will ten o'clock tomorrow morning be all right?"

"Ten o'clock?" Just wait until they hear about this back in Hogs Head. "Yes, ten will be perfect."

"Go to the hall on the second floor. It's on the east end. Tell the messenger to escort you to Housekeeping. You might want to arrive early. There's always a crowd waiting to see the president."

"I will most definitely be there," Kate promised, her heart fluttering with anticipation. Who would have ever thought that a country girl from Hog's Head, Indiana, would have the honor of cleaning the president's carpets?

Just wait till that thieving Mr. Hunter heard about this!

Chapter 8

The following morning, the hansom cab carrying Kate followed a long line of carriages past the gatehouse and up the sweeping drive of the White House. Gravel crunched beneath the wheels of the cab as the driver reined the skittish horse to a slow gait.

Kate glimpsed a handsome German shepherd guard dog sitting at attention by the gate, next to a white-painted doghouse.

Heart pounding with excitement, Kate peered from the open window of the cab, not wanting to miss anything. The long hard winter had taken its toll on the White House lawn, but the many trees bursting with newly sprouted leaves and white blossoms more than compensated for the lack of green grass. Neatly trimmed hedges grew next to the stables and carriage house. Ivy crept along walls, its full twisted vines wrapped around lampposts.

Meticulously kept flower beds were in full bloom. Bright yellow daffodils and scarlet red tulips lined the many graveled footpaths. Massive glass houses stood to the west and south of the White House, providing a year-round selection of cut flowers and potted plants. Mrs. Cleveland was known for her love of flowers, especially pansies.

Kate craned her neck as her cab drew near the large

mansion. She didn't want to miss a single detail of the oval portico with its tall graceful columns.

After paying the driver, Kate hauled her carpet cleaner from the cab and followed the crowd to the steps of the entrance. A man dressed in a suit and wearing a tall hat, helped Kate lift the cleaner up the steps. Kate thanked him and watched him hurry across the polished marble floor to join a group of grim-faced legislators gathered at the foot of a red-carpeted staircase.

The waiting hall was crowded with members of the House and Senate, all dressed in somber dark overcoats and square crown hats. At least half of the men, regardless of age, availed themselves of a walking cane, which was used primarily to emphasize a point of discussion.

Looking less impressive, but no less determined in their quest to see the president, were artists, inventors, and, judging from the number of agitated men holding caged hens, disgruntled chicken farmers.

Kate rolled her carpet cleaner across the floor toward the marble benches that lined one wall. She squeezed next to a red-faced man balancing a black box on his lap. The man gave Kate's machine a cursory glance.

"Don't expect to get a hearing with the president anytime soon," he grumbled. "This is my third day trying."

He turned his head toward the uniformed messenger who had just entered the hall. The various knots of people fell silent as the messenger read off the name of the next person whose long wait to see the president was about to end. The lucky person was a thin toothless man carrying a violin. Kate wondered what possible business a violinist would have with the president.

"Excuse me, sir," Kate called politely, raising her hand to draw the messenger's attention to herself. "I have a ten o'clock appointment with Mrs. Jenkins in Housekeeping."

The messenger glanced down at his notes. "Are you Miss Whittaker?"

"Yes, I am."

"Very well, follow me."

Kate's carpet cleaner rolled easily across the marble floor as she threaded her way through the crowded room. Her cheeks grew warm with embarrassment as several people stopped talking and turned to stare at her.

"Who does she think she is?" someone whispered loudly.

"She hasn't even been waiting an hour."

"And what in the world is that strange-looking contraption?"

The messenger led her through a carved oak door and down a short hall to yet another marble stairway. Kate lugged the carpet cleaner down the stairs, across a wide hallway to a large and stately room.

Never had Kate seen such elegant decor. Thanking the messenger, she gazed around the spacious room in awe. Scallops of red velvet fabric edged the top of half-moon windows. The room was filled with elaborate bookcases and candle stands. A mahogany writing table with a gilded bronze rim stood in front of the window. Two Chippendale wing chairs with carved cabriole legs flanked a Duncan Phyfe curving arm settee. A marble and bronze clock stood upon the mantel of the marble faced fireplace. A fire blazed in the hearth, supplying more color than warmth to the oversized room.

Kate set her carpet cleaner next to a rosewood

lyre table and studied the red floral carpet that stretched from wall to wall.

A voice she recognized as the housekeeper's sounded behind her. "Ah, Miss Whittaker. How nice to see you again. I hope you haven't been waiting long."

Kate turned to greet the housekeeper. "Not at all. I only just arrived."

No sooner had she greeted Mrs. Jenkins than they were joined by a petite and rather demure-looking woman with dark shining hair drawn back into a tidy bun. The woman carried a basket filled with pansies over her arm.

Kate recognized her immediately from the many pictures that had been printed in the newspaper following her wedding to President Cleveland, although her face appeared fuller than it had in previous years.

The housekeeper made the introductions.

"I'm very pleased to make your acquaintance," Kate said.

Mrs. Cleveland set the basket of flowers on the floor and held out her hand to Kate, greeting her with a warm friendly smile. "The pleasure is mine." At thirty-one, Mrs. Cleveland was still a young woman, only six years older than Kate. Even so, she moved with a grace and poise usually found in one much older.

"Mrs. Jenkins told me about your amazing machine. She said you've agreed to give me a demonstration, but I'm really not certain if that would prove to be of much value. As you can see, the carpet has recently been thoroughly cleaned."

The busy floral design made it impossible to see much of anything, but Kate resisted the temptation to say so. "I would be most honored if you would at least let me show you how my machine works."

"I would be most interested to see how it works." Mrs. Cleveland sat herself daintily upon the settee and pressed her lily-white hands into the folds of her skirt.

Kate prepared her machine for use. "As you can see, the inside of the canister is spotlessly clean." This was an important part of her demonstration. It prevented anyone from accusing her of planting dirt inside the canister in advance. She snapped the lid on and attached the rubber hose before turning the crank to start the motor.

Even the vastness of the room could not mute the loud roar of the machine that seemed to bounce off the high sculptured ceiling. The sound so startled the president's wife that she flung herself back against the settee in alarm, a bejeweled hand planted firmly on her chest. Even Mrs. Jenkins, who had heard the machine previously, looked a bit unnerved.

Kate gave the president's wife an apologetic smile, but continued to push the cleaning wand back and forth until she had covered the area between the settee and the fireplace. Satisfied that she had made the carpet as dust-free as possible, she turned off the machine.

"My word!" Mrs. Cleveland exclaimed, trying her best to regain her composure. "That's rather loud, isn't it?"

"It's a powerful machine," Kate explained. "If it were less powerful, it couldn't reach the dirt caught in the deep fibers."

"I suppose some housekeepers would find that a useful feature," Mrs. Cleveland said in a voice that clearly stated she was not one of them. "But of course, Mrs. Jenkins and her staff keep the carpets spotlessly clean."

"I'm sure they do," Kate said tactfully. "But carpets as fine . . . and closely woven at this one, often require special care." She flipped open the canister and tipped it on its side so that Mrs. Cleveland and her housekeeper could see the accumulation of dirt that clung to the fabric bag. Even Kate was surprised by how much dirt had been gathered.

Mrs. Cleveland's eyes widened. "Oh, my."

Mrs. Jenkins looked horrified. "We just had this carpet lifted and taken out back for its semiannual cleaning."

"No more than a week ago," Mrs. Cleveland concurred. "I supervised the cleaning myself."

"Yes, yes," Mrs. Jenkins said, obviously not wanting to take the blame for any lax in cleaning standards.

Mrs. Cleveland glanced at one of the open doorways. "Quick, Mrs. Jenkins, close the door. We wouldn't want anyone to know . . . oh, this is awful."

Kate watched in confusion as the two women ran around, closing all four of the doors leading to other rooms and pulling the draperies shut. "It's just a little dirt," she protested.

Mrs. Cleveland clucked her tongue. "Do you realize that my whole reputation is at stake?"

"Just because of a little dirt?"

"You don't know what it's like being the president's wife. I'm expected to maintain the highest standards. Isn't that so, Mrs. Jenkins?"

"Yes, indeed, Mrs. Cleveland," the housekeeper agreed. "The highest standards."

"How much do you want?" Mrs. Cleveland asked.

Kate blinked. "Want?"

"For your carpet cleaner?"

"Oh, I couldn't sell it. This is my prototype." The two woman stared at her and she explained.

"A prototype is a full-scale model. It's the only one I have. I need this to sell my idea to a manufacturing company."

Mrs. Cleveland sighed in relief. "Manufacturing company? That must mean your machines will soon be available for purchase."

"Oh, I do hope so." Kate hesitated, not certain if she should trouble the president's wife with her own personal problems. "The only problem I might have is if the board of examiners fails to grant me a patent."

Mrs. Cleveland's eyes widened. "Is that a possibility?"

"I'm afraid it could be." Kate explained how a man named Mr. Hunter had made false claims of having invented the machine himself. "He calls it a fertilizer spreader."

Mrs. Cleveland cried out in disbelief. "That's the most ridiculous thing I've ever heard. Why, anyone can see it's a carpet cleaner."

"I quite agree. But Mr. Hunter has the advantage of his sex. You know yourself that women don't always get credit for what they do. Why, I have it on good authority that it was actually *Mrs.* Howe who invented the sewing machine."

"You can't be serious!" Mrs. Cleveland exchanged a horrified look with her housekeeper. "*Mrs.* Howe. Are you certain?"

"Indeed I am," Kate said. "My uncle knew someone who shared a tent with Mr. Howe during the war. This man said that Mr. Howe admitted to spending fourteen years trying to develop the sewing machine. According to Mr. Howe, his wife decided that they would all starve to death waiting for him to figure out how to make the sewing machine work. So she took it upon herself to sit down and solve the problem."

"The woman is a genius!" Mrs. Jenkins exclaimed.

"Absolutely!" Mrs. Cleveland declared.

"Naturally, the patent was in Mr. Howe's name. But even if Mrs. Howe had been allowed to take out the patent in her own name, it wouldn't have been prudent to do so," Kate said, recalling her meeting with Mr. Matthews on the previous day. "I'm afraid no one would have given much credence to a sewing machine if it were known it was even partially invented by a woman."

"Why, that's ridiculous," Mrs. Cleveland said. "Who better than a woman to invent a sewing machine or, for that matter, a carpet cleaner?"

"I quite agree. However, my immediate problem is whether or not the board of examiners believes that I am the true inventor."

The housekeeper clucked her tongue. "Anyone can see that you're the rightful inventor."

"Thank you, Mrs. Jenkins. That's kind of you to say."

Mrs. Cleveland looked less confident than her housekeeper. "I don't think we should leave anything to chance. Who knows what the board of examiners is likely to do?"

"I'm afraid there's not much more I can do," Kate said, ruefully. "I filled out all the correct forms and told the examiners exactly how I came to invent the machine. I'm afraid all I can do is wait."

Mrs. Cleveland rose abruptly to her feet and struck a pose that was more refined and ladylike than determined. "Perhaps the board of examiners might benefit from some gentle persuasion."

A look of pride crossed Mrs. Jenkins's face. "Mrs. Cleveland is an expert on the art of gentle persuasion."

Kate wasn't certain what to make of this news.

The people in Hogs Head preferred the direct approach, and if that didn't work, brutal honesty did. "Does this . . . gentle persuasion work?"

Mrs. Cleveland was obviously surprised that anyone would question her tactics. "Why of course it works, doesn't it, Mrs. Jenkins? Naturally, it means going to the press."

"Oh, dear, Mrs. Cleveland." Mrs. Jenkins shook her head. "You know how the president feels about the press."

"Indeed I do." Mrs. Cleveland turned to Kate. "He has never forgiven the press for hounding us during our honeymoon."

Mrs. Jenkins snorted in disgust. "The press actually followed them all the way up the mountain in Maryland and watched the two of them through spyglasses."

"How shocking!" Kate gasped.

"They stopped at nothing," Mrs. Cleveland agreed. "One morning as we stepped out of our lodge, the president spotted the spyglasses and pushed me back inside to protect me. And do you know what those ghouls of the press did? They reported my husband mistreated me!"

"No!" Kate said, shocked at the thought of anyone accusing the president of mistreating his wife.

"Of course, nothing could be further from the truth." Mrs. Cleveland's face softened. "No husband could be more attentive, kind, or considerate than President Cleveland."

"I can hardly blame the president for distrusting the press," Kate said.

"That's putting it mildly." Mrs. Cleveland thought for a moment. "Perhaps a little gentle persuasion on my part would make him relent, just this once."

The housekeeper smiled as proudly as a new

mother showing off her infant. "Never knew a time when your gentle persuasion failed to work with the president."

The president's pretty wife blushed a most becoming shade of pink. She patted Kate lightly on the arm. "Just leave everything to me."

Chapter 9

Jonas woke early that Monday morning with a sense of well-being. He allowed himself the luxury of lying in bed long past his usual rising time to reflect on his fortunate state of affairs.

How foolish of him to allow that annoying Miss Whittaker to upset him. So what if she had the prettiest blue eyes he'd ever set his sight on? Who cared that her petticoats were the loudest and most shocking shade of red possible?

The board of examiners would certainly see through her ruse and rule in his favor, if they hadn't already done so. In two days, the problem would be resolved and he would be free to market his product. After which time, all he would have to do is let the money roll in.

Life was good, no question about it, he thought as he dressed. Especially here, away from the farm. He was far more suited to the business world than he had ever been to farming. He could hardly wait until the time came to approach manufacturers and distributors with his ideas.

Meanwhile, he was quite content to spend another day in the glorious city of the nation's capital, strolling through its brilliant gardens, luxurious art museums, and that remarkable place known as the Smithsonian Institution.

Whistling to himself, he completed his toilet and

walked down the stairs of the boardinghouse to avail himself of the wonderful home-cooked breakfast that was provided each morning by the proprietor's hefty German wife. The boardinghouse was less expensive than the hotel he'd stayed at the first night, and far more conveniently located. Here he was only two miles from the patent office.

He nodded to the other boarders and took his place next to the window where he could watch the traffic rush by. Bicycles outnumbered carriages by far and businessmen dressed in black suits and bowler hats pedaled toward the business district.

Women seemed to favor the newer safety models that were equipped with ball-bearing wheels and air-filled tires. Dressed in knickerbockers, women zipped in and out of traffic as speedily as their male counterparts. The loose-fitting pants allowed women to maintain decorum as they pedaled, without interference from their garments, but Jonas was quite shocked to note that any ladylike dignity was forgotten the moment anyone or anything slowed a bicycle's progress.

He'd never seen so many aggressive women in his life. Of course, none compared to the likes of Miss Whittaker and her bold attempt to rob him. What was the world coming to? he wondered. What was happening to make women so stalwart and pushy? Was it the advent of electricity that was causing the problem? Were electrical impulses doing something to the female brain?

Soothsayers had been predicting problems for years, declaring electric lights bad for the public's health. Some had warned about electricity ruining ladies' complexions or causing blindness. But as far as Jonas knew, no one had predicted electricity would make women so outrageously aggressive.

His thoughts were interrupted by an odd-looking

bicycle with wings. Never had he seen so many modes of transportation as he had seen these last few days in Washington. He'd even caught sight of several of those gas-powered motorcars that everyone had been talking about. Yes, indeed, life was good.

"Good morning, Mr. Hunter." The owner's daughter, Annie, handed him a copy of *Frank Leslie's Illustrated* newspaper and filled his cup with coffee.

"And it is a good morning," Jonas concurred.

Taking a sip of the rich delicious brew, he unfolded the paper and almost choked. For spreading across the entire front page of the newspaper was a full-blown picture of Miss Kate Whittaker standing between the president and Mrs. Cleveland. All three were shown looking—gloating, more like it—at *his* fertilizer spreader!

Flabbergasted, he turned the page to read every word of the accompanying article.

Mrs. Cleveland had nothing but praise for Miss Whittaker, calling her the most brilliant inventor since Mrs. Howe invented the sewing machine. . . .

Mrs. Howe? Thinking it must be a misprint, Jonas continued to read.

Mrs. Cleveland told reporters that because of Miss Whittaker, the American housewife was about to be freed from household drudgery.

"Ha!" Jonas exclaimed. "And what about the poor farmer? What about men like my father who toil from dawn to dusk only to lose everything to a poor harvest?'' The other boarders turned to look at him.

Ignoring his wide-eyed audience, Jonas kept reading, each outrageous lie bringing a loud cry of protest to his lips. "Why, the little cheat! How dare her suggest that my character is in any way flawed."

He glanced at the other boarders and pointed to himself. "I ask you, do you see a flawed character?"

The boarders shook their heads mutely and, one by one, began to vacate the dining room, leaving their half-empty plates behind as they fled to the safety of their rooms or left for work.

Jonas slammed his fist on the table, rattling the dishes and knocking over a pitcher of cream. So now the woman had roped the president and his wife into her little scheme. By George, she wasn't going to get away with it.

According to the article, Miss Whittaker was staying at the Anderson Arms Hotel. He dropped the newspaper on the table and stared with unseeing eyes out the window. He decided not to go to the art museum or the Washington Monument as planned. He had more important things to do with his day.

He tucked the newspaper beneath his arm, went back to his room for his coat and hat, and hurried outside to hail a cab to take him to the White House.

Settling back against the worn leather seat, he chided himself for being such a fool. He should have known Miss Whittaker would pull something like this. He had been willing to let providence take its course, confident that justice would prevail. Now it appeared that all the time he was taking in the sights of Washington, Miss Whittaker had been busily plotting against him.

The woman had no scruples, no morals, no conscience. To think she had hoodwinked the president and his sweet innocent wife into such a dastardly scheme! Well, two could play the same game, by George!

The cab drew up in front of the entrance to the White House. Jonas paid the driver and followed the crowd of people up the steps.

For the next seven and a half hours, Jonas sat in the cramped waiting room at the east end of the White House, amid cages of smelly Brahma chickens, and listened to a group of chicken farmers complain about the proposed legislation that threatened to levy taxes on hens.

"The worst of it," one farmer confided, "is I've been waiting three days to see the president."

"That's terrible," Jonas exclaimed. "Three days!" How did Miss Whittaker manage to connive a meeting with the president and his wife so quickly?

At the end of the unbelievably long day, the harried messenger boy apologized to the still-waiting crowd. "You'll have to come back tomorrow."

Jonas left the White House, grumbling. He was tired, he was hungry, and he was certain he smelled like an unkempt chicken coop.

He hailed a cab to take him back to the boardinghouse, then changed his mind. He pulled out the newspaper from his coat pocket and scanned the article for the name of the hotel where Miss Whittaker was staying. Finding the information he sought, he leaned out the window and called up to the driver, "Take me to the Anderson Arms Hotel."

Folding the newspaper and slipping it back into his pocket, he eagerly anticipated meeting Miss Whittaker and wringing her pretty little neck.

Chapter 10

Kate was so exhausted, it was all she could do to drag her carpet cleaner across the lobby to the hydraulic piston elevator that would take her to the fourth floor. Although the lobby was wired for electricity, the upper floors of the hotel had still not been converted. Gaslights hung at dreary intervals along the hall leading to her room.

She had spent the entire day cleaning the carpets of the White House. It was the least she could do to show her gratitude to that nice Mrs. Cleveland for all her help. But never had it occurred to her that a single residence could have so many carpets!

What she needed was to take a hot bath and turn in early.

Still, despite her exhaustion, Kate couldn't be happier. The patent examiners couldn't possibly rule against her now that the president and Mrs. Cleveland had gone public to declare their confidence in her. She smiled to herself. She only wished she could have seen Mr. Hunter's face when he saw her photograph in the newspaper.

A knock came at the door, and thinking it was the maid bringing her more towels as she'd requested earlier that day, she hastened to answer it.

Nothing could have surprised her more than to find herself face-to-face with Mr. Hunter. Hard piercing eyes glared at her from a face dark with anger. His brows were knitted together; his nostrils flared.

"What are you doing here?" she stammered.

Much to her astonishment, he boorishly pushed his way inside her room, waving a newspaper in her face. "Of all the low-down, despicable tricks . . ."

Standing her ground, she railed back, "How dare you come charging into my room. I want you to leave at once!"

"I'm not going anywhere until I've said my piece. You orchestrated this whole thing with the president just so the board of examiners would rule in your favor."

"I did no such thing! Now if you would be kind enough to—"

He slammed the door shut behind him and advanced forward. "I'm not feeling especially kind at the moment. I hope you'll find it in your conniving little heart to forgive my poor manners."

Trying to hide her nervousness, she stepped backward, determined not to be intimidated by him, even if it killed her. "If you don't leave at once, I'll . . ."

He followed her step for step across the room. "You'll what, Miss Whittaker? I would be most interested to hear what you intend to do."

The bed prevented any further escape. Still he advanced toward her.

"I want you to leave now," she stammered, falling onto the edge of the mattress. "You have no right to be here."

The menacing look on his face made it abundantly clear that no amount of reasoning was going to convince him to leave.

A change of tactics was definitely in order; she opened her mouth wide and let out an ear-piercing scream.

Jonas momentarily froze in his tracks and stared at her, dumbfounded. Recovering quickly, he lunged forward and pressed his hand over her mouth. Her screams muffled now, she fought him like a wildcat.

"Dammit, keep still!" he hissed in her ear. The last thing he needed was for the hotel management to come storming into the room. "I'm not going to hurt you."

He realized with no small surprise that he was fully on the bed, the woman sprawled beneath him. She was squawking and kicking and carrying on like nobody's business. He, on the other hand, was trying to calm her down, to no avail.

When at last she grew still, he removed his hand from her mouth, ready to clamp it back on at the least indication she intended to resume her screams.

"Get out of here!" she enunciated, her voice low and threatening. "I've had an exhausting day—"

"*You've* had an exhausting day. Lady, you don't know what an exhausting day is until you spend it with six dozen irate chicken farmers."

Not having the slightest idea what he was talking about, she pushed against him. But he quickly grabbed her hands and she was once again firmly trapped between him and the mattress.

More furious than frightened and having had a moment to recover, she fought him with every ounce of strength left. "Let go of me, you thieving ..."

She was no match against his powerful body and she soon realized the futility of trying to physically fight him off. She grew still and glared up at him. Her chest heaved with her labored breathing. "I want you to leave at once!"

"I'll leave when I'm good and ready to leave and not one moment sooner!"

She was tempted to argue the matter, but since her body was crushed helplessly beneath his, it appeared she had little authority over his time of departure.

His breath hot on her face, he held her arms pinned over her head. His powerful chest pressed against her bosom, his strong thighs clamped like steel bars around her hips. She kept her muscles taut, but it did no good. As much as she hated to admit it, he had a definite advantage. "What ... what do you want?"

A look of approval crossed his face. Clearly he thought she was ready to capitulate to his wishes. He released her arms, then straightened until he was sitting on top of her.

"You know damned well what I want," he said curtly, keeping her trapped between his knees. "I want you to go to the board of examiners and tell them how you manipulated your way into the president's favor."

"I did no such thing! If you want to blame anyone, you can blame Dr. Rose and his dyspepsia powder for getting me into the White House."

Jonas stared down at her in amazement. Things kept going from bad to worse. Now she had Dr. Rose on her side.

He regarded her with as much caution as one would give a venomous snake. She returned his assessing look with a bold demeanor that irked him. Never had he seen a woman's eyes flash so dangerously. He had her pinned to the bed and at his mercy. Couldn't she have the good grace to concede he had the upper hand?

He did have the upper hand, didn't he? It was hard to know for sure. For one thing, her closeness was making it hard for him to breathe. Her hair had come unpinned during their scuffle, and her golden red curls spilled across the rumpled bed. The sweet fragrance of her overheated body added to his confusion, making it necessary to remind himself of his state of mind. He was angry—hell, he was mad as hornets—and with good reason. So why in the name of God did he feel tempted to kiss the pretty pink lips that were clamped together in indignant outrage?

He *did* have the upper hand, he told himself.

Of course he had the upper hand.

To prove it, he pulled away from her and rose to his feet. She sat up slowly and glanced at the door.

"Don't try it," he warned. "We're not finished with our little talk."

"I have nothing to say to you." Moving to the far edge of the bed, she glared at him like a cornered bull.

"I beg to differ with you, Miss Whittaker. I think you have plenty to say to me. You might start by telling me how you propose to right the terrible wrong you've done."

"I've done nothing wrong!"

"You stole my idea!"

"You stole mine!"

She was going to stick with her story. Well, he could hardly blame her for that. She knew perfectly well that the chances of the board of examiners deciding in his favor were slim, if not altogether nonexistent, now that she had the support of the president and his wife, not to mention Dr. Rose and God knew who else.

He circled the machine she called a carpet cleaner. Lord, if it didn't look like one of his own! She watched him from the bed, looking like a mother about to fight tooth and nail to save her child.

"If you don't leave at once—"

"Quiet! I need to think!"

The look she gave him was filled with hate and loathing, but she fell silent, allowing him time to gather his thoughts.

Unless she told him how she managed to steal his notes, he was doomed. He was about to lose the rights to the invention he had spent the better part of the last five years working on. Five years of work, and what did he have to show for it? Not a damned thing!

Rubbing his chin, he paced back and forth at the foot of the bed and considered every possible option. He was even more tempted than before to wring her neck and be done with it. Fortunately for her, he was a law-abiding citizen who preferred dealing with his problems with as much civility as circumstances allowed.

Maybe he was going about this all wrong. Perhaps he should let her think he was willing to concede—for a price. Earn her trust. Eventually she was bound to reveal her sources. Women, as a whole, weren't generally known to keep secrets.

It would take some doing, he knew. She was a smart woman—too damned smart, as far as he was concerned. Certainly she was smart enough to know her own limitations. The business world was no place for a woman. Whether or not that was fair was up for debate. Nonetheless, she had to know the reality. Her best bet for success was through him.

As obvious as this was, he knew he'd have to sell her on the idea. One could never assume that a woman, even one as intelligent as Miss Whittaker, would understand logic. If he had any chance of getting her to agree to a partnership proposition, he'd have to make sure she understood the full extent of what she stood to gain. Once he'd gained her trust, it would only be a matter of time before he found out what he needed to know, retrieved what was rightfully his, and let the law deal with Miss Whittaker and her accomplice.

Damn, he hated playing games! But she left him no choice. He cleared his throat.

Her eyes flashed as if she were preparing for another round, and he reminded himself of his own intolerance to violence. Wringing her neck was not an option, however much she deserved it. A moment later, it was necessary to remind himself that neither was kissing her.

"What do you know about French fashions?"

She looked at him incredulously. "I beg your pardon?"

"You know. Ruffles. Lace. That kind of thing." It suddenly seemed imperative to encourage her to talk about the tedious womanly details that never failed to drive him to distraction. Considering the wanton direction his mind was heading, he needed all the distraction he could get.

"Mr. Hunter, if you don't mind, I've had an extremely hard day."

"Very well . . ." His mind raced. He had to get her talking, but this was no ordinary woman. He suspected she had less interest in French fashions than even he did.

He held out his hand to help her to her feet. He told himself it wouldn't hurt to let her think the bargaining ground was level. In reality, he found the bed too distracting, which explained why the thought of kissing her kept popping into his mind. "Perhaps I've been rather hasty in my opinion of you."

Suspicion clouded her face. He was going to have to be extremely careful about how he presented his idea. If he acted too hastily, she would see right through him. Perhaps a bit of charm was in order.

"Perhaps I've been mistaken in assuming that you would do anything as low as to steal another's invention. Anyone can see that you're a charitable woman with high principles."

She had allowed him to finish what he had to say uninterrupted, but the mistrust remained in her face. "I'm certainly relieved to hear you say that, Mr. Hunter. Now if you would be kind enough to leave, I'll try my very best to forget how you bullied your way into my hotel room and held me against my will."

"Bullied, you say?" He managed to look wounded. He took her arm and moved her away from the bed. He had enough to think about without recalling how she looked minutes earlier on the bed, sprawled beneath him, her well-rounded breasts heaving next to his chest, her hair a golden red halo around her head. "I can't bear to think that you think of me in such terms. In reality, I'm a peace-loving man. Perhaps ... Oh, no ... you'd never agree."

Curiosity deepened the blue of her eyes. "What is it that I won't agree to?"

"It's too preposterous to think about. You being a fine lady and all."

"Mr. Hunter, would you please tell me what it is I'd never agree to?"

"I had this crazy idea that we could have dinner together. It would be my way of ... apologizing for the distress I've caused you. It would also allow me to correct any wrong impressions you might have in regard to my character."

She looked taken aback. "I couldn't ..."

"But you might?" He looked hopeful. "What

useful purpose would it serve for us to be at loggerheads?"

Kate ran her fingers along the carved oak bedpost as she considered his unexpected invitation. He was up to something and she knew she'd better be on guard, especially since being near him made her heart pound so quickly she could hardly breathe. "I'm not sure that you and I have anything to discuss, except perhaps how you stole my idea."

"Let's not talk about the ... eh ... your carpet cleaner." He had to fight not to give away his distaste in referring to his invention in such undignified terms. "It's only a patent and it's obvious it will soon be yours, so how can you deny me this small consolation?"

Kate tightened her fingers around the post. It might only be a patent to him, but to her it represented everything she'd worked for these last six years. As for having supper with him, she'd sooner starve to death.

Still, she was curious to know who in Hogs Head had worked as his accomplice. Someone must have stolen her notes; that was the only thing that made sense. But who? Unfortunately, there was only one way to find out.

"Very well, Mr. Hunter. If you would be kind enough to wait downstairs in the hotel dining room while I freshen up. I shall require but a few minutes."

He considered her request. It could be a trick to get him to leave, he thought, but to insist upon staying might make her resist all the more. His best bet was to see if her curiosity would make her play into his hands.

"Very well, Miss Whittaker. I shall meet you downstairs in, shall we say ..." he glanced at his pocket watch, "forty minutes?"

Chapter 11

Jonas sat at a table in the corner of the hotel dining room, his gaze glued to the arched doorway leading to the foyer. Never had he waited for a woman with more anticipation than he waited for Miss Whittaker.

He was shocked to find, after glancing at his watch and shaking it to make certain it was still working, that no more than twenty minutes had passed since he'd left her room.

Due to the awkward placement of an oversized potted palm, he was required to lean over the arm of his chair to get a clear view of the doorway.

The hotel was among Washington's oldest, its glory days predating the War Between the States.

During the last year, the gaslight fixtures in the dining room had been converted to handle Edison's new incandescent lights. A clear glass bulb loomed from the brass sconces on the wall. Each bulb contained a glowing orange filament that threw off a smokeless light, both mild and intense.

A confusing mass of electrical wiring was strung haphazardly across the ceiling. The new lamps cast an all-too-revealing light upon the worn dull green carpet, faded damask draperies, and mended table linen.

Jonas was of the opinion that any businessman

thinking about converting to electric lights should first consider the merits of redecorating.

Exactly forty minutes after Jonas had left her room, Kate Whittaker walked into the restaurant. He was relieved to see her. He honestly thought she would not show her face.

He was more intrigued by her than ever. Did she really believe that he was going to give up so easily and concede defeat? Maybe she wasn't as smart as he thought she was. Then again, maybe she was. *Which is it, Miss Whittaker?*

For a fleeting moment he was taken aback by her beauty. In a remarkably short time, she had managed to contain the thick mass of her hair. It was now piled high on her head, emphasizing her long graceful neck. A few wayward tendrils curled around her forehead, suggesting, perhaps, she was less controlled than she would like him to think.

She was dressed in a simple gray dress that would look plain on most women, but which revealed enough womanly curves to inspire even the most unimaginative man. Whereas the new electric lighting revealed every flaw in the room and cast an unflattering glare upon the other diners, it only enhanced Miss Whittaker's golden red hair and smooth pink skin.

She turned her head to scan the room before her gaze fell on him. Something seemed to pass between them—a spark, perhaps, an electrical impulse. It was gone so quickly, he decided it was Mr. Edison's lighting. The inventor was obviously more of a genius than Jonas had given him credit for, even if he was causing the fairer sex to go berserk.

Rising to his feet, Jonas found himself straining to see her petticoats as she walked. His efforts were rewarded with a beguiling and all-too-fleeting glimpse of a fiery red ruffle. *Well, now,* he thought in wry amusement. *Miss Whittaker would certainly give those French designers a run for their money.*

"I hope I didn't keep you waiting long, Mr. Hunter."

"Not at all." He held her chair for her, wondering if her promptness was due to habit or curiosity. Judging by the bold assessment in her clear eyes, he decided it was the latter.

He took his place opposite her, his leg brushing against hers. The jolt he felt this time could not be his imagination—nor could it possibly be Mr. Edison's doings.

Curious as to whether the red petticoat actually revealed a passionate nature, he let his knee press against hers once again. He wondered how long it would take her to move her leg away. Such dallying was bound to cause her to become all red-faced and flustered. No woman could ignore such brazen behavior, especially if she felt as much as a fraction of the jolt he himself had felt upon initial contact.

The smile died on his face when a full minute passed and she had yet to respond. He moved his leg along hers. Nothing! She continued to study the menu as if it were a scholarly piece of work. *Come on, Miss Whittaker,* he thought with growing irritation. Any woman wearing such blatant red petticoats couldn't possibly be that immune to the opposite sex. Could she?

Kate stared at her menu, unable to make out a single word. She was aware—too aware—of the dangerous game in progress. His leg against hers sent a fiery charge up her spine. Lord forgive her for thinking it, but he was a handsome, devilish rogue. Too bad, in a way. Had she met him under any other circumstances . . . well, who knows what might have happened? But who cared? Certainly not her!

"Your leg, Mr. Hunter," she said with icy politeness, keeping her gaze fixed firmly on her menu. She wished she could have kept up the pretense of not noticing his leg next to hers, but she would never manage to concentrate on the menu if he didn't move it.

She heard him inhale. "I beg your pardon?"

He sounded so astonished at her request, it was all she could do to keep from laughing. What an arrogant man! She allowed her gaze to travel upward until she was looking him straight in the eye. "Your leg is taking up too much space."

Following her rather blunt if not startling observation, she perused her bill of fare with an air of dismissal, as if she had asked nothing more than for him to remove his coat or hat. In reality, she congratulated herself for maintaining her composure, at least on the outside.

Jonas pulled his leg back and, feeling rebuffed, tried to concentrate on the menu. Never had he known a woman so self-possessed. Most women would have been flustered by such a wantonly aggressive overture. But not Miss Whittaker. *Your leg is taking up too much space.* Never had a woman insulted him more.

The waiter came to take their order and Jonas, having had his fill of chicken during the hours spent at the White House, decided to forgo the specialty of the house and chose roast beef instead. The waiter left, taking the bills of fare with him.

Without the distraction of the menu, Jonas was forced to focus solely on his dinner companion. It was a diversion that was an unnerving as it was pleasurable.

"So where are you from, Miss Whittaker?"

"Hogs Head, Indiana," she replied. *As if you didn't know, you two-timing . . .* He smiled and her heart skipped a beat. He had a dimple on his right cheek, which matched the soft impression on his chin. She pressed her hands together and reminded herself that the key word was *two-timing*.

"Hogs Head, eh?"

"And you, Mr. Hunter? Where are you from?"

He grinned at her as if he knew something she didn't know. "Waller Creek, Iowa." Without the shadows normally cast in a room lit by gas or candles, his face looked deceivingly honest. Thank goodness she had the good sense to know it was the lighting and not the man that gave the impression of integrity.

His gaze grew more intense. "Are you familiar with the town?"

"I never heard of it," she replied.

He stroked his chin. "I thought perhaps you might know someone who lives there?"

"Why would you think that, Mr. Hunter?"

"No reason." His benign smile belied his turbulent thoughts. The only way she could steal his notes was by working with someone who knew him and who had access to his family farm. He sighed inwardly. If his leg didn't distract her enough to give away her secrets, what would?

He glanced at her soft pink lips and immediately attempted to dismiss the disturbing desire to kiss her. The only problem was, her lips were every bit as seductively tempting now, in public, as they had been in private.

Their dinner arrived, and while they ate, Jonas kept up a steady conversation that seemed harmless enough on the surface, but was cleverly directed toward earning her trust.

The easy smile playing upon the corners of her mouth told him he was making headway. At least the hostility and suspicion had left her face. Unfortunately, she still maintained the pretense of being an inventor.

Realizing he was being dangerously distracted by her, he kept his eyes glued to his plate as he ate. The slices of roast beef were paper-thin and cooked to perfection. The rice was fluffy and well seasoned, the fresh garden peas tender and sweet.

"That was a delicious supper," she said after a while, pushing the chicken bones to the side of her plate. "Clearly the best meal I've had since coming to Washington."

Congratulating himself for thinking up the idea of inviting her to dinner, he weaved his fingers together and leaned on his elbows. It was time for the kill.

"I wonder if you would be kind enough to accept a proposition of mine."

He almost regretted seeing the smile leave her face, but it couldn't be helped. A lot was at stake and he wasn't about to let a woman, even one as beguiling as Miss Whittaker, cheat him out of what was rightfully his.

"A proposition, Mr. Hunter?"

"Don't look so worried, Miss Whittaker. I was referring to a *business* proposition. I only wish to suggest a resolution to our patent problem that would be to our mutual benefit."

"As far as I know, I don't have a patent problem. If the president and his wife believe I'm the true inventor, I doubt very much the board of examiners will think otherwise."

"Of course they won't, Miss Whittaker."

She greeted his admission with a look of surprise. "Then you admit you're a thief and a—"

He hushed her gently. "I should think you'd be more charitable toward your future business partner."

She gasped. "My what?"

"Getting the patent is only half the battle. You'll have to find a manufacturer willing to work with a woman." His voice was soft and alluring, more suited for an illicit liaison than a business discussion, but he couldn't seem to help himself.

He regretted the loss of soft flickering candlelight, which would have better suited his mood than the harsh glare of Mr. Edison's filaments. Still, as detrimental as electric lights were to romance, he knew they were a blessing in disguise. Candlelight would make it too easy to forget they were in a public place.

He allowed his fingertips to brush against her hand. He knew from past experience how such an innocent though intimate touch could distract a woman. Despite his lack of success earlier in provoking her with his leg, he wasn't willing to concede that she could be so completely immune to him.

He waited for the telltale blush to reach her cheeks, and when none came, he continued, "Then there's the problem of distribution and capital. Do you know how much something like this can cost? With your patent and my know-how, it would be a partnership made in heaven."

He presented such a strong case to favor a partnership, he couldn't understand why she looked so thoroughly unconvinced. "All I'm asking is for you to think about it." He brushed his hand against her velvet-soft skin. "You don't have to let me know your answer until later in the week, after you've had time to think about it."

She moved her hands to her lap. "I don't have to think about it, Mr. Hunter. I have no intention of taking you on as a partner. Now if you will excuse me, I'm quite exhausted."

He frowned. Was that why she seemed so oblivious to him? Because she was tired? God, he hoped so. He hated to think he'd lost his ability to seduce a woman. Maybe he'd been spending too much time, lately, with his inventions and not enough time with womenfolk.

Another thought suddenly occurred to him: Was it possible that electrical lighting was somehow hindering the attraction between the sexes? In the name of Sir Isaac Newton, he hoped not! He looked over at the next table to see if any other couples were being so adversely affected. Two matronly women stared back at him.

Kate pushed her chair back and stood. "I trust I'll see you on Wednesday?"

He rose to his feet. "Oh, I'll be there, Miss Whittaker. Make no mistake about it."

Without so much as a backward glance, she walked with quick, determined, no-nonsense strides through the dining room. Despite her formidable facade, she managed to turn the head of every diner in the room, leaving behind a trail of admiring males and their annoyed female companions.

He watched her until she disappeared through the arched doorway, then sat down and stared into his empty wineglass.

Dammit! What in the world was he doing sitting here? Since when had he been so reluctant to pursue a woman all the way to the logical tryst? He'd already been on her bed once tonight. Surely it wouldn't have been all that difficult to get invited back a second time. Women confessed all sorts of things in bed. His mind wandered as he considered the possibility of her revealing who had put her up to such chicanery amid passionate embraces and hot, tempting kisses. In the name of Sir Isaac Newton, who would ever think that detective work could be so interesting?

Damn! He should have insisted upon escorting her back to her room. He *should* have kissed her! That would have rattled her! Caught her off guard. Made her confess.

Recalling his own confusion earlier in her presence, he stared at her empty chair and wondered how he could so much as consider taking a woman with such unethical deportment to bed.

Still, Miss Whittaker or someone she knew had stolen his notes. Even if by chance the board of examiners voted in his favor, his strong sense of justice wouldn't let him rest until she and her cohort were punished by law.

He frowned at the glaringly bright light bulb over his table and firmly vowed to ban Mr. Edison from any future liaisons.

Chapter 12

Kate left her hotel early that Wednesday morning and hailed a cab to take her to the United States Patent Office. No sooner had the driver helped her out of the carriage than she was swarmed by a mob of waiting newspaper reporters.

"What's it like being a woman inventor?"

"When will your carpet cleaners be ready for purchase?"

"How many carpet cleaners did Mrs. Cleveland order for the White House?"

"Gentleman, please!" Kate beseeched the newspapermen with good-natured tolerance. It was flattering to be the center of so much attention. She might lack all but the fundamental knowledge of business practices, but she knew the value of publicity. She smiled and the reporters were ready to fall on their knees. "I shall be happy to discuss this with you after I've met with the board of examiners and have heard their decision."

The journalists were clearly dazzled by her. They followed her up the steps like puppies, racing to see which lucky reporter would have the opportunity to open the door for her. "Thank you," she said to the earnest young man who had beat out his competitors. Smiling, she turned to wave. She posed for the cameras, then disappeared through the double oak door. Inside, she literally ran straight into Mr. Hunter.

Squeaking out an apology, she stepped back and stared up at his handsome, though stoic face and mocking brown eyes.

He tipped his hat. "Miss Whittaker."

Wondering what in the world he had to look so smug about, she lifted her chin. "Mr. Hunter."

"After you," he said, making a sweeping gesture with his arm.

Taking a deep breath, she started toward the conference room. He followed close behind, and though he didn't say a word, she could feel his eyes boring into her back.

Inside the room, she took her place to the right of the aisle; he took his to the left. She kept her eyes straight ahead, but couldn't resist holding him in her ken. Despite his lack of integrity, she found him—Lord forgive her for thinking it—the most attractive man she'd ever met. This despite his arrogance, his boldness, his attempt to steal from her.

She sensed a danger in him that thrilled her even as she fought the attracting force. It was the same sense of danger she felt when she first began experimenting with electricity. Shaking herself, she decided she'd best treat him like she would a dangerous live wire.

He took off his hat and set it upon the seat next to him. He moved a leg and she swallowed hard as she recalled how that same leg had felt against hers. Forcing the unwanted memory away, she turned her head slightly so she could no longer see him. Now if she could only forget his presence altogether . . .

At exactly five minutes to ten, the members of the board of examiners entered through a side door and took their places around the table. Commissioner Hobbs waited until the men were seated before banging the gavel repeatedly against the table—for what reason, Kate couldn't imagine, since he already commanded everyone's attention. He cleared his throat and, without further ado, made his statement.

"Mr. Hunter, Miss Whittaker, as you know, the board of examiners takes its responsibilities quite seriously. We have spent a great deal of time going over all the notes and drawings that were presented to us. Since we were not able to come to any agreement after reviewing the material, we were forced to take other considerations into account." Mr. Hobbs took a drink of water before continuing.

"It was the general consensus of the board members that the machine in question is much more suited to cleaning carpets than it is to spreading fertilizer. For this reason, the board has decided to award the patent to Miss Whittaker."

Silence followed his declaration, and finally Kate realized the commissioner was waiting for her to say something. "I'm most honored," she stammered, feeling strangely tongue-tied. She had dreamed about this moment for so long, she could hardly believe it had arrived. She was going to have her name on a patent! Not wanting anyone or anything to spoil the moment for her, she refused to look at Mr. Hunter.

The commissioner addressed Kate directly. He took undue care in explaining what amounted to a simple procedure. "I'll require your signature before you leave today. In a few weeks' time, you'll receive the documentation in the mail with your patent number."

One by one, the examiners hastened from the room. Only the commissioner remained.

Kate clasped her hands to her chest and said a prayer of thanksgiving. Finally, she stole a glance at Mr. Hunter, who looked less contrite than she would have liked for her peace of mind.

The man had acted abominably and anyone less charitable than herself would certainly insist he be brought to justice. She had no such desire. She was far too anxious to put the unfortunate episode behind her and concentrate fully on the manufacturing of her machine. She did, however, expect an apology. It was the least he could do for the trouble he had caused her.

Commissioner Hobbs retrieved several documents from his portfolio and invited Kate to join him at the table. He handed her a fountain pen with a golden-tipped nib. "Sign your name on this line," he said, pointing.

Kate dibbed the pen into the bottle of ink and signed her name *Katherine Hoover Whittaker*. She then handed the pen back to the commissioner, who immediately signed his own name on a line marked WITNESS.

"Oh, dear," he exclaimed, glancing about the room. "Everyone has left and we'll need another witness."

"Allow me," Mr. Hunter said, joining them.

Kate whirled about to face him. "I . . . I don't think that would be appropriate."

"Not appropriate?" Commissioner Hobbs looked from Kate to Mr. Hunter. "How do you mean?"

Kate tempered her voice. She was not going to embarrass herself in front of the commissioner. "Mr. Hunter's petition for a patent has been denied. To ask him to serve as a witness would be most unseemly."

Mr. Hunter disregarded her protest with a wave of his hand. "I'm sure Miss Whittaker is simply taking my feelings into account." Avoiding Kate's warning look, he took the pen offered by Commissioner Hobbs. He leaned toward Kate and whispered in her ear. "I ask you now, whose name better belongs on that patent than mine?"

"I'll not have your name on my patent!" Kate whispered back, her lips wooden.

"Sign your name on the line next to mine," the commissioner said, obviously unaware that a tug-of-war ensued. "I say, it's most generous of you to offer to witness the signing of this document. Don't you agree, Miss Whittaker?"

"I doubt that generosity has anything to do with it," Kate lit back. She watched in dismay as Mr. Hunter leaned over the table and signed his name as a witness to her patent. He filled the entire lower portion of the paper with dark thick strokes and underlined his name with such a bold flourish, the other two signatures, including her own, seemed insignificant in comparison.

How she hated having his name on her patent! How dare the man put her in such a position!

Satisfied the required paperwork had been filled out, Commissioner Hobbs gathered up his portfolio and left through the side door.

Not wanting to spend one minute longer than necessary in Mr. Hunter's company, Kate hurried to her seat and gathered up her kid gloves. Turning, she found him blocking her way. "I do not appreciate your little games, Mr. Hunter."

"I'm not playing games, Miss Whittaker." Gone were any attempts to seduce or charm her. Nor, judging by the harsh lines in his face, was he going to accept his fate with any sort of dignity. He was angry and he made no attempt to hide it. "You're not going to get away with this."

Kate narrowed her eyes. She had had about all she could take of this man and his threats. But she had no intention of letting him ruin her victorious day. Forcing a calm she didn't feel, she appraised him with cool detachment. "I have no idea what you're talking about."

"I'm talking about the way you stole my idea. I won't stop until I've found the proof I need to make the board of examiners reverse its decision. The next time that patent is issued, it will be my name on the center line and your name will be mud."

"I'm shuddering in my boots, Mr. Hunter."

Jonas knew she was doing no such thing. If anything, she looked as bold and arrogant as . . . well, a man on a winning streak. But there was nothing manly about her soft lips and delicate nose. He only wished he didn't know what she wore under her somber dark dress.

Kate pulled on her gloves. "If you'll be kind enough to excuse me, I promised those gentlemen from the newspaper I would answer their questions."

"By all means, don't keep them waiting." He stepped aside to let her pass. He watched her like a hawk eyeing its prey, but made no attempt to follow or further delay her departure. "Enjoy yourself, Miss Whittaker," he called after her, his voice thick with ominous threat, "while you still have the chance."

Chapter 13

It was a bright sunny day that afternoon in early June when the Chicago-bound train pulled into the Hogs Head train station.

A wild cheer greeted Kate as she stepped off the train and set her carpet cleaner down on the wooden platform. The train whistled and a blast of steam shot out from beneath the engine. The hazy mist that swirled around her feet added to the dreamlike scene around her. Exhausted from her journey, she stared in surprise and confusion at the mob of people gathered around the weathered-wood depot to greet her.

"Hooray for Kate!"

Smiling in uncertainty, Kate lifted her arm and waved at the cheering crowd. She was joined by her Aunt Hattie and Uncle Barney. Her aunt was, in the words of Uncle Barney, gibber-jabbering up a storm about Kate's wondrous machine.

"Wait until Mr. Shears hears he's not getting his hands on your machine," Aunt Hattie said, smacking her lips with relish.

"That's Sears," Uncle Barney said.

Kate hugged her aunt and gave her uncle a kiss. She glanced over at their wagon, hoping they'd been able to persuade Jimmy to meet her train. The wagon was empty, but she was more disappointed than surprised.

"Is Jimmy . . . ?"

"He's fine," her uncle assured her. "He missed you. Did you get your patent?"

"Indeed I did."

Aunt Hattie wrapped an arm around Kate's. "We saw your photograph in the paper. The one with you and that nice President Cleveland and his dear sweet wife."

Kate was amazed. "I had no idea you would see that photograph here in Hogs Head."

"Ran on the front page of the *Hogs Head Gazette,*" Uncle Barney said proudly. "Not too many people get to have their pictures taken with the president of the United States."

"It was plastered clear across the page," Aunt Hattie added. "You got a bigger headline than Shears and Rhubarb. Quincy did himself proud." Clearly the newspaper editor had worked himself back into Aunt Hattie's good graces by running Kate's picture.

"You're famous, Kate." Uncle Barney was forced to raise his voice to be heard above the small brass band that had started to play.

Kate was nearly overwhelmed with emotion. "Is this . . . is this all for me?"

"No, no, no," Aunt Hattie said. "It's one of those marches by—what's his name? You know the one who played at the Chicago Fair."

"Mr. Sousa," Uncle Barney said.

"You didn't miss the tuba," Aunt Hattie declared. "It's that Eric Chambers. He just can't blow hard enough. Why they give the smallest band member the largest instrument is beyond me."

Accustomed to her aunt's hearing problem, Kate remained speechless as she gazed in amazement at the celebration in her honor. Even Smoky Joe rushed up to shake her hand and congratulate her.

"I knew from the moment you ran your fuel-driven buggy into my wall that you were destined for greatness!" he said.

Sheriff Williams hung his thumbs on his belt. "Is that why you insisted I put her in jail?"

Smoky Joe gave a sheepish grin. "Ah, come on, Sheriff. I didn't really want you to put her in jail."

The sheriff snorted. "You could have fooled me."

The band finished its medley and the mayor took his place on the platform of the train station and yelled through a megaphone. "Ladies and gentlemen. It gives me great pleasure to declare this Kate Whittaker's Day."

The residents of Hogs Head went wild. Loud shouts of approval accompanied the thunderous applause and stomping of hundreds of feet. The band struck up again and a group of laughing young men hoisted Kate into the air and paraded her up and down Main Street for all to see.

Hidden behind the ticket counter, Jonas Hunter watched the festivities with growing amazement. Did all these people actually believe that Kate had invented the carpet cleaner by herself?

Did they not know the years of work that such an invention required? The dedication? The focus required? The commitment? Did they think that such an invention could be whipped up like a batch of gingerbread?

Feeling hungry and tired, Jonas nonetheless kept himself hidden. It wouldn't do for Kate to know he'd followed her to her hometown. He didn't plan on staying more than a day or so—a week at the most. That should give him ample time to gather up proof positive she'd stolen his idea. He would then head back to Washington, go straight to the

Patent Office, and insist the board of examiners right the terrible injustice that had been done.

He scanned the crowd in search of a familiar face. Someone had stolen his notes and given them to Kate. Someone who knew him, someone who had access to his family farm. Someone who had the morals of a snake.

His gaze returned to Kate, who was dancing in the street with the sheriff. Her red petticoats flashed beneath the hem of her dress each time she kicked up her heels. Strands of her sun-kissed hair fell from the confines of her bun and curled around her lively face. Jonas was reminded of how it had felt to be close to her, her rounded breasts pressed against his chest, as they'd wrestled on the bed of her hotel room.

His already fast-beating heart took a flying leap when she flashed a coquettish smile in his direction. Pulling back into the shadows, Jonas watched the sheriff spin her around in time to the music.

The band changed tempos and Kate danced with flirtatious grace from one male to another. A line began to form as every eligible man in town, and a few Jonas suspected weren't so eligible, waited to twirl Kate in their arms.

Jonas watched with an odd combination of envy and disdain. The woman was not only a thief, she was a temptress. Granted, she was a beguiling one—and granted he would give anything to dance with her—but that didn't change a thing. Not a thing.

So what if she had the most intriguing smile he'd ever seen on a woman? Who cared that she had the prettiest eyes he'd ever had occasion to look into? What possible difference could it make that beneath her rather plain and prudish dress she wore the most outrageous but intriguing red petticoats he'd ever laid eyes on? So what if the afore-mentioned frock defined her womanly curves in a way that made a man's heart flutter faster than the wings of a hummingbird. She was a thief!

Craning his head above the crowd, he followed her every movement like a man possessed, quite forgetting the need to keep himself hidden from sight.

A shock of recognition suddenly darkened her face, and he quickly drew back. Kate had looked straight at him. Damn!

Fearing she might come to investigate, he merged with the band, keeping his head hidden behind the flaring horn of the tuba, and took cover by the water tank. It was several moments before he chanced another look. She was surrounded by a group of people, and he breathed a sigh of relief. His solace, however, was temporary, for she cast an anxious glance toward the ticket counter where he had been standing when she had spotted him.

Chastising himself for his carelessness, Jonas pulled his hat down low and turned up the collar of his coat. With a little luck, she would dismiss the sighting, blaming it, perhaps, on exhaustion or an overactive imagination.

He checked his watch. Minutes passed, then an hour, and still she hadn't broken free from the crowd to search him out. Relieved, he nonetheless took great care in keeping himself hidden for the remainder of the day. Next time he might not be so lucky.

It was late in the afternoon by the time the cele-bration ended and people started drifting away from the station.

Kate left with an older couple, whom he pre-sumed were her parents. The man, probably her father, had lifted the newly patented invention onto the back of their wagon along with Kate's baggage, and the three had driven off amid loud cheers.

Free to leave his hiding place, Jonas walked the length of Main Street to get a feel for the town. He guessed there were some thirty buildings in all, fronting a weathered boardwalk that ran along both sides of the street. Planted firmly on one end of town was a three-story hotel with a gabled roof and a wrap-around veranda.

Businesses were strung along Main Street like clothes on a clothesline, stretching between the hotel and the Red Rooster Saloon located on the other end of town. Faded signs hung from the false fronts of each building: HOGS HEAD GAZETTE; HOGS HEAD BANK; ELROY'S SADDLE AND FEED SHOP; BARNARD'S HARNESS SHOP; THELMA PAINE, SEAMSTRESS (LET THELMA TAKE THE PAINE OUT OF YOUR SEWING CHORES); CURLY'S BARBERSHOP; and an assortment of other businesses. Aunt Hattie's general merchandise store was centered in the middle of town. A small sign in the crammed window read U.S. POST OFFICE.

Although the general store was housed in one of the largest buildings, an amazing number of goods spilled onto the covered porch, down the steps, and onto the boardwalk, including two rocking chairs, a baby carriage, several wooden washtubs, and one of those new safety bicycles with wheels of equal diameter.

He counted four saloons in all, less than the number of his own town, and less, he suspected, than most towns of a comparable size.

He rented a black gelding from the stables located behind the hotel. The swaybacked horse had seen better days, but Jonas didn't expect to do much in the way of riding.

"You new to these parts?" the stable owner asked. The man spoke as slow as he moved.

"Yeah," Jonas said. "Do you know anyplace I can get a hot meal and some shut-eye?"

The man's thought processes were equally slow, for a good two or three minutes passed before he finally got around to nodding his head. "The hotel's right there."

Jonas pushed his hat back. "I was looking for something outside of town."

The stable owner stared at Jonas's worn boots and eventually got around to pointing up Main Street. "About a half mile outside of town, you'll find Mrs. Applegate's Boardinghouse. Tell her Speedy sent you."

Jonas stared at the man in amazement. "That's your name? Speedy?"

A grin as slow as molasses inched across Speedy's face. "Yep."

Jonas paid the man, mounted the horse, and rode out of town. He kept his brim pulled down low in the unlikely event that Miss Kate Whittaker might decide to make another appearance.

Shadows crisscrossed the dirt road leading out of town. The sun rode low on the horizon, a fiery red ball that cast a copper glow across the sky. It had been a long day. He was more than ready for a good night's sleep.

A two-story clapboard house with angled bay windows and curlicue scrollwork stood to the right of the road. A wooden sign told him it was the boardinghouse.

Dismounting, he tied his horse to a weathered wooden post next to a water trough. His horse drank thirstily, then dipped its head and neighed gruffly as it rooted for a sprinkling of hay that had been left by the low wooden fence. Jonas patted the long rough neck of the horse, then stooped and reached through the railing to grab a handful of fresh hay. He straightened and held the hay where his horse could reach it and grinned in satisfaction as the soft nose pressed hungrily against his callused palm. "That a boy."

Mrs. Applegate greeted him warily, until he mentioned Speedy's name. Turning an astonishing shade of red, she then melted into a butterball smile.

"A friend of Speedy's is a friend of mine." She giggled and motioned Jonas inside. "What did you say your name was?"

"Hunter," he replied. "Jonas Hunter."

Mrs. Applegate led him down a long hall and into a cozy dining room. The table was spread with a lace tablecloth that looked more yellow than white beneath the gaslit chandelier. A vase of roses stood in the center of the otherwise bare table.

"Sit there," she said, pointing to the ladder-back chair at the end of the table. She disappeared for a few minutes before returning with a tray set with a bowl of hot steaming chicken soup and a basket of fresh bread. She set the bowl in front of him and reached into the drawer of the mahogany sideboard for eating utensils.

"Some wine, Mr. Hunter?" she asked, grabbing a wine decanter from the built-in wine cooler.

"Yes, thank you."

The soup and bread were delicious, the wine satisfying. Mrs. Applegate sat across from him, watching him eat. "Are there no other boarders?" he asked.

"I have two others," she replied. "They all went to town for the big celebration. Mr. Bender plays in the band."

"Celebration?" Just the opening he hoped for.

He tried not to sound too interested. "Come to think of it, I saw something going on down by the train station."

"The Whittaker woman arrived in town today."

The cutting edge in her voice as she said Kate's name told him he had hit pay dirt. "That wouldn't be the same Whittaker who was written about recently in the newspaper?"

"The very same one." She gave a disgusted snort before continuing. "After all the trouble that woman has caused this town, I can't for the life of me figure out why they're making her out to be a hero. Just cuz she got her picture taken with the president."

His sentiments exactly. He reached for another slice of bread. "What kind of trouble has she caused?"

The woman leaned across the table, her imposing bosom supported by her folded arms. She pointed to the ceiling. "See that crack up there?"

Jonas attached his gaze to the jagged line that ran from the crystal chandelier to the far corner of the room.

"She did that!" Mrs. Applegate sniffed.

"Kate . . . eh, Miss Whittaker?"

The widow gave no indication she noticed Jonas's slip of the tongue. "You have no idea what it's like living in the same town as that woman. Always blowing things up with her inventions, she is."

Jonas suddenly felt as if someone had stabbed him. "Did . . . did you say inventions?"

"Why, yes. She calls herself an inventor. What kind of inventor is always blowing up things? That's what I want to know!"

Jonas's mouth ran dry. What kind of inventor didn't? He remembered reading somewhere that

Thomas Edison had been thrown off a train in his youth for causing an explosion. But of course, Mrs. Applegate would have no way of knowing that such mishaps were an occupational hazard. "You say she blows up things?"

"I'll say she does. You should see her house. What's left of it, that is. The chimney's gone. The porch is only half there. I shudder to think what it looks like inside."

Jonas felt a tight knot in his stomach. *It was true, then. She was an inventor.* The woman with her flashing blue eyes and outrageous red petticoats was an honest-to-God inventor!

It took him a full minute to absorb this astounding piece of news. He'd known from the moment he'd met her she was extremely intelligent. No one could have given such an accurate and in-depth presentation before the board of examiners without having a thorough education on the subject. Naturally he'd assumed she had been carefully schooled by someone, possibly the man who had stolen his idea in the first place. It was quite a natural assumption. Understanding how a machine operated was not the same thing as conceiving an idea and designing a working model.

"She's got herself those, what do you call them, new lights?" Mrs. Applegate was saying.

"Electrical lights?" he offered, though he doubted that was what Mrs. Applegate meant. He'd not noticed any electrical powerhouses in Hogs Head.

"Those are the ones. I can't tell you how many times she set the house afire with her lights."

"When did Hogs Head acquire electricity?" he asked, surprised. He'd not even been able to convince the residents of Waller Creek to convert to electricity, though it would certainly be to their advantage to do so.

"We don't have electricity. And after all the problems the Whittakers have had since Kate installed electric lights, we don't want it."

Jonas finished his soup in silence, giving full consideration to this rather startling piece of information. If Kate did, indeed, have electric lights, then she must have a generator.

It wasn't all that difficulty to install electricity. Several articles in the *Electric Age* magazine had described how it was done. By following the step-by-step directions, he had managed to install electricity in his father's chicken coop and barn. Still, it was hard to imagine a woman, any woman, successfully wiring a house for electric lights. Hell, there were few men who would mess around with something as potentially dangerous as electricity. "Are you certain these lights are electric?"

" 'Course I'm certain. Her house was so lit up you could see it for miles. That was before she blew out the windows and had to board them over."

"She blew out the windows of her house?"

"And that ain't all she's done, either. I couldn't begin to describe the mayhem she's brought to this town."

"Does . . . does she live near here?"

"Just a half mile or so away, on Rocking Horse Lane."

"Rocking Horse, eh?" He seemed to remember passing that street on the way to the boarding-house. "Quaint name."

"There ain't nothing quaint about it. Kate Whittaker spooked the horses so badly with her explosions, all they do is rock back and forth. It's nerves, you know. Had an aunt once who did the same thing. Are you going to be in Hogs Head long?"

"I don't expect to be."

"Here on business?"

"Something like that." Hoping to ward off the onslaught of questions plainly written all over the woman's face, he stood. "I hope you don't mind if I retire to my room. I've had a long and extremely tiring journey."

"Of course, Mr. Hunter. You needn't explain. Your room's right at the top of the stairs. Bathroom's down the hall. Breakfast will be served at eight."

He thanked her and carried his valise up the stairs to the second floor. His room was small but comfortable. He glanced through the lace curtains and watched as a lamplighter stopped to light a lamp in front of the boardinghouse. The trees were silhouetted against the dim traces of a sunset. Overhead, the first star twinkled.

This was normally Jonas's favorite time, neither day nor night, but a blending of both that seemed to demand serious reflection and contemplation. Tonight, however, rather than ponder the meaning of the universe, as was his usual custom, he was obsessed with thoughts of Kate Whittaker.

It had never occurred to him that she was actually an inventor. Not that it changed anything. In some ways, it made matters worse. He liked to believe that inventors as a whole subscribed to the highest ethical standards possible. Why, he'd no sooner steal another's idea than he would steal another's wife.

Of course, it did explain why Miss Whittaker gave such a convincing testimony in front of the board of examiners. If she could wire a house for electricity, then she could most certainly understand his notes. One mystery was solved. Now if he could just figure out how she got her pretty little hands on his notes in the first place . . .

He unconsciously narrowed his gaze to follow the lamplighter's retreating back, but in his mind's eye he saw Miss Whittaker dancing in the street, flashes of red showing beneath her gown.

Yes, indeed, he intended to make it his business to learn everything he could about one very intriguing and mysterious woman named Kate Whittaker.

Chapter 14

Jimmy sat on his bed dressed in his white summer nightshirt. His freshly scrubbed face glowed pink; his uncombed hair stuck up in little spikes like half-pulled taffy.

Kate gathered up copies of the *Electric Age* magazines strewn across the bed and floor.

Jimmy's eyes shone bright as he watched her. He'd hardly let her out of his sight since she'd returned earlier that evening.

"Would you read me the story about the wireless radio?" he asked.

He looked so earnest, Kate couldn't help but smile. Lord, what would Mrs. Bagelbauer say about Jimmy's taste in reading material? "I suppose so," she said. "Which magazine is it in?"

"The one with the arc light on the cover," Jimmy said.

Kate rifled through the stack in her arms, finding the one she wanted at the bottom of the pile.

Jimmy worked his way beneath the covers. "Did you really go to the president's house?"

She slid the stack of magazines onto the bookshelf, keeping the one she wanted. "I most certainly did, and what a fine house it was."

"Do you think I can see the president one day?"

"Of course you can. You can even be the president one day, if that's what you want. Then I'll come to the White House to visit you."

Jimmy giggled. "You won't blow the White House up, will you?"

"Well ..." Kate pretended to think about it. "Maybe not."

A look of relief crossed Jimmy's face, then his mouth turned downward. "I can't be the president. I can't walk."

"If I can be an inventor, you can be the president, if that's what you want."

Jimmy wrinkled his nose. "I don't think I want to be the president. I want to be an inventor, just like you."

Kate smiled. "Then that's what you shall be." She held up the magazine with the arc light on the cover. "Ready?"

He nodded and she settled down on the bed by his side and leaned her head against the feather pillow next to his. She flipped through the magazine, finding the page she wanted, and began reading. She stopped on occasion to explain a new word to him or to answer a question.

Jimmy's eyes never wavered from the printed page. "Do you really think they can send sound across the ocean?" he asked when she paused to find the continuation of the story.

"It says here that a scientist named Mr. Marconi is trying to do just that."

Kate continued reading and Jimmy hung on to her every word. He looked disappointed when she came to the end of the article. "Maybe one day I can help Mr. Marconi like I help you."

Kate closed the magazine and placed it on the bed table. "Maybe you can." She pushed a lock of hair away from his forehead. "Oh, Jimmy, I'm going to find you a wonderful family of your very own. With a mother and father and . . . maybe even brothers and sisters. How would you like that?"

"Can I have a dog and my own horse?"

"Maybe."

"Will you come and visit me?"

She leaned over and rubbed her nose against his. "Of course I'll visit you." She slipped off the bed. "You better get some sleep now."

"Kate?"

"Yes, Jimmy?"

"Mr. Marconi won't laugh at me, will he? Because I can't walk?"

She stood by his side and squeezed his hand. "Jimmy, you *can* walk. You just need a little help."

"I won't use my crutches. I won't!"

The plaintive cry almost broke Kate's heart. She tucked his hand beneath the blanket and drew the covers up to his chin. "No one's going to laugh at you, Jimmy," she vowed. "Not Mr. Marconi. Not anyone. I won't let anyone laugh at you ever again."

Jimmy's tight face relaxed and his mouth curved upward. "Promise?"

"I promise." She turned and tugged on the chain hanging from the ceiling. The room was thrown into darkness. "Good night, little one."

Leaving his door ajar, she descended the stairs to the melodious chimes of the tallboy clock. It was only nine o'clock, but it seemed much later.

Upon reaching the parlor, she sank into a comfortable upholstered chair and positioned the footstool so that it covered the charred hole in the floor left over from the time her motorized boot-polishing machine caught fire.

Planting her bare feet on the padded stool, she gratefully accepted a steaming cup of tea from her aunt.

"What a wonderful surprise this day has been." She took a sip of the soothing herb-scented beverage and pulled her woolen shawl tight around her shoulders to ward off a sudden chill.

She longed for a warm crackling fire in the fireplace. The first thing she planned to do once the money started rolling in from her invention was to arrange for the repairs of the chimney and replace the windows. Then, of course, she would hire someone to fix the various holes in the floors to cut down on the drafts.

The central heating and cooling system she'd installed two summers ago worked well enough. Pipes ran along the baseboard, allowing hot or cold water, depending on the time of year, to travel from either the boiler in the cellar or the holding tank in the mudroom behind the kitchen.

Though the cooling system kept the house a comfortable seventy-five degrees throughout most of the summer, the heater proved difficult to regulate. During the blizzard that paralyzed Hogs Head before Christmas, her poor aunt and uncle were forced to stand outside to cool down. In any event, nothing replaced the coziness of a warm crackling fire.

She sipped her tea with a wistful sigh and promised herself to have all the repairs completed by winter, she hoped by the first snowfall.

"Is everything all right with Jimmy?" Aunt Hattie asked. She was sitting on the divan, embroidering. "He simply wasn't himself when you were gone."

"I think he's all right now," Kate replied, frowning. She worried about him growing too attached to her. "I wish I could find him a proper home."

Uncle Barney grunted from behind his newspaper. "What's wrong with Thelma Paine? She's offered to give him a home."

Kate recoiled at the thought. "I wouldn't let him stay with that woman if she were his last chance. She insists upon sewing by hand and won't even use a self-filling fountain pen. Says it's not natural."

"I suppose you can't blame the poor woman," Uncle Barney said. "Her one and only attempt to change to modern ways resulted in the death of her first husband."

"I don't consider changing from kerosene lights to gas particularly modern. In any case, everyone knows you should never blow out a gaslight."

"Hmmm," Uncle Barney said, disappearing behind his newspaper. "Thelma may be a bit odd, but she's harmless. I still think she'd do right by the boy."

Kate didn't agree. Jimmy needed someone who would encourage his natural curiosity and quick intelligence. The boy was a born inventor. Thelma's idea of spending time with the boy was to have him hold her yarn while she wound it into a ball. Or to sort buttons or scraps of fabric according to size and color. Surely someone, somewhere, could provide a more suitable home for Jimmy.

Feeling drowsy, she lay her head against the back of the chair.

Her trip to Washington had been exhilarating, though nonetheless tiring. Perhaps that would explain why she had started to imagine things. Not things, exactly. She thought she saw—could have sworn she saw—Mr. Hunter down by the train station. But of course she'd been mistaken. What possible reason would he have to follow her to Hogs Head? Unless . . . She almost spilled her tea. He was trying to steal another one of her ideas!

Her uncle, obviously sensing her change of

mood, looked up from his newspaper. "Is something wrong?"

Kate shook her thoughts away and gazed in puzzlement at her uncle's anxious face. "Wrong?"

"You seem upset."

"I'm just tired. I think I'll make it an early night."

Aunt Hattie glanced up from her embroidery. "Curly's got every reason to be contrite, if you ask me. After the way he's treated you."

Uncle Barney winked at Kate. "I doubt Curly knows the meaning of contrite, Hattie." He addressed his wife with more tolerance than usual. "Kate said she was going to get an early night."

"Oh." Hattie sniffed and poked the needle into the fabric spread across her lap.

Uncle Barney folded his newspaper and reached for his pipe. "What are your plans now that your machine has been patented?"

"I have to find a way to produce the machines economically. I interviewed several manufacturers while in Washington, with no luck. I plan to write to some companies in New York."

"Don't forget you promised to let me sell your carpet cleaners in my store. If you ever let Mr. Shears and Mr. Rhubarb get their money-grabbing hands on your machine, it'll be your ruin. Mark my words."

Uncle Barney rolled his eyes to the ceiling and waited for his wife to finish her tirade. "How many times do I have to tell you, Hattie?" He struck a match and lit his pipe, filling the room with the smell of fragrant tobacco. "It's *Sears* and *Roebuck*." He waved out the flame and dropped the burned-out match into an ashtray. "Sears, dammit! Not shears!"

Aunt Hattie sniffed, her mouth set in a stubborn line.

"Don't you worry, Aunt Hattie," Kate promised. "No one is going to get their hands on my machine unless I say so." Recalling how Mr. Hunter had tried to seduce her—how he had pretty near succeeded—she set her cup down. "No one! Not even Mr. Hunter!"

She spoke with such vehemence that both her aunt and uncle stared at her.

"Well, don't you worry about a thing," her aunt said at last. "We've all made a blunder on occasion."

Uncle Barney groaned, his patience tried to the limit. "She didn't say *blunder,* she said *Hunter.*"

"Oh, my!" Aunt Hattie exclaimed, dropping her needlework. "I didn't know you were going to change occupations. Does this mean you'll no longer be an inventor?"

Chapter 15

Kate Whittaker is an inventor. Jonas had chewed on this astounding piece of information for most of the previous night. The thought was still very much on his mind when he woke to a dark room early that morning.

He still couldn't believe it. He could accept the idea a woman might invent some household gadget or think up a better way of doing certain feminine chores. But Miss Whittaker was dealing with serious technology. Motors and electricity. Dynamos and generators. Was it possible that Mrs. Applegate was confused about the lights?

Accustomed to rising early on the farm, Jonas rose before daybreak. He lit the gas lamp and poured water into the porcelain basin, anxious to accomplish his mission so as to return to Waller Creek as soon as possible.

He dressed in a fresh pair of trousers and worked the sliding lock he'd had installed in his pants after seeing the amazing metal fastener called a Clasplocker demonstrated at the 1893 World's Columbian Exposition in Chicago. The fastener had actually been made for shoes, requiring him to make a few changes in the original design. After some initial embarrassing episodes, he finally made a fastener suitable for trousers, although it was still too bulky for his liking.

After donning a warm flannel shirt, he tiptoed down the stairs so as not to be heard by Mrs. Applegate, who, judging by the loud clatter of pots and pans, was already preparing breakfast for her boarders.

He slipped out the front door, mounted his horse, and rode the short distance to the crossroads. The eastern sky was edged with a thread of silver light, but it was still too dark to read the road sign. It was light enough, however, to pick out the silhouette of a mare rocking back and forth, and he decided he'd found the street he was looking for.

His guess was that the large white house at the end of the street belonged to Kate. His assumption proved correct when the sky overhead grew light enough to reveal the chimney missing from the house. He waited patiently, not sure what answers he hoped to find.

In due time the sun rose, pointing fingers of bright yellow light toward the damaged porch and boarded windows. Much of the east wall was missing and had been replaced with crisscrossed planks of unfinished wood.

Narrowing his eyes in disbelief, Jonas dismounted and tied his horse to a sapling away from the road. Staying out of sight, he covered the remaining distance on foot until he reached the leaning fence.

What he saw absolutely astounded him. He pulled his hat off, held it to his chest in something akin to reverence, and stared at the house. His disbelief escalated as the light grew more pronounced. His own mishaps and misfires had been impressive, but never had they incurred such structural damage.

What in the world had Miss Whittaker done to

blow the chimney into a pile of rubble? The windows he could understand. It didn't take much of an explosion to break glass. But the whole side of the house? And the porch?

His regard for Miss Whittaker increased by leaps and bounds as the fast-rising sun exposed a yard filled with strange-looking contraptions, including two abandoned dynamos, a metal boiler larger than a stagecoach, and a windmill attached to a bicycle.

He would have continued to stand in front of Miss Whittaker's house indefinitely had the front door not opened, revealing the same older couple who had driven away with Kate the previous day.

He managed to step behind a clump of overgrown bushes sight unseen, but only because the couple was too busy arguing to notice him.

He cocked his ear, but he could only make out one or two words. It appeared that the woman he suspected was Kate's mother was upset about her crop or somebody's crop of rhubarb.

He shook his head in disbelief. One would think, given the sad condition of her house, the woman would have more to worry about than her garden.

He waited until they disappeared into the woods, which provided a shortcut to town, then crept closer to the house. His hope was to find a window in back that was not boarded up.

The yard presented the challenge of an obstacle course with its piles of scrap iron and lumber. He stopped to inspect the remains of a runabout and wondered what Miss Whittaker's intention had been. He hoped that whatever she'd had on her mind, she hadn't required a horse, for certainly no animal could have survived such an unfortunate blast.

At first he missed the little window that opened into the cellar. Squatting down, he pressed his face against the dusty glass. He caught a quick glimpse of Kate and suddenly had trouble breathing.

Inhaling until his lungs were filled with dew-sweet air, he wiped the dust away from the glass with a handkerchief. That was better.

Unable to catch a second glimpse of Kate, he glanced around the cellar, astonished at what he saw. Mrs. Applegate was right about the electrical lights. One of Edison's electric light bulbs dangled from a drop cord, its bright white light radiating from an orange filament.

A dynamo took up one entire corner. The rest of the cellar was packed with various scraps of metal. Steam rose from a bubbling pot providing power to some strange-looking contraption with fast-moving parts. The cellar looked suspiciously like the barn where he worked on his own inventions.

He sat down on the ground, not wanting to believe the idea that suddenly occurred to him. If she stole his idea, then wouldn't it be likely she'd stolen other ideas, other inventions? The question was how.

He left Kate's house like a man possessed. He hurried back to the boardinghouse, ate an enormous breakfast, and then headed for town. Cutting through the woods to save time, he tied his horse to a wooden post in front of the barbershop and hurried up and down Main Street, racing in and out of shops and businesses, talking to anyone willing to talk.

Not wanting to chance bumping into Kate, he started with the businesses that a woman would be less likely to visit. This included predominately male domains like the saloons, the barbershop, and the newspaper office. Normally he would have included the blacksmith, but judging from the amount of iron on her property, he guessed that Kate was a frequent visitor.

He guessed right, for as he was sitting in a barbershop seat, his chin covered in foaming cream, he saw Kate sweep into the blacksmith shop across the street as easily as most women sailed into a millinery.

"Hold still!" Curly growled.

"Forgive me. Eh . . . the woman who just went into the blacksmith shop. Was that the same woman honored by the town yesterday?"

"You must be talkin' about Kate Whittaker. You might have seen her picture in the paper with the pres'dent."

"With the president, you say? Would that be the president of the United States?"

"That's one and the same." Curly honed his razor on the canvas strop, then flipped the band over and smoothed the heated edge on the leather side. "She's an inventor. Claims she invented some newfangled machine that cleans carpets."

One of the customers who was waiting his turn spit a stream of yellow tobacco juice into a rusty spittoon and guffawed. "That's what I got me a wife fer. To clean tem carpets. I don't need no newfangled contraption."

"Don't go lettin' Miss Whittaker hear you talk like that, Hal. The woman is likely to give you an earful." Curly shaved the last of the whiskers away from Jonas's face and finished by applying a hot Turkish towel and a sprinkling of talcum powder.

"It's hard to believe," Jonas said. "A woman inventing a carpet cleaner."

Curly reached for a comb and a pair of shears, and set to work snipping Jonas's hair. "Kate sure in blazes ain't like no ord'nary woman. She has big plans to sell her machines in her aunt's shop, and you know what? She'll prob'ly be a big success."

Not if I have anything to do with it, Jonas thought. "You say her aunt owns a shop in town?"

"Yep. Right across the way. Aunt Hattie's Gen'-ral Merchandise. Be careful. The ole woman's al-most as crazy as her niece."

"Crazy?" He thought about Miss Whittaker. He could think of a lot of ways to describe her, but the word *crazy* had never entered his head. Still, he'd heard it said that a fine line existed between genius and madness. "What do you mean, exactly, when you say she's crazy?"

"Both Kate and her aunt are always up in arms about somethin'. The aunt parades up and down the street with those ... whatshamacallits? Picket signs. She once got Madam Miranda and her girls so mad, they refused to work for a whole week. If that didn't cause an uproar."

"Don't take too much off," Jonas said, looking in dismay at the amount of hair falling around him.

"Hold still, willya?"

"Eh ... you were saying about Madam Miranda ... Who is she?"

"Why, she's just the owner of the best whorehouse this part of the country. That's who she is. Just tell them Curly sent you and they'll take good care of you."

"Yes ... well, thank you."

"As I was saying, Kate's as crazy as her aunt. Why, she's been carryin' on somethin' awful tryin' to get the town to install 'lectric lights."

"Nothing wrong with that," Jonas said. "A lot of towns are installing them." Could it be there really *was* a connection between electric lights and women like Kate Whittaker being out of control? God, he hoped not.

Curly made a noise of contempt. "Kate installed them in her house. She makes her own 'lectricity with one of those dynamo things. Every night for three months it was the same old thing. Kate turned on her lights and the volunteer fire department had to race over to put out the fire. We had to make a deal with her not to turn on her lights on Wednesday nights, so as not to int'rupt lodge meetin's."

"Sounds reasonable," Jonas said. "Is she still having trouble with her lights?"

"Not as far as I know. But no one wants to go through that trouble agin. As far as I'm concerned, there ain't nothin' wrong with them there gaslights."

"Gas lights are nowhere near as efficient as electric lights," Jonas explained. "The least amount of wind can blow out a gaslight and I don't have to tell you how much oxygen the damned things consume. I'm amazed we haven't all become asphyxiated."

"I'd rather become 'ph'xated than 'lectrocuted," Curly grumbled. Curly removed the towel from around Jonas's shoulders and swept the snippets of hair from the back of Jonas's neck with a horsehair brush.

Jonas ran his hand along his neck and frowned. Curly had cut his hair in one of those short styles he noticed were so popular in Washington, and it no longer reached his collar. He dare not show his head in Waller Creek or he'd be the laughingstock of the town. "It's kind of short, isn't it?"

"It's the fashion," Curly assured him. "Trust me, the women will go wild when they see you."

"Wild, you say?" Interesting thought, but he wasn't convinced. In any case, since he was in town solely on business, he wasn't likely to find out if

Curly's claim was true. "Does Miss Whittaker have an assistant?"

Curly's forehead wrinkled. "What do you mean?"

"Someone who works with her. It's hard to believe that a woman can be an inventor without some sort of assistance."

Curly shook his head. "That's no more difficult to believe than what I heard recently. It seems that there're two lady barbers in San Francisco."

One of the customers waiting his turn looked up from a dog-eared copy of the *Police Gazette* in disgust. "Not a woman barber!"

"I ask you, what'll be next? A lady pres'dent?" Curly sneered at the thought.

"It seems to me that learning to cut hair and shave a beard is a lot easier than learning about electricity," Jonas said.

"It's not *that* easy to learn my trade," Curly exclaimed, looking offended. "The next thing we know, women will be pinnin' velvet bows on razor stands and hand-paintin' flowers on barber poles. I tell you, the way women are takin' over, there ain't nothin' sacred."

Jonas hung around the barbershop for a while longer, making small talk with Curly and his customers. All the while he kept an eagle-eye on the blacksmith shop across the street. At last Kate left the shop carrying a large wicker basket. He couldn't see what was in the basket, but it appeared heavy, requiring her to use both hands.

He waited until Kate was out of sight before he took his leave. Darting across the street, he weaved his way around the various horse-drawn vehicles parked haphazardly while farmers loaded supplies into the back of the wagons. Dodging the numerous bicycles proved an even greater challenge and the heel of his boot was clipped by a speeding two-wheeler.

He ducked into the blacksmith shop and glanced around. A man wearing a leather apron and covered in axle grease stood beating a gun barrel into shape upon an anvil. Sparks accompanied the loud clanging of metal against metal. Behind him a blazing fire crackled in the red-hot forge.

Jonas called out twice before he could get the smith's attention.

The man looked up, his ebony face streaming with sweat, and lay his hammer next to a pair of angle tongs. "Haven't seen you 'round these parts."

"That's because I'm new in town."

The man wiped his hands on a rag. "New, eh? My name's Spencer. But you can call me Duke. How can I help you?"

"Pleased to meet you, Duke. I'm an inventor and I was told that ... the woman who was recently pictured in the newspaper lives in Hogs Head."

Duke ran his arm across his forehead. "You just missed her. Her name's Kate ... Kate Whittaker."

"Just missed her, you say?"

"Yep. She wanted me to weld something for her."

"Do you often weld things for her?"

"All the time."

"What kind of things?"

Duke shrugged. "How the hell should I know? I made the mistake of asking her once. She went into a detailed expl'n'tion that I couldn't make heads nor tails outta. I don't ask no more. She comes in and tells me she wants this piece of metal attached to that piece of metal and that's what she gits, with no questions asked."

"I see. You don't happen to know where she was going after she left here, do you?"

"I'd say she was goin' home. She seemed anxious to try out some newfangled idea. She's an inventor, you know. I often wonder where she gets all those crazy ideas from."

"I've been wondering that myself." After a moment he asked, "Do you happen to know if Miss Whittaker has an assistant? You know, someone who helps with her work."

"She ain't got no one to help her. Fer as I know, she works alone."

Jonas thanked the blacksmith and left. He walked the short distance to Aunt Hattie's General Store, keeping his head low. Before entering, he peered through the crammed windows to make sure Kate wasn't inside.

Bells jangled on the door when he opened it, announcing his arrival. The air was spiced with cinnamon, licorice, and tea. Wicker baskets, cast-iron cookware, and rubber boots dangled from the rough wooden rafters, along with strings of strong-smelling onions. The goods were hung high enough for most customers to walk under, but Jonas's height made it necessary for him to duck.

Two counters ran the length of the store. One counter was lined with shiny glass bins filled with licorice strips, peppermint candy, and chocolate bonbons. The other counter was bare except for some folded calico yardage and a pair of shears. The walls were lined with shelves stacked high with bolts of fabric and other merchandise. One portion of the wall was divided into alphabetized mail slots. All manner of kegs, bins, and barrels brimmed with crackers, coffee beans, rice, and other bulk foods.

The woman he now knew to be Miss Whittaker's aunt was sitting behind a small desk in back of the store, next to a round heater stove. She glanced up from her ledger as he approached. "How can I help you, young man?"

He glanced at the glass case filled with cigars. "Let me have a twofer," he said, though he didn't smoke. Maybe they would come in handy in the future. The easiest way to get a man to talk was to offer him a cigar. By contrast, women usually needed no more persuasion than a compliment.

Aunt Hattie shuffled toward him. "I'm sorry. I don't carry blue fur."

"Uh ... twofer." He pointed to the cigars and held up two fingers. He then pulled an envelope out of his pocket and placed it on the counter. "I also want to mail this letter."

No sooner had he pulled the coins from his pocket than the door flew open. Fearing it might be Kate, he threw a quick glance over his shoulder. It was an older woman whose generous girth would clearly be challenged by the cluttered aisles. The hat she wore was three stories and an attic high and burdened with enough feathers to warm a flock of birds.

The woman ducked beneath the amazing array of goods dangling from the rafters and still managed to keep her feathers intact. She was apparently unaware of the onion that had stuck to the top of her crown as she swept beneath a string of the pungent white bulbs.

Aunt Hattie smiled at the woman. "Good morning, Ellie May. I received that new shipment of hats I told you about. Arrived on yesterday's train." She walked behind a counter, lifted a hatbox from a shelf, and set it in front of the woman.

"Wait till you feast your eyes on this beauty." Slowly, and as reverently as a new mother handling a firstborn, Kate's aunt removed the lid and drew out the contents.

To Jonas's way of thinking, the hat was the most hideous thing he'd ever laid eyes on. Amazingly enough, neither woman shared his opinion.

Oohing and aahing, Ellie May took the black felt hat and held it up, her face radiating a zealous awe that struck Jonas as excessive. One would think the Lord himself had paid a visit, the way these two women carried on.

Ellie May turned the hat this way and that to examine it from every possible angle. She squealed upon touching each sweeping quill that was arranged around a bright red taffeta rosette.

"It is every bit as beautiful as I had hoped," Ellie May whispered in awe. "I can hardly wait until my hat gets here." She set the hat on the counter almost as gingerly as a guilt-ridden mortal might set a candle down on an altar.

"Next year?" Aunt Hattie frowned in annoyance. "What's the matter with you, Ellie May? You can't wait till next year. It'll be out of style by then."

"Oh, for goodness' sakes, Hattie. You can't hear a thing anyone says." She gave Jonas a helpless shrug. "I said"—she lifted her voice—"I can't wait till it gets here." She drew a sealed envelope from the pocket of her coat. "I ordered the very same hat from the Sears, Roebuck mail-order catalogue."

"You did what?" Aunt Hattie's face grew red with rage. "I'll not have you post your letter in my store!"

"You most certainly will. This is the official Postal Office for Hogs Head. If you fail to give proper and official attention to my letter, I shall report you to the president of the United States."

"Is that so? You whining, conniving, bellyaching . . ."

Ellie May's mouth dropped open in disbelief, but

she soon recovered enough to respond in kind. "Why you ..."

The most unfortunate name-calling followed, punctuated with all manner of insults the likes of which Jonas had not heard in his life. "Ladies, ladies," he said, aghast. His efforts to restore civility resulted in both women trying to get him to take sides.

"She can buy the same exact hat here for less money than what Shears and Rhubarb ..."

"I believe that's Sears and—" he began.

Ellie May shouted to be heard over him. "It's worth a little extra money for the convenience of shopping through the catalogue."

"Convenience! What convenience? You had to come to my store to mail the order and then you will have to wait for the order to come!" Aunt Hattie continued to glare at Ellie May, but she addressed Jonas. "Now I ask you, young man, what convenience is that?"

Jonas searched for some way to bring peace. "Well ... I ..."

The door flew open and Jonas decided the tall man with graying sideburns was Kate's uncle and not her father as he'd previously assumed. "What are you two ladies squawking about? I can hear you all the way down the street."

Aunt Hattie was all too glad to inform him. "This ... this woman is a hard-nosed traitor!"

Barney leveled his gray eyes on Ellie May. "So you went and ordered through the Sears, Roebuck catalogue, did you?"

"I most certainly did, and from now on I intend to make all my purchases through them." Ellie May slapped her letter on the counter and flounced past Jonas, the feathers on her hat brushing against his face, the onion wobbling dangerously on top of the crown.

"Over my dead body!" Aunt Hattie shouted after her.

The woman slammed the door as she left and Hattie stormed back to her desk, where she busied herself opening and slamming shut drawers.

Barney sighed and took his place behind the counter. He nodded to the cigars still in Jonas's hand. "I'll take your money, if you like."

"Eh ... yes. Much obliged." Jonas placed his coins on the counter and Kate's uncle swooped them up with one large callused hand and dropped them into the money drawer of the cash register.

"Sorry about the little altercation."

Jonas blinked. Little altercation? Is that what he called it? "Your wife is rather a ..."

"A human dynamo?" Barney suggested.

For want of a better word, Jonas nodded in agreement.

"You haven't seen anything yet," Barney added. "You should see my niece."

"Your ... niece is a ... takes after her aunt, does she?"

Barney scowled beneath his dark thick brows. "I just hope you never have occasion to find out how much she's like her aunt."

Chapter 16

Kate stood in the cellar, hands on her hips, and studied the window over her head. Dressed in a full, ankle-length skirt and a neatly pressed linen waistshirt, she wore her thick hair in a bun at the back of her neck. Her smooth white forehead was speckled with grease, her full pink lips pushed together in thought.

She could have sworn she saw something move outside the cellar window earlier that morning. It could have been a cat, of course. Mable Cummings's cat, to be exact. The annoying animal was always popping up in unexpected places. Kate sighed. Maybe she was just being paranoid.

Still, someone had stolen her idea for the carpet cleaner. If it happened once, it could happen again. She regretted not having taken precautionary measures years ago. No matter. She had put an end to any attempts to steal from her again! No longer would she leave her notes lying around the house. From now on she intended to keep her notes locked up in a strong metal safe.

Still unable to shake the feeling that someone had been on her property earlier, she finally climbed the cellar stairs and walked around the house to the little square window in back. Cautiously, she checked the trip wires on her skulker's alarm. The wire protecting the back window was loose, which could explain why the alarm had not sounded that morning. She pulled the wire taut and reattached it to the pistol that was hidden in the bushes. Making certain the wire would not be detected, Kate returned to the cellar to concentrate on the task at hand.

She lifted a pistol from her workbench and stared down the cocked barrel. There had to be a way to make the safety pin fit snug enough to prevent dangerous gas from escaping from the chamber upon firing. Her Uncle Barney liked to take the old pistols from his vast collection into the woods and practice his aim. The pistols had been in the family for years, and included a flintlock "Harper's Ferry" pistol used by his father during the second war for independence, fought in 1812.

She dropped the pistol onto her worktable. She'd been working on the problem at her uncle's request for most of the day. It was one of many such projects she planned to devote her time to while waiting for her patent notice to arrive from Washington. Meanwhile, she continued to write letters to various manufacturing companies, outlining her plans for the carpet cleaner and requesting information as to how to proceed.

She hoped to begin full production by early fall. With a little luck, she could have a carpet cleaner on sale in time for Christmas.

She wondered how many carpet cleaners to order. According to a book she'd read on the sound principles of conducting business, the higher the number produced, the lower the manufacturing costs. Was five thousand too few? Twenty thousand too many? And what name should she use? Kate's Carpet Cleaner sounded too simplistic. She'd adopted her uncle's surname shortly after she'd arrived in Hogs Head, when she was still dressed in pinafores. Her legal name was Hoover, Katherine Hoover. But who in their right mind would purchase a carpet cleaner called Hoover?

It made her head spin just thinking of all the decisions facing her. She only wished she had someone to consult, someone who would make up for her own lack of business experience. Someone like . . .

The name that came to mind astonished her, though it shouldn't have. Mr. Hunter had been on her mind almost constantly since she'd left Washington. Twice she thought she saw him, once on the train and then again at the station during the celebration in her honor.

She'd been imagining things, of course. What unearthly reason would he have to follow her to Hogs Head? If the truth were known, he was probably somewhere in . . . where did he say he was from? Waller Creek. No doubt plotting some other dastardly way to swindle yet another poor and unsuspecting victim.

Why he continued to haunt her, and why she was forever recalling bits and pieces of the conversation they shared over dinner, was a puzzle. Perhaps the sheer boldness of his ploy was what had made such a deep and lasting impression on her and not the memory of his leg pressing against hers in the restaurant, on the bed, and—Lord forgive her—even in her dreams. She shuddered to think what her aunt and uncle would do if they knew a man had forced himself into her hotel room. . . .

Feeling her cheeks grow warm, she hastily pushed these thoughts away. The man was a thief, a liar, and a womanizer.

She hastened over to the workbench in search of a vise. Feeling anxious and not at all like her usual self, she glanced up at the window.

Had she only imagined seeing something move outside earlier? She sincerely hoped so. It concerned her that the tripping wire had fallen from position. Had someone purposely detached it, or was it a result of that terrible windstorm they'd had a few weeks back? She decided to check the wires at least once a week in the future. No one was ever going to steal from her again!

Jonas mounted his horse and proceeded up Main Street toward the boardinghouse, his mind troubled. Everyone in town had confirmed that Miss Whittaker was an inventor. He had no argument with that. What disturbed him were the number of people who'd insisted Kate had worked on her carpet cleaner for years, with no assistance.

The sheriff said as much. As did the owner of the Red Rooster Saloon. The seamstress, who introduced herself as Thelma Paine, thought Kate had been working on the carpet cleaner much longer. Thelma also had a lot of other things to say about Kate, none of which supported his theory that Kate was stealing ideas and marketing them as her own. Mostly they had to do with Kate not having a husband.

Despite the growing evidence to the contrary, he held fast to his contention. Kate stole his idea. To think otherwise meant he would have to consider the possibility of them both coming up with the same exact idea independent of each other, and that would be unthinkable. Kate had to be a thief. It was the only idea that made perfect sense.

Maybe . . . she had purposely set out to fool the whole town. She'd offered to produce witnesses for the board of examiners. After what he had seen and heard in the short time he'd been there, she would have had no trouble finding people to sup-

port her claim. Hell, the whole town would probably have jumped at the chance to testify on her
behalf, if, for no other reason, but to get their
names in the newspaper.

He debated at great length whether to pay another visit to Rocking Horse Lane or to simply
head back to the boardinghouse. The sun had
dipped behind the cottonwoods and it had grown
noticeably cooler in the last hour.

He probably wasn't going to learn much more
about Kate and her work even if he was lucky
enough to catch her a second time in the cellar. He
knew she was working on a new invention, but
what exactly she was doing was anyone's guess.

As tempted as he was to call it a day, the only
way he could think to find out the answers to the
many questions that still remained was to catch her
in the act. Taking into consideration the unseemly
ways a man could force a woman to reveal information, spying on her seemed almost honorable in
comparison.

His mind made up at last, he left his horse in
front of the boardinghouse and ran the short distance to Kate's house on foot, cutting through the
woods. Since most of the downstairs windows were
boarded, his chances of being discovered seemed
remote. Still, he took care to keep himself crouched
low to the ground, darting from tree to tree, bush
to bush until at last he reached the back of the
house.

Stooping low, he sneaked up closer to the house.
The electric light in the cellar was still on. Kate
was apparently still at work. Sucking in his breath,
he inched closer.

This time he noticed something he'd not seen
earlier. Several abandoned canisters were stashed
in a corner of the cellar. He had a sinking feeling;

it looked as if Kate had experimented with different sizes and shapes before settling on the identical canister he'd used for his own machine. Why, if she'd stolen his notes, was such experimentation necessary? He'd explained in thorough detail why that particular canister worked best.

As much as he hated to admit it, it was beginning to look as if she really did invent the fertilizer—carpet—whatever the machine was called!

How could this have happened? How could two people living hundreds of miles apart invent what was essentially the same machine?

He caught a glimpse of Kate and, seeing her back was toward him, momentarily abandoned his cover to stoop on hands and knees, intent on getting a closer look at those canisters. Confident that he would have time to duck should she turn around, he pressed his nose closer to the mottled windowpane.

The blast was so unexpected, Jonas practically jumped out of his skin before landing on his backside next to a stack of firewood.

At the sound of the gunshot, Kate spun around to face the window overhead. Although not a soul was in sight, someone had set off the skulker's alarm and she intended to find out who the culprit was!

Grabbing one of the pistols she'd been working on, she lifted the fabric of her skirt and raced up the wooden steps to the first floor. Now she would find out once and for all who had the audacity to peer in her windows and steal her ideas!

Calling to Jimmy and telling him to stay in his room, she raced through the house, and burst out the front door. Tearing around the side of the house as fast as her feet and the obstacles in her path would allow, she swore revenge on the person setting off the alarm.

She held the pistol in front of her as she ran, shouting, "Don't move, whoever you are!"

Upon reaching the cellar window, she stared in disbelief at the man sprawled on his back. This time she was not imagining things.

Chapter 17

"Mr. Hunter!"

His eyes widened upon seeing the barrel of the gun pointing at him. Frowning, he sat up, his face white. "What the hell happened? Did you shoot at me?"

Kate straightened her aim, pointing the pistol directly between his eyes. "So you're the culprit who set off my skulker's alarm!"

"Your . . ." He stared in astonishment at the wire he had apparently tripped. "You could have killed me!"

"The pistol is aimed away from the person tripping the wire, and you should thank your lucky stars for that. But it would have served you right had the bullet gone right through your thieving little heart. Of all the devious, underhanded . . ." She was so incensed, she barely took a breath between insults. "You . . . you're nothing but a low-down, thief. A tail-buzzing, thimble-rigging . . ." On and on she went, spouting off every slanderous slur she'd ever heard and a few invented on the spot.

Feeling dazed and a bit overwhelmed by Kate's impressive ode to a thief, Jonas raked his hair with his fingers and reached for his hat.

"Don't move," Kate said in a tone of voice clearly meant to discourage any argument.

He held his hands shoulder high as he rose to

his feet. He distinctly remembered Curly saying Kate was crazy. Normally, he would jump at the chance to test a theory, but this time he was content to accept the barber's conviction unchallenged. Despite the precarious and perhaps even dangerous situation he was in, there was one cheering thought: If Curly was right about Kate, maybe he was right about the haircut. "I can explain what I'm doing here."

Kate's eyes flashed dangerously. "I know what you're doing here. You came to steal my ideas ... you ... you ... Put your hands up!"

His hands were up, but he wasn't going to argue with her. Instead he raised them a tad higher. "Now calm down, Miss Whittaker. I wasn't stealing a thing."

"Oh, no? Then suppose you tell me what you're doing on my property."

"I was trying to find out how you went about stealing from me."

"You don't give up, do you? I thought after the board of examiners ruled in my favor, you would graciously admit defeat." The barrel of the gun was wagging like the tail of a friendly dog. This was not particularly encouraging. Friendly-looking dogs had been known to bite.

"Perhaps this will help you along." She pressed the barrel closer to his chest.

"No pistol in the world could make me admit defeat," he growled. She may be crazy, but if he died, he intended to do so with some measure of dignity. Besides, his backside was sore and his head ached. He wasn't feeling particularly gracious or even charitable at the moment.

"I wouldn't be so certain of that, Mr. Hunter." She jerked the pistol. Something broke loose from the weapon and flew into the tall grass that covered most of the backyard.

A slow smile spread across Jonas's face. One didn't have to know much about guns to know that the pistol was missing its firing pin. He reached out and grabbed her wrist, forcing her to drop what remained of the weapon. "I'm very certain I won't be admitting defeat, Miss Whittaker. Gracious or otherwise. How about you?"

She fought him like a wildcat. Although he had been exposed previously to her fighting spirit, he was no more prepared for the strength of her than he had been the first time he'd encountered it. He finally managed to contain her in the steel-tight confines of his arms, but not without a major struggle.

"Let me know the minute you are prepared to admit defeat," he said, gasping for air.

"Never!" she heaved, her enraged face mere inches from his.

"Very well." He pushed her back against the house and pressed his body next to hers to hold her in place. A moment of uncertainty crossed her face as she assessed his advantage over her, but the look passed quickly and was replaced with such bold countenance, he feared the yard might be further booby-trapped. There had to be some reason why she looked so damned self-assured.

If he wasn't struggling so hard to contain her, to contain the way his body reacted to hers, he would have looked for more telltale wires. Promising himself to watch his step, he turned his full attention to the bundle of energy in his arms. "Keep still," he growled irritably. "You and I have something to talk about. I suggest we have a quiet dinner somewhere like two civilized adults."

"Dinner?" She spit the word out. "I've eaten all the meals I intend to eat with you."

He tightened his hold. Dammit, if she would just stand still for a minute. "In that case, you leave me no choice but to hold you prisoner until I've said my piece."

"You won't get away with this, you thieving, scalawaging . . ."

She showed every bit as much imagination as her aunt in thinking up unflattering names.

He assessed the situation as thoroughly as was possible under the circumstances. He was having a hard time containing her. Lord almighty! He'd known alley cats with less fighting spirit. "I told you I won't admit defeat, but I do admit to misjudging you."

She stilled in his arms, her eyes shining with triumph. "Is that so?"

Relieved at having found a way to keep her from fighting him, he nodded. "It appears you are, indeed, an inventor."

"And you're a two-timing swindler—"

"Now, now, Miss Whittaker, let's not forget who has the advantage."

Kate was so incensed, her sputtered curses sounded much like a cornered cat.

"Shame on you, Miss Whittaker." His head was pressed against hers, allowing him to talk softly into her ear. "I'm shocked to hear such vulgar words coming from a woman. Sailor talk belongs on the high seas."

Having run out of names to call him, she pressed against his chest with open palms. His body felt hard and lean next to hers, his breath like a warm summer breeze.

"Despite your rather colorful undergarments, you might concern yourself with acting like a lady."

"My un—" She looked up at him aghast, hating the amusement that softened his mouth. Was the man referring to the glimpse of her petticoats she knew he'd seen on occasion, or had he somehow managed to spy on her further?

Dear God, she thought, *on top of everything else, please don't let him be a peeping Tom!*

Mr. Hunter used her stunned silence to his full advantage. "As difficult as it is to believe, I'm quite willing to explore the possibility we both invented the same type of machine, albeit for different purposes. It's possible—as unlikely as it seems, mind you—that neither of us stole a thing."

"I don't believe that for a moment." She hesitated, not sure what to make of this change in tactics. "Why, that's the most ridiculous thing I've ever heard!"

"Maybe not as ridiculous as you think. The only way we can know for sure is if you allow me access to your notes."

She pulled back and this time he let her go. "I knew this was a trick! Do you really think I would be so foolish as to allow you to see my notes?"

"What are you afraid of? That I will find out how you stole your notes from me?"

"I stole nothing from you. You're the one who stole from me. Now you're trying to steal other ideas. That's what all this is about, isn't it? You're trying to make me think that you believe me so that you can steal more of my inventions."

"That was never my intention."

"Then why did you follow me to Hogs Head? What do you want?"

"I want what is rightfully mine."

"If you think I stole something from you, then I suggest you talk to the board of examiners."

"If you will recall, Miss Whittaker, I *did* talk to

them. I told them precisely how I invented that machine. What's more, they believed what I said was true. Had it not been for the president's intervention on your behalf, I would be holding the patent on our little invention, not you."

"I'm not going to listen to any more of this!" She spun around and stalked away.

"It took me five years to perfect that machine," he called out. His voice broke and grew husky. "Five long years."

Surprised by the plaintive note that unexpectedly touched some deep and needy part of her, she stopped and turned. She searched his face for his usual arrogance, was ready to confront it. What she wasn't ready to do was fight the raw emotion on his face that looked for all the world like the emotions of a man about to lose something that meant the world to him.

"I had plans for it, big plans." His voice was barely above a whisper. His eyes revealed a pain so deep, she could almost feel it. "Do you know what it's like to have five years wasted?"

Confusion clouded her thinking. Was it possible he was telling her the truth? Could they really have invented identical machines?

Not knowing what to think or even what to believe, she tempered her suspicions. "Let's suppose for a moment what you say is true. That you did invent a machine similar—"

"Identical."

"—to mine. . . . I'm not saying I believe you, mind you."

"Of course not."

"But just for the sake of argument, were it true, what do you expect me to do about it? The board of examiners has already made its decision."

His soft brown eyes never left her fact. "I would

expect you to act in accordance with your moral and ethical convictions."

She folded her arms in front of her. This was a trick; it had to be. He was trying to confuse her. "My moral and ethical convictions?" she asked, curious. A strange choice of words from a man she suspected of having neither.

He gave her a knowing, yet infinitely charming smile. His arrogance had returned and it was, as usual, unbearable, but infinitely better than the other, more worrisome expression that had made her doubt her own instincts. Upon discovering that her low opinion of him remained fully intact, she heaved a sigh of relief. He was a transgressor of the worst kind. Of that she had no doubt!

"I've decided to give you another opportunity to go into partnership with me," he said magnanimously. For someone who was lacking something as basic as a patent on the machine in question, he looked amazingly sure of himself.

She couldn't help but laugh. He was simply too outrageous to take seriously. "Why should I agree to such a thing?"

He rubbed his chin and studied her. "I'm going to be honest with you."

"That's a refreshing thought."

"You have something I want."

She inhaled, telling herself that he was talking about her invention. Still it was hard to ignore the way his warm gaze traveled up and down the length of her.

It was even harder to keep her own gaze from wandering. Reminding herself it was most improper to stare, she let her gaze sweep across his broad shoulders and work down his length. He certainly knew how to take full advantage of his clothing. His wide shoulders and well-muscled chest stretched the fabric of his well-worn shirt to the limits. His powerful thighs provided no less of a challenge to his otherwise unremarkable trousers, which appeared to be fastened together with a rather intimidating, though ultimately intriguing metal track. Could a man really be that endowed as to need such a heavy-duty fastener?

"And I have something you want."

Her gaze flitted upward to meet his, but it was obvious by the look on his face that she'd been caught with her hands in the cookie jar, so to speak. Her cheeks tingling with warmth, she fought to regain her composure. "What . . . what might that be, Mr. Hunter?"

He arched a dark brow. "My business acumen. What else?"

"I'm quite capable of handling my own affairs."

"Manufacturers aren't used to working with women. Most will refuse to work with them altogether."

That was true, and it was probably why she'd received no replies to the many letters of inquiry she'd mailed out to manufacturers. Still, she wasn't about to admit it to him. "If they want my business, they'll have to get used to working with a woman."

"You might be cheated."

"Don't count on it, Mr. Hunter. Now if you'll excuse me, it's getting late." It would soon be dark and Jimmy would be wondering where she was. Then, too, her aunt and uncle would be home at any minute, if they weren't already.

The side door was boarded up, having been blown off its hinges when the first boiler she'd ever installed blew up. She walked around to the front door, conscious that Mr. Hunter followed close behind.

"Does this mean you won't have dinner with me to talk over our partnership?"

She sighed. The man never gave up. "We have no partnership to discuss." She sidestepped an old boiler and hurried up the steps to the porch, staying clear of the damaged area. Her hand froze on the door handle when she heard a thud from behind, followed by a curse.

A quick glance over her shoulder revealed her uninvited guest sprawled on the ground.

Chapter 18

"Mr. Hunter!" she gasped, rushing back down the steps. "Are you all right?" He failed to reply or even to move as she hurried to his side. He was lying on the ground, facedown, his right leg going in one direction, his left in another. "Mr. Hunter!"

She shook him, but all she could solicit was a groan. "Stay here. Don't move." Lifting the hem of her skirt, she raced into the house, praying that either her aunt or her uncle had returned home while she was out back. "Uncle Barney! Aunt Hattie. Anyone home?"

Her uncle looked up from his newspaper and frowned.

"A man has been hurt. Hurry!" She raced outside with her uncle at her heels.

Uncle Barney leaned over Mr. Hunter's body. "What happened?"

"I'm not sure. I think he hit his head when he tripped and fell. Oh, Uncle Barney, do you think we can get him inside?"

"We can try. You take his feet."

"Barney, is that you?" It was Aunt Hattie calling from the doorway.

"Come and help us," Barney called back. "We have an injured man."

"Well, now, isn't that nice?" Aunt Hattie said, obviously misunderstanding. Aunt Hattie shuffled back to the doorway, disappearing inside. Uncle Barney and Kate had no choice but to carry the unconscious man up the steps by themselves. From the porch, they carried him through the door and into the foyer, where they stopped to rest before lugging him into the parlor. It was quite a struggle. Mr. Hunter was solidly built; his legs were as strong and powerful as tree trunks.

When at last they managed to lay him on the divan, Uncle Barney pulled out his handkerchief and mopped his beaded forehead.

"Sakes alive!" Aunt Hattie declared upon seeing the injured man stretched out in her parlor. "Why didn't you tell me someone was hurt?"

After giving her husband a proper scolding, Aunt Hattie plodded upstairs to fetch a pillow and blanket, calling to Jimmy and otherwise "gibber-jammering" all the way.

Throwing his hands up, Uncle Barney headed for the kitchen to search for a bottle of whiskey.

Meanwhile, Kate examined Mr. Hunter's head, taking care not to cause further injury. She ran her fingers through his hair in search of a lump or contusion. His hair was shorter than when she had last seen him, barely reaching the collar of his shirt, and giving him a boyish charm that struck a responsive chord in her.

Finding no signs of injury, she withdrew her hand from his head and gently shook him. "Mr. Hunter . . ."

Deriving great satisfaction from the concern in her voice, Jonas allowed his eyes to flicker as he feigned a groan. It was tempting to sound melodramatic, and of course, that would never do. Just a little whimper now and again was all that was needed. No sense overdoing it and making his charming, though exasperating host suspicious.

He tried not to move when she leaned over him. Harder still was resisting the urge to open his eyes fully so he could better absorb her. The only thing that prevented him from doing so was the stark white glare of electric lights. The Great White Way in New York City couldn't possibly be any brighter than Kate's parlor. In the name of Sir Isaac Newton, did she actually install all these lights herself?

She squeezed his hand and he concentrated on the warm, gentle pressure of her fingers. "Mr. Hunter."

Not wanting to worry her more than necessary, he blinked against the glare and tried for a dazed look. It was harder than he would have thought. How could a man concentrate around the likes of Kate Whittaker? Faking an injury required a focused frame of mind, and she was clearly the most distracting female he'd ever encountered.

What in hell was she doing looking at him with eyes all soft with concern? Who did she think she was, pressing her firm round breasts next to him while she rubbed her hands through his hair? Didn't she know she was practically suffocating him with her delicate fragrance that reminded him of warm summer days?

She was a one-woman torture chamber, that's what she was. She might not have stolen his idea, but heaven only knew she could very possibly steal a man's heart if she had half a notion.

Aunt Hattie hurried into the room, arms piled high with bedding, complaining up a storm. "No one lets me know anything that goes on around here. Why, if I hadn't seen it with my own eyes, I would never have known a man was dying in my very own parlor."

Good Lord. Dying. He was a better actor than

he'd thought he was. Perhaps he missed his true calling.

"He's gained consciousness." Kate took a pillow from her aunt and turned back to him.

"Well, that's something," Aunt Hattie said. "I can't afford to lose any more of my customers."

"He's a customer of yours?" Kate asked, surprised.

"He most certainly is," Aunt Hattie declared.

Kate leaned over the divan. "Do you think you can sit up?"

He rubbed his head gingerly, remembering to grimace. "I . . . think . . . so." Taking full advantage of the situation, he slipped an arm around her slender waist, laid his head against the firm mound of her breasts, and held on to her as he lifted himself up. He continued to hold on to Kate while she arranged the full feather pillow behind him.

"Lie back," Kate said.

His arm still around her waist, he lowered himself against the pillow, surprised to find himself reluctant to release her.

She covered him with a fine knitted afghan, pulling it to his chin. He was momentarily reminded of how little nurturing he'd received in the past from his poor overworked mother. Illness, injury made no difference, any and all physical complaints were ignored for the more important task of putting food on the table.

He recalled the time he fell off the roof at the age of ten, breaking both legs. A long and painful convalescence followed, and he felt guilty for adding yet another burden to an already overburdened household.

During his long weeks of recovery, he'd thought up gadgets that would help him dress and get through his day. He recalled making a pulley for the purpose of lifting himself up and down the stairs. Next came a hand-propelled wagon that provided him enough mobility to do his chores and attend school. He learned early in life to do for himself, and it was this quest for independence that led him to becoming an inventor.

His childhood memories faded as he felt Kate's cool hand on his forehead. Her administrations were unlike anything he had ever experienced. The original intent of his staged accident had been to gain entry into her house and to learn everything he could about Kate and her inventions. But Kate made it all but impossible to think much beyond the gentle fingers at his brow and the softly spoken words of encouragement she offered.

"There, there, Mr. Hunter. Just lie still."

Kate's uncle walked into the room. "This will cure you," he said. He held the rim of a glass next to Jonas's lips and tilted it gently.

The whiskey blazed a fiery path down Jonas's throat. His eyes watered. He coughed, which didn't do much to clear his throat, but did bring more attention from Kate.

"Are you all right?"

Jonas held her wide-eyed gaze. He felt a surge of guilt for taking advantage of her kindness, but he couldn't seem to help himself. It was too late to admit his deception. She would never talk to him again if she knew the truth, and suddenly preserving whatever tenuous bond they shared became of utmost importance. "I . . . I think so."

Aunt Hattie made a face. "What you need, young man, is my famous chamomile tea." The older woman disappeared into the kitchen.

Kate glanced up at her uncle, who was refilling Jonas's glass. "Maybe you better go and fetch the doctor, Uncle Barney."

"No!" Realizing he'd overreacted, Jonas coughed to hide his gaffe. He adjusted his voice to sound weak, without sounding like he was on death's doorstep. He wouldn't put it past Kate's aunt to start planning his funeral. "I'm feeling much improved. I just had a nasty fall. After some rest . . ."

Kate brushed his hair away from his forehead. Her fingertips slid across his brow as easily as warm butter slid across hot rolls, and he felt a worrisome stirring inside. He felt all quivery and jittery—not at all like himself. Was it possible that he actually *had* injured himself when he'd fallen?

"If you're sure," she said. It was clear by the look on her face that she was unconvinced.

It took sheer willpower not to put his arms around her and kiss her tempting full lips right then and there. Heaven help him had her uncle not been present. "I . . . I'm quite sure."

"Are you warm enough?"

Hot. He was hot. Boiling hot. *Must be the lights,* he thought. "Perhaps you could tuck the blanket around me."

She tucked the afghan around him, her hands as gentle and soothing as a tropical breeze. The wool blanket added more warmth to his already over-heated body, but Kate's presence more than compensated for his discomfort.

"My head hurts." He moaned. "Would it be asking too much for you to . . . rub it?"

"I'll be happy to." She dropped down on her knees and pressed two fingers against his temple. "Where does it hurt?"

He absorbed the feel of her and sighed inwardly. Heavenly days. "All over," he replied, hiding his smile beneath a corner of the knitted spread. He glanced over at her uncle and was vastly relieved to discover the older man had disappeared behind his newspaper, a hazy cloud of blue smoke rising from his pipe.

"I feel so guilty," Kate said, stroking Jonas's neck with soft feathery caresses. "I should never have left that pile of iron sitting in the yard."

It had never before occurred to him how useful guilt could be. Especially coming from someone as beguiling as Kate Whittaker.

"Don't feel bad," he murmured as if each word required great sacrifice. "I don't blame you for . . . my injuries."

"I can't help but feel responsible," she replied. She had worked her fingers down to his shoulders.

"That feels so . . ." He'd almost said *good.* "Sore."

"I'm not pressing too hard, am I?"

"Not at all."

"Where else does it hurt?" she asked. "Here?" She ran her hands down the front of his shirt and began massaging his chest.

He wanted to shout out in glee. He had Kate where he wanted her, by George! Ho, ho. It would only be a matter of time before she begged him to be her business partner. Damn it, what was he thinking? If she kept doing what she was doing, he'd be the one doing the begging—and his pleas would have nothing to do with business.

Fortunately, good sense prevailed and he managed to keep his unchaste thoughts hidden. Not trusting himself to speak, he tried not to stare at her, and every time he felt the irresistible urge to grab her, he let out a gut-wrenching moan that brought a startled glance from Uncle Barney and a worried look from Kate.

"I didn't mean to hurt you," she apologized after one such loud groan.

"It's all right," he assured her. "Keep going."

She met his gaze. "All this from one fall?"

"I think I twisted myself as I hit the ground." He moved his leg and grimaced. "My ... leg ..."

"Oh, dear. I really think we should fetch the doctor."

"It's nothing more than sore muscles. What could a doctor do that you're not already doing?"

Looking unconvinced, she turned the afghan back and pressed her fingers into his upper thigh. Her hands felt so heavenly, he almost blurted out his desirous feelings then and there. Catching himself just in time, he let his voice rumble in his throat. "Yes, that's the spot." After a moment, he added, "A little higher."

She studied his face for a while and, apparently satisfied his discomfort was real, pressed her fingers below his waist and began massaging his hips. Her hand accidentally brushed against his most intimate part and a jolt shot through his body. He immediately tried to cover his somewhat explosive response with a muffled, "Hurts."

Watching her face through slitted eyes, it was all he could do to stifle a yearning sigh when her cheeks grew a most becoming shade of pink. So Miss Whittaker wasn't quite as oblivious to his masculinity as she had tried to make him think during their dinner together in Washington. What a damned inconvenient time to find that out. It made his job of keeping his hands to himself all the more difficult.

He let out a self-pitying groan and, thinking he was still in pain, she resumed the massage.

Oh, heavenly days! "That feels ... so much better," he murmured. What ecstasy! What unbelievable torture! It was the latter that convinced him that if he didn't do something soon, he wouldn't be responsible for his actions.

Besides, she owed him for what she'd put him through—was putting him through even now with her soft gentle touch and concern-filled eyes. It was time to make her pay.

"Down lower," he said, and this time he didn't have to feign the hoarseness in his voice. He felt her hand tremble at his waist before her massaging fingers began to inch downward.

Chapter 19

Much later that same night, Jonas lay in his own bed and recalled the events of the evening. He stared up at the dark ceiling, his fevered body still tingling with the memory of Kate's touch. He cursed himself for the guilt that darted in and out of his thoughts like a swarm of crazed bees. So what if he'd faked an injury? He hadn't meant any harm.

If Kate Whittaker had agreed to have dinner with him, had so much as considered the possibility he was telling the truth about the two of them inventing what was essentially the same machine, he would never have stooped to such an outright, flagrant deception.

His intention had been to endear himself to Kate in some small way, earn her sympathy and trust. Women couldn't resist a man who was in need of maternal consideration. So he took advantage of a woman's innate nature. That didn't mean he was evil. So why in heaven's name did he feel so damned guilty? So damned foolish? *So damned deprived?*

He flopped to his side and considered the hard facts. Never had he wanted a woman more than he wanted Miss Kate Whittaker. Never had he known a woman so intelligent, so feminine, so gentle, so sexy.

Thinking of Kate in these terms only increased his agony; he was ninety-nine percent sure she'd not stolen from him, but she still believed he had stolen from her. And if she ever found out how he'd tricked her that night, he'd never be able to convince her of his innocence.

Maybe he hadn't acted as despicably as he thought. Wasn't he the one who'd called a halt? She had wanted him to stay the night, had practically begged him to, but he hadn't wanted to take any more advantage of her.

After arguing with him, she finally accepted his decision, but not without regret. "I'll worry all night," she'd said.

He wondered if she was worrying about him at that very moment. It gave him a warm glow to think of Kate laying in bed, thinking of him. Thinking *nice* thoughts of him. It was enough to make him put his guilt aside and concentrate fully on the body-warming memory of her gentle hands on him.

Recalling with infinite detail the feel, the pressure, and even the warmth of her caressing fingers, he sighed. He wondered if it was only guilt that made Kate such an attentive nurse. Lord knew she had enough to feel guilty about. She almost blew his head off with her—what did she call it?—Skulker's alarm. If that wasn't enough, she led him on a merry chase through a dangerous booby-trapped yard. He *could* have been seriously hurt, dammit!

Yes, indeed, if anyone had a reason to feel guilty, it was Kate Whittaker. With this thought firmly in mind, he rolled over and closed his eyes. He hoped by morning he would have thought up a way to make Kate feel more guilty still.

Meanwhile, Kate lay in bed, unable to sleep. She should never have allowed poor Mr. Hunter to leave the house. He could have had a concussion, for all she knew. Internal injuries, perhaps. *People died from internal injuries.*

Why, the poor man couldn't even stand on his own two feet without holding on to her. Maybe it had been a mistake not to have sent for the doctor despite Mr. Hunter's objections. How like a man not to seek medical attention when he needed it. Thank goodness Uncle Barney had insisted upon driving him back to Mrs. Applegate's Boarding-house in the mud wagon.

Her uncle had returned a short while later and told her Mr. Hunter had made a remarkable recovery. "It must have been the night air that revived him."

Despite her uncle's comforting words, Kate couldn't help but worry. The man did fall and injure himself on her property. So it stood to reason she should worry. Even if he was a thief.

She thumped her pillow with her fist and turned over. She had almost fallen asleep when she could have sworn she heard his voice floating out of the darkness: *Down lower.*

Eyes flying open, she lay poker still. Her heart pounded so wildly, it felt like the entire feather mattress beneath her heated body had come alive. Just thinking about touching him on his thighs made her quiver all over. Twice she'd accidentally brushed her arm against his manhood and another time—Lord, forgive her—she'd touched her finger to the intriguing metal fastener on his trousers. . . . It wasn't exactly on purpose, but it wasn't entirely by accident, either.

All three times she thought she'd felt a jolt shoot through his body, but his eyes remained closed and the pain on his face was so evident, she was convinced he hadn't noticed any impropriety on her part. Thank her lucky stars for that!

Never had she touched a man so intimately.

Did a man always feel so, well ... uh ... hard?

Forget it, she told herself. *Put it out of your mind.* Touching him was a simple necessity. Why, a doctor wouldn't have thought twice about what had occurred in the parlor that night. She did what any reasonable or charitable person would have done for an injured man.

It was new to her, that was all, this touching a man, rubbing him, pressing her fingers into the hardness of his firm lean body, knowing how he felt beneath his clothes ... *between his thighs.*

New! She would have felt the same embarrassed, disconcerted mishmash of feelings had she given the same treatment to ... say, the sheriff, for example—or Smoky Joe. Of course she would!

Feeling considerably better, Kate rolled over. She felt herself drift upon a velvet-soft cloud. She might have fallen into a peaceful sleep had a whispery voice not called from some unknown void, repeating those same damning words: *Down lower.*

Jolted to full wakefulness once again, Kate clutched at her pillow and tried to still her quivering body.

Early the next morning, Jonas took his place at the dining room table along with Mrs. Applegate's other two boarders.

"You're up bright and early," Mrs. Applegate said, cheerfully. She was dressed in a black skirt and a starched pleated shirtwaist that was buttoned all the way up her neck. "Considering how late you came in last night."

It had been after midnight by the time Kate's uncle had driven him to the boardinghouse. Mrs.

Applegate poured him a cup of coffee. Her curiosity about why he was out so late was obvious as she looked him up and down. Apparently thinking it impolite to ask him outright, she tried an indirect approach. "I trust you slept well?"

He hadn't slept a wink. "Yes, thank you."

"And you found everything all right? In town, I mean."

"I did."

Her mouth tightening ever so slightly, Mrs. Applegate handed Jonas his coffee and introduced him to the others. There was a Reverend Jenkins, a traveling preacher. The man interrupted a rousing rendition of the good Samaritan to peer at Jonas through his gold-rimmed eyepiece before reaching across the table to shake Jonas's hand. "Bless you, son, bless you."

"And this is Mr. Bender," Mrs. Applegate said, referring to a thin hollow-chested man whose tangled mass of gray hair and beard seemed to weigh him down. "He's a philosopher and a stargazer. He's also the gentleman I told you about who plays in the band."

"And a fine band it is," Jonas said, shaking the man's limp hand before taking his seat again.

"And what is your profession?" Mr. Bender asked.

"I'm an inventor."

"Oh, no!" Mrs. Applegate almost dropped the platter of flapjacks she had lifted from the sideboard.

"Is something wrong?" Jonas asked.

Mrs. Applegate looked embarrassed. "If you don't mind my saying so, I think perhaps you best not tell anyone in town the true nature of your profession."

Jonas sipped his coffee thoughtfully. Did the

woman misunderstand, perhaps? Think he'd said something else? "Is there something wrong with being an inventor?"

"Oh, no!" Mrs. Applegate was clearly disconcerted. "I never meant to imply there was." She handed the platter to Mr. Bender and lowered her voice. "It's that terrible woman. You know, the one we talked about yesterday. Kate Whittaker. Remember my telling you she's an inventor?"

"As a matter of fact, I do." At the mere mention of Kate's name, he was forced to battle the memory of her touch. He could almost feel her fingers on his brow and on his thighs. Warding off the shivery feeling that shot down the length of him, he pointed to the ceiling cracks and Mrs. Applegate gave a firm nod.

"Let me tell you, that's nothing compared to what she did to poor Smoky Joe."

Jonas disliked gossip and would normally go to great extremes to avoid it. Today, he relished hearing every last tidbit on one Kate Whittaker.

After Mrs. Applegate finished her anecdote, Jonas shook his head in amazement, the minister looked positively shocked, and the stargazer clucked his tongue and drew his napkin to his mouth.

Jonas tapped a finger on the edge of his plate. "You say she actually made a wagon travel without benefit of a horse or other means of transport?" He himself had done some preliminary sketches on a two-cylinder motor wagon, but he was nowhere near ready to put his idea into practice, and from all the horseless carriages he'd seen during his recent trip to Washington, most of his ideas were already obsolete.

"It traveled the entire length of Main Street!" Mrs. Applegate exclaimed. "It practically scared

everyone to death, and then ran right into the Red
Rooster Saloon. You never heard such a commotion in your life. It took the sheriff and three men
to calm the owner, Smoky Joe, down. What a mess.
The town smelled like the inside of a whiskey barrel for a month."

"And what happened to the buggy?" Jonas
asked, curious.

"Oh, that! It caught fire and had to be hauled
away. More coffee, Mr. Hunter?"

"Oh ... ah ... yes, thank you."

She refilled his cup, then lifted the platter from
Mr. Bender's hands and offered it to Jonas. "Help
yourself to some flapjacks."

He took the platter, but he was more interested
in persuading Mrs. Applegate to talk about Kate
than he was in breakfast. "It's rather unusual for a
woman to be an inventor, wouldn't you say?"

Mr. Bender sniffed. "That's no more unusual
than a woman stargazer. I heard tell that a woman
works at the Yerkes Observatory in Wisconsin. Can
you imagine? It's getting so that women don't know
their places anymore."

"I heartily agree," Mrs. Applegate said. "Why,
in my day, a woman got married, had children, and
didn't go around blowing up the town."

"Does she do it often?" Jonas asked, helping
himself to the flapjacks before passing the platter.
"Blow up the town?"

"More times than you can shake a stick at," Mrs.
Applegate replied. "Last time, the sheriff put her
in jail."

Jonas sat back in his chair, the pitcher of maple
syrup in his hand. "Did you say jail?"

"I most certainly did. It was the first time anyone
used that old jailhouse since the Brannon brothers
were captured back in the sixties. The cell lock is

broken. Kate was on her honor to stay there all night. Of course the poor sheriff felt obliged to stay with her to make sure no harm came to her. Said the jail was no place for a lady. Ha! Some lady!"

Jonas recalled Kate and the sheriff dancing together in the street and wondered just how much of a hardship the sheriff had endured to protect his prisoner.

The widow practically drooled as she leaned closer to Jonas. All three of her chins quivered with anticipation. "Why, that Kate Whittaker is never going to find herself a husband." It was obvious that she enjoyed an opportunity to express her views on the subject. "I ask you, what man in his right mind would want a woman like that?"

"Certainly not me," harrumphed the stargazer.

"Nor me," added the preacher.

Mrs. Applegate looked positively righteous. "There you have it."

Jonas stared down on his flapjacks as the conversation drifted away from Kate and turned to the weather. Dribbling syrup onto his plate, he tuned out the astronomer's predictions of rain and considered the possibility that Kate's lack of marriage prospects might be of use to him.

Mrs. Applegate's opinion that Kate's prospects of marriage were dismal if not altogether nonexistent had been expressed verbatim a day earlier by Thelma Paine, the town seamstress.

Could it really be true? Was it possible that Miss Whittaker—Kate, as he'd come to think of her since last night—was doomed to remain that socially bereft anomaly known as an old maid?

Admittedly, he knew little if anything about marriage, and to hear the two women talk, it was obvious he didn't even know something as basic as what made one woman more marriageable than another.

Obviously, it had nothing to do with a woman's appearance or intelligence, or even her exceptional nursing skills, or certainly Kate's chances of marriage would be more favorable.

If Kate was like most women, she probably dreaded the thought of facing a future without the security of a husband, although he couldn't for the life of him imagine Kate a spinster. Still, a woman facing such a dreary prospect might be willing to make certain concessions.

He smiled to himself as an idea began to form. He'd been going about this all wrong. Instead of trying to talk her into taking him on as a business partner, he should be working on the marriage angle.

If the seamstress and Mrs. Applegate were right, then maybe, just maybe Kate was desperate enough to think twice about letting her last chance at a normal life pass her by.

His grin grew wider. As soon as he and Kate tied the knot, the ownership of the patent would revert to him as her husband.

Admittedly, marriage to such a woman would be no rose garden. She was far too mule-headed to allow for domestic peace. Still, she was pleasing to the eye, understood his work, and would, judging from their few lively encounters, make a spirited bed partner.

His heart began to pound. Imagine touching her in return. Imagine . . .

"I see you think the idea amusing, Mr. Hunter."

Jonas turned his head toward the stargazer. "I beg your pardon."

"You don't believe the stars are trying to tell us something about the future?"

"I consider myself a scientist as well as an inventor. I must confess that when I look up into the sky, I see balls of gas. I suspect they tell us more about the past than the future."

Mr. Bender was obviously not amused. His right eye twitched and the muscle at his temple began to bob up and down. "How fortunate that more visionaries than scientists walk the earth."

Before Jonas could reply, an explosion ripped through the air. The force shook the house and rattled the dishes. Directly overhead, the crystal prisms of the chandelier vibrated and a loud tinkling sound filled the room.

No sooner had the boom sounded than Mrs. Applegate dropped on all fours and crawled under the table, followed close behind by the stargazer.

The preacher's eyepiece popped out of his hand, but otherwise he stayed frozen to his chair. "Good heavens! What was that?"

"It's that foolhardy Kate Whittaker!" the widow yelled from beneath the table. "And if I ever get my hands on her, I'll . . ."

Jonas didn't stay around long enough to hear what Mrs. Applegate planned to do to Kate. By then he'd already dashed out the door. Pressing his hat to his head, he ran down the steps of the porch, quickly mounted his horse, and raced toward Rocking Horse Lane, praying all the while his dear, sweet future bride had not been injured in the explosion.

Chapter 20

It was cool outside, the smell of rain in the air. Unbroken gray clouds stretched across the sky. It looked and felt more like November than June.

Making his horse practically fly, Jonas reached the Whittaker house ahead of the volunteer firemen and even the sheriff. Dogs barked furiously and the horses on Rocking Horse Lane ran in frantic circles, whinnying loudly. Bellowing grunts rose from Bexler's hog farm, all but drowning out the distant sound of fire bells.

Kate's Uncle Barney opened the door to Jonas's frantic knock, looking amazingly calm in view of the fact that the upper part of his body, from his shoulders to his head, was covered in a thick layer of ceiling plaster.

"Didn't expect to see you so early. Come in, come in." Uncle Barney turned his head and called over his shoulder. "Kate, Hattie. We have a visitor."

Jonas whipped off his hat and entered the house, glancing around for signs of disaster. No one else was in sight. "Is everything all right?"

Uncle Barney looked surprised by the question. " 'Course it's all right. Why wouldn't it be?"

"I heard a loud blast and I thought—"

"That was just Kate. She still hasn't gotten that

damned temperature gauge to work right on the boiler."

"What brings you out here so early, Mr. Hunter?"

He spun around at the sound of Kate's voice. The pulse that had hammered through his body earlier when he thought she might be in danger had almost returned to normal. But his veins fluttered at the sound of her voice, and his heart quickened at the simple act of looking at her.

"I ..." Suddenly he was having trouble with his throat. She looked even more beautiful than he had recalled. She was dressed in a simple calico dress that emphasized her tiny waist. She wore her gold-red hair in a neat and tidy bun that made the dark smudge centered on her forehead that much more incongruous. And her hands—her amazingly soft and wonderful hands—were by her side.

"He heard the boiler blow up," Uncle Barney explained, brushing the plaster off his shoulder.

"Really? All the way at the boardinghouse?" She sounded surprise.

"I'm not the only one who heard it," he explained. The fire bells were growing louder, but she seemed not to notice.

Dismissing the subject with a shrug of her shoulders, she eyed him shrewdly. "I see you've made a rather remarkable recovery."

Jonas fingered the brim of his hat and met her probing gaze. A man could get lost in those eyes and never find his way out. "Only because of the wonderful care I received."

Uncle Barney shuffled out of the room, leaving the two of them alone.

A sizzling sound behind him made Jonas jump away from the wall. He turned to study the metal pipe that ran along the baseboard.

"It's just our heater," Kate explained. "As you may have noticed, our fireplace is out of commission."

"I did notice." His gaze followed the heated pipe around the room. "This is most ingenious."

Kate accepted his compliment with more wariness than gratification. "It keeps the house warm in winter. In the summer, I run cold water through the pipes. It keeps the temperature somewhere around the seventies."

"That's amazing." He stepped to the foot of the stairs. "I see the pipe goes up to the second level."

"It only goes to the master bedroom. Aunt Hattie is very sensitive to the cold."

"Your uncle said you are having problems with the temperature gauge on the boiler."

"I can't get it to regulate properly."

"Doesn't your boiler have a safety valve?"

"Yes, but it keeps getting stuck. I ... I hope it didn't alarm you."

"Well ... I ..." Of course it alarmed him. He feared something might have happened to her. "No, no, of course not." He pressed his fingers into the felt of his hat. "I've had a few explosions myself."

"You have?" She tilted her head and gave him a look that told him she was interested in him, no matter how hard she tried not to let her interest show. His heart greeted this knowledge with a startling leap.

"I guess it's what you call an occupational hazard. If you would permit me to have a look, I might be able to offer some help. I installed a temperature gauge on a boiler back home and I might even be able to figure out why the safety valve keeps sticking."

She studied him a moment, as if to ascertain his

motivations for wanting to help. "Actually, what I would like to do is get rid of the steam boiler. Use electricity instead. Now that I have the house completely wired, I think it would be a simple matter to convert the house completely." He glanced upward at the unbelievable tangle of wires over his head. It was a wonder she hadn't burned the entire house down.

"Don't you think it possible to heat a house satisfactorily with electricity?" she asked, obviously mistaking the apprehension on his face for doubt.

"Of course it's possible," he replied. "I've proven it to some extent. I ran a conductor through a chicken coop."

Her eyes widened. "A chicken coop, Mr. Hunter?"

He grinned. "You'd be amazed what electricity does to a rooster's prowess."

She had the good grace to laugh at his feeble attempt at humor. She had a rich throaty laugh, filled with exuberance.

"That's only the beginning," he added. "I see a day in the not too distant future when our meals will be cooked on electric rather than wood stoves."

A dreamlike expression crossed her face. "I read about such stoves in the *Electric Age* magazine."

She never failed to amaze him. "You read the *Electric Age* magazine?" How different she was from the dull girls back home. He was right in his earlier assessment of her; she would never be content to sit around and discuss fashions.

She nodded. "That's how I learned to wire the house. But I'm not sure about the stove. Do you think an electric stove will really work?"

"I saw one work with my very own eyes."

"Really?"

"Indeed I did. At the Chicago Fair."

She gazed at him with bright shining eyes. "You went to the Chicago Fair?"

"Yes, and I saw the most wondrous things imaginable. I walked through an electric house, complete with an electric stove."

"Oh, do tell me more," she pleaded softly, her face radiant with awe and wonder. "Please, you must."

His voice rising with excitement, he talked about the fair, then described his dreams for the future. "One day we'll wash our clothes in electric machines. Who knows? Maybe we'll even have horseless carriages that run on electric currents. Certainly everything we do domestically will be done with electricity. I envision a future with electric irons, electric butter churns, even electric sewing machines." He raised his arm as he spoke, as if to illustrate the future in midair.

Eyes bright with interest, Kate followed the invisible lines he drew, her face telling him his dreams for the future were fast becoming her dreams.

He sucked in his breath. No one—not a single soul—had ever shared his vision. For as long as he could remember, people had told him to stop talking "crazy" talk. He couldn't have been more than fourteen or fifteen when he'd finally come to accept he was destined to live a lonely existence. That was the day he vowed never to share his dreams with another soul, not ever again. That's why he was so surprised—stunned, actually—to find himself breaking the promise he'd made to himself all those years ago.

Once the floodgates had been cracked open, though, there was no holding back. He could no sooner deny himself the pleasure of sharing his dreams with her than a starving man could refuse food.

"Just think, Kate!" He hadn't felt this much enthusiasm in years. "Think of the wonderful things that lie ahead."

She was so engrossed with what he was saying, she lay her hand on his arm, unaware of her action. Jonas, equally unaware of his own gesture, cupped her elbow with his hand, locking the two of them in some sort of half embrace.

Kate's mind fairly danced with all the amazing things he had predicted. The two of them stood facing each other with only a few inches separating them. But the dreams they shared bonded them so close, it was as if the space between them didn't even exist.

"Oh, Jonas. If only I could get the people of Hogs Head to embrace the idea of installing an electric plant just like they built in Muncie, Indiana. Did you know that the new electric lights cost Muncie only thirty-four dollars a year?"

"Unbelievable," Jonas murmured.

"That's considerably less than the eighty-five dollars a year it cost Hogs Head to maintain its gaslights!" she declared.

"Think what a boon electricity will be to farmers," Jonas said. He hadn't considered the fact that electricity would be cheaper than gas. Kate obviously had a better head for business than he'd given her credit for. "Since I installed electricity in my father's chicken coop, egg production pretty near doubled."

Kate gazed at him and wondered if she could have possibly misjudged him. It was hard to believe, considering she had caught him red-handed trying to spy on her. Still, she'd never met anyone who inspired or excited her more. She would have gladly stood and listened to him all day had Uncle Barney not interrupted.

"Kate, the sheriff wants to see you. Says you disturbed the peace."

"Oh, no, not again." Reluctantly, she pulled away from Jonas and quickly followed Uncle Barney from the parlor.

Jonas followed Kate and her uncle onto the porch and stopped in his tracks. He was astonished at the number of people gathered in front of the Whittaker house. He had been so engrossed in his conversation with Kate, he'd forgotten about the fire bells, forgotten about the blast, forgotten about anything but the pleasure of having found someone with whom he could share his dreams.

Everyone talked at once, heated tempers giving way to raised fists. A horse-drawn fire truck pulled up behind the hook-and-ladder wagon already parked in front of Kate's house.

The sheriff looked beleaguered, if not altogether overwhelmed. It was only after the mob looked about ready to storm the house that he lifted his hands and yelled, "Quiet!"

Having gained some semblance of order, the sheriff turned to Kate. "I'm afraid I have no choice but to haul you off to jail. D'turbin' the peace is a mighty serious o-fense."

"You tell her!" Smoky Joe yelled.

Cheers of approval rose from the others. "That'll teach her!" Thelma Paine shouted. "The blast scared me so much I almost sewed my fingers together!"

Curly shook his head. "It didn't teach her last time. Why should this time by any diff'rent?"

"That's cuz she only stayed in jail overnight," Quincy Litton pointed out, scribbling notes furiously as he did whenever he was hot on the trail of a story. "She was in and out so fast, I didn't even have a chance to interview her for the newspaper."

Jonas listened in growing amazement at the argument that raged back and forth. Only a short time ago, Kate had been treated like royalty. Now the very same people who had thrown a party in her honor were demanding that the sheriff throw her in jail. All because of one little explosion. He'd never seen such a changeable group of people in his life.

"Wait!" he yelled, no longer able to listen to the disparaging remarks about Kate. He lifted his hands, and because he was a relative stranger in town, the crowd fell silent. Everyone stood watching him, faces filled with curiosity.

Jonas had never spoken in front of a crowd this size. He didn't even know what to say. Still he had to try. "Eh . . . you can't put Kate in jail."

The sheriff scratched his temple. "Why not?"

"Why not?" Jonas repeated, stalling for time. He glanced at Kate, who was watching him with big round eyes. This was his chance to ingratiate himself with her, his golden opportunity to earn the approval of her family, and he couldn't think of a damned thing to say. "Because . . ."

Seconds passed. No one said a word. Everyone stood frozen in waiting silence. Jonas prayed that a bolt of pure inspiration would favor him.

Finally the sheriff leaned toward him. "Because why?"

"Because . . ." Jonas glanced up at the sky. Anytime now, inspiration was bound to strike, just like it did whenever he got around to sparking with the girls back home.

He swallowed hard as an idea began to form. Kate was standing on the other side of the sheriff. That left only Kate's aunt within easy reach. Aunt

Hattie had wandered outside to shake out her feather duster, unaware that a crowd was gathered outside her front porch.

"Forgive me, Aunt Hattie," he said beneath his breath. He grabbed her by the waist and gave her a resounding kiss on the mouth, pretending she had just bored him with hours of idle gossip. The crowd gasped, Kate's eyes widened in astonishment, and Aunt Hattie dropped her feather duster.

But, by George, Jonas had his inspiration.

He faced the stunned spectators and lifted his voice. "You can't put Kate in jail because the president and his wife would be most upset to hear that their dear friend Miss Kate Whittaker has been incarcerated."

Curly blinked and scratched his bald head. "Who said anythin' about incarc'rating her? All we're gonna do is put her in jail."

"It's the same thing," Smoky Joe explained. "Ain't it?"

"Sort of," the sheriff said, looking unsure.

Jonas continued, "What I'm trying to say is that putting Kate in jail could do the president of the United States great harm."

"How do you figure that?" Kate asked curiously.

Jonas spoke over the sheriff's head. "Hush, dammit! I'm trying to keep you out of jail."

Kate's eyes flashed. "Well, don't let me stop you."

Sheriff Williams looked worried. He was a patriotic man. Everyone knew he could recite the entire Constitution by memory. And hadn't he personally seen to it that every citizen of Hogs Head who was qualified to vote in the last presidential election had done so? "How do you figure that my puttin' Kate in jail is gonna harm the president?"

"I'd like to know that myself," Kate added.

Jonas flashed Kate a look of irritation. The least she could do was keep from being a hindrance and help him out. He turned back to the crowd and lifted his voice in what he hoped was a proper orator style.

"The question, ladies and gentlemen, is how would Kate going to jail hurt our president. Well, I'll tell you. . . . How do you suppose it would look if word gets out that one of the president's friends is a criminal? Why, the president has been fighting graft and corruption in the government since the day he took office." Jonas paused for a moment to relish the look of approval on Aunt Hattie's face. If only Kate looked half as appreciative.

Turning back to the crowd, he continued, "The president's motto that 'a public office is a public trust' would have no meaning if it's known he cavorts with criminals."

"We hardly cavorted," Kate said, but her protest was drowned out by Curly.

"By jove, he's right! Puttin' Kate in jail could create a nat'nal scandal."

"It most certainly would," the editor of the newspaper agreed. "It would be a terrible thing to do to that nice Mrs. Cleveland."

Everyone seemed to agree. "A terrible thing."

Amazed at how easily Jonas had swayed public opinion, Kate locked gazes with him. What a strange man he was: one moment stunning the crowd by kissing her aunt, and the next moment having everyone worried about the president's wife.

She wasn't sure if he was brilliant or insane. She only wished he didn't look so unbearably handsome, with the breeze in his hair and his dark features touched by a sudden glint of sunlight breaking through the clouds.

Thelma Paine turned out to be an unexpected

ally by pointing out that an act of treason would be even more scandalous with Independence Day just around the corner. She raised her bandaged pin-pricked hand to make the point. "If you're going to commit treason, at least do it on another holiday," she declared.

She received a thunderous applause. Fortunately for Kate, no one bothered to point out the irrelevancy of her argument, and gradually the crowd began to drift away.

Jonas flashed her a beguiling though nonetheless arrogant smile.

"An act of treason, indeed!" she muttered to herself, though she had to admit it was clever of him to conceive of such an argument. Too clever, if you asked her. She wondered what other clever things he'd been up to recently.

The sheriff flung his arm across Jonas's shoulder in a fatherly fashion. "I bet you've never heard anyone recite the entire Constitution of the United States."

"I can't say I have," Jonas admitted. He gave her a beseeching look. "Kate and I . . . were in the middle of something."

She folded her arms in front of her. She could, if she had a mind to, rescue him from the sheriff. But thinking Jonas acted a bit too sure of himself and, in view of the nasty fall he'd had the night before, looked far too healthy, she decided he deserved to be thrown to the wolves. "That's all right. I wouldn't want to deprive you of hearing the sheriff recite the Constitution."

The Sheriff looked beside himself with joy. "Well, come along, lad. You're in for a real treat."

Aunt Hattie gazed after Jonas as he and the sheriff walked away. She dangled her feather duster from her hand, her ruddy face all aglow. "What a wonderful man. And does he know how to kiss!"

"Aunt Hattie!"

Aunt Hattie shrugged. "Well, he does. And you, young lady, might want to give it a try sometime." Before Kate had recovered from her shock, Aunt Hattie stomped inside the house to change her clothes. She was late opening the store.

Kate followed her aunt into the house and stood at the bottom of the stairs, calling up to her. "I wouldn't kiss Jonas Hunter if he were the last man on earth." It surprised Kate to find herself trembling suddenly, and she quickly grasped the newel post to steady herself. "I'd sooner kiss a hog!"

Aunt Hattie stopped halfway up the stairs and glanced over her shoulder at Kate. "Now, you don't need to go catching yourself a dog. You have your hands full taking care of Jimmy."

After Aunt Hattie had gathered up her belongings and left for the general store, Kate pulled the carpet cleaner from the storage cupboard beneath the stairwell and proceeded to clean up the plaster that had been dislodged from the ceiling during the early morning blast.

Much to her dismay, not even the loud roar of the motor could prevent her from thinking about the remote yet intriguing possibility of being kissed by Jonas.

She gave a deep sigh and stared into space, unaware that she ran the cleaning wand repeatedly over the same section of carpet. Not that she cared for him in any romantic sense, she told herself. Her interest in him was purely professional. How it warmed her heart and pleased her soul to hear him talk about his dreams! Never did she think it possible to find someone whose vision for the future so completely matched her own.

She wondered if people with passionate dreams kissed with equal fervor. Her old beau, Harold Davenport, had talked about the future in a dull, monotone voice. Kissing him had been like kissing a wet towel. She narrowed her eyes as she recalled, with increasing distaste, the various men who had attempted to court her in the past. There hadn't been a passionate dream among the bunch. No wonder their kisses had been as bland as milk and water.

Startled by her thoughts, she decided it was all Aunt Hattie's fault for making such a fuss over a friendly little buss.

Come to think about it, what could possibly be so special about a kiss? Knowing Aunt Hattie, she was probably exaggerating.

Kate was grateful, of course, that Jonas had managed to talk the sheriff out of putting her in jail, for Jimmy's sake. Even so, she still didn't trust him. How could she? He'd followed her to Hogs Head. Spied on her. For all she knew, had stolen from her. Who knew what else he was capable of doing?

And does he know how to kiss!

Hearing her aunt's words echo in her memory, she turned off the carpet cleaner.

It was then that she heard Jimmy calling to her from his room.

"I'm coming, Jimmy." She hesitated at the foot of the stairs, her gaze riveted to the divan in the parlor where Jonas had lain the previous night. Her face grew hot as she recalled the feel of him.

"Down lower," he'd murmured, his voice barely louder than a whisper. But, oh, how her heart had pounded when he'd said it. Oh, how her body had trembled, was still trembling, just thinking about it.

How was it possible that he could make her heart do cartwheels when no man previously had made her lose so much as a train of thought? Unless . . .

Narrowing her eyes, she tightened her fingers around the oak newel post as a nagging notion took hold.

She was right to be suspicious of his injuries. Less than sixteen hours ago he had suffered a severe head injury, at least severe enough to be rendered momentarily unconscious—or so he claimed! Yet he'd looked in perfect health when he stood in her parlor that very morning telling her about the Chicago Fair. Perfect health hardly described how he looked on her porch giving his ridiculous though infinitely persuasive argument on her behalf. Oh, yes, indeed. He looked exceedingly robust, in a rakish, handsome sort of way, and all the time he was manipulating the crowd, he was also cleverly manipulating her.

No wonder she'd not discovered any outward signs of injury following his fall. The two-timing thief had feigned his injuries, all right. She only wished she'd suspected his little game earlier. If she was lucky, the sheriff would recite not just the Constitution, he would also recite the Bill of Rights, the Declaration of Independence, *and* the Articles of Confederation. It would serve Mr. Hunter right!

The question was, why would he fake an injury? Unless, of course, his intention had been to get inside the house hoping to steal yet another one of her ideas.

She knew it! She ran up the stairs. Knew it all along. She tore open the door to Jimmy's room.

The man was up to no good.

Chapter 21

The following day, a large bouquet of summer flowers was delivered to Aunt Hattie's General Store by Maizie Campbell, who was known throughout the county for her magnificent gardens and artistic flower arrangements.

Shaped like a flower pot, with narrow hips and wide shoulders, Maizie was a walking advertisement for her flower business. A ruffle of bright red posies trimmed the hem and neckline of her floral print dress.

The small features of her face almost disappeared beneath a chimney-squat hat that was covered with Taffetine rosettes. Tiny violets dangled from slender ribbons and swung back and forth in front of her forehead like well-regulated pendulums.

The bouquet she delivered was enormous. Golden marigolds and red carnations offered a striking contrast to the purple delphiniums. Wrapped in tissue paper, the bouquet was tied together with a big red satin bow.

Kate, who just happened to be in the store to check for mail, clapped her hands together. "What beautiful flowers! You're bound to walk away with all the blue ribbons at this year's fair."

Maizie looked pleased. "This is my best arrangement so far and I did it special for you. I was on my way to deliver them to your house. But I happened to notice you through the window."

Kate drew back in surprise. "For me?"

"Says so right here on the card." Maizie drew the envelope from among the blooms and handed it to Kate. The handwriting was large and bold, definitely masculine in nature.

Aunt Hattie sniffed the bouquet. "You must have a secret admirer."

Kate's hands shook as she tore open the envelope and pulled out a single folded sheet of paper that read, *"With my gratitude. Jonas Hunter."*

"Well, what does it say?" Aunt Hattie asked impatiently.

Her pulse racing, Kate struggled to keep her voice normal in tone. "It's just a thank-you from Mr. Hunter." For Maizie's benefit, she added, "He injured himself and we nursed him back to health."

"You never told me the man had wealth," Aunt Hattie said, looking impressed.

"I said health."

"Well, speak up. How can I hear you when you go around mumbling?"

"Do you know this man, Hattie?" Maizie asked.

"Mr. Hunter? Well, of course I know him. Do you think I would let a perfect stranger have his way with me?"

Maizie's mouth dropped open.

"He didn't have his way with her," Kate hastened to explain. She gave her aunt a scolding look. "He kissed her, is all."

"But Hattie's a married woman." Maizie gasped.

"She's also old enough to be his mother," Kate pointed out.

"You didn't tell me his mother was coming to town," Aunt Hattie said. "Hope she's as nice as her son. You never saw anything like it, Maizie.

Lay right there on my sofa like a perfect gentleman."

Kate frowned. Perfect gentleman indeed! He managed to trick her into giving him a massage. Feeling sorry for him, she'd willingly complied with his every request. How could she have been so foolish as to fall for such an underhanded attempt to seduce her? Oooooooh. If she ever got her hands on him again, she'd not be responsible for her actions.

The more Aunt Hattie rambled on about Mr. Hunter, the more confused Maizie looked. "Did he injure himself before or after he took advantage of you?"

"He didn't take advantage of her," Kate protested.

Aunt Hattie looked puzzled. "I can't imagine what you mean, Maizie. What possible advantage could there be to an injury? Anyway, as I was saying, he's a very nice man. When the boiler blew up, he came flying to the house to see if Kate was all right."

Maizie looked from Aunt Hattie to Kate. "Flying? But I thought you said he was injured."

"He made an amazing recovery," Kate explained. Yes, indeed, most amazing.

"That was because of your good care and my herb tea." Aunt Hattie nodded in satisfaction. "Works every time." She glanced up at her niece and frowned. "And why are you looking like a dried-up fig? It is you who should be thanking that nice Mr. Hunter. If it wasn't for him, you'd be sitting in jail and that poor President Cleveland would be facing political doom."

At the mention of President Cleveland, Maizie threw up her hands in despair. "None of this makes any sense."

"It doesn't make any sense to me, either," Kate said. She was amazed by the number of people who apparently believed Jonas's ridiculous contention that anything happening in Hogs Head would have an effect on the president. "All I can say is I don't trust him. And I don't think you should, either, Aunt Hattie."

"Maybe Kate's right," Maizie said, her violets swinging furiously. "Any man that would take advantage of an old lady . . ."

Aunt Hattie's eyes widened. "My word. He took advantage of an old lady?"

"And a lot worse," Kate replied. "He tried to steal my carpet cleaner."

"Seal?" Her aunt looked confused. "Are you saying it had a leak?"

"Steal, Aunt Hattie. Steal!"

"That's preposterous!" Aunt Hattie declared.

Maizie agreed. "Besides, what possible use would a man like him have for a carpet cleaner?"

Before Kate could explain, Jonas walked into the store and all heads turned in his direction quicker than a compass needle pointed north.

He was dressed in a pair of plain black trousers held up with red suspenders that stretched over his shoulders and crisscrossed in back. He wore a red and blue work shirt and a rawhide hat. It was pretty near the same outfit worn by most of the local farmers, but because of his impressive height, he bore his clothes with an air of importance that few men achieved, even those dressed in city clothes.

Kate had never seen Aunt Hattie carry on so. She was all a-twitter, suddenly, smiling and fussing with her apron and hair, and "gibber-jabbering," as her uncle called it. "Why, Mr. Hunter. How nice to see you again. We were just talking about you, weren't we, Kate? As you can see, your flowers have arrived, and my, do they smell good. Why, it's like a breath of spring and summer all rolled into one."

"I'm mighty happy you like them." He talked to Aunt Hattie and gave Maizie a polite nod, but his eyes quickly sought Kate. "The red bow seemed an especially appropriate way to . . . express my gratitude."

If Kate had the least doubt he was making a brazen reference to her red petticoats, it was quickly dispelled when his gaze dropped to the hem of her dress.

He lifted his eyes and arched a dark brow. "I hope you like them, Kate."

Aunt Hattie nudged her niece. "Well, of course she does. What girl wouldn't? Tell him, Kate."

Not wanting to make a scene in front of her aunt, Kate bit back the urge to tell him what she thought of him and his fake injuries. Just let him try and deny it! "You shouldn't have troubled yourself, Mr. Hunter."

"It was no trouble, thanks to this lovely lady." He bowed to Maizie, who turned pale and held him at arms' length.

"I'm a married woman, Mr. Hunter, and don't you forget it!"

Jonas gave Kate a questioning look. Kate responded with a mocking smile. "We were telling Maizie about your unfortunate *accident*."

"Well, thanks to you both, I have completely recovered from my concussion." He studied Kate as he spoke, as if to read her thoughts. It gave her great pleasure to see the smile die on his face as he apparently realized she was no longer fooled by him. "Concussion, my foot," she said, keeping her voice low so that her aunt wouldn't hear. "No one recovers that quickly."

"I only wish I could recover from the sheriff's recitations as quickly," he whispered back. He leaned across the counter. "Would you look at that hat?" He reached past her to pluck a man's hat off its wooden stand, his arm brushing against her shoulder.

The hat he chose was a black felt fedora, so unlike anything one would expect him to wear that Kate knew immediately he was up to one of his tricks.

He removed his old hat and placed the new one atop his head. Twisting his head this way and that, he turned for all to see. "What do you think?"

"It's perfect!" Aunt Hattie cooed.

"You can get the same thing in the Sears and Roebuck mail-order catalogue," Maizie said.

Aunt Hattie glared at Maizie. "Now, why would he want to do that?"

"Now, don't go getting yourself on a high horse, Hattie. You know as well as I do that it's much more fashionable to shop through the mail-order catalogue," Maizie said defensively. "Everyone's doing it."

"Why do you suppose that is?" Jonas asked. "If I buy the hat from Aunt Hattie here, I can take it home with me at once." He lay the hat on the counter. "I won't have to wait for weeks."

"Reeks, you say?" Aunt Hattie lifted the hat and sniffed. "It does have a peculiar smell. It's probably the glue. But I don't think it reeks, particularly."

"I'll buy it," Jonas said, winking at Kate and making her heart do flip-flops.

He reached into his pocket and drew out his leather billfold. He paid for his purchase, placed the hat on his head, and, bidding everyone a cheery good day, stepped outside.

"What a fine young man." Aunt Hattie clasped

her hands to her ample bosom. "He can take advantage of me anytime he wants."

Maizie looked shocked. "Why, Hattie, you should be ashamed of yourself. You're an old married woman." With that she hurried from the store, slamming the door shut behind her and streaking past the window in a colorful blur.

"If you ask me, she's just jealous," Aunt Hattie declared with a knowing nod. It was how Aunt Hattie habitually explained another's ill manners or bad temper. To Aunt Hattie's way of thinking, half the town was jealous of her on any given day.

Kate pressed her fingers into her palms and bit back the urge to argue. She probably had a greater chance of getting her aunt to say a civil word about Mr. Sears than convincing her Mr. Hunter was a liar and a thief. Aunt Hattie would no doubt insist Kate was jealous of the man—as if she could be!

If he left town, which she hoped he would do soon enough, she might be able to protect Aunt Hattie from the terrible truth.

Two weeks later, the man still had not left town. Kate knew this because everyone who walked into Aunt Hattie's store couldn't seem to say enough about him.

"He's wonderful," Thelma Paine declared. "Helped my Harry build that fence he's been putting off for months. And he even helped me pick out one of those fancy Singer sewing machines."

Kate couldn't believe her ears. "I've been telling you for years how much easier your work would be with the proper equipment. Why, a high-grade sewing machine with all the attachments will make perfect stitches in far less time."

With a haughty sniff, Thelma flung the end of her shawl over her shoulder. Obviously she resented the implication that she could so readily be replaced by a machine. "Mr. Hunter said that my artistry was not in the fine even stitches I worked so hard to achieve, but in my designs. He said it was only good business to concentrate on things that no machine could produce. I'm no longer a seamstress. I'm a designer."

"Well, I wouldn't go around advertising it," Aunt Hattie said. "No one likes a whiner."

Before Thelma had a chance to correct Aunt Hattie's mistaken notion, Curly walked into the shop and the conversation immediately reverted back to Jonas.

"That Mr. Hunter is a fine man, aw-right. Fixed my barber chair so it goes up and down again."

Even Smoky Joe, who stopped by to pick up some dry goods, had unprecedented praise for the man. "Some troublemaker came to town and I thought he was gonna shoot up the place, but ole Jonas stood right up to him, he did. Never saw so much bravery in all my life."

Kate was convinced that if she heard one more complimentary word about Mr. Hunter, she would scream.

In the days to follow, it seemed she couldn't move without bumping into him. Five out of the six times she stopped into her uncle's harness store, he was there. At least four or five times a day, he stopped by the general store to charm her aunt with unflattering anecdotes about Mr. Sears or to otherwise amuse her.

He was everywhere. Kate met him in the blacksmith shop when she dropped off a piece of metal for Duke to weld. She found him there later in the day when she returned to pick up the same piece of metal, and still again when she had dodged into the barbershop trying to avoid the director of the school board, Mrs. Baglebauer.

"I swear the man is following me!" she complained one night after supper while helping her aunt with the dishes.

Her aunt rinsed the suds off a stoneware plate and handed it to Kate. "Since he's already in the store when you get there, how can he be following you? It seems to me you're the one doing the following."

"I most certainly am not!" Kate protested. She wiped the plate dry and stacked it on the shelf over the sink. "I have legitimate business in town."

"Seems to me you have a lot of business, lately. It was not so long ago that you came to town once or twice a month. Now you're in town three or four times a day."

"I'm working on a special project," Kate explained, feeling suddenly defensive.

"A special project, you say?" Aunt Hattie smiled and nodded in satisfaction. "I guess that's as good a name for it as any."

Kate studied her aunt. "What is that supposed to mean?"

"I just hope this special project of yours is a success, that's all."

"It will be," Kate said, wondering why her aunt had suddenly taken such an interest in her work. If Mr. Hunter would stop distracting her, her project was likely to be a big success. The problem was, just knowing he was in town was distraction enough.

Uncle Barney walked into the kitchen, looking grim. "The new catalogues have arrived," he announced.

Aunt Hattie dried her hands on her apron. "What? What did you say?"

"I said the new Sears and Roebuck catalogues arrived. They came on today's train."

Aunt Hattie flew into a rage. "How dare those men trespass on my territory."

Alarmed by her aunt's red face, Kate tried to placate her. "Now, now, Aunt Hattie. Don't get yourself all upset."

"Upset! Those men are putting me out of business. I have every right to be upset."

"There's nothing we can do about it," Uncle Barney said.

"Maybe there's nothing *you* can do about it. But there's plenty *I* can do about it!" Aunt Hattie ripped off her apron and flung it to the floor.

A look of dread crossed Uncle Barney's face as he and Kate followed her out of the kitchen. "Now, Hattie, there's no sense in getting all riled up."

"I'm not riled up!" Aunt Hattie declared. "I'm mad!" She marched through the parlor and out the front door, slamming it so hard that one of the few picture frames to survive Kate's many explosions fell off the wall.

Kate started to follow her, but Uncle Barney held her back. "Let her go."

"You don't suppose she'll do anything drastic, do you?"

"Drastic? No. She's probably going to blow off some steam. Tomorrow she'll picket up and down Main Street and that'll be the end of it."

Her uncle was probably right, Kate thought as she hastened upstairs to give Jimmy his bath. Still, it was hard to shake off the feeling that her aunt had reached her very last straw.

Chapter 22

The fire alarm sounded just after ten o'clock that night. The loud clang of fire bells was accompanied by a chorus of barking dogs.

Kate was upstairs in her room, sketching plans for the fuel-driven buggy she'd been working on for so long. Upon hearing the bell, she threw up the sash of her window and leaned over the sill.

The grove of cottonwoods blocked off the view of the town, but the orange glow flickering above the treetops told her that the fire was in the direction of the train station. Craning through the open window, she caught a whiff of acrid smoke.

The sound of horses' hooves thundering in the distance indicated members of the volunteer firemen's brigade were already racing to town. Closing the window to keep out the smoke, she grabbed her wrap and checked to make certain Jimmy was asleep before hurrying downstairs.

"It looks like the train station," she called to her uncle, who was hopping around on one foot as he pulled the pants of his volunteer fireman's uniform over his long underwear.

"Hurry," she urged, helping him into his jacket.

"When you're my age, this is as fast as you go!" Uncle Barney protested, grabbing his leather fire helmet.

Together they left the house and, not wanting to

waste time harnessing the horse to the wagon, cut through the trees on foot, the rosy glow of the fire lighting their way.

A large crowd had already gathered around the train station. Crackling flames had engulfed both the ticket office and waiting room. Sparks shot high into the sky before falling to the ground in a shower of red embers. Uncle Barney ran to help several volunteer firemen who were busily priming the pump.

Spotting Maizie, Kate called to her, "What happened?"

Maizie sputtered and coughed. "I'll tell you what happened." She coughed again before continuing. "Your crazy aunt set the station afire, that's what happened!"

Shocked by Maizie's accusation, Kate gave her shawl an indignant tug. "My aunt would never do such a thing."

"Oh, no? Then you tell me why the sheriff hauled her off to jail like a common criminal."

Kate's throat went dry. "Sheriff ... Sheriff Williams took Aunt Hattie to jail?" This simply couldn't be true.

Smoky Joe's eyes gleamed menacingly in the light of the fire. "I think we ought to name the jail after the Whittakers, here. They're the only ones who use it. What do you say?"

"I say anyone crazy enough to burn down the train station should be hung!" someone shouted.

A cheer rose up from the crowd. "Hear, hear!"

Tears flooded Kate's eyes. What was happening to her town? To the people she loved? To the dear aunt who had taken her in at the age of five and raised her like a daughter?

"Maizie, do me a favor, please. Go back to the house and stay with Jimmy until I get back."

"Well ... I ..."

"Please."

"Oh, all right. But you better not be gone too long." Maizie shuffled off in the direction of Rocking Horse Lane.

Kate searched for her uncle and, unable to spot him in the confusion, picked up her skirts and raced down Main Street to the jail.

Aunt Hattie was in jail, all right, and Kate could hear her aunt's high strident voice drifting from the open window of the sheriff's office even before stepping inside. "I demand that you let me out of here at once. Did you hear what I said, Sheriff? At once! If you don't, you'll live to regret it. Mark my words ..."

Kate opened the door and the sheriff, leaning against the cell door so that Hattie couldn't leave, greeted her with a weary wave of his hand. "Hello, Kate."

"Sheriff." She closed the door behind her, hastened over to the cell, and grabbed hold of the iron bars. "Aunt Hattie! What is the meaning of this? They said you are the one who set fire to the train station."

"I did no such thing," Aunt Hattie protested. "I set fire to the Shears and Rhubarb catalogues."

"Aunt Hattie!"

"That's arson," Sheriff Williams told Kate. "And it's against the law." He turned to Aunt Hattie, lifting his voice so she wouldn't misunderstand him. "It's also against the law to escape from jail."

"Not if there's no lock on the door," Aunt Hattie argued.

"She has a point," Kate said, though she was no authority on the law.

"Lock or no lock, she better not escape, because if she does, it'll be over my dead body. And, Hattie, just so you don't get no fancy ideas, murderin' a sheriff is a mighty serious o-fense."

"So is locking up a friend!"

"Friend or no friend, I can't let you go around burnin' down public buildin's."

"I never made your billings public and you know it! What people owe on credit is always kept in the strictest of confidence!"

The sheriff sighed. "I wonder if there's a law that says I can't lock up a person who's hard of hearin'?"

"What are you mumbling about now, Sheriff? If you have something to say, speak up and say it!"

"Aunt Hattie, please calm down." Kate reached through the bars to pat her aunt on the arm. She spoke in a loud voice, saying each word distinctly. "You've committed a very serious crime."

"I've done no such thing. I burned those catalogues in self-defense and the sheriff knows it!"

Kate spent the next hour trying to reason with her aunt, to no avail. Finally she gave up in despair.

The door to the sheriff's office flew open and in walked Uncle Barney, followed by Jonas. Both men were covered in soot.

"It's about time," Aunt Hattie complained. "Here I am rotting in jail while you take your own sweet time getting here."

"Uncle Barney was putting out the fire," Kate said, aware of Jonas watching her. She met his gaze with unflinching eyes. "I'm not sure what Mr. Hunter was doing."

"Helping us put out the fire," Uncle Barney explained. "The man's a born firefighter."

Jonas grinned and managed to look halfway modest. "I've had a lot of experience. I can't tell you how many times I've set my pa's barn afire."

Barney walked up to the jail cell. "For God's

sake, Hattie, why didn't you just picket like you usually do when you're upset about something?"

"You dummy, what good would a ticket have done me? I didn't want to *ride* the train. I only wanted to protect what was mine."

Uncle Barney sighed. "Let me take her home, Sheriff, so you can get some rest."

"Sorry, Barney, I can't let you do that."

"You can't keep her here all night," Kate protested.

"I plan to give it a damn good try."

"How much do you think it would cost to repair the damage?" Jonas asked.

Sheriff Williams's forehead creased. "Damage? You mean to the train station? I don't know." The sheriff scratched his head. "A couple hundred dollars. We'll have to build a new waitin' room and ticket office."

Jonas reached into his pocket and pulled out a wad of currency. He picked out several crisp bills and handed them to the sheriff. "Does that take care of it?"

Kate's mouth dropped open in surprise. She couldn't believe what Jonas was doing. "We can't possibly allow you to pay for a new train station."

"We can't let your aunt spend the night in such a place. Please, let me do this—"

"But—"

"Let him do it," the sheriff said, plucking the money out of Jonas's hands. " 'Course this doesn't cover everythin'. There's that little matter of d'turbin' the peace. Why, most people were woken out of a deep sleep to put out the fire."

Jonas handed him another bill.

"Then there's a cell fee."

"What do you mean, sell fee?" Aunt Hattie cried out. "I'm not for sale!"

"All right," the sheriff said. "Forget the cell fee." The sheriff folded the bills in his hand. "Thank you, Hunter. Come to think of it, I saw the perfect lock in the Sears and Roebuck catalogue. Maybe there'll be 'nuff money left over to order it."

Aunt Hattie glared at him. "I ain't mailing your order."

"You have to, Hattie. Your store is the o-ficial 'Nited States post office. Not mailin' my letter would be a fed'ral o-fense."

"I don't care how many fences you want to build. I ain't mailing it and that's final."

Uncle Barney rolled his eyes to the ceiling as he pulled the cell door open. Aunt Hattie marched from the cell with a huff. Without so much as a backward glance, she stormed out of the office, gibber-jabbering all the way.

"Lord help us," Barney said, running after her. "Hattie!"

That left Kate alone with Jonas, or that's how it seemed, for neither one paid any attention to the sheriff, who was busy carting his Independence Day decorations back into the empty cell.

Kate didn't know what to say. She couldn't believe Jonas would pay out so much money just so her aunt wouldn't have to spend the night in jail. "I don't know how to thank you for what you did for my aunt."

"I don't want gratitude. All I want is . . ." He stopped himself. "Do you mind if I walk you home?"

Kate hesitated. As grateful as she felt, she was still reluctant to trust him. Still, he had done a very kind and generous thing tonight. What kind of person would she be if she didn't acknowledge his generous act? "I would like that. But first, let me help you clean up. I'm sure the sheriff could let us have a washcloth and some water."

Jonas's eyes never left her face. "Sheriff?"

"Hold on a minute." The sheriff disappeared into the back room, returning a moment later with a small basin of water and a piece of Turkish toweling. He placed the basin on the edge of his desk.

Jonas sat on a ladder-back chair. "Thank you, Sheriff."

Feeling suddenly nervous, Kate dipped the towel into the tepid water, squeezed out the cloth, and lifted it to Jonas's blackened forehead. "Let me know if I'm hurting you."

"You wouldn't hurt me, would you, Kate?" he drawled.

Her hand stilled. Her eyes collided with his. Some tangible, yet invisible force snapped between them, like electricity jumping a gap in a circuit.

It was the sheriff's voice in the background, grumbling about having to move his Independence Day decorations every time he needed to use the jail cell, that jolted Kate and Jonas back to reality.

Kate pulled her eyes away from his and concentrated on the blackened portion next to his nose. "I'll ... I'll try not to," she murmured. She drew the towel down one male-rough cheek, across the bridge of his fine nose to the other. The dingy yellowed towel looked sparkling white next to his bronzed skin. Some would call it a farmer's skin, weathered by the sun and the wind into a ruddy brown glow.

For the first time since his injury, she was close enough to discern the fine lines around his eyes and the golden tips on his lashes.

Leaving the area around his mouth for last, she rubbed the soot away from his laugh lines and tried not to notice him running his tongue along his lower lip. It was his smile she couldn't ignore, and no sooner had the corners of his mouth tipped upward than she quickly withdrew her hand.

Not wanting him to know how he affected her, she tried for a cool appraisal, but his knowing look told her how much she had failed. Feeling uncomfortably warm, she stepped toward the open window to take advantage of the slight breeze ruffling the gingham curtain.

After carrying the last of his cartons into the cell, the sheriff brushed his hands together. "If your crazy aunt behaves herself and you, young lady, don't go d'turbin' the peace no more, I won't have to move those boxes again till the Fourth."

Jonas took the washcloth from the basin where she'd left it, and wiped the soot away from his hands. After he was finished, he dropped the cloth into the basin and stood. "Shall we?" He opened the door of the office and waited for Kate.

"Good night, Sheriff," Kate said.

" 'Night. And remember what I said about not d'turbin' the peace."

Chapter 23

Pulling her wrap around her shoulders, Kate stepped outside into the welcome coolness of night. The air hung thick with the smell of smoke, but was otherwise clear. Countless stars dotted the black velvet sky.

They walked side by side down Main Street, careful to avoid stepping into the puddles of water that remained from the firefighting efforts, and taking even more care not to touch each other.

"I still think it was a very kind thing you did for my aunt," Kate said. She still couldn't believe it.

"I'm very fond of your aunt."

"She's fond of you, too. I don't have much money ... but I intend to pay you back."

He stopped and, because she had stepped ahead of him, she was forced to turn around to face him.

"That won't be necessary," he said. "I ... I won't be needing that money. Not now."

She looked up at him, seeing only the outline of his head against the jeweled sky. "You won't?"

"I'll be honest with you, Kate. I was going to use that money for capital to start my own company. But now that I no longer have a machine to market ..."

"Oh." She felt so bad for him, she could hardly stand it. Was it possible ... could they really have invented the same machine? She didn't want to believe it was true, but she could no longer, in good conscience, ignore the facts.

Jonas Hunter was a knowledgeable, capable, and imaginative inventor. It was hard to imagine him having to resort to stealing ideas. Still, how could one explain the fact that he'd invented a machine identical to hers? Could it be true that they were both victims of circumstance?

Feeling as if she were about to step off a dangerously high cliff, she clutched at her wrap. "I've been thinking. Perhaps I could hire you as an assistant and adviser." Naturally, she wouldn't let him anywhere near her work area. Just in case her earlier suspicious were true. "I'd pay you a salary."

"A salary?"

"It would be a small one at first," she admitted. "But as soon as my business is established, I could pay you more."

He touched a finger to her lips, sending a deliciously warm wave of pleasure shooting all the way to her toes. "You are a most capable woman. You don't need anyone to advise you."

His touch elicited so many sensations she could hardly speak; his words reached even deeper, finding the needy part of her that wanted—needed—validation. It was something she had sought for most of her life, since the time she was put on a train with nothing more than a note pinned to the bodice of her thin calico pinafore, and was made to sit in the baggage car because no one had wanted a child who was "wild and disruptive."

Blinking away the tears that those past memories elicited, she swallowed the lump in her throat. "But if you really did . . . I mean, if what you said is true about us both inventing—"

"It *is* true, Kate, I swear it." A lone horseman left the Red Rooster Saloon and galloped up Main

Street. Jonas pulled her out of the way, then resumed walking.

"Then it's only fair . . ." Kate began tentatively, "we must find a way for us both to benefit—"

"I want you to have it all, Kate. You deserve it. Me? I'll just go back to the family farm and . . . Don't worry your head about me. My pa always wanted me to be a farmer. It'll make him very happy."

Kate felt her spirits plummet, though she couldn't imagine why. She wanted him to leave her alone, leave Hogs Head, leave her to work in peace. So why did she have the strange feeling she was about to suffer a great loss when he left?

"What about you? What about your happiness?"

"Don't worry about me, Kate. I have other inventions I'm working on. Of course, none so far have the commercial potential of my fertilizer spreader."

"When . . . when will you be leaving?"

"I was hoping to leave by the end of the week."

"So soon?"

"I planned to leave sooner, but I want to avoid traveling around Independence Day. You know how crowded the train is on holidays. Besides," he added with a laugh, "I don't think the sheriff will ever forgive me if I leave town without seeing his Independence Day decorations."

Kate laughed, too. "You're right." Her laughter died away, and once again she battled the lump in her throat. "My aunt will miss you."

"And you, Kate? Will you miss me?"

She glanced at him from the corner of her eye. "Perhaps. A little." She could hardly lie. Besides, she *would* miss him. His presence was so noticeable, anyone would miss him.

By unspoken consent, they walked the long way

down Main Street, avoiding any shortcuts that would lessen their time together, and turned on Rocking Horse Lane. Her skirt brushed against the legs of his pants. His arm inadvertently skimmed her shoulders.

"I don't know if I have the right to ask this of you ..." He hesitated and she stopped by his side to face him.

"Ask me what?"

"Your aunt told me that Hogs Head always had a big Independence Day celebration and I thought ... since it's my last week in town ..."

"Oh, you really should attend," Kate said hastily. "We have a big parade and a picnic down by the creek. After dark, there's always a fantastic fireworks display."

"Would you do me the honor of letting me be your escort?"

"Well . . . I . . ." A number of polite excuses raced through her head.

"Please. It would mean so much to me."

For some reason she was shaking, but not from the cold. She knew it wasn't from the cold. "I'm not sure what my plans are...."

"You're not thinking of missing the festivities, are you?"

She took a deep breath. "I don't know. I'm taking care of a young boy named Jimmy. He's an orphan who came to town on the train and I've not had any luck finding him a home."

"Bring him along."

She sighed, wishing it was that simple. "He refuses to leave the house. You see, he has a bad leg and can't walk. He's been rejected by several families because of it."

"Kate, this is terrible."

"I know. I just hate to leave him alone on a holiday."

"Do you think that your staying with him is a good idea? I mean ..." He paused a moment before adding, "I'm sorry, I have no right to interfere."

"No, please. I'd like to know what you think."

"It seems to me that your staying with him gives him less incentive to want to leave the house."

"I never thought of it that way," she said. "Do you think that's possible?"

"I don't know." He raked his fingers through his hair. "I don't know anything about raising children. I'm being selfish to want to spend Independence Day with you. I apologize."

"Don't apologize. The truth is I would like to spend the day with you."

"Really, Kate?"

"Really," she said.

"If you like, we can both stay home with the boy."

Kate pulled her shawl so tight around her shoulders, the woolen fibers were stretched to the limit. "Maybe what you said about incentive is true. I don't know. Sometimes I feel so alone. I want to do what's right by Jimmy, but I don't always know what that is."

"Kate, please. Spend this one day with me. I'll soon be gone and ... I'm only asking for one last day together."

Kate bit her lip. During the last six months Jimmy had lived with her, she had always put his welfare first. Not once had she considered her own needs. Until tonight. "I would be delighted if you would escort me to the Independence Day celebration," she said, making up her mind. Jonas was right. It did no good to mollycoddle the boy. "But only if I can find someone to stay with Jimmy."

"Of course."

"And even then, I'll want to check on him during the day."

"Kate, we'll work it out."

They walked the remaining distance to the house in silence. Never had the walk seemed so short.

"Be careful," Kate said, grabbing his arm to keep him from walking into a discarded wagon wheel. She could feel his breath on her forehead as he looked down on her. Her cheeks growing warm, she drew her hand away from him. "I wouldn't want you to injure yourself . . . again."

"You . . . needn't concern yourself with my welfare."

Kate chewed on her lower lip, hating the doubt that still lingered. "You made a most remarkable recovery from your fall."

"Which I attribute to the wonderful care I received from you and your aunt. Then, of course, there's my strong constitution, derived, I'm told, from my German heritage."

"German, you say?" Maybe he really had been injured. Anything was possible, wasn't it? Lord, moments ago she was even willing to believe that two people could invent the same machine independent of each other.

"Good night, Mr. Hunter." She held her breath and waited. He was so close that it was only natural to think he might conceivably kiss her. Not that she wanted him to, of course. But if he did, she probably wouldn't object. After all, he was leaving town. So what harm could a little tiny kiss do?

"I really do appreciate what you did for my aunt. I'll pay you back just as soon as I get my carpet cleaner business going."

"That won't be necessary."

"I want to," Kate insisted.

Silence hung between them for a moment or two before Jonas bid her good night.

Feeling somewhat chagrined by his remote, though polite salutation, and not wanting him to think she had been waiting for anything more, she spun around and hurried up the steps of the dilapidated porch. She hesitated long enough to give him a chance to halt her departure, and when it was obvious he had no intention of doing so, she hurried into the house feeling hurt and angry and, more than anything, feeling like a foolish schoolgirl.

Hearing the door shut with more force than necessary, Jonas whirled about to face the house, a smile playing at the corner of his mouth. He could have kissed her, of course, and judging by her trembling and the warmth he'd heard in her voice, he would have most assuredly gotten away with it.

Though his instincts told him his decision not to kiss Kate was wise and necessary, it was no less frustrating. Depriving himself of what surely would be a most pleasurable experience put his spirits at an all-time low. His only consolation was the belief that such self-control would assure handsome dividends in the very near future.

A vision of her soft pink lips came to mind and he smiled in anticipation. Ah, yes.

What a stroke of good luck. He'd sat in his lonely room earlier that evening, brooding over his failure to win Kate over, when fate stepped in, offering him a chance to rescue Kate's aunt. What better way to ingratiate himself with Kate than through her family? Of course his generous deed would put him into a serious financial bind. But once he and Kate were married and he had control of the patent rights, he'd never have to worry about money again.

Feeling a twinge of conscience, he justified his actions to himself. He had worked long and hard on his fertilizer spreader. He was only taking what was his. He'd allowed Kate every opportunity to right the wrong, and what had she done? She'd offered to hire him as an adviser and pay him a salary. A salary! As far as he was concerned, it was fifty-fifty or nothing!

She gave him no choice. If it was true they had both invented the machine simultaneously, then it only made sense for the two of them to reap equal benefits. Besides, Kate needed a husband. Everyone in town said as much. He would be a good husband to her and a good father to the boy in her care, if she would let him.

Of course, he wasn't opposed to the idea of having a wife. Especially a wife by the name of Kate Whittaker. No, indeed. Suddenly he was grinning like a fool. He wasn't opposed in the least.

Feeling considerably better, he picked up speed. He couldn't believe his good fortune; he was going to spend an entire day with Kate Whittaker. Oh, heavenly days. Just thinking about it made his heart skip a beat.

Suddenly he remembered leaving his horse tied up in front of the Red Rooster Saloon. He would have to go back to town.

As he strolled briskly along the dark dirt road—and recalled his pleasure moments earlier while covering this same ground with Kate by his side—he continued to savor the extraordinary circumstances that had occurred that evening, starting with the fire.

It was providence, that's what it was. Pure and

simple providence. He glanced up at the brilliant stars just as a fiery streak shot across the sky.

God bless Aunt Hattie.

God bless Sears and Roebuck.

God bless Independence Day.

Hands in his pants pocket, he strolled down Rocking Horse Lane, whistling to himself. Upon reaching Main Street, he jumped up and clicked his heels together.

Who would have ever thought that Kate Whittaker would be such an easy conquest?

Chapter 24

The Fourth of July dawned in rose-colored splendor. A fiery red halo fanned the eastern sky before the sun emerged. The brilliant gold rays lit the distant church steeple, then spilled across the rooftops of downtown Hogs Head and trickled through the trees.

The sound of hammers echoed along Hogs Head Creek as residents scrambled to put the finishing touches on carnival booths for the big Independence Day celebration.

Main Street was abuzz with activity. Young girls wearing pretty calico dresses, and boys dressed in knee pants, rolled large wooden hoops along the boardwalk, their excited voices piercing the air.

Shopkeepers scrambled about, tacking red, white, and blue bunting onto the front of their stores and attaching American flags to lampposts. The flags fluttered and flapped in the early morning breeze.

Despite the flurry of activity, the shopkeepers could not outdo Sheriff Williams, who had emptied the jail cell of its numerous crates and boxes and had turned the entire front of the sheriff's office into a giant American flag complete with forty-five stars representing each state of the Union, including the newest state, Utah. A giant figure of Uncle Sam guarded the doorway, and a picture of every

president, from Washington to Cleveland filled
each diamond-shaped windowpane.

The strains of patriotic music floated down Main
Street. Anyone who could pluck, toot, or beat out
a musical scale had been asked to join the Hogs
Head Patriotic Band, and the field outside of town
was filled with people warming up their instruments. Unfortunately for the few music virtuosos
in town, the musicians manifested more enthusiasm
than musical ability.

Trying to ignore the tuneless rendition of the na-
tional anthem, Kate stood in front of the general
store holding pieces of red and blue fabric. Next to
her, Aunt Hattie issued orders to Uncle Barney,
who was balanced precariously atop a wooden
ladder.

Kate wore the red checkered dress her aunt had
made special for the occasion and not one of the
"awful Shears and Rhubarb atrocities!" as her aunt
put it, that a number of the other women donned.
The ready-made catalogue dresses appeared in such
large numbers, they seemed to be the official uniform of the day.

"Disgusting," Aunt Hattie declared loudly as
three matronly women passed by, each wearing the
exact same dress. "What's the matter with them?
Can't they see that dress was designed to be worn
by a cow?"

Kate hushed her aunt. "Today's a holiday. We're
here to celebrate, not to pass judgment on what
others are wearing."

"Don't think they're not looking you over,"
Aunt Hattie said, feeding Uncle Barney more
fabric.

"They can look all they want," Kate said. Her
dress had been expertly designed to show off her
small waist and full rounded breasts. The hem was

finished in a wide ruffle trimmed with little red bows. The skirt was full enough to allow Kate to wear her favorite double-skirted red, white, and blue petticoats. Her thick waving hair cascaded down her back to her waist. She wore a wide-brimmed straw hat with trailing red ribbons.

Her aunt gave her a shrewd look. "If you're so intent upon celebrating, why are you frowning?"

"I'm worried about Jimmy," Kate said.

She had tried her best to persuade Jimmy to come into town for the festivities. As usual he'd refused, insisting he would only be laughed at.

"They won't laugh," Kate had protested. "I won't let them laugh." But no matter how much she talked about the parade and fireworks, she failed to change his mind.

Her aunt brushed away Kate's concern with a wave of her hand. "Jimmy is fine. Despite your opinion of Thelma, she will take very good care of him. But if it will make you feel any better, your uncle and I will check on Jimmy. Don't you go worrying about it. Your job is to have a good time with your nice young man."

"He's not my nice young man," Kate argued. "Besides, he's leaving town."

Her aunt looked surprised. "Really? I thought he looked nice in brown. No matter. If you don't like the color of his clothes, perhaps I could try to sell him something more to your liking. It would take tact, of course. Nothing I can't handle."

Uncle Barney let out a loud laugh. "Since when have you ever been tactful?"

"I'm always thankful," Aunt Hattie replied, looking up the ladder. "Mercy me, Barney. I want the bunting higher, to the roofline."

"The ladder won't go that high," Barney barked back.

"What we need is an extension ladder," Kate said.

"Then why don't we have one?" Uncle Barney asked grumpily.

"As far as I know, no one has invented one," Kate replied, her mind working away. "It wouldn't be all that difficult to add a track along the sides of the ladder and . . ." Her mind immediately began to work on the problem. She was so engrossed in her thoughts, she failed to notice Jonas until he spoke.

"Good morning, Aunt Hattie, Uncle Barney." Jonas addressed the older couple, but he only had eyes for Kate. "Miss Whittaker." He tipped his derby to her. "My, if you don't look as pretty as a picture."

She greeted him with a smile. "Good morning, Mr. Hunter. You look most handsome yourself." Disconcerted by the smoldering look in his eyes, she was greatly relieved when at last he directed his gaze to the top of the ladder. She took advantage of the reprieve to secretly study the man.

Dressed in a blue serge sack coat, with matching vest and trousers, topped by a festive red bowtie, he cut a striking figure, to be sure. Of course, his appearance had nothing to do with the way Kate's heart was pounding. He surprised her, was all, coming up from behind like he did.

Aunt Hattie leaned over and whispered in Kate's ear, "You're right about the brown. He looks better in blue. Guess I won't have to use any of my tact, after all."

Jonas steadied the ladder with his hands. "Would you care for any assistance?"

Uncle Barney made a gruff sound. "I don't need assistance, I need someone to do the job."

"If you will kindly come down from the ladder, I shall be happy to finish the job for you."

"Isn't that nice?" Aunt Hattie beamed up at Jonas like he'd performed a holy miracle. Her aunt's adoration and her own traitorous awareness of him added to Kate's uneasiness.

"First you save Kate and me from jail, and then you keep Barney from breaking his neck. What did we ever do without you?" Aunt Hattie gave Kate a meaningful look, which Kate ignored.

Kate still wasn't all that certain if she could trust Jonas. She wanted to—Lord, how she wanted to. The other night, when they had walked beneath the stars, she was willing to believe anything he told her. But it was the hot blazing sun, not the stars, that shone in her eyes at the present time, and it was harder to ignore her instincts in the harsh light of day. Especially when those instincts told her there was too much at stake to make a mistake in judgment.

Uncle Barney climbed down the ladder, complaining all the way. "Why do womenfolk always have to decorate every damned thing in sight?"

"It's not just us women, Uncle Barney," Kate pointed out. "Look at how nice the sheriff's office looks."

"It looks ridiculous. Show me where it says we have to decorate every blasted time a holiday rolls around. Can't leave well enough alone."

"Don't be such an old grump." Kate gave her uncle an affectionate kiss on his rough-whiskered cheek.

"Old grump, indeed!" But the look on his face belied his gruff voice. Uncle Barney enjoyed holidays as much as the next person.

Jonas handed his hat to Aunt Hattie for safekeeping and climbed the ladder with none of the grunting and groaning that had accompanied Uncle Barney's earlier ascent.

"Do be careful," Aunt Hattie called.

"Don't worry, Aunt Hattie," Kate said, "Mr. Hunter has a strong constitution. He's part German."

Aunt Hattie looked momentarily disconcerted. "Like I always said, a few germs never hurt anyone."

Jonas grinned down at Kate, then, taking the end of the bunting, drew it up to the roofline. He was at least six, probably eight inches taller than Uncle Barney, which allowed him to reach the roof without difficulty.

After the last piece of bunting was tacked into place and Jonas had safely reached ground, Aunt Hattie clapped her hands. "It's going to be a glorious Fourth!" she declared.

Jonas placed his hat back on his head. "I think you're right, Aunt Hattie." The look he gave Kate shot shivers down her spine. "Don't you agree, Miss Whittaker?"

"I think I prefer to reserve judgment," Kate said.

He gave her a lazy grin that contradicted the intense glow in his eyes. "I like a woman who takes her time making up her mind. Shall we?" He held out his arm. He gave her such an endearing smile, she couldn't help but smile back as she slipped her hand through the crook of his elbow.

By this time, the citizens of the town were already lined up on both sides of the street, making it difficult to find a vacant spot to stand. Fortunately, Uncle Barney had roped off a place in front of his harness shop.

Sheriff Williams rode back and forth on his horse, looking unbearably important as he shouted on the top of his lungs, "Git back. Git back."

A rumbling drum roll announced the start of the parade, followed by the appearance of the red-uniformed drum major, who stepped from behind the hotel and started down Main Street. His spotless white spats kept perfect time, adding a rhythm that was otherwise missing from the blare of horns and drums behind him. The sun flashed against the shiny brass buttons of his gold braided jacket. The golden fringe on his epaulets danced merrily.

The crowd cheered and applauded as the band came into view, the shiny instruments gleaming in the sun. No one seemed to mind the strange squeaks and alarming honks produced by the earnest, yet woefully inept musicians. "The Star-Spangled Banner" sounded remarkably like foghorns battling it out in a stormy sea.

Next came the volunteer firemen's brigade pulling a bright red pumper behind them, followed by a horse-drawn hook-and-ladder truck. Spotting her uncle carrying a hose, Kate waved. "There's Uncle Barney!"

The firemen were followed by Curly and his Harmonizing Quartet singing a cappella and providing the only melodious sound in the parade. Next came Madam Miranda, dressed in a garish purple satin dress that separated in the most alarming places. Madam Miranda was headmistress of the "finishing" school for girls outside of town. But everyone knew this was just a fancy name for a whorehouse. The "girls" followed their flamboyant leader, waving and blowing kisses to the crowd.

"This is absolutely scandalous," gasped the wife of the newspaper editor, looking through the silver-rimmed lorgnette that hung from a golden chain around her neck. The eyeglasses made her startled eyes look big enough to pop out of their sockets.

She was standing next to Ellie May, who wore her new catalogue hat.

Aunt Hattie waved to Madam Miranda. "Stop by the shop next week. Your red satin fabric just arrived."

Kate tugged on her aunt's arm. "This is no time to be conducting business."

"I should say not!" Ellie May huffed.

Aunt Hattie tapped Ellie May on the back with the tip of her fan. "At least the woman doesn't buy her hats from Shears and Rhubarb. She understands about loyalty and friendship."

Ellie May glared back at Aunt Hattie. "Except when it concerns other women's husbands."

"Speaking from experience?" Aunt Hattie retorted.

Ellie May's mouth dropped open for an instant before she found her voice. "I most certainly am not. How dare you suggest that my sweet Harvey would take up with such a woman!"

"You're the one who brought it up."

Kate grabbed her aunt's arm. "Aunt Hattie, please!"

"Look at the clown," Jonas said, gently steering Aunt Hattie's attention back to the parade.

Kate gave Jonas a grateful smile. "That's Woody," she explained. "I went to school with him. He was always in trouble for his antics. I'm afraid the teacher didn't think he was funny. I only wish that Jimmy could see him."

Jonas studied her face, his eyes warm with concern. For too long he held her gaze and might have continued to look at her indefinitely had she not averted her eyes to search out Woody. She needed the clown's antics to calm down her raging senses.

The crowd roared when Woody spotted Ellie

May's hat and mimicked it. But no one enjoyed the joke more than Aunt Hattie.

The clown moved on and Aunt Hattie called after him. "Woody, your order arrived at my store."

Ellie May folded her arms across her chest. "First whores and now clowns. Won't Mr. Sears be jealous?"

It took fast action from Jonas and Kate to prevent Aunt Hattie from attacking the woman physically. Although the parade had barely begun, they pulled Aunt Hattie away.

Aunt Hattie protested loudly. "I want to see the parade."

"We'll find another spot," Kate said.

"It's not *that* hot," Aunt Hattie argued, fanning herself.

Jonas took Aunt Hattie by the arm and engaged her in a lively conversation regarding the town's history. Kate marveled how Jonas could so easily distract Aunt Hattie. She was obviously charmed by him. At one point, Aunt Hattie whispered in his ear, and by the smile on Jonas's face, Kate could only assume he had been privy to some outrageous gossip.

Since her aunt appeared to be in good hands, Kate started for Rocking Horse Lane to check on Jimmy and to try one last time to talk him into coming to town.

Chapter 25

After the last of the parade had marched down Main Street, the spectators followed the marching band to the picnic area, where a lively auction ensued. Serving for the fifth consecutive year as auctioneer, Smoky Joe stood on a wooden platform and held up each wicker picnic hamper in turn. The money generated from the auction would go to the Hogs Head Christian Church to purchase a new organ.

"Which one is yours?" Jonas whispered in Kate's ear.

"That's not fair," Kate whispered back. "We're not supposed to tell."

He lifted a dark brow as if wounded. "Do you always play by the rules?"

"Of course. Don't you?"

He smiled and Kate's heart did flip-flops. Surely the good Lord wouldn't give one man so much charm and good looks and not give him the integrity to match. She wanted so much to believe they had both invented the same machine and there had been no deceit or theft involved. In her heart she did.

Smoky Joe held up a large wicker hamper topped by a big red bow. He lifted the lid and sniffed the contents. With a appreciative swoon, he asked,

"What do I have for this delicious lunch with the big red bow?"

Jonas raised his hand and called, "Five dollars."

Surprised, Kate glanced up him and knew she had given herself away.

"It's for a good cause," he explained.

"Good cause, indeed! How did you know that's my picnic hamper?"

He smiled mysteriously, then promptly raised the bid higher than a man named Harold Davenport. Another man by the name of Joseph Brinker jumped into the act and soon a lively bidding war was in progress. Jonas, however, prevailed and when the bidding stopped at the shockingly high amount of twenty-two dollars, he ran to claim his prize.

After the auction was over, the sheriff called out. "When do I get to recite the Constitution?"

"Later, Sheriff, Later." Smoky Joe grabbed Madam Miranda's picnic hamper and hurried away.

Kate followed Jonas to a shaded area along the meandering stream. She ducked beneath the low-hanging branches of a weeping willow where Jonas had already staked out a spot. "Are you going to tell me how you knew this was my hamper or aren't you?"

"One good turn deserves another." He shook out the blanket that came with the hamper and spread it upon the grass.

"And what is that supposed to mean?"

"I bailed your Aunt Hattie out of jail and she told me which picnic basket was yours."

"Well, of all the . . . I can't even trust Aunt Hattie."

"Come on, Kate, admit it. You're delighted I won the bid on your basket and you know it."

"I know no such thing."

"You agreed to let me escort you to the festivities."

"I didn't say I'd eat with you."

"Consider this an added bonus." He pulled off his jacket and sat down on the blanket. One leg drawn to his chest, he looked relaxed and very much at home in his shirtsleeves.

The dark handsome man with the laughing eyes was alluring enough, but combined with the seductive cool shade offered by the delicate branches, she simply could not resist the invitation. "I really can't stay long. I should go and spend some time with Jimmy. Thelma is making the poor boy sit and hold her yarn. What a dreary way for a seven-year-old to spend a holiday."

It wasn't only Jimmy she was worried about. She was worried about herself. It wasn't normal the way her heart was pounding and her knees were knocking together.

"You and I can go and see him after we eat." He patted the ground next to him. "Come on, now, be a good sport."

His eyes sparkled with mischievous humor as he looked up at her, and she couldn't help but laugh. Swallowing her apprehension, she sank down on the blanket. She straightened her crisp skirt until it made almost a perfect circle around her and provided, at least in her mind, a safe barrier between them. If she kept up the conversation, maybe she would get her senses back under control. It was the silences she dreaded, for it was during the little pauses that stretched between them at times that her awareness of him—while always keen and perceptive—knew no boundaries.

"A good sport like you were when the patent was rewarded to me?"

"You can't hold that against me. I worked five

long years on that project. It's hard to walk away from something I poured my heart and soul into. Could you?" He was looking at her with keen earnestness. The mottled sunlight revealed a sensitivity in his face she'd not previously noticed. Suddenly she could hardly breathe. All around them was the sound of other picnickers calling to each other, talking, laughing, their cheerful voices drowning out the song of birds, the hum of bees, the gurgling rush of running water.

But nothing seemed to penetrate the intimate circle they shared. It was as if the shade of that particular willow tree had the ability to make time stand still.

"Could you walk away from something you'd worked so hard to achieve?" he persisted.

"Maybe not." At last she turned her head away, not sure how to handle the powerful pull between them. He was like a huge magnet that held her in its powerful grip.

She was greatly relieved when he diverted his attention to the bountiful picnic hamper. Aunt Hattie had outdone herself. Soon a vast array of cheese, smoked meat, and fresh fruit was spread across the blanket.

"What's this?" he asked, holding up a metal flask.

"It's a beverage keeper," Kate explained. She took the vessel from him and unscrewed the top. "It keeps cold drinks cold and hot drinks hot." She poured the lemonade her aunt squeezed fresh that morning into a glass and handed it to him.

He took a sip. "It *is* cold," he declared, clearly impressed. "And it's been sitting in the hot sun all this time." He took the flask from her and stared down the narrow neck. "What did you use for insulation?"

"Glass. I had a glassmaker in Springfield form the insides. It only keeps things cold for a few hours. Not as long as I would like. I need to find something better to use as insulation."

Jonas thought a moment. "Have you thought about coating the glass with silver?"

"Silver?"

"I saw a demonstration at the Chicago Fair showing how silver prevented heat transfer. It seems to me it would be a simple matter to coat the glass."

"That might work," she agreed. "I'll write to my glassmaker and ask him if it's something he can do." Kate screwed the top back onto the flask and watched Jonas slice the loaf of fresh bread. "I'm amazed at how well you get along with Aunt Hattie."

He glanced up at her. "Why would that amaze you?"

"Aunt Hattie's not that easy to get along with. She tends to be ... how shall I say it ..."

"Spirited?" he offered.

Kate smiled at his tactful choice of words. "I was thinking more along the lines of opinionated. But yes, you're right. Aunt Hattie is spirited." Kate thought of the years she'd lived in Hogs Head. They had been happy years. She wouldn't have traded a single one for all the money in the world. "I love both my aunt and uncle dearly."

"How is it that you're living with them? What happened to your parents?"

"They died when I was only five."

"I'm sorry," he said, looking for all the world as if he'd regretted reminding her of the past. "I didn't mean—"

"It's all right," she hastened to assure him. "I don't mind talking about it." She moistened her lips before continuing. "I was put on a train and sent to my aunt and uncle with no more warning than a note pinned to me. I'll never forget that ride as long as I live." She could still remember riding in the baggage car, not knowing what was going to happened to her. "My mother had never gotten along with her family. Mother told me that her sister Hattie was a bit strange in the head. You can imagine my fear when I found myself being shipped off to live with her."

"How awful for you, Kate." Jonas's eyes were soft with sympathy. "I've always been surrounded by family. I never considered what it would be like to be an orphan."

"It *was* awful until I reached Hogs Head. Sheriff Williams found me wandering around town, and after reading the note pinned on me, he took me to my aunt." Kate smiled at the memory. "Aunt Hattie took one look at me and declared me the daughter she never had. She also had a few choice words for the people who'd put me on the train with no supervision. She made it her business to give them a piece of her mind in a flurry of letters."

Jonas laughed. "I can just imagine it!"

His laughter was like a cool breeze rippling across the meadow. Taking a deep breath, she reached for a red strawberry at the same time he did, their fingers touching as gently as a butterfly landing on a rose petal.

Her cheeks warming beneath his gaze, she quickly withdrew her hand and lifted the strawberry to her mouth. His gaze riveted firmly upon her lips, he lifted his hand and tasted his own fruit.

Her mouth filled with a spill of warm juice that was strangely bland to the taste buds compared to the kiss she imagined hung between them. Popping the rest of the fruit into her mouth, she let her hand drop. What was she thinking? Kisses don't hang. A kiss doesn't even exist until two people . . .

She gazed at a leaf floating along the stream, watching it until it disappeared around a rocky bend. A gentle breeze carried a soft cool mist to her torrid flesh. Inhaling the damp musky smell that rose from the mossy rocks, she searched for something to say to break the timorous silence that suddenly stretched between them. Her senses alert, she was aware of his every movement, no matter how small. It seemed to her there was a definite change in his features whenever their gazes met. She sensed rather than saw a softening of his mouth. Caught the smoldering lights in his gold-flecked eyes. Felt in him an overall intensity that told her he was reading a few subtle messages of his own.

Embarrassed at the thought of what he might see in her face, she glanced away. "I guess that's why I object to the way orphans are put on a train and sent away to farmers whose only interest is acquiring labor."

"Don't be too hard on farmers, Kate. It's a hard life. They simply can't afford to feed a mouth without expecting labor in return."

She glanced back at him. "I'm talking about children, Jonas. Children like Jimmy."

"I know. I don't like the idea any better than you do. That's why I wanted so much for my fertilizer spreader to be a success. I have ideas for other labor-saving machines that will make a farm run more efficiently. That'll make child labor a thing of the past. Children should be in school, not working in the fields."

His voice held a bitter edge that puzzled her. She studied him. His concern for orphaned children seemed genuine, but he'd admitted he never gave much thought to the problem. So where did the bitterness come from? What was the root of the pain and regret she saw within the depths of his eyes?

Curiosity made her lower her guard. That was a mistake, for without the mental barrier, the intensity seemed to grow between them, like the pressure building inside a boiler.

His gaze lingered on her lips and his eyes became two smoldering flames that threatened to set her afire. Suddenly, all the new words and phrases she had learned in recent years having to do with electricity came to mind, and each one of them, from *electrifying* to *recharging*, seemed to take on special meaning when applied to Jonas.

Her heart pounding wildly, she reached for the picnic hamper intent upon trying one of the plump ripe peaches, but then decided against it. "Are you saying the fertilizer spreader could make that much difference?"

"Absolutely. Last year, my father lost a whole crop of corn because of the cutworm. The year before that, we had an invasion of locusts that left nothing but destruction behind. And look what the boll weevil has done to the cotton in Texas." His voice resonated with passion which could only come from the heart. "Some people believe that the proper use of fertilizer can make crops healthier and more resistent to pests. The problem has been that it takes days, sometimes weeks, to do a thorough job by hand."

Kate felt a surge of guilt, though she couldn't imagine why. She had invented her machine fair and square. She had every right to benefit from her honest hard work. Not wanting to spoil the festive occasion by resuming what had become a familiar argument between them, she changed the subject.

"Tell me about your youth, Jonas. What was it like growing up on a farm?"

Jonas studied the pretty round face that looked at him from beneath the straw brim of her hat, and he felt the need to burn the lovely vision into the farthest reaches of his heart.

It wasn't the first time he'd seen approval in those big beautiful blue eyes of hers, and if he had his way, it wouldn't be the last. The very fact she wanted to know about him seemed to indicate her feelings for him ran deeper than she was willing to admit. What was even more surprising was to discover his own feelings for her were a lot stronger than he had ever thought possible. "I worked in the fields starting at the age of five." He fell silent as bits of the past came to mind.

"So young?" Kate prodded gently, as if she sensed the need to tiptoe around the subject.

He nodded. At the time, it hadn't seemed so young. It had seemed like the most natural thing in the world. "My ma was a schoolteacher before she married my pa. I remember her following us in the fields as we worked, giving us lessons in history and mathematics. I learned to read literally while behind an oxen and plow. My ma would stand at the end of a row of corn, holding up a word, and I'd have to keep repeating the word and spelling it until I completed the row. Then she'd give me another one." He grinned. "It took me three long rows to learn to spell *Mississippi*."

Kate laughed and Jonas likened her laughter to music. "When did you first start inventing things?"

He thought a moment. "I think it grew out of necessity. I always wanted to go to school. You know, one of those fancy eastern schools. The only way I saw to do that was to read everything I could get my hands on. The problem was lack of time.

As the youngest of six boys and seven girls, the worst chores always fell to me. So I started to think up ways to make the work go faster so I would have more time to read. Then when I broke both legs falling off the roof—"

"Oh, no!" She gasped.

He grinned. "Right here." He pointed to the calf of one leg and to the ankle of the other, and in so doing pushed against her skirts with his foot, closing the distance between them.

"My family didn't have time to spend with me," he continued, "so it was either figure out a way to move around or die of boredom." His eyes never left her face as he spoke. "I devised myself a chair with wheels. By turning the wheels by hand, I could pretty much get around. It worked so well, I started experimenting with other ideas and eventually started to work with engines. After a while, I forgot about the fancy schools. I became consumed with changing a farmer's life." He paused for a moment. "What about you? How did you become an inventor?"

"I take after my papa," she replied. "He was always thinking up new ideas." It was her father who thought up the idea of color-coding his children's clothes to prevent confusion. Kate, next to youngest of seven children, picked red, knowing it was her father's favorite color. To this day, she couldn't don her red petticoats without remembering the pleased look on her father's face upon learning that his little Katie-Did, as he had called her, had chosen his favorite color as her own.

Swallowing back the lump that had risen to her throat, she took a sip of lemonade. "What ... what are you going to do when you go back to the farm?"

The question brought such a frown to his face, she immediately regretted having asked it.

"Work on my inventions. Continue to repair the

gas tractors for the local farmers. That's how I managed to save so much money—by repairing motors. I also have a few other projects I'm working on. Mostly farm equipment. Did you know that over forty-three percent of all gainfully employed men work in agriculture?"

"No, I didn't," Kate said.

"It's true. There're a lot of ways I could make my pa's work—every farmer's work—easier. Maybe even solve the labor problem that causes so many orphans to be mistreated." His gaze settled on her lips. "You must be hungry," he said dryly, feeling the need to explain his reason for staring.

"I ... didn't eat much breakfast," she said, and popped a strawberry into her mouth.

As they ate, Jonas continued to talk about his inventions and his theory regarding magnetic fields. "I'm working on a system of electric fans for the cattle shed. I've already installed electric pumps to keep a fresh supply of water in the barn, and already I've noticed an increase in milk production."

"Really? How amazing."

She laughed when he told her about putting incandescent lights in the chicken house. "Surely it can't be good for the chickens to be kept up all hours of the night."

He grinned. "They haven't complained so far. Well, maybe Ole Red. She's a Rhode Island Red that kind of reminds me of Aunt Hattie."

"Oh, no!"

They spent the next hour or so discussing their various projects and mishaps. Kate described her somewhat disastrous experiments with a horseless buggy.

"I heard about that," Jonas said.

"It's the steering mechanism. The tiller won't work over three miles an hour," Kate explained.

Jonas talked about the time he rigged the schoolhouse clock so that it ran faster during school hours and slower at night. "The clock was only accurate at eight o'clock in the morning when we arrived. One day I actually got the school day down to four hours. The poor teacher couldn't figure out why the sun was still overhead at the end of the day."

Kate giggled. She hadn't noticed how close they had moved to one another until Jonas took her hand and held it in his own, studying it as if he meant to memorize every line of her palm.

"I never knew a woman could be so knowledgeable about dynamos and motors," he said. "I can't tell you how good it makes me feel to be able to talk to you about my experiments and not have to worry about boring you to death."

"You could never be boring," she whispered. A thrill shot down her spine as he ran his thumb across her wrist.

He chuckled. "You'd be surprised. I once put a young woman to sleep at her own birthday party explaining the theory of combustion to her."

"It sounds perfectly fascinating to me."

"Somehow I knew you'd think that." He leaned closer, his gaze on her lips, his fingers tight around her wrist. A little closer and she would feel his breath. Closer still and their lips would touch. . . .

"Kate, do me a favor," he begged.

"What?" she murmured, eyes half closed.

"Tell me everything you know about French fashions, and hurry."

Her eyes widened in confusion. "I'm afraid I don't know a thing."

"That's what I was afraid of." He'd have to find another way to calm his rampaging emotions.

"I have a problem I've been working on," he said softly. "Gasoline tractors don't do well in the mud. They're so heavy, the wheels keep sinking into the ground. I'm trying to find some way to prevent the problem."

"Have you thought of any ideas?"

"Not yet."

She moistened her lips. "Does it help to talk things out?"

"I don't know. This is the first time I've ever tried. It takes a little getting used to."

"Really? What do you usually do? When you're having a problem with one of your inventions or are trying to come up with new ideas?"

He looked embarrassed. "I . . . I usually . . ."

She glanced down at her lap. "Go sparking?"

A startled look crossed his face. "How would you know about that?" His eyes narrowed in suspicion. "Don't tell me . . . Why, Miss Whittaker, you never fail to amaze me."

"That's not the only way I get my ideas," she protested. "Sometimes they come to me while I'm in bed."

His eyes widened. "In . . . in bed?" he stammered.

It wasn't until she saw the astonished look on his face that she realized how her statement could be misinterpreted. Blushing, she hastened to explain, "Oh, I don't mean . . . It's not what you think. I'm always alone in bed."

"What a pity," he murmured softly, stretching the full length of his body across the blanket. "Why do you suppose sparking stimulates the thought processes?"

Plucking a little white daisy from the grass and keeping her head low, she shook her head. "Maybe it's not sparking. Maybe it's being with the wrong person."

He took her hand in his and pulled her down on

the blanket until their heads almost touched. Lord, he hoped that was true. "What do you suppose would happen if you and I . . ."

She couldn't breathe. "I don't know. Maybe we would think of some wonderful invention that would change the entire world."

Lord, he hoped not. He hoped that what she said about being with the right person was true. He wanted to kiss her and not think of anything but how her lips felt on his. Oh, heavenly days, he wanted to take her in his arms and hold her tight. "In that case," he said, trailing a finger up her arm, "it seems we have an obligation . . . to the world, I mean. To try a little sparking of our own."

She looked him full in the face. "I . . . I suppose we do."

At first she ignored the agitated buzz among the other picnickers, but an angry shout forced Jonas to draw away just as it appeared that the burning need trembling on her lips was about to be satisfied.

Kate glanced through the leafy veil of the willow tree, surprised to discover that most of the other picnickers had abandoned their hampers and were marching toward town.

She felt a sense of alarm. "What do you suppose is wrong?"

Jonas had already jumped to his feet and had stepped out from under the tree to stare in the direction of Main Street. "I don't know," he said as she joined him. "It looks like trouble's brewing." He looked at her ruefully. "I'm afraid folks will have to wait a while longer for that invention of ours. The one that's going to change the world." The one he hoped to God would never exist.

Chapter 26

With a sense of awareness that practically crackled like lightning between them, Jonas and Kate quickly gathered up their picnic supplies. When everything had been packed into the hamper, he helped her to her feet, holding her hand longer than necessary. Yearning for the promised kiss, Kate held her breath and felt a sense of disappointment when he released her hand.

"Come on," he said, hooking his jacket over his right shoulder. Spurred by the sense of urgency in the air, they cut across the grass and through the trees. She planted one hand firmly on the crown of her hat to keep it from flying off, and lifted her skirts above her ankles so she could more easily keep up with Jonas's long even strides.

They slowed their pace upon reaching Main Street, emerging from behind the hotel. Without the protective shade of the picnic grounds, the heat and glare of the midday sun was almost unbearable.

A large noisy group was gathered in front of her aunt's general store. Kate couldn't make head nor tail out of the angry words that were being shouted.

"Oh, dear!" Kate grabbed hold of Jonas's arm. "You don't suppose something has happened to Aunt Hattie or Uncle Barney?" She craned her head to see over the crowd.

Jonas squeezed her hand. "They're all right. See? They're over there."

Kate followed his finger and breathed a sigh of relief mingled with dismay upon seeing Aunt Hattie shouting back at the crowd. "What do you suppose has Aunt Hattie so upset?"

Sheriff Williams came running down the middle of the street, his face grim. He pushed his way through the crowd and took his place next to Aunt Hattie.

"Quiet!" he yelled. "That means you, too!" he shouted in Aunt Hattie's ear. Aunt Hattie folded her arms in front of her chest and clamped her mouth shut. A strained silence washed over the crowd.

"That's better," the sheriff said. "Everyone who wants to will get a chance to talk." He glared at Mable Cummings, who was whispering something to Maizie. "But only if I say so."

The sheriff scanned the crowd, his gaze falling on Smoky Joe, who was waving his hat over his head. "Aw-right, Smoky Joe, let's start with you. Come up here so we can all hear what you're bellyachin' to say."

Smoky Joe stomped onto the porch of the general store, his boots pounding against the wooden planks. "The fireworks display has been canceled."

A gasp rose up from those in the crowd who had not previously heard this disconcerting news.

"Oh, dear," Kate said in a hushed voice, glancing up at Jonas. "Jimmy will be so disappointed. He was looking forward to watching them from his bedroom window."

The sheriff held up his hands. "Quiet!" He then nodded at Smoky Joe. "Maybe you better explain why."

"I'll be glad to. When the volunteer fire department put the fire out at the train station ..." he stopped to glare at Aunt Hattie, "the boxes of fireworks that had been shipped all the way from Chicago got soaking wet."

Hearing that her aunt was responsible for the cancellation of fireworks, Kate cupped her hand over her lips. "Oh, dear."

Jonas slipped his arm around her shoulders. "It'll be all right, Kate," he whispered. "We'll think of another way for the town to celebrate."

Curly hopped onto the porch next to Smoky Joe. "I say Aunt Hattie should go back to jail where she belongs."

"I agree!" declared Ellie May. "Why, ruining fireworks is treason, pure and simple."

The crowd rallied in agreement, and a loud buzz of angry voices filled the air. "Jail Aunt Hattie! Jail Aunt Hattie!"

Kate turned to Jonas. "You've got to do something."

Jonas felt himself drowning in Kate's big blue eyes. Lord, how did she do it? How did she always manage to find that one needy part of him that had never been touched before, and therefore had never developed any sort of protective armor?

As difficult as it was to deny her request, the reality was she asked the impossible. How in the name of Sir Isaac Newton could he possibly combat such an angry crowd? He'd already bailed Kate's aunt out of jail once. He couldn't afford to do it again; he'd used up almost all of his savings. And the crowd wasn't likely to let him get away a second time with that presidential hogwash he'd pulled for Kate's benefit. "Kate ... I ..."

"Please," she whispered, her eyes shimmering with tears.

The tears touched him like nothing had ever touched

him in his life. This beautiful capable woman who knew how to tame the elements of nature most men feared was now appealing to him to save her beloved aunt. Never had he felt so tall. Never had he known what it was like to have someone believe in him.

"I'll see what I can do," he said softly, knowing his voice had been drowned out by the angry shouts around them. No matter; she understood him, even if she hadn't heard his actual words. Her face softened and a hint of a smile touched her mouth. His last bit of resistance melted away.

Sucking in his breath, he felt like his heart was going to take flight.

Determined to make good on his word, he tore himself away from her side, and pushed through the angry crowd. Lord, he hated speaking in front of a large group of people, and here in less than a week he was about to do it for a second time.

"Sheriff Williams, may I please address the crowd?"

"I guess it'll be aw-right. Quiet, everybody!"

Jonas stepped onto the porch next to the sheriff, his jacket folded over his arm, and faced the sea of agitated citizens. His mind was blank. He couldn't think of a thing to say that would save Aunt Hattie's neck, let alone save the day. A group of wide-eyed children watched him from the front row. One little girl who couldn't be more than five years old stood crying her little heart out.

"I want fireworks," she sobbed, burying her face into her mother's taffeta skirts.

Feeling like the world's biggest failure, he sought Kate out in the crowd, and realized too late his mistake in doing so. Lord, he couldn't seem to think whenever he looked at her. And this was no time to go completely blank in the head.

"Well?" the sheriff demanded impatiently by his side. "Do you have somethin' to say or don't you?"

"Eh . . ." Feeling desperate, he turned to look at Kate's aunt, intending to apologize for being unable to help her. Instead, he thought of something. "As a matter of fact I do. . . ." He grabbed Aunt Hattie by her upper arms. "Sorry, Aunt Hattie, but it's for a worthy cause." He then gave her a resounding kiss smack on the lips, closing his eyes as he did so and trying to recall every dull, boring description of French fashions he'd ever had the misfortune of hearing.

Finally, he felt the familiar surge of energy course through his body as his inventive mind clicked into place.

His rather unorthodox behavior brought a gasp from the crowd. After kissing Aunt Hattie, Jonas glanced around with a sheepish expression on his face. The sheriff shook his head in puzzlement, Aunt Hattie blushed, Maizie's mouth fell open, but, by George, he had his inspiration.

"Thank you, Aunt Hattie," he said, releasing her and facing the crowd. Almost by instinct, he rested his eyes upon Kate, who nodded in understanding.

Feeling a sense of closeness with her that negated his dislike of public speaking, he lifted his voice in what he hoped sounded all at once confident and commanding. "As you know, Kate is quite an expert in explosions. What you probably don't know is that I've also had some experience in this regard."

"So what are you saying, Hunter?" An angry voice shouted out. "You and Kate want to blow up the town? What?"

"Nothing quite as drastic as that. I'm merely suggesting that if you would all go back to your picnics, Kate and I would be more than happy to whip up a batch of firecrackers for tonight."

"You can do that?" the sheriff asked, looking amazed.

"Guaranteed."

Relief washed over the sheriff's face. "Well, you heard the man, back to your picnics. Fireworks will start at nine o'clock as promised."

Many expressed doubts about Jonas's and Kate's ability to replace the fireworks, but with the sheriff's urging, the crowd soon began to disperse. The band struck up another strident tune, presumably of a patriotic nature, but due to the brassy squeaks and rasping bleats, no one knew for certain.

A short distance away, Smoky Joe could be heard shouting through a megaphone. "Time for the relay races."

The sheriff called over to him. "When do I get to recite the Constitution of the United States?"

"Later, Sheriff, later."

Kate waited until the last of the crowd had dispersed before joining Jonas on the porch of her aunt's store. "I don't know how to make fireworks."

Jonas took her by the arm. "I'll teach you." He led her into the relative coolness of the store, followed by Uncle Barney and Aunt Hattie.

Uncle Barney leaned against a counter and mopped his forehead with a handkerchief. "I thought for sure your aunt's goose was cooked this time."

Aunt Hattie shook her head. "Mercy me, Barnard, you can't be hungry already. Not after the lunch you ate."

Jonas pulled off his bowtie and rolled up his shirtsleeves. "We need sulfur and charcoal."

Barney headed toward the back of the shop. "There's a bucket of charcoal by the stove."

"I have sulfur at home," Kate offered.

"Great." Jonas glanced around, then lifted a handful of saltpeter from a barrel. "This will supply potassium nitrate. Now all we need is something to hold the ingredients." His eyes fell on the bundle of bamboo fishing rods stacked by the wall. "Is it all right if I use these?"

Aunt Hattie gave a disgusted grunt. "That fool man Curly insists he never ordered them. Said he ordered some special shampoo. Now I'm stuck with a bunch of bamboo rods that no body wants!"

Jonas grinned. "Aunt Hattie, you're a genius!" He grabbed hold of the poles. "Do you think we can go back to the house, Kate? We'll have more room to work."

Kate nodded. "We can work in the cellar. It'll be cooler there."

"I'll get the wagon ready," Uncle Barney said.

A short time later, Uncle Barney pulled the wagon in front of the house and Kate led the way. "Careful," she said, pointing out the various obstacles cluttering up the path to the front door. "Jimmy, we're home."

"It's about time!" Thelma called from the parlor.

Kate stepped through the archway and blinked her eyes, not believing the startling sight that greeted her. "Thelma! What happened to you?" The woman was pinned to Uncle Barney's favorite chair, wrapped from head to toe in yarn.

"That ... that ..." The woman literally sputtered. "He's as crazy as you are."

Kate glanced down at Jimmy, who was sitting on the floor at her feet, a pair of scissors in his hand. "Jimmy?"

"Mrs. Paine made me hold her yarn so she could wrap it in a ball."

"Harrumph!" Thelma glared at the boy. "He talked me into putting the yarn on one of those newfangled machines that should be outlawed!"

"She means the flour mixer," Jimmy explained. "It worked real good until—"

"It went berserk!" Thelma declared.

"I'm so sorry," Kate said. "Here, let me do that." She took the scissors from Jimmy and quickly cut away strands of yarn.

"Now, don't you worry, Thelma," Jonas said, reaching in his pocket for a penknife. "We'll have you out of there in no time at all."

"I've never been so humiliated in my life," Thelma muttered.

"I can't tell you how sorry I am," Kate said. "Jimmy only meant to help."

"Help? The boy is a menace to society. And if you think I'd consider giving him a home after this, you're sadly mistaken."

"There you are," Jonas said, pulling the last piece of yarn away.

Leaping up from the chair, Thelma stormed about the room, gathering up her reticule, her parasol, and her knitting basket. "Never in all my days have I been so humiliated!" She gave Jimmy a tight-lipped scowl, then slammed out the front door.

Jimmy looked close to tears. "I didn't mean to get her mad. Honest."

Kate wrapped her arm around his shoulders. "I know."

"Come on," Jonas said impatiently. "We've got work to do."

In no time at all, they had carted all the supplies into the cellar and had spread everything across

Kate's workbench. Uncle Barney carried Jimmy downstairs and set him on a stool.

"Can I help, too, Kate?" Jimmy asked, staring at the strange combination of supplies with interest. "Are we going fishing?"

"No, we're going to make fireworks," Kate replied. "And yes, you can help." To Jonas she explained, "Jimmy is my assistant."

Jonas chuckled as if he had been privy to some private joke. "So you do have an assistant, after all."

"I'm going to be an inventor like Kate."

Jonas smiled at the boy. "A mighty noble profession, if I say so myself." He laid the fishing rods on the table, glancing around the cellar for a saw. "Kate, cut these fishing rods into ten-inch lengths. And Jimmy, help Aunt Hattie grind up that saltpeter."

Uncle Barney tramped down the stairs, carrying a bucket of charcoal. "Where do you want this?"

"Over here," Jonas replied, clearing off yet another workbench. "What's this?" he asked.

Kate glanced over at him. "I call that Harold's automatic potato peeler." She took the gadget from him and demonstrated. "You put the potato in here, close the lid, and turn the handle."

He frowned. "Harold? That wouldn't be named after the same Harold who was bidding on your hamper today?"

Kate blushed. "As a matter of fact, it is."

"I see," he said stiffly.

"And this gas-powered iron is named after Joseph, the other man who was bidding. And that automatic flour sifter is named after Billy, and see that metal—"

"I think we better get to work," Jonas said brusquely. Harold and Joseph and Billy. Lordy, how many other sources of inspiration did she have?

After Kate and her aunt had finished the tasks he'd assigned them, Jonas combined the ingredients into a metal washbasin.

"Would you like to use my David Brown egg-beater?" Kate asked. "It's much more efficient than a spoon."

"No!" he said curtly, wondering why the man rated both his first and last name on her beater.

Kate looked surprised. "You don't have to be rude."

"I don't have to be nice, either," he growled.

He grabbed a length of the fishing rod, wrapped a piece of butcher paper around one end, then stuffed the smelly concoction into the length of bamboo.

"That should do the job."

Aunt Hattie looked amazed. "My stars! No one told me it was this easy to make fireworks."

"Don't get any idea, Aunt Hattie," Kate cautioned. "And the same goes for you, Jimmy. Fireworks are dangerous." Following Jonas's example, she picked up a piece of bamboo and proceeded to fill it. "Uncle Barney, Jimmy, you two stuff and I'll wrap."

Aunt Hattie fanned herself with her hand. "It is a bit stuffy in here."

For the remainder of the afternoon, the five of them packed the ingredients into the hollow rods, then wrapped each individual length of bamboo with butcher paper.

Kate felt grateful to Jonas for so quickly solving the fireworks problem. She was hurt, however, by his sudden bad mood. Since it had occurred so abruptly after she had described some of her other inventions, she could only assume he was jealous of her work. Well, let him be jealous, she decided. What did she care?

Oh, but she did care. She wanted so much for them to return to the same easy rapport they had shared earlier, beneath the shade of the old weeping willow.

Her heart fluttered just thinking of how the two of them had whiled away the time, talking inventions while studying each other. Just thinking of the kiss they almost shared only served to increase her awareness of him. Every time she looked his way, her heart ached anew with longing and need.

Had Jonas felt the same wondrous and magical things she'd felt? She studied him from across the table, but it was obvious by his dark, silent, though efficient demeanor that he was more interested in the task at hand than anything having to do with her. Feeling oddly disappointed, Kate dropped her gaze to the half-finished firecracker in her hand.

Jonas's disposition improved somewhat during the afternoon. He bantered with Aunt Hattie, talked politics with Uncle Barney, and playfully teased Jimmy, who teased him back. He said nothing to Kate, although on occasion she thought she felt his eyes on her, but every time she glanced up, his attention was directed elsewhere.

"What kind of a rocket is that?" Uncle Barney asked, watching Jimmy struggle to wrap a length of bamboo in paper.

"A messy one," Jimmy admitted.

"The only thing that counts is performance, not appearance," Jonas said, taking the loosely wrapped firecracker from Jimmy and placing it on the growing stack. "I would say your rocket is going to fill up the entire sky. Why, they might even see it as far away as Chicago."

Jimmy's eyes shone. "All the way in Chicago?"

"You never know," Jonas said.

It was late afternoon by the time they had produced enough fireworks to equal the number destroyed. The five of them stood staring at the impressive stack of skyrockets.

"I hope I didn't put in too much saltpeter," Jonas said.

"What would happen if you did?" Uncle Barney asked.

Jonas glanced at Kate. "Let's just say we might all be spending the night in jail."

"Me, too?" Jimmy said, looking intrigued.

Kate picked him up and gave him a big hug. "I hope not. Someone has to come and bail us out. What do you say we clean up this mess?"

Kate, Jonas, and Jimmy cleaned up the workbench and Uncle Barney swept the floor. Aunt Hattie went upstairs to make lemonade to go with the gingersnap cookies she'd baked special for the holiday.

"I'm glad that's done," Uncle Barney said, standing the broom and dustpan in a corner.

Kate nodded. "I think we better go upstairs and get you cleaned up." Jimmy was covered in black charcoal smudges. For once, he didn't try to talk Kate out of a bath. Instead, he looked from Kate to Jonas and back again. "This is the bestest Independence Day ever. I just wish I got to see the parade."

"There'll be other parades," Kate said. "Besides, we've got fireworks to watch. Come along, my little one." She lifted the boy in her arms. "Upstairs we go."

She glanced back at Jonas. "I'll be back soon."

Jonas studied Jimmy. "Thank you . . . . I'll be gone for a short while. Your aunt and uncle will need help taking the fireworks into town, and I have something to do while I'm there. I'll be back before you know it."

Kate held Jonas's gaze, wondering why he suddenly seemed in a hurry to leave. Before she had a chance to ask, he'd already raced up the stairs ahead of her out of the cellar.

Later, Jimmy sat on his bed, freshly bathed and dressed in a clean pair of knee pants and a white shirt. He played with his metal toy soldiers while Kate combed his hair, parting it at the side. "There, now," she said, looking him over. "My, if you don't look handsome."

"Do you think the fireworks are going to work?" he asked.

"Of course they're going to work," Kate said. "We're inventors. We can make anything work."

"I didn't make the yarn machine work."

"That's because you haven't thought through all the problems. I suspect you turned the speed too high." Recalling how indignant Thelma looked wrapped in yarn, it was all Kate could do to keep from laughing aloud. "Next time, you might do well to try out your ideas in advance."

"Why can't I work out the problems with my leg?"

Kate ran her hand along the part of his leg showing beneath his knee pants. His bad leg, though slightly smaller and less developed than his good leg, looked so normal it was hard to believe that a problem existed.

Shortly after rescuing Jimmy from the orphan train six months earlier, she had taken him to see Dr. Trinner. The doctor recommended she take Jimmy to Boston to be examined by a specialist. The examination and therapy would cost a great deal of money, more than she could afford to pay.

That's why it was so important to begin manufacturing her carpet cleaner.

She was growing impatient. She'd fully intended to be in production by this time. She bit her lip in irritation. What was taking those manufacturing companies so long to reply to her letters? For that matter, why hadn't she received her patent in the mail as promised? Perhaps that's what was causing the delay with the manufacturers. Without the official document and patent number, it was hard to prove she actually held the patent. Promising herself to post a letter to the commissioner of patents first thing in the morning, she directed her attention back to Jimmy.

"Inventors work with machines," she said. "The human body . . . now, that takes special knowledge. Doctors go to a special school to learn how the body works."

"Dr. Trinner didn't fix my leg," Jimmy said.

"That's because he wasn't the right doctor."

"Can the right doctor fix my leg?"

She touched her forehead to his, not wanting to make promises that might never become reality. "That's what we're going to find out." Hearing the sound of a drum roll, she pulled away from Jimmy. "What in the world?"

Dashing across the room, she kneeled on the wooden seat in front of the window and threw open the sash. Jonas waved to her from below. "Where's Jimmy?"

"On the bed. Why?"

"Bring him to the window. I have a surprise for him."

Kate hurried back to the bed. "Come, Jimmy." She slipped one arm around his shoulder and the other beneath his knees. "Mr. Hunter has a surprise for you."

She carried him across the room and set him on the smooth painted window seat. Jimmy ducked his head beneath the open window and leaned over the sill. Seeing Jonas below, Jimmy waved. "Hello, Mr. Hunter."

"Hello, Jimmy," Jonas called back. "Stay where you are." Jonas turned and waved his hands over his head like a flagman signaling a train. The drum major standing at the start of Rocking Horse Lane lifted his baton in response. Almost simultaneously, the air filled with a horrendous and tuneless rendition of John Philip Sousa's "The Thunderer." The music grew louder—and even more tuneless—as the band marched down the middle of the street toward the Whittaker house.

Kate kneeled on the window seat next to Jimmy and gazed down at Jonas. The music drowned out her words of gratitude. Jonas winked back at her and turned to salute the passing band.

"Oh, Jimmy!" She threw her arm around his slight shoulders and gave him a quick hug. "Isn't this wonderful? A whole parade just for you."

And it was the whole parade: Woody the clown, Madam Miranda and her girls, the volunteer firemen's brigade and their bright red hook-and-ladder truck, Curly and his Harmonizing Quartet. The parade marched up Rocking Horse Lane just as it had done earlier on Main Street.

At first Jimmy didn't say a word, but his eyes were wide as saucers. "Don't laugh!" he said at one point, looking worried. "You'll hurt the clown's feelings."

"The clown wants us to laugh," Kate assured him. "That's how he knows we're having a good time. If we don't laugh, we'll hurt his feelings."

Jimmy turned his head. "He wants us to laugh?"

She took his hand in hers and squeezed it tight.

It saddened her that a child so young would be afraid to laugh. It was as if he'd lost the ability to distinguish the difference between happy, joyful laughter and laughter that was derisive in nature. "Absolutely."

Woody imitated the drum major and with Kate's encouragement Jimmy laughed aloud. He laughed tentatively at first, his forehead shadowed with uncertainty, but when the clown reacted favorably, Jimmy's stilted chuckles grew into wholehearted guffaws.

It was the first time Kate had heard Jimmy laugh aloud. Lord Almighty, it had taken her three months just to get him to smile. She felt as if her heart would burst with happiness at seeing the young child at her side so filled with joy.

The parade spun a U-turn in front of the house and started back up the street. All too soon, Sheriff Williams rode past the house astride his horse, signaling the end of the parade.

Jimmy waited until the very last musical note had faded away before leaving his post. Kate wished she'd had a photograph of Jimmy's beaming face. All Kate wanted to do was race downstairs and throw her arms around Jonas and thank him for the wonderful miraculous thing he'd done.

"Come on, Jimmy." She lifted him in her arms and started for the door. "Let's go and tell Jonas how much we enjoyed the parade."

They found Jonas standing on the porch, his closed fist lifted as if he'd been about to knock. He pulled off his hat and smiled at Jimmy, who was clutched in her arms. "Did you like the parade, Jimmy?"

Jimmy nodded his head, his face still flushed with excitement. "I liked those funny ladies."

Jonas lifted a dark brow. "So you like Miranda

and her . . . eh, friends?" He took Jimmy from Kate and carried him into the parlor.

Kate closed the door and followed them. "Oh, Jonas . . ." She swallowed hard to keep from making a fool of herself by bursting into tears. "He loved it. How . . . I mean . . . what made you think of the idea of bringing the parade to Jimmy?"

"I thought of the idea during our picnic. Remember my telling you how we couldn't attend school when we were young? How my mother brought school to us? She once told me that you didn't have to leave home to see the world. Anyway . . . I started thinking about Jimmy and the idea just followed." He held Kate in his gaze for a moment longer, before looking back at Jimmy. "So tell me what else you liked about the parade." He glanced up at Kate and gave her a wink. "Besides Miranda."

"The clown was really funny and I laughed 'cuz Kate said I would hurt the clown's feelings if I didn't and—"

"Whoooa, son. Slow down." Jonas tousled Jimmy's hair. "I'm mighty pleased to hear you laughed." He frowned and studied Jimmy, as if puzzled by the boy.

"Kate said she's going to stay with me tonight while we watch the fireworks."

Jonas met Kate's eyes. "Am I invited?"

"Of course," Kate said. The ill temper he'd showed earlier was no longer evident. He looked relaxed and, to Kate's way of thinking, more handsome than ever. "J-Jimmy would like that, wouldn't you, Jimmy?"

Jonas picked up a scrap of yarn from the floor and suddenly started to laugh.

"What's so funny?" Kate asked.

"I was just thinking . . ." He laughed so hard, he

could hardly speak. "I was just thinking about ... about Thelma. She looked like a tightly wrapped cigar."

The laughter that Kate had tried so hard not to give in to earlier bubbled out of her like water bubbled out of a fountain. "I . . . I thought she looked like a mummy."

The three of them laughed until tears rolled down their cheeks.

Chapter 27

The first rocket shot into the sky, tracing a fiery arc high above the town. An impressive boom shook the ground and was followed by a flash of light so bright it brought cries of alarm from the crowd of spectators gathered in the empty field outside of town.

Fearing Hogs Head would burst into flame, the crowd fell silent following the first display of aerial lights. All eyes were riveted to the bright sparks that fell from the sky and rained upon the dark wooden buildings along Main Street.

Moments passed, and when no sign of smoke or fire appeared, the crowd broke into loud applause, followed by shouts of "Bravo!" and "More!"

Jimmy, his head out the window, watched the amazing flashes of light weave fiery patterns across the velvet black sky, and cried out in delight. Tonight, he needed no encouragement to laugh. "That's the biggest and the bestest rocket I ever saw!"

Jonas grinned and slipped his arms around Kate's waist. "Come to think of it, it's the best I've ever seen myself."

Turning in his arms, Kate gazed up at him. "I do believe you're a genius."

"It takes one to know one," Jonas said, staring deep into her eyes.

"Wow!" Jimmy exclaimed when another loud boom rattled the windowpane. "Look at that!"

"It's wonderful," Kate said dreamily, although in reality the only fireworks she could see were the ones in Jonas's eyes.

"Kate," Jonas whispered, "this has been a wonderful day for me."

She moistened her lips and willed her knees to stop shaking. "It has been for me, too."

"I hope you mean that."

"I mean it with all my heart," she whispered.

"Look at that, Kate!" Jimmy yelled out.

"Amazing," Kate agreed, unable to take her eyes off Jonas.

"Astonishing," Jonas echoed. He held her gaze and thrilled to the sparks of desire in the depths of her eyes, matching his own desire.

He lay his hand next to her satin-smooth cheek, and she pressed her face against his palm. He lowered his head closer to hers, pausing just short of her lips as if to wait for the pull of gravity to close the maddening gap. When at last their lips finally touched, they were like two inventors about to embark on a tricky experiment—excited about what they were about to do, but cautious and careful, wanting to thoroughly test each new stage before proceeding to the next.

He withdrew his mouth and she stared up at him, her mind anticipating what it would feel like when they got past the experimental stage.

"I have an idea," she whispered.

He looked crestfallen. "Dammit, Kate! This is no time to be thinking up ideas." With that he crushed her mouth with his own, intent in wiping her mind clear of anything but the sensations of being kissed by him. He'd be damned if he'd end up nothing more than a name on one of her inventions!

He could tell by the dazed, dreamy look on her face when he released her that he'd succeeded. Succeeded so well, in fact, that even he hadn't thought of an idea. That was a first. Never could he remember kissing a woman without thinking up something, if only something as small as a way to redesign an ax handle.

No sooner was the fireworks display over than Jimmy started talking up a storm. He appeared completely oblivious to the rather dazed behavior of the two adults. "Did you see that last one? It made almost as much noise as you made, Kate, when you blew up the boiler, and did you see the one that went straight up—"

Jonas lifted Jimmy off the window seat. "See? What did I tell you? Our fireworks were an overwhelming success." He glanced at Kate.

"Why don't we go downstairs and I'll make us all some hot chocolate," Kate suggested.

They trooped downstairs just as Aunt Hattie and Uncle Barney walked into the front door.

Jimmy couldn't get his words out fast enough. "Did you see the fireworks?"

"We most certainly did, young man," Uncle Barney said. He lay his arm across Aunt Hattie's shoulders. "They were the best fireworks ever, if I do say so myself."

Aunt Hattie beamed proudly. "Much better than any of the fireworks we've had in the past. Now aren't you glad I ruined the ones from Chicago?"

"Come on, everyone," Kate called out, heading for the kitchen. "Let's make some hot cocoa."

Later, after Jimmy had been tucked into bed, Kate walked outside with Jonas. Rocking Horse Lane was deserted, and the gaslights had been turned off in town. The only light came from a silver-bladed sickle of a moon.

Kate gazed up at Jonas. "I can't tell you how much I appreciate everything you did for us today. Saving Aunt Hattie from jail for a second time. The fireworks. The parade for Jimmy . . ."

"Kate . . ." They were in each other's arms so quickly, it was impossible to know which of them had made the first move.

Holding her tight, he traced her mouth with the tip of his tongue. Much to his delight, she met his tongue with her own before parting her lips to him. He flicked his tongue in and out of the lovely sweet recesses of her mouth, his hand lovingly at her throat. He withdrew his tongue slowly, delighted to discover her tongue following his in an erotic dance that seemingly sparked another round of fireworks. She stood on her toes to deepen the kiss; he bent over her slightly. She arched her back to conform to his frame, her arms wrapped around his shoulders.

One silky soft hand worked up his neck and dived into his hair, sending his hat flying off. He let his hands slide down the lovely valley of her spine, all the way to her buttocks. Pressing her as close as was possible in their clothed state, he continued to nip, tug, and dance his way in and out of her mouth. She matched him move by move, coming up with a few inventive nips that sent his already staggering senses careening into another direction.

He kissed her long and hard, leaving no room for inspiration to interfere. He slid one hand over her gentle curves, following the soft lines of her hip, her tiny waist, and settling finally on the round fullness of her breast. His touch brought a happy sigh from her fevered lips and a satisfied curve to his own. The little rosebud tip grew taut to his touch, straining against the thin fabric of her shirtwaist.

By the time Jonas had finished kissing her, Kate was gasping for breath. Kate gasping for breath, he decided, was a wonderful and glorious thing.

"Jonas." For once in her life, her overly active mind couldn't seem to put a thought together. "I—"

He took both her hands in his. "Marry me!"

There was nothing else he could have said that would have surprised her more. "What?"

"I said marry me. You know as well as I that something wonderful happened between us today. Please, Kate, you've got to marry me."

She pulled away from him, her emotions in a whirl. "Why . . . why do you want to marry me?" she asked, her voice amazingly controlled considering the enormity of the discussion.

"Because . . . because I kissed you and nothing happened."

"Nothing?" She squeaked the word out, barely able to find her voice.

"I don't mean nothing. I mean everything happened. It was just as you said, Kate. I'd never before kissed the right person. That's why I kept thinking up all those ideas while sparking with others. If you're the right person for me, then it only stands to reason that I'm the right person for you."

"I . . . I don't know," Kate stammered, feeling confused. "I'm not sure."

Feeling crushed, he stared at her. "You're not sure? Did you think of any ideas while kissing me?"

"Ideas? Well, not exactly, but—"

"Then how can you not be sure? Oh, Kate, I really care for you. I've never met a woman like you before. Not ever. There isn't another woman like you!"

She stared at him, feeling a strange sense of disappointment. He cared for her? As flattering as this was, it wasn't the same as loving someone. "I don't know what to say. It's all happening so fast."

"I know. It's happening fast for me, too."

"There's so much to think about. Jimmy."

"He can live with us, Kate. I'd like that. I'd be the best father a kid could ever want."

"I'm sure you would be...." She managed to catch her breath, but the next one stuck in her chest. "I'm truly flattered, Jonas. Really I am. But I always promised myself that if I ever did marry, it would be for love. I couldn't possibly settle for anything less, not even for Jimmy's sake."

Jonas slipped his finger into the collar of his shirt. His body was on fire and if they didn't get this matter settled quickly so they could finish what they had started, he was going to explode in a burst of flames. "Love is a good reason to marry," he readily agreed. "And I told you, I've come to care for you."

"Caring isn't what I want." She lowered her voice to barely a whisper. "I want someone to love me. Someone I can love in return."

"I'm sure that could be me, Kate, given time."

"I . . . I don't know." She broke away from the intimate circle of warmth they'd created, and suddenly felt cold. "What about your parents' farm?" she asked at last. "You said they needed you. Wouldn't your getting married pose a problem for them?"

"As soon as you and I start our company, we'll make enough money to hire them all the help they need and—"

An icy chill ran down her spine. She'd wanted

so much to believe that his proposal of marriage, if not made out of love, was at least sincere. "That's what this is all about, isn't it?" Her voice was edged in anger, but her heart, her soul, the very essence from which she drew breath, ached with a sudden squeezing pain. Hiding her inner misery, she choked back the hot burning tears that blurred her vision and lashed out at him. "The only way you can get your hands on my patent is by marrying me!"

Jonas stiffened. Good lord, he thought in astonishment, he'd forgotten about the patent. He walked back and forth in front of her, trying to gain control of the situation. He just wished his male member wasn't cutting into the damned metal fastener on his trousers. What an inconvenient time to have a serious discussion!

"Maybe at first," he conceded. He didn't have the heart to lie to her and he wasn't even certain she would believe him if he did. "But not now. Not after the day we spent together."

"So you admit it! You planned to marry me from the start just so you could get your hands on my patent!"

"That's before I knew you. Before I came to care." He took a deep breath. "Before I fell in . . . in l-love with you."

Just hearing the word *love* fall from his lips almost shattered what little control she had left. It appeared he would do anything to get his hands on her patent, even lie. "Don't, Jonas. Don't lie about your feelings. It's only going to make matters worse!"

"I'm not lying, Kate. At least I don't think so. These things I'm feeling inside . . . they feel too strong to be just caring." His voice grew thick. "It's like I said. Not once during all the time I kissed you did inspiration strike." That wasn't exactly true. He thought up all kinds of wonderful things to do with his hands and lips, and if she'd give him half a chance, he intended to try out every last one of his ideas on her. "What I mean to say, Kate, is that I didn't think up a single invention. If that's not proof of love, I don't know what is!"

Kate had to admit this had been a first for her, too. But she was less willing to regard this as proof of anything, let alone love. "I'm not sure it proves anything."

"Kate, listen, I'm not used to this sort of thing. I've never been in love. Not the kind of love that inspires poets and artists. How can you expect me to be an expert in something I've never done before?"

"I'm not asking you to be an expert. I just want you to . . . oh, never mind! How could I have been such a fool? I knew you were up to something and I let my own feelings—"

"What feelings, Kate?"

Mortified by her own slip of tongue, she haughtily lifted her chin. "I won't marry you, Jonas. Not ever!" She turned to the gate, but he grabbed hold of her arm and spun her around to face him.

"Kate, please, don't leave like this. Talk to me."

"All right, I'll talk to you and I hope you listen and listen well. You'll never get your hands on my patent! Did you hear what I said? Never!"

He held her at arms' length. "Forget the patent! It has nothing to do with this strange, confused, topsy-turvy feeling inside. Great Scot, I can barely remember my own name when I'm with you. Does this sound like a man who's out for his own gain?"

She pulled away from him. "It was for your own gain that you followed me here."

"I don't deny that, Kate." His mind spun. He

tried to think of something to say, some way to prove to her he was a changed man. There was far more at stake than his immediate physical discomfort. Far more at stake than he had ever imagined.

"Kate, listen to me," he pleaded. "You're the first one I ever met who actually speaks my language. Do you know how much it means to me to find someone I can talk to? Share my ideas? I never thought I'd find a woman who could build a dynamo and not be intimidated by a little explosion. Never did I think such a woman existed. God, do you know how wonderful it makes me feel to be able to share my work with another person?"

Of course she knew how it felt. She felt the same way. No one, not even her dear aunt and uncle, was able to understand her work. No wonder she'd lost her head and acted like some innocent schoolgirl who'd never been kissed. Not that she had been kissed, of course, at least not like Jonas had kissed her.

What began as an ache was now a full-fledged stabbing pain inside. Why he could hurt her so, she had no idea. It wasn't as if she were in love with the man. Just because his kisses filled her with ecstasy was no reason to imagine herself having feelings for him. And yet . . .

It was this confusion that put a shrill ring in her voice. "You planned this whole thing, didn't you? You know that once a woman marries, everything she owns becomes her husband's." Angry at him, angrier at herself—feeling more hurt than it seemed possible to bear—she charged toward him, swinging her arm.

He backed away. "Now, Kate, calm down. Like I said, it was true in the beginning. I can't lie about that. But not now. You've got to believe me. I don't care a red hen about the patent."

"After all the years you supposedly worked on it? Do you honestly expect me to believe you suddenly no longer care?"

"It's true, Kate, I swear."

She closed her eyes for a moment. It was so hard to think with him looking at her as he was. Marriage must have been in his plan from the start, the reason he'd followed her to Hogs Head. "It was probably you who ruined the fireworks just so you could save the day for Aunt Hattie and win my heart."

He searched her face, his moonlit eyes practically setting her afire. "Then I did win your heart?"

"You did no such thing!"

"You said I did."

Furious, she placed her hands on her hips. "Don't you go putting words into my mouth, Jonas Hunter!" She turned and walked away, slamming the gate shut behind her.

He watched her disappear into the house, her last words echoing in his head. He meant to put words in her mouth. That he did. Loving words, caring words, words that only a woman in love would know how to say. He wouldn't rest until the words he himself had the sudden urge to yell to the treetops fell from her soft pink lips.

Shocked at the reality of what he was thinking, he hurried up Rocking Horse Lane and tried to make sense of what was happening to him. What was going on here? Why was he acting so unlike himself?

It was his own fault for allowing himself to have feelings for her. Had he kept his fool head, he would have waited before proposing marriage until after a proper courtship. It's what any reasonable man would have done.

He pressed his fists against his forehead and

walked in circles. "Fool, fool, fool." He'd practically had Kate in the palm of his hand. What had possessed him to push her so hard? And what was all that stuff about love? Where in the world had that come from?

True, her lips were the sweetest lips he ever had kissed. And she made him feel like no other woman had ever made him feel. Lord, he still couldn't get over kissing her without a single marketable idea popping into his mind. All he could think about when kissing her was how good she felt in his arms and how very wonderful she made him feel.

Still, that was no reason to imagine himself head over heels in love. No reason at all. Why, falling in love could mean an end to his creative ideas, if his experience kissing Kate was any indication. Without his inventions, where would he be? He'd have to go back to farming, and he hated the thought of returning to such a life.

No, he must keep his fool head at all costs. He must keep to the original plan. Marry her, be a good husband. Get his name on her patent. Conduct their business affairs. Be a father to Jimmy and keep love out of it, no matter what his feelings!

All right, so he had a selfish reason for wanting to marry her. He wanted the patent, dammit! Was that so bad? Was it his fault that he and Kate had both invented the same machine? Besides, look at all she had to gain. A father for Jimmy; a husband for herself. Love.

There it was again, that annoying word *love*. Make that *security*. Yes, that's better. He couldn't be—wasn't!—in love. He simply wanted to offer Kate security. He felt somewhat relieved. Falling in love was by its very nature a selfish thing to do. A person in love demanded love in return.

Giving a person a sense of security seemed so unselfish ... so much more noble. Why, he owed it to Kate to insist that she give him a second chance. For her own good.

The problem was he'd already lost one major battle and probably the whole war.

He stopped in his tracks. How was it possible that a man could invent the most amazing machines known to mankind and couldn't do something as basic as persuading a woman to marry him?

"Is that you, Jonas?"

Jonas recognized the sheriff's voice. "Yes," he said, not wanting to make conversation. He wanted to be alone. He had serious thinking to do.

"I wonder ... I know it's late ..."

Hearing the plaintive tone of the sheriff's voice, Jonas sighed. "What is it, Sheriff?"

"The celebration was rather hectic today and I didn't get a chance to say my piece. It just doesn't seem like the Fourth without paying homage to those noble men who made it all possible. Know what I mean?"

Jonas had no idea what the sheriff was talking about. "Well, I—"

"Do you have time to listen to me recite the Constitution of the United States?"

Chapter 28

After leaving Jonas, Kate rushed into the house and, without a word to her aunt and uncle, flew up the stairs and dashed into her room.

Throwing herself facedown on the bed, she made no effort to hold back the tears. Never had she felt so humiliated in her entire life. The way she had allowed that ... that conniving, cheating man to kiss her. Had kissed him back. Had wanted him to—oh, Lord, forgive her for thinking it—do more than just kiss her. What in the world had come over her?

True, he was the most attractive man she'd ever met. She could hardly deny that his kisses had swept her off her feet. But marriage? Did he honestly think she would be so foolish as to marry him?

How dare he make a mockery out of love? He didn't know the meaning of the word. He couldn't even say it without stuttering. "Well, I don't love you, Jonas Hunter," she said aloud, and for some reason her tears started to flow again.

A knock sounded at the door and Kate quickly sat up and wiped away her tears.

"Kate?" Aunt Hattie stuck her head into the room. "Are you all right, child?"

Kate knew better than to try to hide her feelings from her aunt. The best she could hope to do at this point was to assure her aunt of her well-being. "Of course I'm all right. Why wouldn't I be?"

"You looked upset when you came in."

"I'm not upset, Aunt Hattie. I'm perfectly happy. I'm just . . . tired."

"Hmmmm." Aunt Hattie plopped herself on the edge of the bed. "Maybe you haven't tried hard enough."

Kate blinked. "What are you talking about?"

"I'm talking about you and Mr. Hunter. I saw the way you two looked at each other in the kitchen while we were drinking cocoa. And the way you two sat talking by the river having your picnic today. . . . Why, the whole town's abuzz. There's even talk that he kissed you right in the middle of Main Street."

"He kissed *you* on Main Street. Not me."

Aunt Hattie gave a wicked smile. "He did, didn't he? There's been nothing so scandalous happen on Main Street since I staged that all-night hunger strike."

Kate sniffed. "As for the picnic, we mainly talked about work."

Aunt Hattie frowned. "Work?"

"Our inventions, magnetic fields. That kind of thing."

"Dear me." Aunt Hattie gave Kate the same look of dismay she gave Mabel's cat when it had decided to have its litter atop the cookstove. "How do you expect to land a husband talking about athletic fields?"

"I have no intention of landing a husband, and certainly not one by the name of Jonas Hunter!"

Aunt Hattie shook her head in puzzlement. "Why ever not? The man is a saint if I ever saw one."

"He's a crook!"

"Really? I thought he was an inventor." She shrugged her shoulders. "I suppose there're worst things than having a man in the kitchen. Take your Uncle Barney. Time was when he snored up a storm."

"He still does," Kate pointed out. Sometimes he made such a racket, Kate, whose bedroom was two doors away from her aunt's and uncle's room was required to sleep with her head underneath the pillow.

"Oh, no, he hardly snores at all anymore," Aunt Hattie declared.

Kate saw no reason to inform her aunt of how loud Uncle Barney's snoring had become over the years. Hard as it was to imagine, there appeared to be at least one advantage to a loss of hearing.

Her aunt leaned forward in the way of hers that signaled she was about to impart some profound wisdom. "I can tell you that snoring is much more of a nuisance than having a man in the kitchen."

"I dare say you're right," Kate said, too tired and upset to argue.

"So does that mean you intend to give Mr. Hunter another chance?"

"It means nothing of the sort. I have my patent and I don't need Mr. Hunter or any other man!" She felt immediate remorse at using such a harsh tone of voice with her aunt. She took her aunt's hand. "I know you mean well, Aunt Hattie, and I love you every much for your concern. But believe me, I have no romantic interest in Mr. Hunter." She spoke slowly and in a voice loud enough so her aunt could hear, but not loud enough to drown out the memory of his lips or—Lord forgive her for thinking it—the touch of his hand on her breast.

"All I want to do is to get my carpet cleaner produced so you can start taking orders. Just think." She forced a smile. "We're going to be rich. We don't need Mr. Hunter or anyone else. All we need is the carpet cleaner."

"Dear me, I don't understand." Her aunt looked positively dismayed. "Why on earth would an intelligent woman like yourself choose a carpet cleaner over a nice young man like Mr. Hunter?"

Jonas lay on his bed, staring up at the ceiling, and knew he was in for a long night. If the sheriff reciting the United States Constitution hadn't put him to sleep, nothing would.

What a mess he'd made of things. How could everything have gone so wrong? More important, what was he going to do about it?

He turned on his right side in an attempt to get another perspective on the problem. He could, of course, apologize. Or he could tell her he'd been so caught up by her beauty, he didn't know what he was saying when he proposed. No sooner had the idea come to him than he knew it would never work. Kate was too smart to be persuaded by flattery, no matter how sincere it might be.

He turned onto his left side. Of course, he could always admit the truth. He wanted to marry her for the sole purpose of getting his hands on the patent. He thought about this for a moment and decided something wasn't right. He tried out various ways of saying this: He wanted to marry her mostly for the patent. Partly for the patent. Not for the patent.

He rolled over on his back. So why did he want to marry her, if not for the patent? If he didn't love her and he didn't not love her, what was left?

Flopping from side to side and using the same precise, problem-solving techniques he used whenever he worked on an invention, he thought of a way that might help him get Kate to give him another chance, but it took him until dawn to do so.

Still, once the idea struck, it hit him like a bolt of lightning. He sat straight up in bed, smiling. How foolish of him not to think of this before. Why, it was plain as the nose on his face. The way to Kate's heart was through her Aunt Hattie. Convinced he'd found a solution to at least one of his problems, he decided to get some sleep.

He buried his head beneath his pillow to drown out the crow of a rooster and after a short while realized he was too anxious to sleep. He wouldn't rest until he had Kate in the palm of his hands. His idea of reaching Kate through Aunt Hattie had better work. For if it didn't . . .

Not wanting to consider the possibility that he'd made such a mess of things that even Aunt Hattie couldn't help him, he tossed his pillow aside and rested his head against the headboard, his arms folded across his chest. He pictured Kate looking up at him with adoring eyes, her face framed by her hat. He could recall with startling detail every line, every curve, every nuance of her face, every one of the many different types of smiles he'd seen on those full pink lips of hers.

He imagined her voice, saying the words he wanted so much to hear: *Of course I'll marry you, Jonas Hunter. You're the most handsome, smartest, most wonderful man in the world.* Jonas smiled to himself. *I love you,* she said, or so it seemed.

His heart stopped. Her voice had sounded so real to him, the vision of her was so clear, he blinked his eyes and glanced around the dimly lit room as if to make certain he was still alone.

He heaved a deep sigh and, feeling hopeful if not entirely confident, threw his bedclothes back and slid out of bed.

Later that morning, he stood in front of the general store waiting for Aunt Hattie to open up for business.

Key in hand, she hurried up the steps of her front porch and greeted him with a warm smile. "Why, Mr. Hunter. What a nice surprise. What brings you here so early?"

"Why, you did, of course."

She giggled. "Oh, Mr. Hunter, you make me feel like a schoolgirl again." She unlocked the door and let him in. "Is there anything I can do to help you?"

"I just came to browse, if you don't mind."

"Oh, dear. I don't expect my order to come in until the end of the week."

Curious as to what she thought he'd asked for, Jonas wandered along one of the neatly arranged counters, trying to decide if his best bet was to tell Aunt Hattie everything and plead for her help. He stopped to examine an ebonite hand mirror, thinking it might make a nice gift for his mother.

Unable to make up his mind how little or how much to tell Aunt Hattie, he continued to examine the various goods on display. All the while, he kept his eye on Kate's aunt. Somehow she was going to help him win the hand if not the heart of her reluctant niece. All he had to do was figure out the right tactic.

The bells on the door jingled and a woman dressed in a black taffeta skirt and tailored white shirtwaist swept into the store.

"Good morning, Hattie."

"Florence."

"Has my order arrived?"

"Yes, indeed." Aunt Hattie pointed to a granite grave marker that was propped next to a barrel of pickles. The headstone was engraved with the letters R.I.P.

Florence stared down at the grave marker and turned a ghastly shade of white. She made a strange gagging sound and her hand flew to her chest. "That's not what I ordered! I ordered a gray new-market," she exclaimed, naming the coat that was in fashion. "I wanted to have it in plenty of time before the weather turns cold."

Aunt Hattie's face grew red with fury. "Then why did you order a grave marker?"

"I didn't, you fool. I should have known better than to order anything from you. Next time, I'll order through the Sears and Roebuck mail-order catalogue!"

"You do and you won't get another thing from me!"

"See if I care!"

Florence stormed past Jonas, knocking over a display sign in her haste, and slammed out of the store.

"Of all the foolhardy, stubborn—" Aunt Hattie stopped her tirade midstream as the door flew open and an odd-looking man with an uneven handlebar mustache strolled through the door.

"Why, Mr. Narrowsmith, how nice to see you."

"It's nice to see you, too, Hattie." He nodded at Jonas and sneezed.

"Bless you," Aunt Hattie said.

"Most obliged to you." He sneezed again. "My order in?"

"It certainly is." Hattie handed him a yellow cardboard carton.

"Eh . . ." Nicholas rubbed his chin and turned the most alarming shade of red. "You must have my order mixed up with someone else's order. I ordered something to help me with this infernal sneezing problem. This package plainly says it's for female diseases."

"So what's the problem?" Aunt Hattie asked.

"The problem is I'm not female and I don't have a female disease." He placed the carton on the counter and started toward the door, sneezing as he went.

"Well, I *am* female and I don't have a female disease, either!" Aunt Hattie yelled after him.

Similar scenes were repeated with other customers throughout the morning.

Jonas watched in amazement as one after another of the various customers stormed out of Aunt Hattie's store, angry or otherwise upset about their orders. He knew Aunt Hattie had a hearing problem, of course, but had no idea how adversely it was affecting her business.

He pulled a small writing tablet from his shirt pocket and began jotting down notes.

Trying to determine the range of Aunt Hattie's hearing difficulties, he talked to her, alternating the various pitches of his voice. Was it possible, he wondered, to come up with a device that could help people like her with a hearing loss?

He'd read a lot about Mr. Alexander Graham Bell's telephone and had even examined the inside mechanism of one firsthand at the Chicago Fair. By using a series of wires and batteries, Mr. Bell had managed to transmit the human voice by transforming sound into electrical resistance, which was then translated back to sound at the other end of the wire. The question was whether the same principles of transporting sound could be used to increase the volume of the human voice.

Jonas was no expert on the human ear, but he had seen a replica at the Chicago Fair and had been fascinated by the demonstration that showed how efficiently the bones in the ear could amplify the tiniest of sounds.

He moved around the store, pacing from counter to counter. He talked about the weather, about the various goods on display. About Kate.

He scribbled down his observations based on Aunt Hattie's response or, in some cases, lack of response.

Kate's aunt seemed to have more trouble hearing from her left ear than she did from her right. She had the most difficulty hearing low-pitched sounds.

Aunt Hattie was clearly growing frustrated with him. She swung around to face him. "What did you say? Speak up? My word, Mr. Hunter, can't you keep still?"

"My apologies, Aunt Hattie," he said, keeping the pitch of his voice high until it sounded more feminine than masculine. As he suspected, she heard his every word.

"No apologies are necessary, Mr. Hunter."

Returning to his normal voice, he continued, "Your store is so interesting." He lowered his voice to a deep bass. "It's incredible the amount of goods you carry."

Sensing he'd paid her a compliment, Aunt Hattie flashed a wide smile. "Don't you worry about a thing, Mr. Hunter. You can tarry here as long as you want."

He left her shop at noon and hurried back to the boardinghouse to work on his idea.

It took a full day and a half to draw the sketches to his satisfaction. It took another two days and numerous trips to the blacksmith to make a working model of what he called a hearing facilitator. Shaped like a small cone no larger than a cigar case, it was designed to be held over the ear by hand or to be affixed to the hair or a hatband. A

wire ran from the hearing device to a dry-cell battery, which could be tucked into a large pocket. He
hoped eventually to make the battery case less
bulky, but for now it would do.

At present, his main problem was how to convince Aunt Hattie to give his hearing facilitator a
trial. Suddenly it occurred to him that another
golden opportunity had presented itself. He would
simply ask for Kate's help.

He smiled to himself. He knew Aunt Hattie was
the way to Kate's heart. And now he knew exactly
how she was going to help him.

Chapter 29

Later that same afternoon, he rode his horse over to Kate's house.

It took much in the way of pounding on the door and pleading with her before she finally relented. Even then, she cracked the door but a few inches wide and stared at him with only one eye visible. It was clear his troubles were far from over. "What are you doing here?" she demanded.

"I'm here about your aunt."

The door opened wide. "Is Aunt Hattie—"

"Healthwise she's as strong as a horse," he hastened to say, not wanting to worry her unnecessarily. "Her mental condition ... now, that's another thing."

"I saw Aunt Hattie this morning and there was nothing wrong with her mental condition—" She broke off and studied him with narrowed eyes, hands at her waist. "If this is another one of your tricks ..."

"I swear to God it isn't."

She regarded him suspiciously and, apparently believing him, invited him inside.

His right hand wrapped tightly around the leather handle of his valise, he whipped off his hat with the other. "I appreciate this, Kate. There's nothing I like more than a woman who keeps an open mind."

"Just tell me what you're doing here and leave. Now, what were you saying about my aunt's mental condition?"

"Have you forgotten how she recently set fire to the train station?"

"Of course I haven't forgotten. But she never meant to burn down the station."

"Even so, setting fire to those catalogues seemed a bit drastic, don't you think?"

"Aunt Hattie tends to feel things more passionately than most people."

"Is that so?" He wondered if passion was an inherited trait. Certainly he'd never known a woman with more fervent lips than Kate's. He still couldn't forget that when he had kissed her not a single idea for an invention had come to mind. "Is that why she threw nine customers out of her shop the other day?"

The suspicion on Kate's face dissolved into concern. "Nine?"

"That's not counting the customers who walked out on their own accord. I'm amazed she's still in business."

"She's been in the town for many years. I suppose some people feel they owe her their loyalty. Aunt Hattie is a wonderful person. She really doesn't mean any harm."

"Your Aunt Hattie has a hearing problem."

"Don't let her hear you say that."

"Either she's going to have to hear it or she's going to go out of business."

Kate's forehead creased in puzzlement. "I'm afraid she's going out of business regardless. Now that the Sears, Roebuck mail-order catalogue is so popular. I'm afraid there's no way to stop progress."

"The townspeople are ordering through the catalogue because your aunt keeps messing up their orders."

"So what do you propose we do?"

He set his valise on an end table and drew out his cone-shaped instrument. "This is a hearing facilitator. Sound travels through this opening and is amplified before reaching the ear."

Kate took the instrument in her hands and studied the skillfully molded wood that had been sanded smooth as satin and varnished. "Do you think it'll work?"

"That's what we're going to find out." Jonas stepped away from her, turned his back, and spoke in a low voice that was little more than a whisper. "Did you hear what I said?"

Kate shook her head. "Not really.

"Now put the hearing facilitator to your ear."

He waited for Kate to do as he asked, then repeated what he had said earlier in the same soft voice, before asking aloud, "Now did you hear me?"

Kate looked startled, then delighted. "Yes . . . yes, I did hear you." She ran to the door and held the hearing aid to her ear. "I can hear the birds as if they were in this very room with me. And the Richmond twins! Yes, yes, listen. I can hear the twins from clear down the block and . . . everything!" She turned to face him. "This is wonderful!"

He grinned. He wasn't used to someone showing so much enthusiasm for something he'd invented. His father certainly never had. Even his mother viewed each new idea with skepticism, convinced that any machine able to perform better than a person could not be trusted. "So what do you say? Do you think we can persuade your aunt to use it?"

Kate's eyes shone with excitement. "I think it's worth a try, Jonas."

Gone was the suspicion on her face of moments before. Gone was the unforgiving edge to her voice. Gone was his own resolve to never again think of the word *love* in relation to Kate.

"When . . . when do you think would be the best time to approach her?" he stammered, feeling all cotton-mouthed and awkward. How did she always do this to him? He was perfectly sane and rational whenever he was away from her. But no sooner did she come into sight than suddenly he no longer acted like himself.

"Well . . ." She thought for a moment. "She might be embarrassed if we discuss it in the store with customers walking in and out. Why don't you come to dinner tomorrow night? I'm sure Aunt Hattie would like that. Perhaps you could bring up her hearing problem after dinner. In a casual way, of course."

Dinner. Oh, heavenly days, she invited me to dinner. Hot blood rushed through his veins; his spirits soared. His smile broadened. "I would be delighted to accept your invitation."

"Could you be here by seven?"

Seven, seven, she wants me here by seven! He pretended to think for a moment, as if to make a mental check of his social calendar. But it really was hard to think with his heart pounding so quickly. "I think I can manage that."

"Are you sure? We can make it later if you like."

"Seven would be fine."

There really was no reason for him to stay. Indeed, he told himself, it would be a grave mistake to linger one moment longer than necessary. Still, he couldn't seem to pull himself away. And so he stood looking at her—and she at him, with only the chimes of the tallboy clock and the low swishing sound of cool water rushing through the complicated network of pipes along the baseboards to break the silence.

He found it necessary to remind himself that the reason he wanted to marry her was for business purposes. Love had nothing to do with it, no matter how fast his heart was beating as he gazed into her eyes. Yes, indeed, business purposes. *Business!* He would gain control of her business affairs; she would gain the social status that comes with being a married woman.

They both stood to gain a lot from such a marriage. And there would be none of that self-serving thing called love that always, to his way of thinking, interfered with marital bliss. A marriage without love would allow the participants to act like mature adults, with no jealousies, no hurt feelings, no demands made on each other—nothing to distract them from their all-important work. It would definitely be a marriage made in heaven.

Kate averted her gaze, and without the pools of blue to distract him, he actually managed to catch his breath.

"It would be wonderful if you could persuade Aunt Hattie to use the hearing facilitator," she said. "I'd be so grateful to you."

Grateful was a start, he thought. Lots of women married out of gratitude. He felt encouraged. "Let's hope it works."

"You know she's a stubborn woman. It won't be easy."

"I don't imagine it will be," he said, surprised to find himself looking forward to the challenge. "I hope you won't be too disappointed if we're less than successful on our first try."

"No, of course not."

"Just to be on the safe side, I think I'll take the added precaution of clearing my calendar for the remainder of the week." As if he had a calendar, he thought, let alone a social life. "I'm even willing to postpone my leaving town indefinitely, if need be."

"It . . . hardly seems fair to ask you to postpone your departure."

Her face showed no change in expression, but there had been a slight hesitation in her voice. What did it mean? he wondered. Did she or did she not want him to leave? "Convincing your aunt to try out this hearing facilitator is at the very top of my priority list."

"It's very generous of you. I can't tell you how much this means to me."

The softness in her eyes touched a deep chord within him. He felt almost dizzy with hot confusion. He opened his mouth to speak. "Will . . . will . . ." He forced himself to inhale, hoping this would help clear his voice. "Will you be able to clear your calendar?"

Kate lifted a delicately arched brow. "My calendar?"

"Your aunt might be suspicious if I show up on her doorstep and you're not here."

"Oh, yes. Of course. You're right."

"Then it's agreed." He really did need to leave before he said the wrong thing. If only he could get his feet moving in the proper direction.

Kate walked toward the door, giving him no choice but to follow. "I'll see you tomorrow, then?"

He gazed at her, annoyed that the worrisome word *love* resurfaced again. He couldn't seem to help himself. He couldn't be around her for long without imagining himself hopelessly in love. Dear sweet heaven. What a selfish clod he was!

He tried to recall all the things Kate stood to gain from marrying him. Respect, status, security. *Love.* "Damn it, can't you remember? Security!" he said aloud, talking to himself as he so often did when he was alone.

She looked startled. "I . . . I beg your pardon?"

His heart stopped. Dear God, what had he done? "I'm sorry," he gasped, biding for time. "Did I say something wrong?"

"You said security."

"Eh . . . yes, yes. Security. That's the name of my . . ." He held up the hearing aid. "The security hearing facilitator."

"That's a nice name," she said. "It gives one a feeling of confidence. Yes, I think that would help matters immensely as far as Aunt Hattie is concerned."

Relieved that she so readily accepted his explanation, he nodded. "I think so, too."

"So we're all set for tomorrow?" she asked.

"Tomorrow?" For a moment his mind was too occupied with the fragrance of her perfume to function properly. What in blazes were they set to do tomorrow?

Chapter 30

Exactly twenty-seven hours eighteen minutes and fifty-seconds later, Jonas arrived at the Whittaker home. Since he was early, he was obliged to wait down the road for an additional ten minutes to pass so that he would not appear too anxious. At precisely seven o'clock sharp, he snapped shut the silver lid of his pocket watch, galloped the short distance to her house, and tied his horse to a fence post.

Kate's uncle answered his knock and led him into the parlor, issuing stern warnings of the possible dangers along the way. "Be careful of that door. It's missing a hinge. Kate needed the metal for one of her inventions. Take care not to step into that hole. Oops! Watch your head!"

Jonas stepped around the hole in the floor and dodged beneath a cluster of electrical wires dangling from the ceiling.

Aunt Hattie sat in the parlor, embroidering. Upon seeing Jonas, she jumped to her feet, knocking a card of thread on the floor, and greeted him with an enthusiastic smile.

"Why, Mr. Hunter, I can't tell you how happy I was when Kate told me you were coming to dinner!" Her hands fluttered like two butterflies looking for a place to land.

"It's my pleasure." He set the valise holding the

hearing facilitator on the floor next to the divan and held his hat in his hands, fingering the brim nervously. "Since I call you Aunt Hattie, it seems only fitting that you should call me Jonas."

"I would love to call you Locust." Aunt Hattie took her place on the divan and indicated for Jonas to sit next to her.

"Eh, Jonas."

Aunt Hattie looked slightly flustered. "Jonas."

Jonas sat on the divan and balanced his hat on his knee. He glanced about the room. Now that he knew the extent of Aunt Hattie's hearing problem, it was easy to adjust his voice to accommodate it. "Is Kate here?"

"She'll be down in a moment," Aunt Hattie explained. "I had to practically drag her out of the cellar. When she gets to working on something, she forgets about time."

He smiled politely. He often lost track of time himself when working on his inventions. Still, it was disappointing, not to mention a blow to his ego, to learn that Kate was more interested in her work than she was in him.

Kate's uncle lifted a meerschaum pipe off the mantel. "How long do you expect to remain in town?"

"Not much longer, I'm afraid."

"Oh, dear." Aunt Hattie jumped to her feet looking all red and flustered. "Please forgive my poor manners. Of course you may have some lemonade. Squeezed it fresh this afternoon."

She hustled out of the room just as Kate entered the room carrying Jimmy. The boy's face lit up at the sight of Jonas. Jonas tossed his hat on the end table and rose to his feet.

"Say good evening to Mr. Hunter," Kate said.

"Good evening, Mr. Hunter."

"And a good evening to you, young man." Jonas held out his arms, indicating he wanted to hold Jimmy. "May I?" He took Jimmy from her and gave the boy a gentle jostle. "And how are you this evening?"

Jimmy held up a metal toy soldier attached to a tiny hot-air balloon made out of fabric and yarn. The solder stood in a tiny metal box next to a stub of a candle. "See what I made? And it really works."

Jonas examined the toy and nodded in approval. "I would say you're proving to be quite an inventor."

"I quite agree," Kate said, her voice warm with pride. Jonas wondered how it was possible she could look more beautiful each time he saw her. She wore what could only be her Sunday best. The blue crepon skirt was trimmed with matching velveteen. An inverted plait in back trailed down the length of the skirt from the waist to the hem, ending in a small train. The skirt was topped by a white waistshirt trimmed in a blue velveteen bow, matching the ribbon in her hair. For him? he wondered, his heart skipping a beat. Did she wear her Sunday best for him?

"Do you really like it?" Jimmy asked, snapping Jonas out of his reverie.

Feeling guilty for having momentarily forgotten the boy in his arms, Jonas set him on the divan and made a wholehearted effort to concentrate fully on the balloon.

"I like it a lot. You did a mighty fine job, Jimmy," he said, and he meant it. It was unusual for someone so young to understand even the fundamental laws of aerodynamics. But judging by the ingenious way Jimmy had balanced the hot-air balloon, he obviously understood more than simple basics. "I hope you're careful with fire," he cautioned.

"I'm allowed to light the candle only when Kate's with me," Jimmy said seriously.

Jonas nodded in approval. "That's good. I definitely think you're going to be a great inventor. Just like Thomas Edison."

Jimmy looked pleased. "And I'm not going to blow things up."

Uncle Barney stood by the boarded-up fireplace. "I can't tell you how relieved I am to hear that, young man." He tamped his pipe. "I doubt if this old house can handle many more explosions." He exchanged a look of affection with his niece before continuing. "Jonas was just telling me about his plans." He waved his pipe. "I believe you said you were leaving soon?"

"I'm expected back on the family farm," Jonas explained, watching Kate's face. It was Jonas's opinion that it was harder to read a person's face in the glare of electric lights than with more traditional illumination. Gas or kerosene lighting, and even candles, were better at transposing the most subtle changes of expression into telling shadows. Still, it seemed to him that Kate's smile was just a bit forced, her eyes a trifle too bright.

Aunt Hattie walked into the room carrying a tray. She set it down on the coffee table and poured Jonas a glass.

"Thank you, Aunt Hattie." Recalling his earlier experiments, he knew that her hearing loss prevented her from hearing low-register sounds. For this reason, he kept his voice pitched high. Kate looked at him curiously, but said nothing.

Aunt Hattie poured a glass for her husband. "We're having baked chicken and rice."

"It smells delicious," Jonas said, his voice high.

"You'll have to give me some of your recipes," Aunt Hattie said.

"My what?"

"Recipes. Kate said you were a cook."

"Did she, now?" He couldn't help but wonder what Kate had actually told her aunt about him. By the look of guilt that suddenly crossed her face, he could well guess.

Dinner was wonderful and because Kate and Uncle Barney unconsciously followed Jonas's lead and talked in high-pitched voices, Aunt Hattie heard most of what was said, and the conversation took less sharp turns than usual. Soon, even Jimmy caught on and raised his voice to a higher octave.

Jonas spent considerable time complimenting Aunt Hattie on her cooking. He watched Kate carefully, to monitor his progress with her. Or at least that's what he told himself, but in reality, he couldn't keep his eyes off her.

Kate tried to avoid Jonas's eyes, but it was hard to do. Especially since she felt his eyes burning into her even when she wasn't looking at him. She was grateful her aunt commanded most of his attention. She would hate to have him turn his considerable charm full-force on her. Even so, it was necessary to keep reminding herself that just because a man was charming, kind to old ladies, and kissed heavenly didn't mean he was trustworthy.

Still, it had become clear to her that as preposterous as it seemed, the two of them had invented their machines independent of each other. There was no thievery or other chicanery at work. For whatever reason, through whatever twist of fate, they had both been attuned to the same creative plane. Who could explain such a thing?

All she knew is that he wasn't a crook in the sense of trying to steal her ideas. But he had misrepresented his intentions, making her think he cared for her when all the time he only wanted her patent. She could never forgive him for trying to trick her in such a despicable way. How dare he toy with her affections as if he were a cat playing with a mouse. It was a cruel and terrible thing he did, hurtful in ways she didn't fully understand. How could she forgive such a thing? How could she forget?

Still, it was hard to keep her eyes off him, and despite her best efforts, she found herself locking gazes with him more often than not. She only wished he would do her the courtesy of not staring at her so she could look at him undetected.

Just when she thought she had a moment's reprieve from his scrutiny and could study him without censor, he lifted his eyes and caught her red-handed. Trying not to look guilty, she gazed at him until a question from her aunt required her to turn away.

After dinner, they adjourned to the parlor. Jonas carried Jimmy and set him down on the floor. Kate sat on the divan and Jonas planted himself right next to her, leaving far less than the customary distance between them.

She moved her legs to the side so that her skirt no longer touched his trousers legs.

"Here we go," he whispered in conspiratorial tones, his shoulder rubbing against hers.

Feeling the warmth of his breath on her neck, Kate wished she'd opted for a chair. She was beginning to feel as fluttery as her aunt was acting.

Jonas cleared his voice. "Aunt Hattie, I wonder if you would be willing to help me with one of my inventions."

Aunt Hattie looked uncertain. "Why, Jonas, I don't know much about inventions. I'm sure Kate could help you, though."

"What I need is business expertise." He reached over the arm of the divan for his valise and opened it on his lap.

"I thought an astute businesswoman such as yourself would have some advice as to how something like this could be marketed." He lifted the hearing facilitator out of the valise and held it up for her to see.

"My, my," Aunt Hattie exclaimed. "How interesting. Is it an instrument of some sort?"

"Not exactly, not the kind that plays music," Jonas explained. "It's a hearing facilitator."

"A hearing what?"

"Facilitator." He glanced at Kate. "Actually it's called a security hearing facilitator. You would be amazed at how many people suffer hearing loss as they get older."

"Really?" Aunt Hattie looked startled, as if the idea had never occurred to her.

"It's true. Why, even Mr. Alexander Graham Bell has a hearing problem. I'm sure you've heard of him?"

"The man who invented that newfangled gibber-jabbering machine?" Uncle Barney asked.

"It's called a telephone," Jimmy said, his eyes shining bright. Sitting in a chair across from Kate and Jonas, Jimmy watched the two of them and gave Aunt Hattie a surreptitious glance on occasion, as if he sensed some sort of game in progress.

"I call it a waste of time," Uncle Barney said. "I'm willing to wager that not only is Bell stone deaf, he also doesn't have a wife. Anyone who has to listen to a woman gabbing around the clock isn't likely to be foolish enough to invent a talking machine!"

"Your uncle has a point," Jonas said, grinning. Ignoring Kate's visual daggers, he pressed the device against his ear and flicked on the battery. "If you hold this up to your ear like this, the sounds are amplified."

Jimmy laughed. "That looks funny."

"It's not polite to laugh," Kate said gently.

"But you said I could laugh at the clown," Jimmy argued.

"That's different," Kate explained. "The clown wanted you to laugh at him."

"Kate's right," Jonas agreed. "I agree, though, it does look funny, but only because we've not seen one before. If everyone with a hearing problem wore one of these, we wouldn't think it was funny at all. Just as we don't think people who wear spectacles look funny. So what do you say, Aunt Hattie? Would you like to try it out? For marketing purposes, of course."

"Oh, yes, of course, marketing purposes. You can't sell something you don't believe in." Aunt Hattie took the hearing aid from him and held it to her ear.

"Can you hear me?" Jonas asked.

Aunt Hattie looked unimpressed. "Of course I can hear you."

"What about if I go into the other room?" Ducking beneath a tangle of electrical wires, he walked into the dining room. "Can you hear me now?"

This time Aunt Hattie looked amazed. "Why, yes! You sound like you're talking in my ear."

He walked back into the room. "I'm actually talking very softly. . . . If you move the cone away from your ear, you will probably have trouble hearing me."

He continued talking while Aunt Hattie tried to hear him both with and without the aid. "Why, this is truly amazing!" she declared. "Amazing! Here, Jimmy, you try it."

Aunt Hattie held it to Jimmy's ear. "What do you think?"

Jimmy pushed it away. "It's too loud."

"That's because you don't have any trouble with your hearing," Jonas said.

"And neither do I," Aunt Hattie declared.

Kate and her uncle exchanged worried glances. Kate leaned toward her aunt. "Do you think Jonas's invention will be beneficial?"

"Of course it will be," Aunt Hattie declared. "I'm sure there're a lot of old folks who would benefit from such a thing." She handed the instrument back to Jonas with a shrug of dismissal that dashed Kate's hopes.

Kate looked so disappointed, Jonas was tempted to put his arm around her. Instead, he sat back with casual confidence and moved his hand across the upholstered distance between them to squeeze Kate's hand sight unseen.

Kate kept herself rigid and avoided meeting his eyes. Only the most discerning eye would have seen the slight color that showed beneath her soft smooth cheeks. Smiling to himself, he withdrew his hand and turned his attention back to Aunt Hattie. "I plan to ask Mr. Sears to carry it in his next catalogue." His voice was high so that Aunt Hattie wouldn't miss a word.

"Mr. Hunter! Locust!"

"Eh, that's Jonas."

"Jonas!" Aunt Hattie's face was flushed in an alarming red color. "Surely you can't be serious about doing business with that—"

"Now, now, Auntie, do calm down," Kate cautioned.

Eyes as deep and as blue as twin mountain lakes looked at him beseechingly. Cursing himself for trying to get to Kate through an aunt who obviously meant the world to her, he relieved his guilt by committing himself anew to the task of getting Aunt Hattie to use his instrument. This time, he had only the purest of intentions. The hearing aid would greatly benefit Aunt Hattie and those who loved her.

"I'm a businessman, Aunt Hattie."

Aunt Hattie leaned back in her chair and fanned herself with her lace handkerchief. "I can't believe that a fine gentleman like yourself would even think of doing business with that money-grabbing scoundrel."

Jonas winked at Kate and took enormous satisfaction in watching Kate turn the same shade of red as the petticoat that showed so prettily beneath the hem of her skirt. Curbing the urge to laugh out in glee, he leaned toward Aunt Hattie. "You think I shouldn't allow Mr. Sears to carry it in his catalogue?"

"You're damned right that's what I think!"

"Aunt Hattie!" Kate scolded, shocked that her aunt would use such language, especially in front of Jimmy. She glanced at her uncle, who continued to puff on his pipe as if nothing Aunt Hattie said or did surprised him.

Jonas remained unperturbed. Encouraged by Aunt Hattie's increasing agitation, he brushed a piece of imaginary lint from his trousers. "Then how do you propose I market this?"

"I'll sell it for you and I'll do a lot better job than that horrible man!"

"You?" He widened his eyes in feigned surprise.

"Yes, of course me," Aunt Hattie said. "In my store. As a matter of fact, I know a lot of people who could benefit from one of these. I can't tell you how many of my customers have mixed up their orders just because they can't hear a thing.

But will they admit it? Not for the world. It's always my fault. I'm telling you, I could sell more than that greedy, good-for-nothing catalogue merchant any day!"

"I don't know." Jonas pretended to mull over the idea. "The person who sells this item must be prepared to demonstrate how to use it."

"And you think Shears will? Harrumph! The man is too busy counting his money and stealing other folks' territory to demonstrate anything but his mean spirit."

He hesitated, not wanting to look too eager. "I would expect the person handling my product to use it both in and out of the store."

Aunt Hattie narrowed her eyes. "Did your Mr. Shears agree to use it?"

Jonas managed to look appropriately chagrined at such a question. "Do you think I would agree to allow him to put something of mine in his catalogue if he didn't agree to my terms?"

Kate made a hiccupping sound behind him. He glanced back at her and realized she was trying to keep from laughing aloud. He gave her a warning look. She lowered her head and begin working on her own imaginary lint.

Aunt Hattie, fortunately, was too occupied with her own thoughts to notice what her niece was doing. She grabbed the hearing facilitator out of Jonas's hands. "I'll use it, but only if it's sold in my store."

Jonas made the mistake of tossing Kate a conspiratorial glance. Her shining eyes and joyful smile almost made him lose his own composure. "I suppose I could give you exclusive rights."

"I don't want exclusive rights. I want your promise that I will be the only one allowed to sell it, and you won't let that belly-cheating rogue put it in his catalogue."

"You drive a hard bargain. . . ."

Aunt Hattie looked downright smug. "You have to get up pretty darn early in the morning to pull the wool over my head. Tell him, Kate."

Kate managed to keep a straight face. "No one has ever pulled the wool over Aunt Hattie's head." She gazed at Jonas through lowered lashes, her eyes bright with challenge.

He rubbed his hand across his chin, pretending to give the matter full consideration. His long fingers hid the confident smile he gave Kate. "I suppose I could persuade Mr. Sears to tear up our agreement."

"Who's better at persuasion than you?" Kate said softly.

"And it's a good thing," Aunt Hattie agreed. "Persuasion is a fine art that only a few of us have perfected."

Surprised that Aunt Hattie responded to something she had meant for only Jonas to hear, Kate realized she'd have to be careful what she said now that her aunt had a hearing aid.

Jonas rose to his feet and almost got his head entangled in the electric wire over the divan. "As Mr. Sears is so fond of saying, no business deal is complete without a handshake."

"That sounds like something the man would say!" Aunt Hattie retorted.

Jonas held out his hand. "Shall we?"

Aunt Hattie lifted her head stubbornly.

"Come on, Aunt Hattie. I believe Mr. Sears stole that idea from Abraham Lincoln. Remember him? Honest Abe?"

Aunt Hattie relented. "I suppose if it's all right with Honest Abe . . ." She reluctantly gave Jonas her hand and allowed him to shake it. "You really are a smart businessman," she said. "For a cook."

Chapter 31

It was nearly ten o'clock by the time Jonas bid Aunt Hattie and Uncle Barney good night and took his leave. Jimmy had fallen asleep earlier and Jonas had carried him upstairs for Kate. Together they had tucked the boy in bed, then returned to the parlor, where Aunt Hattie had served tea and gingersnap cookies.

Now Kate walked him to the door, surprised at how quickly the evening had passed. "I better walk you out to the street so you don't fall over something. I wouldn't want you to injure yourself again."

He lifted an electric wire that dangled in front of his face and grinned at her. "I'll say one thing for you, Kate"—he looked up at the tangled web of wires over his head and stepped around the hole in the floor—"you sure do know how to keep a man on guard."

Kate took his hand as they reached the porch. "Careful, now." His hand felt warm and sturdy in hers.

She led him down the porch steps and through the narrow path leading to the gate. It was dark, with only the stars lighting the way. Upon reaching safety, she quickly released his hand.

Although they stood but a few feet apart, she couldn't see his face. Only the fine turn of his head was revealed, outlined against the star-studded sky. She inhaled the fresh outdoorsy scent of him, so different from the usual tobacco and alcohol smell of most men, and oddly enough, so much more masculine.

Her heart thumped so hard, she was positive he could hear it. She tried to think of something, anything, to say to break the tension that had been building all night between them and was now threatening to explode.

"I can't believe the difference your hearing facilitator made to Aunt Hattie. Did you see how she kept lifting it to her ear?"

"She did seem to like it, didn't she?" His voice was low, velvety soft. "Though I doubt she'll ever admit it."

Her knees threatened to buckle. Feeling the need to catch her breath, she took a step back. If only she could breathe normal, she might manage to say good night without making a fool of herself.

"I really am grateful to you." Her voice grew husky. "Aunt Hattie was actually able to participate in the conversation without going off in a different direction. I can't tell you how very much it means to me." She had almost grabbed his arm, but fortunately managed to catch herself just in time.

She'd already made the mistake of touching him once tonight. To touch him again would be sheer torture. "I know Uncle Barney feels the same way," she continued, her voice breathless. She waited for him to say something, but he made no attempt to fill in the silence, and seemed to be content to stand quietly by her side.

Just as she began to think the strained silence would never end, he surprised her by reaching for her hand and lifting it to his mouth. It was only her hand, dear God, but the way her heart was beating, it could just as easily have been her lips he kissed or—Lord forgive her for thinking it—a breast.

"I'm glad it worked out, Kate. You're right. Your aunt is as stubborn as they come." He chuckled to himself. "I think she'd do anything to get back at Sears."

Kate laughed, too, but not because of the humor he evoked. Her laughter, instead, was a desperate attempt to cover her nervousness. "I think you're right."

He released her hand and they fell silent again, but the night was anything but quiet. Crickets chirped, toads croaked, and a hoot owl flapped its wings overhead. It seemed to Kate that nature was urging them on, and her heart pounded in nervous anticipation.

She held her breath, waiting. If only the light were better. Why hadn't she thought to run the wires outside the house for incandescent lighting?

Did it seem like his head had moved? Tilted forward, perhaps, closer to hers? She swallowed hard and reminded herself how he'd tried to trick her out of her patent.

What she knew in her head to be true was overruled by the foolish yearnings of her heart. She wanted so much to believe the warm lights in his eyes as he'd gazed at her all evening long had been sincere. But how could she know for sure? Could she really trust her instincts?

She imagined she could see his mouth in the darkness, Lord, his wonderful, magical, velvet-soft mouth. With the image came the memory of his kisses, and it was so vivid, her mouth trembled with sweet longing. Her body ached with sweet urgent need.

Propelled by a force so strong she could no

longer fight it, she raised herself on tiptoes and lifted her face upward. In the deep recesses of her mind, she knew there was a reason why she shouldn't be doing this, flaunting herself, but she didn't care. She didn't care about anything but the kiss she knew was hers for the taking.

"I think your hearing facilitator is going to be a big success." Her voice caught in her throat.

"Do you think so?"

Ah, yes, he had lowered his head a mite closer. It was obviously an invitation for her to raise herself a teeny-tiny bit higher. "Will you be able to make enough to fill the orders?"

"I'm sure that won't be a problem," he said. His voice sounded forced, as if the very act of speaking were difficult. This time he left no doubt as to how close he was.

Her heart practically stopped when his lips suddenly brushed against hers. Swooning next to him, she was more than ready when at last he took her in his arms.

But rather than kiss her as she wanted and—Lord, forgive her—practically demanded of him, he whispered a grating accusation in her ear. "You called me a crook!"

Thrilling to both the power and danger she felt in him, she gasped in momentary confusing. "What . . . what did you say?"

"You didn't tell your aunt I was a cook. You told her I was a crook!"

Living with Aunt Hattie all these years, she was accustomed to abrupt changes in mood or conversation. Even so, she felt too disoriented to deny it. "I know."

"I may be many things, Kate, but I'm not a crook."

His mouth closed over hers, and her rather unladylike response was blissfully quashed between them. His hot, possessive lips ignited a fireball of passion that seemed to fill the night with a heated pulse. Pulling her tight against his hard lean body, he filled her mouth with an electric current that sizzled a path all the way to her toes. Flames of desire sparked inside her, then erupted into an all-consuming blaze that took her breath away.

His hungry lips raced along her neck; his heated breath seared her skin. One fiery hot palm covered her breast. The torrid blaze of his hand burned through the thin fabric of her shirtwaist, setting her heaving breast afire.

Clinging to him, she lay her hand on top of his and urged him to press harder. Her breast tingled beneath his touch; the flames of need and want jumped wildly from one part of her body to the next.

He captured her lips again and nipped her lower lip with his teeth. Not to be outdone by his inventiveness, she nipped back and then ran a series of sensuous kisses down his firm jaw and neck, tasting the dampness of sweet passion that beaded his skin.

Tugging wildly at his shirt, she felt a sense of triumph when his buttons popped open, as if she'd managed some death-defying feat. Inspired by his brazen mouth and spurred on by the sensations of his hot skin beneath her lips, her mind swung into high gear. What would happen if she kissed him on the hollow below his neck and there, along his shoulder blade and—dear Lord forgive her for thinking it—here. The latter place was the part of his chest exposed by the open shirt. Growing braver by the second, she let her tongue trail down his chest to his—

Gasping, he pushed her away. "My God, Kate!"

Startled by the abruptness of their separation,

Kate stood frozen in place. "Is there something wrong?"

"Wrong? Nothing is wrong! In the name of Sir Isaac Newton, Kate. I never knew a woman who kissed like you do. . . . Come back to the boarding-house with me. Please, Kate, say you will."

It took her a moment to realize what he was asking her to do. She was shivering, suddenly, and more than a little overwhelmed by her own behavior. "I . . . I can't."

"Why not?" He clearly sounded surprised and maybe even confused. Lord, who could blame him?

"It would be . . ." She stopped. She'd almost said *dangerous*. After the way she had run her mouth down the length of his heated torso, she could no longer trust herself to follow the rules of propriety she had so virtuously upheld until now. "I . . . I have to go."

She moved away quickly, reality sinking in faster than a rabid dog's teeth. Lord, what had she done? How could she allow herself to kiss a man whose character was so questionable? Goodness, what was she thinking? She hadn't just kissed a man, this time, she had . . . well . . . *kissed* him. And if he hadn't stopped her, who knows where her curiosity might have led her?

Oh, no, you don't, Kate Whittaker, she scolded herself. *You're not getting out of it that easily. You know full well where it would have led you.*

How could she have confused gratitude with feelings of caring and trust? True, he'd done a wonderful thing for Aunt Hattie. Had done wonderful things for Jimmy. But that was no reason to think that he . . . that she . . . that things had changed. The only thing Jonas Hunter wanted was her patent. Why was she having such a difficult time re-

membering that? She pushed open the gate leading
to the house.

"Wait, Kate—"

She slammed the gate shut between them.

The door to the house flew open and Aunt Hattie peered outside. "Are you still out there, Kate?"

Thanking her lucky stars she had not installed
electricity outside the house, Kate quickly checked
the buttons of her shirtwaist and prayed that her
aunt could not see the condition of Jonas's shirt.
"Yes, Aunt Hattie, but I'm coming in. Good night,
Mr. Hunter."

Chapter 32

The sound of his horse's hooves thundered along the dark dirt road as Jonas raced back to the boardinghouse. His blood pounding through his veins, he pressed his knees against the horse's flanks, urging the animal onward as if his own life depended on it.

The night air did little to cool down Jonas's heated body. He wasn't sure how to assess his progress with Kate. Good God, she had kissed him like no other woman had kissed him—kissed him the way every man dreamed of being kissed. What did she expect him to do? Not respond? Not want to take things a step further?

Had he pressed too hard? Not hard enough? Had it been a mistake to ask her to come back to the boardinghouse with him? Dammit! Of course it had been a mistake. Why couldn't he have been contented to let her have her way with him—and the way she was burning up his chest with her hot, passionate lips, he could well imagine what that way might be—and politely bid her good night.

As if he could!

No woman had ever affected him like Kate Whittaker affected him. No woman had ever touched him, tantalized him, thrilled him, or taunted him like Kate Whittaker had. He wanted her in his bed. More than that, he wanted her in his life.

Patent or no patent!

* * *

The next day, when Jonas bumped into her at Aunt Hattie's General Store, as, of course, he'd hoped he would, it was painfully obvious that Kate had no intention of allowing a repeat of what had occurred the previous night.

She kept herself aloof, though polite, with not a hint of the passion that had kept him tossing and turning through the long, seemingly endless night. Without a plan or even a prayer of winning her over, he did his best to follow her lead.

"Mr. Hunter."

"Miss . . . Whittaker." This wasn't working. Not for him, and he suspected not for her, either. "Kate, about last night . . ." He felt a surge of hope and satisfaction when a spot of color appeared on her otherwise pale cheeks. Just as he'd hoped. "I apologize for my actions last night." He learned a long time ago that taking the blame was always the best policy when dealing with a woman, as long as it was within reason, of course.

Kate looked him square in the eyes. "If you'd have worn a shirt with proper fasteners, things most certainly wouldn't have progressed as far as they did."

"Proper fasteners?" He'd made up his share of excuses in the past for pushing propriety beyond the limits. But even he had never thought to blame a woman's fasteners. "Are you saying that I should put the same sort of fastener on my shirt as is holding my pants together?"

Kate's gaze dropped down to the metal sliding fastener below his waist. Catching herself, she quickly drew her eyes away. "That would be an improvement, I suppose, over those ridiculously small buttons. In any case—I encouraged you. I accept full responsibility."

She should. She was the one who popped his buttons. "Why don't we just say we're both responsible?"

"Very well, if you insist." She continued on her way without a backward glance. He watched her bustle down Main Street, no doubt in a hurry to work on some invention or other. Recalling the feel of her mouth feathering down his chest, he shook his head with regret that things had come to such an abrupt conclusion.

What an inventive mind she had. She might not have thought up a marketable idea while he kissed her, but never had he known a woman think up so many intriguing things to do with her lips. He only hoped that one day he would have the pleasure of knowing just how inventive she could be in other areas.

He almost got his wish the following day as he stood on Main Street talking to the sheriff. A terrible commotion was followed by shouts and a blaring horn. When the strange *chuggity-pop-pop* sound grew louder, he spun around and gasped, for heading straight at him was a runaway buggy.

Diving for cover, he peered out from behind a wooden keg as Kate whizzed by, yelling for everyone to get out of her way. His eyes wide with astonishment, he realized that Kate was driving a fuel-operated machine.

"Hold your horses," the sheriff yelled after her, waving his hat.

Ignoring the sheriff, Kate rattled down Main Street, zigzagging from one side to the other, honking and shouting and otherwise creating havoc. Farmers dived headfirst beneath their vehicles. Their wives dropped their wicker baskets and ran screaming down the street. One horse managed to pull away from a hitching post and galloped away, fast on the trail of Mable's poor cat.

Meanwhile, the internal combustion engine continued to hiss and sputter and belch black smoke.

In no time at all, Kate had driven through town, but she left a path of destruction behind her. Water spilled from overturned barrels. Fresh fruit and vegetables lay scattered in the dirt next to the capsized cart. A group of indignant bicyclists fought to free their two-wheelers from a tangled heap.

The sheriff's face was red with rage. "Dammit, I told her to hold her horses!"

Jonas stood and brushed off his trousers. "I don't know if you happened to notice, Sheriff, but there weren't any horses to hold."

Kate and her vehicle had disappeared, but the *chuggity-pop-pop* sound could still be heard in the distance. Jonas and the sheriff ran for their horses and gave chase.

They found Kate standing next to her overturned carriage about a mile outside of town. It was hard to know which looked the worse for the wear: the driver or the vehicle. Kate's straw hat was askew and she was covered from head to toe in dust. Even the veil she had tied prettily beneath her chin had failed to keep the dust off her face—or the spattering of slick motor oil from her forehead.

Kate wasn't concerned about her appearance. She was too busy kicking the undersides of the buggy and giving the vehicle a piece of her mind.

The motor sputtered and died, but the two left wheels kept spinning.

Jonas leaped off his horse and ran to her side. "Kate, are you all right?"

"Of course I'm all right." She brushed off her skirt. "I just had a little mishap is all."

"Sakes alive, Kate!" the sheriff complained.

"You give me the jim-jams with your death-defyin' tricks. Next time, I'm placin' you under arrest for reckless drivin'."

"I wasn't driving reckless," Kate protested. "My steering mechanism failed to work."

"You could have killed yourself," Jonas added, his voice hoarse. He suddenly realized the full extent of his feelings for her and he didn't care how selfish such a notion was. Terrified she would do serious injury to herself with her fancy contraptions, he vowed to win her back, no matter what it took. Then, by George, he intended to see that she find less hazardous ways to occupy her time.

"See!" Kate said, pointing to the tiller. "As soon as I go faster than three miles an hour, the steering fails."

The sheriff showed not the least bit of sympathy. "The least you could have done, young lady, is apply the brakes. This thing does have brakes, doesn't it?"

"Of course it has brakes," Kate retorted. "They just take too darn long to lock into place."

"I've done some work with brakes," Jonas offered. "And I read about this new type of steering . . ."

They locked gazes and an electric charge seemed to snap like summer lightning between them.

"I best be going home," Kate said, at last. She was frowning, but the irritation had left her voice.

"But—"

She started toward town, walking with long, determined strides, leaving the two men to stare after her.

How did he always manage to do that to her? she stewed. Make her heart alternate between beating up a storm and seeming to stop altogether. It was darn annoying, to say the least, and most inconsiderate of him. She wouldn't put it past him to have some sort of electrical device in his pocket that controlled the way a heart beats or lungs took in air. Maybe this same device altered a person's feelings. That would certainly explain the strange behavior on her part whenever she was with him.

She slowed her stride, coming to almost a stop. Was it possible, could it be, that this strange confusion—not knowing what she was doing, how she was feeling, believing, or thinking—was love? Shaking her head, she picked up speed. Dear God, what a thought.

She couldn't be in love with a man who tried to trick her into marrying him for his own devious purpose. Still, she couldn't deny the fact he was the most attractive man she had ever met. And his kisses were the most passionate kisses to ever cross her lips. Then there was that little problem with her erratic heartbeats.

Maybe he did have more good qualities than bad. He was kind to Jimmy and showed the most amazing patience with her aunt. His feelings for them seemed sincere. But it still didn't make up for the way he tried to trick her in the past and, for all she knew, was trying to trick her again.

She would never marry him. She would never marry a man she didn't trust and, more than that, didn't love.

But if she didn't love him and she didn't not love him, what was left?

Such were her confused thoughts as she trudged home, with the sun beating down and the dust rising up. Her head still ached from the gasoline fumes. And the muscles in her left shoulder were sore. She was in no condition to sort out her mixed-up feelings for Jonas.

When at last she spotted her house and saw

Jimmy watching for her from his bedroom window, her spirits lifted. She waved.

He waved back and cupped his hands around his mouth. "Where's the fuel-driven buggy?"

"It's in a ditch," she called back.

Despite the rather abrupt end to her test drive, Kate was satisfied with the results. The engine still sounded rough, but there was less smoke than during previous tests and this time the gasoline hadn't leaked out of its tank.

Of course the steering and brake problems still needed to be worked out, but she had already thought up some ideas she was anxious to try. And hadn't Jonas said there was a new type of steering?

Although she went straight to the cellar intent on working out the problems with her steering, she was unable to keep her mind on her work. She kept thinking of Jonas and how worried he'd looked when he'd found her. The concern on his face looked genuine. But then, of course, she'd been fooled by him before. How was she to know he wasn't trying to fool her again?

She only wished he would leave town. Then, surely, she could forget him, forget the way his lips felt. Forget she had ever met him.

Sheriff Williams couldn't find anything in the town ordinances that said driving a wagon without benefit of horses was illegal.

Jonas breathed a sigh of relief.

"It should be!" Smoky Joe insisted. He'd paced back and forth in front of the sheriff's desk the entire time it took Williams to pore over the journal that listed the various laws that had been added to the town ordinances through the years.

"It's against the laws of nature," Curly added, rubbing his bald head.

"I can't put anyone in jail for breakin' the laws of nature," the sheriff said, closing the journal. "As unb'lievably as it seems, gentlemen, Jonas here is right. Miss Whittaker did not break any law in regards to drivin' without horses. Now, of course, there's that little matter of d'turbin' the peace. . . ."

Fortunately for Kate, the sheriff never got around to arresting her. The controversy over Kate's wild ride through town was quickly diffused by news of Jonas's amazing hearing facilitator.

By the end of the first week, Aunt Hattie had taken two dozen orders.

"Never knew we had so many people in Hogs Head with a hearing problem," Aunt Hattie said when Jonas stopped in to pick up his orders.

Jonas thumbed through the stack. "If it wasn't for your merchandising talents, these people would never have considered purchasing my product."

Aunt Hattie accepted his compliment with her usual lack of modesty. "You're darn tooting I've got merchandising talent, and that's something Shears and Rhubarb can only dream about!"

Jonas didn't know what to make of the initial success of his hearing facilitator. He couldn't imagine making much money from the things. He was convinced once the novelty wore off, the orders would drop.

Meanwhile, he was having a difficult time keeping up with the demand. Not that he minded the work, of course, nor did he object to the profit he made from each hearing aid sold. The Lord knew he needed the money. His work also gave him a legitimate excuse for staying in town and spending time with the Whittakers.

Since he worked all day long filling orders, he didn't have much time to visit Aunt Hattie's General Store. This required him to stop at the Whittaker house during evening hours to pick up and deliver orders. Naturally, he always timed his visits so that Aunt Hattie would insist he stay for dinner. Naturally, his sudden interest in social mores wouldn't allow him to do anything as ill-mannered as eat and run.

So he read aloud to Jimmy, played whist with Uncle Barney, and planned marketing strategy with Aunt Hattie. His patience nearly always paid off, for the evenings often ended with a lively conversation with Kate, who joined them in the parlor after finishing her work in the cellar.

At such times, they discussed their inventions, the weather, the state of affairs of the town, the nation—everything, in fact, but what he really wanted to talk about. On one such occasion, he leaned across the divan and whispered loud enough to be heard over the tinny tune rising from the spring-motor gramophone. "Come outside with me, Kate."

She hesitated a moment as if tempted. "I . . . I really don't think that would be a good idea."

"Are you afraid of what would happen if you do?" he challenged.

"Nothing will happen." The stubborn and determined look on her face was enough to convince him that if he meant to win her over, he'd better put his own inventive mind to work like it had never worked before.

Chapter 33

The train whistle sounded in the distance just as Kate put the finishing touches on a new safety valve she'd designed for the boiler.

The whistle signaled the arrival of the noon express carrying mail from the East Coast. Maybe today she would receive the patent on her carpet cleaner or, at the very least, a response to one of the letters she'd written to countless manufacturing companies.

She glanced across her workbench at Jimmy, who was sitting on a stool making his metal toy soldiers move with the help of a large magnet. "I'm going into town for the mail. If you be a good boy, I'll bring you back some peppermint."

"Will you see Jonas?"

"That's Mr. Hunter to you. I don't plan to see him. Why?"

"Just asking." Jimmy scrunched up his nose. "When is Aunt Hattie coming home?"

Kate was surprised by the question. "The same time she always comes home. Just as the sun is setting. Are you asking for any special reason?"

"I like talking to her. She's really smart now. She doesn't say stupid things anymore."

Kate walked around the workbench and lowered herself onto the stool by his side. "Aunt Hattie was never stupid, Jimmy. She made mistakes because she couldn't hear properly. Now that she wears the hearing facilitator Mr. Hunter made for her, she doesn't make those mistakes anymore."

"How come her ears don't work well?"

"I don't know. It's hard to say. Sometimes as we get older, we can't hear or see as well as we used to. Mr. Henry used to keep driving his bicycle off the road until he started wearing his spectacles, and now he sees just fine."

"Is that why you keep driving your fuel-driven buggy off the road? Because you can't see well?"

"I see perfectly well," Kate assured him. "I just have some problems to work out with the steering. I don't need spectacles, but if I did need them, I would most certainly wear them."

"When Elizabeth Davenport was made to wear spectacles, the children at the orphanage laughed at her."

Elizabeth had been Jimmy's friend at the orphanage.

"Sometimes we laugh when something's new and unfamiliar because we don't know what else to do," Kate told him.

"Did you laugh when Mr. Henry started wearing spectacles?"

"No. But then a lot of people wear spectacles. It's not all that unusual."

"What about crutches? Do a lot of people wear crutches?"

"Some people. Especially men who fought in the war. And Mr. Hopkins uses a cane."

"The children laughed at me when I walked into the orphanage with my crutches."

"I know, Jimmy. People laugh at my inventions."

Jimmy frowned. "They do?"

"Yes, indeed."

"Why?"

Kate shrugged her shoulders. "Some people laugh because they think it's funny that a woman is an inventor."

Jimmy's serious face made him look older than his seven years. "I don't think it's funny that a woman's an inventor."

"I know you don't, Jimmy."

"What do you do when they laugh?"

"I ignore them, and you know what? They don't laugh so much anymore. I have a feeling that no one laughs at your friend Elizabeth anymore, either."

"Do you think they would still laugh at my crutches?"

"You mean the children at the orphanage? Maybe at first. Until they got to know what a special person you are. When that happens, no one will even notice your crutches."

"But no one wants me in their family."

"That's not true," Kate said. "There's been several people who want you. Mrs. Paine, for one."

"She's still mad at me for tying her up."

"That was an accident. If she doesn't understand how such accidents can happen, then she's not the right mother for a budding inventor. Meanwhile, you're part of our family. And one day soon, we'll find you the best family in the world. You'll see. But ... Jimmy, you really do need to try to get around by yourself."

"I won't use my crutches. I won't!" His eyes filled with tears, but because he was obviously trying to hide them from her, she pretended not to notice.

She gave an inward sigh of frustration. Never had she felt so inadequate. Although she was born into a large family, she basically grew up as an only child; she had no idea how to relate to a child of seven. She really did need to find Jimmy a family. He needed both a father and a mother who, preferably, was experienced in raising children. Maybe with the right parents to love him, Jimmy would gain the confidence he needed to use his crutches and maybe even learn to walk again. "Come on, Jimmy. I'll take you upstairs."

She carried Jimmy to his room and lay him on the bed for his afternoon rest. She dropped a kiss on his forehead. "I'll leave as soon as Uncle Barney arrives for his afternoon nap. I'll be back in no time."

"Don't forget the peppermint," Jimmy called after her.

Pausing at the doorway, she glanced back over her shoulder. "I won't."

A line of people snaked down the porch of her aunt's store and ran the length of the boardwalk clear to the hotel.

"What in the world?" Kate muttered to herself as she pushed her way past the crowd, through the door, and up to the counter, where Aunt Hattie was demonstrating how the hearing aid worked.

"Personally, I don't have a problem," Aunt Hattie assured the crowd gathered around her. "But I like to use the hearing aid just because it's so much fun to use."

Thelma Paine took it upon herself to be the unofficial spokesperson for the hearing aid. "I ordered ten spools of red thread and it was the first time Hattie got my order right."

Aunt Hattie glared at Thelma. "Like I said, I don't have a hearing problem, but some *older* people fall into the bad habit of mumbling. The hearing facilitator helps to clarify the words of mumblers."

"I want one of those!" shouted Duke, the blacksmith. "My wife has gotten to mumbling somethin' awful lately."

"Get me one, too," Curly said.

Sheriff Williams shook his head. "What do you want one of them for? You have perfectly good ears."

Curly rubbed his hand over his bald head. "I used to have perfectly good hair, too. It doesn't hurt to prepare for the future."

Kate was the first to notice the handsome stranger who stood watching from the sidelines. Dressed in a blue serge coat with matching vest and blue plaid pants, he sported a full mustache and wore his slick hair parted in the middle. Curious about who he was, Kate threaded her way through the crowd toward him.

"I'm Kate Whittaker," she said. "I don't believe we've met."

"Well, howdy, ma'am. Richard Warren Sears at your service."

Kate couldn't believe her ears. "You're Mr. Sears? The one from Sears and Rhu . . . eh . . . Roebuck?"

"That I am, ma'am. I understand there was a problem with an order of catalogues we shipped. Thought I'd see for myself what the problem is. Second time we had a problem with catalogues in this town." He nodded in Aunt Hattie's direction. "I noticed someone at the train station with one of those things attached to his ear. He said it was a hearing facilitator. Thought I'd stop by and see for myself. Maybe meet the inventor. Is the woman behind the counter the owner of the store?"

"Yes, that's my Aunt Hattie."

"Aunt Hattie, eh? Well, I'll just go and introduce myself."

"That's probably not such a good idea," Kate said.

"Oh? And why might that be?"

"She's, eh ... occupied. She doesn't like to be interrupted when she has customers. She says that the customer should always come first."

Mr. Sears looked impressed. "Now, that's the kind of person I like to do business with. Nice to have met you, ma'am."

"But—"

Already Mr. Sears had worked his way politely through the crowd and reached the counter, where Aunt Hattie was writing up another order for a hearing facilitator.

"Excuse me, ma'am," Mr. Sears said, his full vibrant voice rising over the excited chatter of the customers still standing in line, waiting to experience firsthand Jonas's miraculous hearing facilitator. "Richard Warren Sears, ma'am. Perhaps you've heard of my company?"

"Sears?" Aunt Hattie exclaimed. "Did you say your name was Sears?"

"That's right, ma'am. I'm pleased to make your—"

"What are you doing in my store?" Aunt Hattie's sharp grating voice could be heard over the murmur of her customers. The crowd fell silent as all eyes turned to gaze at the stranger.

The man looked positively startled. "Well, I—"

"Out. Get out!" Aunt Hattie set her hearing aid on the counter and grabbed a broom.

Before anyone could stop her, she had shot from behind the counter and had chased poor Mr. Sears clear out of the store.

Horrified, Kate turned to Sheriff Williams, who looked as startled as the rest of the crowd. "Can't you do something?"

The sheriff made a face. "I knew it! I knew I should have gotten the lock on the jail cell fixed." He marched outside. "Hattie! Hold your horses!"

"Oh, dear," Thelma protested. "Mr. Sears seemed like such a nice man. If something happens to him, will we still be able to order from the catalogue?"

Kate threw her hands in the air. "Is that the only thing anyone cares about?" Unable to stand around while her aunt did heaven knew what to an innocent man, Kate whirled toward the door and dashed outside. She was moving so quickly, she didn't see Jonas until she practically mowed him down in his tracks.

"Hold on," he said, his hands on her shoulders to steady her. "Where are you off to in such a fired-up hurry?"

"Aunt Hattie is trying to murder Mr. Sears."

Jonas's eyes widened. "That wouldn't be the same Mr. Sears who heads that mail-order house, would it?"

"It's one and the same. You've got to do something, quick!"

"Do something?" Jonas glanced around.

"They went that way." Kate pointed down the street. "Be careful, Aunt Hattie is armed."

Jonas paled. "Don't tell me she has a gun!"

"No, no, nothing like that. She has a broom!"

Jonas mounted his horse and rode away, leaving Kate to deal with Aunt Hattie's startled customers. Kate put Thelma Paine in charge of demonstrating the hearing facilitator. After assuring everyone that everything was under control, Kate raced back outside.

Twisting her handkerchief in her hands, she paced back and forth on the porch and prayed with all her might her aunt would come to her senses before any real harm was done.

Aunt Hattie finally returned. She walked down the center of Main Street with the broomstick still in hand. Dressed in black, her shawl trailing from her shoulders, she made a formidable figure. Muttering to herself, she ignored the curses from drivers who were forced to steer their wagons around her.

Kate picked up her skirts, dashed down the wooden steps, and raced to her aunt's side. "I've been so worried. Where . . ." She squinted her eyes against the sun. "Where's Mr. Sears?"

"Harrumph!"

"What happened to him? Aunt Hattie!"

"Oh, all right! Your Mr. Hunter whisked him away on his horse like some damned knight in shining armor."

Kate never thought she'd hear her aunt use such a disapproving tone of voice in referring to Jonas. "Was Mr. Sears all right?"

"He wouldn't have been had Mr. Hunter minded his own business!" Aunt Hattie hurried up the steps to her store.

Kate followed close behind, trying to reason with her. "You have no right to try and hurt him."

Reaching the porch, Aunt Hattie ignored the line of people still waiting for a demonstration of Jonas's miraculous hearing facilitator. She jammed the tip of the broomstick against a wooden plank and held the broom like a warrior holding a spear. "He had no right trespassing in my store!"

"He wasn't trespassing. Anyone can walk into the store. It's a free country."

"The country might be free, but my store is off limits to the likes of that man!"

Kate watched her aunt disappear inside. There

was still no sign of Mr. Sears or Jonas or even the sheriff. Not wanting to listen to any more of her aunt's rantings, she decided to return home until Aunt Hattie had calmed down.

Chapter 34

Kate hurried down Main Street past the train station toward Rocking Horse Lane. The air vibrated with the sound of hammering. Already the platform had been replaced and the frame for the waiting room had been rebuilt.

A table and chair had been arranged beneath a tattered umbrella to serve as a temporary ticket booth. Jonas and Mr. Sears were standing near the table in deep conversation. Much to her relief, Mr. Sears looked none the worst for the wear following his encounter with Aunt Hattie.

Standing next to the renowned businessman, Jonas looked tall and lean, radiating the same virile strength that never failed to fill her with the overwhelming need to be close to him.

She started toward them, telling herself that her only intent was to apologize to Mr. Sears for her aunt's behavior.

She stopped dead in her tracks upon seeing the two men shake hands. It was as Mr. Sears turned toward the waiting train that she noticed he was holding a hearing facilitator to his ear. Obviously, Jonas had made some sort of business deal with Mr. Sears.

Surely he hadn't agreed to let Mr. Sears put the hearing facilitator in his catalogue? After promising

Aunt Hattie he wouldn't? Kate didn't want to believe it, but what else could she think?

Desolation swept over her; tears sprang to her
eyes. She had believed Jonas when he promised her
aunt exclusive rights. Just as she'd wanted to believe
him when he had said he loved her. Well, look where
that got her. What in the world made her think she
could believe anything Jonas told her?

Thank God she'd had the sense not to go to
the boardinghouse with him. Oh, but she'd been
tempted. Was still tempted, and knowing how very
tempted she was filled her with anguish and grief.

Jonas waved one last time at the train before
walking to his horse. Upon spotting Kate, he lifted
his hand in greeting and called her name.

Barely able to make him out through her tears,
she turned and ran blindly toward the woods. Upon
reaching the thick cover of pines, she raised the
hem of her skirt and raced along the narrow dirt
path as if a tornado were at her heels. The shortcut
saved time, but not enough. Astride his gelding,
Jonas was able to catch up to her with little effort.

"Kate!" He dismounted from his horse, raced
toward her, and tackled her before she reached the
gate to her yard. He dragged her down into a
grassy patch by the fence.

"Let me go, you brute!"

"Not until you tell me why you're so upset."

He rolled her over and pinned her to the ground,
her hands over her head. "Tell me."

"You promised Aunt Hattie the exclusive right
to sell the hearing aid in her store."

"Agreed."

"And then as soon as a better offer comes along,
you forget all about poor Aunt Hattie and—"

He raised his dark eyebrows. "*Poor* Aunt Hattie.

She didn't look so poor a short time ago when she was beating on Mr. Sears."

"Don't change the subject. How could you do such a thing? I know you tried to cheat me. But to try and take advantage of an old lady—"

"I turned him down."

"She trusted you, Lord only knows why, but she did. And what does she—"

"I turned him down."

"She gets broken promises and—" Her eyes widened. "What did you say?"

"I said I turned him down." He released her hands and stood, brushing off his trousers.

Kate sat up. "You ... you turned him down? But why?"

"He only offered to make me rich and famous."

"What's wrong with that?"

"Nothing. But since your aunt threatened to kill me if I did business with Mr. Sears, there's no point in letting fame and fortune be wasted on a dead man."

"Be serious, Jonas."

"I *am* serious." Looking deep into her eyes, he relented. "All right. I promised your aunt exclusive rights, and despite what you may think of me, I am a man of my word."

She stared at him in disbelief. "You passed up all that money because of Aunt Hattie?"

Jonas glanced skyward. "God, I must be out of my mind."

"Not out of your mind, Jonas." A lump rose at her throat. "It's ... it's a wonderful thing you did."

"I'm not sure how wonderful it is," he said. "My family back home could use that money. I would never forgive myself if something happens to my father because I failed to get him the help he needs."

"Oh, Jonas ..." She swallowed hard, not wanting

to give in to the tears that burned her eyes. "Life has become so complicated. It was so much easier when we had fewer choices to make, less chance of success. I wish that I . . . that you . . . that we never invented that ridiculous carpet cleaner—"

"Fertilizer spreader," Jonas said, as a matter of pride. He held out his hand and helped her to her feet.

"You know what I mean." She started for the house.

"Wait!" He ran to catch up to her. "We have to talk about this. Where are you going in such a gosh-darn hurry?"

"I just installed a new pressure gauge on the boiler and I want to make sure it's working right."

"Great Scot, Kate! What are you waiting for?" He followed her through the gate and the littered yard. They reached the front door just as Uncle Barney emerged.

"I thought I heard you, Kate. I promised your aunt to help her out at the shop as soon as you returned. Jimmy's still in his room, resting." Uncle Barney waved and headed for the path leading into town.

"Thank you, Uncle Barney," Kate called after him.

"Eh, the boiler?" Jonas reminded her.

"Oh, yes." Kate raced into the house and down the steps to the cellar, with Jonas close behind.

The huge sizzling boiler filled an entire corner of the cellar. While Kate checked the gauge, Jonas studied the array of pistols spread on her workbench, some dating back to before the war. "I'm not sure I know what you meant earlier when you said you wished you never invented your . . . our machine."

She joined him. "It's not fair that I should get rich from the carpet cleaner when you turned down the one chance you had of getting rich from your hearing facilitator."

Jonas could think of a lot of emotions he'd like to see in Kate's eyes. Pity was not one of them. But at least it wasn't anger or suspicion, and he was desperate enough at the moment to consider this a step forward.

"I'm sorry, Kate, for causing you so much trouble. This should be a happy time in your life. I didn't mean—"

"I don't blame you," she said. "The two of us inventing an identical machine. Who would ever think such a thing possible?" After a moment, she continued, "Maybe . . . maybe we can take a lesson from Mr. Sears and Mr. Roebuck. Why, they have over a million dollars in capital and assets. Or so they say. Why can't we do likewise, you and me?"

He didn't want to talk business, not when she was looking so enticingly soft and he was aching to take her in his arms. "I don't understand. What do you propose?"

"I'll write to the patent board and request that both our names be put on the patent."

"I don't think that will work. A patent can only be issued, as is clearly stated in the rules of practice, to the first and true inventor."

Undaunted, she considered other possibilities. "Forget the patent. We can still form our own company. We'll share the profits fifty-fifty. We can call it Whittaker and Hunter: producers of fine carpet cleaners and fertilizer spreaders." Her face grew more animated, her voice full and vibrant. "Think how wonderful this would be. We could call it the all-purpose machine. Our motto . . . oh, dear, we need a motto." She walked around the table. "I know." She stopped and faced him. " 'Use it inside and out.' Don't you think that has a nice ring?"

Caught up in her enthusiasm, Jonas nevertheless stared at her in astonishment. After all these weeks of trying to regain what was rightfully his, she was offering it to him on a silver platter. The strange part was that he didn't feel the slightest inclination to accept her offer. Admittedly, a few short weeks ago, he would have jumped at the chance, but not now—now he had only one goal, and it had nothing to do with business.

"I don't want the damned machine!"

A startled look crossed her face. "But this is what you've wanted. You've been trying to get your hands on my patent since I've known you."

"I know what I've been trying to do, dammit!" Did she always have to make him sound like some heartless money-grabbing rogue? "The only way I'll even consider accepting your offer is if you agree to be my wife."

"I'm offering to make you a partner without marriage."

"And I'm telling you the only thing I care about is you, us—the two of us together."

"Please, don't, Jonas. I can understand why the patent is so important to you, and I quite agree. It's only fair that we both benefit from our work. But don't lie. Please don't lie."

"I'm not lying, dammit. Listen, Kate . . . I'll sign something that would allow you to keep full rights. We can have a lawyer draw up an official paper. If this state won't allow a married woman to hold property in her own name, then we'll move to a state that will. Kate, I'll do anything—anything at all—to prove to you I'm telling the truth."

She searched his face. "You . . . you really mean that? You would sign something?"

"What do I have to do, Kate, to prove how much I love you? Yes, love you. There, now I've said it, and this time I have not the slightest reservation. I don't care about the patent. I don't care about anything but you."

Her gaze was riveted on his face, searching for some telling line or movement that would prove or disprove his declaration of love. Much to her utter joy, everything her heart told her was true was readily confirmed by what she saw in his face.

Love shone like the sun from his eyes. It radiated from his face and danced upon his lips as he kept repeating the words over and over. "I love you, Kate."

"Oh, Jonas!" She threw her arms around his neck. "I was so afraid to believe.... I thought you were only interested in my patent.... I love you, too!"

His arms around her waist, he crushed her to him. Kate loved him! The words wrapped around his heart like loving arms. She loved him!

And he loved her!

Warm desire erupted into heated passion as his lips met hers. Dropping kisses on her forehead and nose, then capturing her mouth again, he reached for the tiny pearl buttons on her dress. Vowing to talk her into replacing such annoyingly small buttons with a much more sensible and expeditious metal fastener, his fingers trembled as he worked her bodice free. Finally, he was able to slip his hand inside her chemise.

The warm firmness of her breast filled his hand and he lowered his head to capture the rosy peak between his teeth. Moaning with pleasure, she arched her back.

He released the tie at her waist and her skirt puddled at her feet in a whisper of fabric. Trailing feathery kisses down the length of her, he eased her bright red petticoats upward and ran his hand up one shapely leg all the way to her warm smooth thigh.

Deepening the kiss, he eased her onto the wooden table, pushing the pistols and tools aside to make room.

"You're so beautiful, Kate." He held her gaze as he lowered the metal fastener on his trousers and released his pulsing hard member.

"Oh!" Kate gasped, looking every bit as impressed as any man could hope for.

Jonas beamed from ear to ear. "Do you like it?"

"Oh, yes," she whispered in awe. "Do you have metal fasteners on all your trousers?"

It took him a full stunned moment to see the teasing lights in her eyes. He burst out laughing. "Oh, Kate." He captured her face in his hands.

"Look at me," he whispered.

Something flickered in the depths of her eyes as she understood his meaning. Her gaze traveled the length of him. "Touch me," he whispered.

Her eyes flew up to meet his. "I never touched a man before."

He looked at her in wonder. She worked with things that most men would never dare touch, experimented with explosives and electricity, elements that even he hesitated to tackle at times. There was so much she could teach him; never had it occurred to him that she would ever need him as a tutor.

Awed by the responsibility suddenly placed on him, and wanting to do right by her, he took her hand in his and dropped a kiss on her fingertips before guiding her palm to him and encouraging her to explore. "Touch me," he whispered again.

He felt her trembling fingers upon his male hardness. At first she touched him with tentative strokes, but her boldness grew and the pressure of her fingers increased accordingly.

The teasing lights had left her eyes and had been replaced by the smoky look of passion and desire.

But he read something else in her eyes, something that fervently meant her love for him was every bit as deep and abiding as his own.

No shyness remained on her face and even less remained in her hands, which were fast becoming increasingly inventive. She wrapped her fingers around the length of his penis and squeezed him tight, sending warm shivery waves racing through his body. Feathering a gentle touch across the sensitive head, she made it impossible for him to lie still.

Writhing in ecstasy, he moaned her name. "Oh, Kate. Dear, sweet, Kate. What are you doing to me?"

Feeling him shudder beneath her touch, Kate felt a hot surge inside that filled her heart with feelings that could never be expressed with words. How she loved knowing she could bring him so much pleasure. Knowing what she was capable of doing to him made her feel both powerful and weak. Her inventive mind had never been so imaginative, her hands so brazen.

"Good God," he gasped aloud. "I thought you'd never done this before!" He grabbed her by the shoulders and rolled on top of her. The heat of his body coursed down the length of her. "Are you ready?" he whispered.

For answer, she spread her legs, opening to him like a flower opens to the sun. He released the tie at her waist and eased her lace-trimmed drawers down the length of her legs. Tossing the lacy garment aside, he reached beneath her petticoats to touch the silky moist warmth between her thighs.

Kate shuddered and sighed happily. It was something else she had never done, let a man touch her so intimately, and she absorbed all the new and wondrous sensations his touch elicited, squealing with delight when he pressed his fingers against a particularly sensitive spot.

"Oh, God, Kate. I've wanted this so much."

With slow deliberate movements, he removed his hand, and when she protested, he kissed her feverish lips and whispered, "I have something better." He touched her with the tip of his throbbing manhood, rubbing it against the soft nestled curls before gently entering her.

She braced herself for the pain she'd heard young women talk about, surprised it was nothing more than a sweet burning sensation that was soon replaced with divine ecstasy.

Instinctively, she followed his lead, matching the rhythm he set, slow at first, increasing with speed and urgency. She sensed something beyond her reach, some divine prize that seemed outside the realm of reality.

Not knowing what it was she was so desperately trying to capture, she lost herself to the whirl of exciting new sensations until she was overcome by tingling, shivering, and freeing waves that told her she had reached her goal.

The trembling release of her body matched his shuddering response. They clung to each other until the final tremors faded away.

He rolled off her, took her in his arms, and dropped a kiss onto her smooth damp forehead. "It was every bit as wonderful as I had imagined," he whispered, and when she didn't reply, he added, "I know the first time is never as wonderful for a woman. But it will get better, Kate. I swear."

"I can't imagine it being any more wonderful than it was today," Kate said, and there was no mistaking the honesty in her voice.

His heart was so filled with love, he felt as if it would burst. Despite his amazing performance of moments earlier, he suddenly felt so inadequate, so undeserving of her love. "I'm sorry, Kate. Our first time shouldn't have been on a table in the cellar. It should have been . . . I should have made it more special for you."

She reached up to push a strand of dark glossy hair away from his forehead. Looking deep into his eyes, she trailed her fingers along the side of his face. "It was special," she whispered in awe. "I simply can't believe how everything works so well together. You know, the male parts. The female parts. Who would ever think that two people could fit so splendidly together? It was as if we had both been carved from a single source."

"A single source. I like that idea."

"It's astounding." Her eyes shone as she considered all the possibilities that suddenly occurred to her. "Has anyone ever made love standing up?"

"Well, I suppose so," he said.

"What about sitting down?"

"Of course, why not?"

"And what would happen if the woman was on top?"

He chuckled. "Why don't we find out?" He pulled her on top of him, her petticoats bunched between them at the waist. She sighed as she wiggled next to him; he moaned in pleasure when her body conformed so perfectly to his.

"You're right, Kate. Everything fits perfectly." He nuzzled her ear and moaned in ecstasy as a fresh surge of energy raced to his groin. Pressing his body against hers, he tried to ignore the hissing sound that filled the room. Finally, the sound grew too loud to ignore. "What is that strange noise?"

"Noise?" Kate lifted her head to listen. "Oh, no. The boiler!"

Chapter 35

The explosion jolted the entire town, sending its residents running for cover. Aunt Hattie, who had the misfortune of demonstrating the hearing aid during the time of the explosion, dropped to the floor in panic. "It's the end of the world, Barney, and don't you try to tell me it's not!"

"It's Kate, and we better go and see what damages she's done this time."

Aunt Hattie and Uncle Barney joined the throng of people marching down Main Street toward Rocking Horse Lane. Sheriff Williams was running alongside the crowd, waving his hat and trying to maintain order.

"Hold your horses!" he shouted. "I'll handle it."

"What good are you going to do?" Smoky Joe shouted back.

"Stop your arguing!" Aunt Hattie said. "My niece could be injured."

"She ain't never been injured before," Curly said.

"That don't mean she's not injured this time!"

"It looks like Kate's okay," Uncle Barney yelled out. "Look."

Kate stood next to Jonas on the front porch. The two of them were covered from head to toe in plaster and soot. Jonas held Jimmy in his arms. Jimmy, still sleepy-eyed from his nap, was the only one of the three who didn't look a wreck.

"That must have been some explosion," Sheriff Williams said, eyeing Kate's red petticoat and still unbuttoned bodice, which she held together with her hand.

"My word!" Aunt Hattie gasped. "Do something, Barney!"

Barney pulled off his vest and quickly wrapped it around his niece. "Are you all right?"

Kate nodded and glanced at Jonas. "The safety valve on the boiler still doesn't work."

Uncle Barney looked Jonas up and down. "What happened to your shirt, young man? And why is my niece standing in public dressed in her undergarments?"

"Barney!" Aunt Hattie scolded. "What are you thinking of? Anyone can see that Kate and Mr. Hunter barely escaped with their lives. We're lucky the blast did nothing more than blow off their clothes."

"Heaven help us," muttered Thelma, tugging at her high-collared shirtwaist as if she feared another blast would blow off her own apparel.

"We're lucky they didn't blow the whole town up," Smoky Joe yelled out, his face gray.

"I say throw them both in jail," Narrowsmith demanded, sneezing.

"You can't do that!" Jonas said. He handed Jimmy over to Uncle Barney and then turned to face the sheriff.

"And why can't I throw you in jail?" Sheriff Williams demanded to know.

"Because . . ." The crowd fell silent and waited. Jonas cleared his throat and tried again. Inspiration was bound to strike. But as the seconds began to stretch into minutes, he knew that if he didn't think of something fast, jail was exactly where they were heading.

Sighing, he accepted the inevitable. He needed an idea and he didn't have time to go through the usual thought processes. He glanced at Kate, but knowing how his mind went blank when he kissed her, he grabbed Aunt Hattie instead, and conjuring up all the boring descriptions of French fashions he had the misfortune of knowing, he gave her a resounding kiss. "Sorry, Aunt Hattie," he said upon releasing her. "This is an emergency."

"Don't apologize," Aunt Hattie said, fanning herself with her hand. "I love emergencies."

Jonas turned back to Sheriff Williams, who was looking at him as if he'd gone mad. Jonas made a mental note to explain the inner workings of an inventor's mind to the sheriff at a later time. Now his only thought was to keep Kate out of jail. "You can't put us in jail, Sheriff, because ... Kate has agreed to be my wife."

Kate's mouth fell open and it was then he remembered she hadn't actually said she would marry him. Her big blue eyes searched his and for a moment he feared she was going to dispute his claim.

"You are going to be my wife, aren't you, Kate?" He searched her soot-covered face. Her hair fell to her shoulders in a mass of tangled curls, the ruffle on her red petticoat was torn, but to his eyes, she had never looked more beautiful. His heart was so filled with love, he doubted he could survive if she turned him down again. "I love you."

For the longest time, Kate made no reply. The sheriff rolled his weight from one foot to the other. Aunt Hattie checked the battery on her hearing facilitator. Curly scratched his head, and Jimmy grew restless in Jonas's arms.

When at last Kate spoke, her clear melodious

voice floated over the crowd like music from a symphony orchestra. "I love you, too, Jonas Hunter." She lifted her voice so loud, Aunt Hattie didn't need her hearing aid to hear. "And if you still want to marry a woman that looks like something the cat dragged in the house, all I can say is, I would be proud to be your wife."

Aunt Hattie let out a whooping sound. "Did you hear that, everyone? Kate's getting married."

Her cry echoed throughout the crowd. "Kate? Married?"

"Married, you say?"

Thelma looked downright impressed. "Who would have ever thought it?"

A farmer's wife nudged her tall homely daughter. "What did I tell you? There *is* a lid for every pot."

While the crowd exclaimed and cheered, Kate and Jonas stood staring at each other in starry-eyed wonder.

Smoky Joe crossed his arms in front of him. "Does this mean she'll stop trying to blow up the town?"

The sheriff looked confused. "I don't understand what Kate gettin' married has to do with anythin'. There's still the little matter of d'turbin' the peace."

Aunt Hattie looked horrified. "Why, Eugene, what are you thinking? You're not going to put this young couple in jail, are you? Anyone can see how much they love each other."

"One has nothin' to do with the other—"

"I can't believe it!" Maizie Campbell piped in, her arms filled with fresh-picked daisies. "Them being engaged and all."

"But—"

Angry shouts rose from the crowd, all directed

at the sheriff. "How dare you lock up these two innocent people?"

"What kind of heartless person are you?"

"Your father would not have done such a thing!"

The sheriff pulled off his hat and threw it to the ground. "My father, my father! I'm mighty tired of hearin' what my father would or would not do. I'm the sheriff around here and I'll decide who gits to the spend the night in my jail."

Curly tried to placate him. "You don't hafta git yourself all riled up."

"I'm not riled up. I'm just tellin' you how it is." The sheriff turned to Kate and Jonas. "D'turbin' the peace is a serious o-fense. I'm givin' you just a few minutes to get yourselves decent and then you're comin' with me."

"Well, I never!" Aunt Hattie declared.

"Of all the heartless . . ."

". . . them engaged to be married and everything."

The sheriff looked chagrined. "Do you think I like this any better than you folks? It's damned inconv'nient to have a prisoner, let alone two. It means havin' to clean out the jail cell agin. Where am I goin' to put my Independence Day decorations? That's what I want to know."

If the sheriff thought he would solicit sympathy or even approval from the folks of Hogs Head, he was sadly mistaken. The crowd was clearly on Jonas and Kate's side and remained with the couple long after the sheriff had escorted the two to the cellar to retrieve their clothes and hauled them down to the jailhouse. The crowd waited outside as Sheriff Williams cleared out the cluttered cell, and continued to camp on the street throughout the remainder of the day.

For his part, Sheriff Williams sulked and pouted.

He paced back and forth in front of the cell, complaining about his lot in life. "Do you know what it's like bein' the son of a hero?" he moaned.

Kate, feeling sorry for him, shook her head. "I have no idea."

"Well, I'll tell you what it's like—"

"Do you have a file?" Jonas asked.

The sheriff stopped his pacing. "What?"

"A metal file. Or something with a pointed tip. I'm trying to fix this lock so you won't have to stand guard all night." He winked at Kate.

"That's mighty thoughtful of you," Sheriff Williams said. He dug in the top drawer of his desk. "Will this do?" He held up a steel file.

"I'm most obliged."

The sheriff handed Jonas the tool and proceeded to tell Kate his tale of woe. "Is it my fault," he asked after explaining about the nine Brannon boys his father had captured, "that the town has no crim'nals?"

"Of course it's not," Kate said. "If you had your way, I'm sure the town would be filled with criminals."

"Absolutely!" Sheriff Williams agreed. "Why, I'd have the cell filled twenty-four hours a day. 'Course, that would mean I'd have to find me another place to store my Independence Day decorations and—"

"Do you have any oil?" Jonas asked.

"I have a can in my desk."

While the sheriff went to fetch the oil can, Kate leaned over Jonas's shoulder. "I think it's downright thoughtful of you to fix the lock for the sheriff."

Jonas glanced over his shoulder, his eyes smoldering. "Of course you know if I fix the lock, the sheriff will most likely go home?"

"I dare say he shall."

"It'll be just you and me. Alone."

She gave his neck a playful nip and whispered in his ear, "Does that mean we can try it standing up?"

Grinning, he speeded up his efforts to repair the lock. "Why not?"

"What about if . . ."

His eyes widened. If he didn't get the damned lock working, the blasted metal fastener in his trousers was going to come apart without any help from either one of them.

The sheriff returned with the oil can. Jonas took the can and gave the lock a generous squirt. He closed the cell door and shook it. The lock held tight.

The sheriff looked pleased. "I'm mighty obliged to you. I've tried gettin' that lock fixed for years."

"It was my pleasure."

"Anythin' I can do to repay you?"

Jonas avoided Kate's eyes. "Nothing, Sheriff. Consider it my gift."

"Well, I can't tell you how much I appr'ciate your gen'rosity." The sheriff thrust his hand between the bars and shook Jonas's hand.

"Why don't you go home and get some rest, Sheriff? Miss Whittaker and I aren't going anywhere till you get back."

"Well, now, isn't that nice of you to be concerned over my welfare?"

Kate smiled. "We only have one sheriff. I guess we better take care of him."

"It's mighty decent of you both." The sheriff plucked his hat from the wooden peg by the door. "I'll send the missus over later with some grub."

"Take your time," Jonas called after him.

No sooner had the sheriff left the jailhouse than

Jonas slipped his hands around Kate's waist. "I believe we have some inventing to do."

His lips felt warm and demanding on hers. Raising herself upward, she wiggled her pelvis against his and forced him to deepen the kiss.

Pressing his cheek against hers, he circled her breast with his hand. "I apologized the first time for taking you on a table. Little did I know there would be worse places to make love."

"Worse places than a jail cell?" Kate looked positively intrigued.

He threw his head back and laughed. "You're right. It would be fun trying to find a worse place than this." He ran his warm moist lips down her neck. "Now, what was your idea about making love while standing up?"

The door flew open and Aunt Hattie's voice floated in. "Kate, Jonas ... guess what? We decided to celebrate your engagement."

Kate and Jonas quickly pulled away from each other. Kate smiled sheepishly at the small gathering. "Celebrate?"

"Yes, of course celebrate," Aunt Hattie said, clearing off the sheriff's desk to make room for the food. "It's a crying shame that a young couple decides to get married and then has to spend the night alone in jail."

"Terrible," Jonas said grimly.

Kate looked up at him with beseeching eyes. "Aunt Hattie means well," she whispered, forgetting that Aunt Hattie had her hearing facilitator attached to her hat.

"You're damned right I mean well. I have a surprise for you," Aunt Hattie continued. She turned to the door and nodded to Uncle Barney, who had been blocking the doorway. Uncle Barney stepped aside, spreading his arm in a wide arc, as if he were a master of ceremonies introducing a performer.

Jimmy grinned from the open door, a crutch beneath each arm.

"Jimmy!" Kate grabbed at the bars with both hands. "You're walking!"

Jimmy beamed happily and pushed out his chest. "And I don't care if anyone laughs at me," he said. "Once they get used to me, they aren't gonna laugh."

"He insisted upon coming to visit you both in jail," Aunt Hattie explained. "Couldn't keep him away."

Kate's eyes filled with tears. "Oh, Jimmy . . ." Never had she felt so happy. First her engagement to Jonas . . . now Jimmy walking. What more could she possibly ask for?

Jonas slid his arm around her waist. Even he looked pleased. "Aunt Hattie's right. This calls for a celebration."

Curly did a little jig and held up a bottle of his moonshine. Thelma plopped herself upon a stool and proceeded to work on her "designs."

"She's a regular designing woman," Aunt Hattie muttered beneath her breath.

"Shhh, Aunt Hattie," Kate said. "This is a celebration."

"It's no reason for her to go around putting on airs," Aunt Hattie whispered. In a louder voice, she asked, "Anyone for fresh rolls and cheese? Or roast beef and ham?" She leaned toward the cell door. "Now, don't you two worry about a thing. We brought along our bedrolls so we can stay the night."

Jonas glanced at Kate as if to confirm what he'd heard. To Aunt Hattie he said, "Did you say bedrolls?"

"Why, yes." Aunt Hattie looked pleased with herself. "They're outside in the wagon. You didn't think I'd let two of my most favorite people stay all night alone in this dreadful place, did you?"

It wasn't easy to keep the disappointment from his face. "No, Aunt Hattie, we never thought that."

The sheriff arrived at his office the following morning to find the floor littered with sleeping bodies. "What in blazes?"

Bedrolls came alive as everyone woke and began talking at once. Jimmy had spent most of the night walking around on his crutches, anxious to make up for lost time. Kate had finally convinced him to lay down, but he'd gotten very little sleep and was now on his feet, trying to maneuver his crutches around the prone bodies and rumpled bedrolls.

"Quiet!" Sheriff Williams yelled. "Or I'll put you all in jail for d'turbin' the peace."

"You don't have to get yourself in a huff!" Aunt Hattie protested, pulling her nightcap off her head and shaking out her faded red hair. "We were only doing our civic duty."

"Well, you can do your civic duty and get out of my office."

He stepped over Curly, who was still sound asleep and, judging from the smell of alcohol, would probably remain so for the rest of the day. Lifting the key off a nail over his desk, the sheriff unlocked the cell. "Now, remember, you two. No more trouble."

Jimmy insisted upon walking home on his crutches. Kate walked beside him, encouraging him all the way, while Jonas headed back to the boardinghouse to clean up.

Upon arriving home, Jimmy fell exhausted across

the divan in the parlor and Kate hurried upstairs
to bathe.

Kate pulled off her clothes and stared at herself
naked in the mirror. Never had she looked at herself with such uncritical eyes. Since making love
to Jonas, she'd come to appreciate her body in a
completely different way. Yes, indeed, she thought,
turning this way and that, studying each feminine
line without embarrassment. The human body was,
indeed, a wondrous thing, far more wonderful than
anything man or woman could ever invent.

"Oh, Jonas," she whispered, feeling a tender
warmth in her heart as she said his name. "I can
hardly wait to be your wife."

After a long leisurely soak in the bathtub, she
washed her hair, brushed it dry, and arranged the
burnished curls on top of her head. She was in love.
In beautiful, magical, wonderful love. And nothing—nothing!—was ever going to change that.

Chapter 36

Fresh from her bath and feeling so happy she could hardly keep still, Kate decided to go to the general store to pick up the mail. Jimmy insisted upon going with her.

"Are you sure?" she asked. "I don't want you to tire yourself."

Jimmy balanced himself on his crutches and tried to open the front door. "I won't tire myself."

"We could take the wagon."

"I want to walk."

"Very well."

They arrived at the general store feeling hot and thirsty. Aunt Hattie, who was sorting through the day's mail, greeted them with a smile. "You're getting better all the time with those things, Jimmy. Come and pick out a piece of sugar candy, and I'll pour you both a glass of lemonade." She hustled to the back of the store.

A local hog farmer by the name of Hank Bexler was standing at the counter. He was a wiry man with an unruly shock of white hair and a slight limp. He looked Jimmy up and down and nodded approval. Kate knew him as a kind, hardworking man but, because of his age, had not thought to ask him to give Jimmy a home.

"You handle those crutches mighty fine, young man," he said. He bent over to look Jimmy square in the face. "You're that orphan boy Jimmy, aren't you?"

Jimmy nodded.

"How'd you like to come and live with me? My wife is bedridden and she could use someone like you to keep her company. What do you say?"

Kate moved to Jimmy's side. "That's a mighty generous offer, Mr. Bexler. I . . . we'll have to let you know."

Mr. Bexler straightened. "It's probably the best offer the boy'll get."

"You're probably right," Kate said. "I'll let you know." Kate felt a sense of dismay, though she couldn't imagine why. Mr. Bexler and his wife had raised a fine family of eight boys and three girls. Not only were they experienced parents, but they had attended church every Sabbath—come rain, shine, or snow—until Mrs. Bexler's health failed. They would be good to Jimmy. There was no reason Kate shouldn't accept Mr. Bexler's generous offer. No reason at all. And yet . . .

Mr. Bexler studied her sharply. "Very well, Kate. I trust you'll let me know when you make up your mind."

"Yes, of course. I appreciate your offer."

Mr. Bexler grunted in response, took his purchase, and left the store.

Kate suddenly felt depressed, but because Jimmy was watching her, she forced a smile. "Pick out your candy."

"Am I going to live with that man?" Jimmy asked.

"I don't know. We'll see. He and Mrs. Bexler are very kind, very good people. Now, what kind of candy do you like?"

"I don't want any."

Kate looked at him in surprise. "But why not?"

"I just don't want any."

"Here we are," Aunt Hattie said, carrying a tray with three glasses of lemonade. She set the tray down on the counter. "Oh, by the way, Kate, you have a letter. From the United States Patent Office."

Kate's heart leaped with excitement. "Why didn't you say so? You know how long I've been waiting for that letter."

Aunt Hattie shuffled behind the counter. "I can't think of everything." She pulled a large envelope from the w slot and slid it across the counter toward Kate.

"Finally!" Kate picked up the envelope and held it to her fast-beating heart for a moment before ripping open the envelope. "Oh, look!" she cried out. Her name was written on the parchment certificate in broad script. The patent was signed by President Cleveland and the secretary of state and, of course, witnessed by Mr. Hobbs and Jonas. She even had her very own number.

She held the document up for her aunt and Jimmy to see. Aunt Hattie scanned it, looking unimpressed. "Mercy me, is this what you've been waiting for? A piece of paper?"

"This piece of paper makes everything official. Jonas and I intend to move full speed ahead with our production plans. We were going to call our company Whittaker and Hunter. But after we're married, I suppose we'll have to change the name to Hunter and Hunter." She smiled. "I know what we'll call our machine. We'll call it the Hunter and Hunter Miracle Machine." She hesitated for a moment, trying to recall the motto she'd thought up previously. " 'Use it inside and out.' What do you think?"

"It doesn't seem right to me that Mr. Hunter . . .

Jonas . . . should get all the credit. You're the one who invented it."

"That's true. But so did he. We both invented the same machine. So it seems only fair that he should get part of the credit as well. That's why I'm calling it Hunter and Hunter."

"It still don't seem right to me. You should have your own name on it."

"You think I should call it Whittaker?"

"Either that or the name of your parents."

"Hoover." Kate made a face. She always hated her real name. "I think the name Hunter has a much better ring to it."

"Well, if you say so. Just as long as you don't let that awful Mr. Sears put it into his catalogue." Aunt Hattie gave her a stern look. "You won't, will you?"

"Of course not, Aunt Hattie. You'll be the sole distributor."

"Then I say the Hunter and Hunter Miracle Machine calls for a celebration. Why don't you ask Jonas to come to dinner?" Aunt Hattie slid an arm around Jimmy's shoulder. "What do you say to that, young man?"

Jimmy shrugged with a look of indifference and said nothing.

Kate glanced at Jimmy, wondering what had put him in such a melancholy mood. Perhaps the walk had been too exerting. "I'll stop by the boarding-house and invite him now. Can Jimmy stay here with you?" Jimmy liked spending time with Aunt Hattie, especially now that she could hear.

"Of course he can. Since you're going to see Jonas, why don't you take him this letter?" She pulled an envelope from the H slot. "It looks mighty important. The return address says it's from the Stanley Manufacturing Company in New York."

Kate felt like her whole world had suddenly crashed to the ground. "Stanley?" She recognized the name from the list she'd obtained while in Washington. She had written to the company a few weeks earlier, but had yet to receive a reply. How did Jonas get such a quick response? Unless . . .

She took the letter from her aunt and studied the envelope.

"Is there something wrong, Kate?" Aunt Hattie asked.

"I don't know. I just don't know."

She left the store and drove her aunt's wagon to Mrs. Applegate's Boardinghouse. No sooner had she driven up in front than Jonas hurried outside to greet her. It was obvious by his wide grin how happy he was to see her.

"Kate!"

Without saying a word, she thrust the envelope in his hands and watched his face, hoping her suspicions proved untrue. "You wrote to the Stanley Manufacturing Company about my machine!"

He stared at the envelope for a long while before raising his eyes to meet hers. "Our machine, Kate. You agreed that we both invented it."

"Not until recently. You had to have written the letter weeks ago, long before we agreed upon anything. I wrote to the same company myself shortly after returning from Washington, and I've yet to receive a reply."

"I'm not going to lie to you, Kate. I wrote the letter on the day I arrived in Hogs Head. I mailed it from your aunt's store. But you have to understand. At the time, I honestly believed you had stolen my invention. I was convinced it was only a matter of time before I found enough evidence to prove it."

"But the patent had been given to me. How did you explain *that* to Mr. Stanley?"

"All I said in my letter was the patent was pending."

"I see. So naturally Mr. Stanley would assume that you owned the patent. It all makes sense. I offered you part ownership, but that wasn't enough. You want to marry me just so you can have the entire patent for yourself, in *your* own name."

"That's not why I want you to marry me."

A knot rose from her stomach, seeming to choke off her very breathing. "It's all so clear. How long did you intend to remain my husband?"

"Forever, Kate. I swear."

He reached for her arm, but she pulled away. "Don't touch me."

"Would you at least listen to what I have to say?"

"There's nothing you can say that will make me believe you. I should have known better than to trust you. I thought . . . Oh, God, I can't believe how foolish I was." Her eyes filled with tears. "I thought you really cared for me."

"Care?" He looked at her incredulously. "My God, Kate, I love you! You've got to believe me."

She couldn't believe him, not ever again. No matter how much she wanted to. Wracked with the most unbelievable pain, she picked up the thin leather traces and snapped the whip over the horse's head.

"Kate, wait!"

The wagon lurched forward, leaving him in a cloud of dust.

Chapter 37

The train was over an hour late arriving in New York City. Exhausted from the long journey, Kate hired a hansom cab to take her to the Walston Arms Hotel. Despite its pretentious name, the hotel was nothing more than a dark, dismal building with no modern conveniences, not so much as a single incandescent light.

The dated hotel did have one thing in its favor; it provided relatively inexpensive accommodations. Her invention had already cost her most of her savings. If she didn't earn back some of the money she'd spent in recent weeks, she would have to find some other means of support.

After checking into the cramped room, with its threadbare carpet and stained walls, Kate stared out the open window. The room was stifling hot, with not a breath of air.

She leaned over the peeling sill to stare down upon an unbelievable tangle of telephone, telegraph, and electrical wires strung from a forest of tall poles. Kate had read about New York's amazing network of wires. Critics said they provided an aesthetic blight and safety hazard. More than one building had reportedly burned to the ground while firemen fought to free a hook or ladder or other apparatus from the muddle of overhead wires. Years earlier, the mayor had ordered some of the unsightly poles to be chopped down, "wires and all!" In Kate's estimation, the mayor would do well to reissue the order today.

Seemingly oblivious to the unsightly wires strung above their heads, a throng of businessmen, dressed in dark suits and derby hats, hurried home after a hard day's work in the many office buildings that made up the city. The street teemed with horses and carriages, their iron wheels rattling along the flagstones. Bicycles, including big-wheelers known as boneshakers, weaved in and out of traffic. Hawkers pushed their wooden carts. A bill-poster stopped to stick a paper advertisement onto one of the electric poles, his bucket of paste swinging from his arm. The air reverberated with city sounds. Never had she seen so many people at one time. Never had she felt so lonely.

"Oh, Jonas," she whispered, tears burning her eyes. "I wanted so much to trust you." Kate would never have believed it possible for a heart to literally break in two. But what else could explain the unbearable pain she felt inside? The numbness on the outside?

No matter how hard she tried, she couldn't seem to put an end to the terrible cloud of unhappiness she felt. Growing weary of the rushing crowds, she pushed away from the windowsill and glanced about the room, wondering how she was ever going to get through the night that loomed ahead, let alone the days, the months, the years to follow.

Catching a glimpse of herself in the beveled mirror over the chest of drawers, and horrified by what she saw, she walked over to the washstand and scrubbed her tear-stained face. She glanced in the mirror again. Her face was clean, but her eyes were still red from all the crying she'd done. She'd closed herself in a private compartment on the train and sobbed her heart out all the way to New York. No wonder the clerk at the desk downstairs looked so reluctant to rent her a room.

She hadn't cried so much since she was five years old and was made to sit in the baggage car all the way to Hogs Head.

Well, she wasn't a child anymore and she had no intention of sitting around and feeling sorry for herself. Nor was she going to pine away for a man. Especially one who was a conniving, cheating ... handsome and endearing ... thief!

Fighting back fresh tears, she yanked the hairpins out of her hair and reached in the valise for her hairbrush. She drew the bristles through her tresses and tried not to recall Jonas touching her hair.

When she could no longer hold the memories at bay, she tossed the hairbrush onto the dressing table. Then, grasping the entire bulk of her hair in one hand, she wound it into a bun at the back of her head, securing it with hairpins.

She had no one else to blame but herself. She had known he was a scoundrel on the day they first met. Still, she'd allowed him to ingratiate himself to her family, to Jimmy, to the whole town. More than that, she had allowed him to wheedle his way into her heart, her soul, her very being until it felt as if he were a permanent part of her.

She stared at the mirror, barely recognizing the grim pale face staring back. "Oh, Jonas," she whispered. "How could you?"

Jonas pounded on the Whittaker door hours after good manners dictated. Uncle Barney opened the door with a fierce scowl. "Have you any idea what time it is, young man?" He was dressed in a white cotton nightshirt that barely reached his knobby knees.

"I've got to talk to Kate."

"Who is it?" Aunt Hattie called from the top of the stairs, her ever-present hearing facilitator attached to her nightcap.

Barney half turned to answer. "Jonas. Says he wants to talk to Kate."

Aunt Hattie rushed to her husband's side. "Well, it's about time you showed your face. What kind of a man would let Kate take off for New York and not try to stop her?"

Jonas felt sick. "Kate's in New York?" It had been a terrible mistake to wait so long before trying to talk to her. He should have followed her home immediately and insisted she hear him out. Maybe it he hadn't been so angry and hurt that she would question his motivations after everything they had shared, he would have.

Hattie studied his face and apparently thinking his distress was sincere, nodded. "Left on yesterday's train."

"Damn! What am I going to do?"

Uncle Barney shook his head in disgust. "If you had any sense, you'd go home and get some sleep." He turned and shuffled up the stairs, leaving Hattie to deal with the problem.

"You look awful."

He was surprised by the note of sympathy in Aunt Hattie's voice. Lord, he must look like hell.

"Come in and I'll fix you a cup of my famous herbal tea."

She led him through the darkened parlor into the kitchen. Jonas sat at the table holding his head while she put the teakettle on to boil. After setting out cups and saucers, Aunt Hattie sat on the chair opposite him.

"This has been a horrible couple of days," she

moaned. "What with Kate taking off and Jimmy refusing to leave his room."

Jonas lifted his head in alarm. "What's wrong with Jimmy?"

"Wish I knew. He won't talk to me. Won't even talk to his uncle."

Jonas glanced up in the direction of Jimmy's room. "Do you mind if I look in on him?"

"Don't mind at all."

Jonas rose. "I'll be back for that tea." He hurried through the darkened parlor, remembering to side-step the holes in the floor and duck the wires overhead, and took the stairs two at a time. The door to Jimmy's room stood ajar. He pushed it open further and sensed a movement on the bed.

"Jimmy?"

"Jonas?"

"It's me." Jonas felt for the light chain overhead and pulled. He blinked against the glaring white electrical light that flooded the room. "Aunt Hattie said you're not doing too well." He walked to the side of the bed. Jimmy's crutches were on the floor, broken in two. Jonas bent over and picked up a piece of the splintered wood.

Jimmy looked away.

Jonas tossed the wood aside and dragged a chair across the floor next to Jimmy's bed. He straddled the chair backward and rested his arms on the upper rail. "I think you'd better tell me what's going on. Did someone laugh at you?"

Jimmy shook his head.

"Did someone say something unkind?"

"No."

"What, then? Speak up, son. It'll help to talk about it. Is it because Kate's gone?"

Jimmy made no reply, but the stricken look on his face told Jonas more than any words could.

"I'm your friend," Jonas said, keeping his voice low. "You can't keep secrets from a friend."

Jimmy wiped away a tear. "Mr. Bexler said he wants to give me a home."

Jonas had only met Mr. Bexler once, but he seemed like a rather pleasant man. "Isn't that what you want? A real home. Parents?"

"I already have a real home."

"But this was only meant to be a temporary home. Besides, you need a mother *and* a father."

"I don't care about that. I want to stay with Kate."

Jonas pressed his fingers into the back of the chair. "Is that why you broke your crutches? So Mr. Bexler wouldn't want you?"

Jimmy didn't answer the question. He didn't have to.

Jonas heaved a sigh. "Have you told Kate you want to live with her?"

Jimmy nodded. "Kate said she doesn't know anything about raising children. All she knows is how to invent stuff. But that's not true. She knows about raising me."

Jonas rubbed the palms of his hands together. "I wish I could help you, Jimmy."

"Will you tell her I think she's the bestest ma in the whole wide world?"

"I'll try, Jimmy." Jonas stood, then leaned over and kissed Jimmy on the forehead. "Now, how about getting some sleep?" Jonas replaced the chair and tugged on the light chain. Jimmy's voice floated out of the darkness.

"Jonas? Mr. Hunter?"

"What is it, Jimmy?"

"I think you're the bestest pa in the whole wide world."

Taken aback by the unexpected compliment,

Jonas left the room quickly. But once outside Jimmy's room, he could hardly contain the overwhelming feelings of loss and defeat.

He pressed his fevered forehead against the cool wall of the hallway. Jimmy had unwittingly done the equivalent of reaching inside his chest and pulling out his heart. The pain was so real, so excruciatingly real, Jonas grimaced and sank to his knees. *I think you're the bestest pa . . .*

He didn't deserve Jimmy's love. Hell, he didn't even deserve Kate's.

How in the world did he ever get himself in such a mess? Moaning over a woman. Moaning over a child. All he ever wanted to do was be an inventor, make his mark on the world. Now he wouldn't care if he never invented another thing.

He pushed himself to his feet and reached for his handkerchief. He dabbed his face and blinked back the moisture in his eyes.

Catching a whiff of Kate's fragrance, he realized the door across from Jimmy's led to Kate's room. Pausing in front, he lay his hand on the door as if to absorb her essence. "Oh, Kate." Her name was an anguished cry that threatened to shatter his last thread of control. Dragging himself away from her door, he staggered down the stairs.

Jonas joined Aunt Hattie in the kitchen just as a strange whistling sound filled the air. He turned to stare at the stove, not sure if he should dive under the table or run from the house. "What in the world?"

Aunt Hattie jumped to her feet. "It's a teakettle Kate invented. It whistles when the water boils." She grabbed a pot holder and moved the kettle away from the flame.

"That's a clever idea," Jonas said. "Wish I'd thought of it." He sprawled on the chair and looked so dejected that Aunt Hattie took pity on him.

"I don't know what you and Kate fought about, but when a woman takes off for another state, it can't be good."

"It's not." Jonas had felt terrible before, but since talking to Jimmy, he felt ten times worse. On some level, it felt as if he'd failed the boy. "Kate thinks I want to marry her so I can gain ownership of her patent."

"Is she right?"

"No." He heaved a sigh. Kate's aunt had been good to him. He couldn't lie to her, no matter how ugly the truth might sound. "I admit that was my intention at first. But that was before I fell in love with her."

Aunt Hattie studied him, her eyes narrowed. "Have you told her the truth?"

"I told her I loved her. I even told her about my original intent to marry her for the patent. I explained that once I got to know her, none of that mattered. Why is it so hard for Kate to believe I love her for herself and for no other reason?"

Aunt Hattie pursed her lips. "Kate's always had to prove herself. I think it goes back to when her parents died. Kate was the only one of my sister's orphaned brood who couldn't find a home. No one wanted her. Said she was wild and destructive." Aunt Hattie grinned. "Takes after me." After a while, she added, "They shipped her to me as a last resort. After so much rejection, I suppose it's only natural that Kate would have trouble believing anyone could love her just for herself."

"What do I have to do to make her believe I do?"

"Don't ask me," Aunt Hattie said. "You're the inventor."

"If only that letter hadn't arrived." He raked both hands through his hair. "Now she won't even talk to me. What am I saying? Her not talking to me is the least of my problems. She's no longer in town. What am I going to do?"

"If I were you, I'd take my bones back to the boardinghouse, get myself a good night's sleep, and make it my business to be on the next train heading east."

"New York's a big city. I don't even know where she's staying."

"That does pose a slight problem. She wouldn't even tell me, her own aunt. But I can pretty much guess where she'll be heading first thing Monday morning."

Jonas looked up. "Of course. The Stanley Manufacturing Company." He jumped to his feet, practically knocking over the teacups. He grabbed Aunt Hattie and kissed her soundly on her cheek. "If I leave tomorrow, I'll be there in plenty of time. Aunt Hattie, you're an angel."

Aunt Hattie looked offended. But after a moment's consideration, she threw up her hands and shrugged philosophically. "Oh, well. I've been called worse things than an angel."

Chapter 38

The Stanley Manufacturing Company was an old brownstone building overlooking the muddy waters of the Hudson River. A row of windows painted green faced the street. A nickel-plated maroon-colored bicycle leaned against one wall. The cab pulled in front of the single door and stopped.

"Please be kind enough to wait," Kate told the driver, who lifted her carpet cleaner off the luggage rack and placed it alongside the narrow cobblestone road.

Kate lugged the cleaner the short distance to the door and pushed her finger against the oak push button attached to the electric doorbell. A muffled buzzing sound was all but drowned out by the deep horn of a steamer ship. She pressed the button again and waited. Overhead, seagulls gave an answering call. She was just about to ring a third time when the door opened, revealing a balding middle-aged man dressed in a dark suit.

He was clearly surprised to see a woman. "May I help you?"

"I would like to speak to Mr. Stanley."

"Do you have an appointment?"

"Mr. Stanley wrote a letter," she said vaguely, hoping to give the impression that the letter had been addressed to her.

"Very well. Follow me." He led Kate down a

dark narrow hall. The carpet cleaner rolled easily along the dull wood floor. He tapped at a door at the far end of the hall before turning the dull brass knob. "Someone to see you, sir."

Kate rolled her carpet cleaner to the doorway, but because the office was carpeted, it was necessary to lift the machine over the threshold.

"She said you wrote her a letter," the man at the door explained.

Mr. Stanley dismissed the man with a nod of his head and rose behind his desk. He was a tall, rail-thin man with sallow skin. "I'm George Stanley. And you are?"

"Kate Whittaker."

He frowned. "You said I wrote you a letter?"

"Not exactly. The letter you wrote was addressed to a Mr. Jonas Hunter."

"Ah, yes, Mr. Hunter." He walked around his desk and studied Kate's machine. "I believe he said something about this being—"

"A carpet cleaner," Kate said. "If you would be kind enough to step aside, I shall give you a demonstration."

The carpet was faded and worn and she decided it wasn't necessary to sprinkle any additional dirt on it.

She flashed Mr. Stanley a smile, surprised to find herself forcing it. She suddenly had no heart to sell her machine. What had been easy for her in the past, even a joy, now seemed like a chore. The machine was a poor substitute for the love she'd found—and lost.

Still, she had a job to do and she would do it, if it killed her. She described the machine's unique capabilities and when her words sounded hollow to her own ears, she borrowed the extravagant adjectives found in the Sears, Roebuck mail-order catalogue. If Mr. Sears saw no reason for modesty, why should she?

"This is truly the most astounding, magnificent, spectacular machine you'll ever set your eyes on." Extravagant words proved a poor substitute for genuine enthusiasm, and when it was obvious she'd failed to impress the grim-faced man, she cranked up the motor, grateful that the loud roar prohibited further speech.

Mr. Stanley leaned back against his desk as if he were about to be attacked by a wild animal. Eyes wide with dismay, he covered his ears against the blaring sound.

Kate gave him a wan smile and quickly set to work cleaning the carpet. She made the mistake of glancing at him as she worked the wand back and forth. He looked so horrified, she felt sorry for him. She was tempted to turn off the machine, but decided to finish the task she'd set for herself.

Satisfied that the carpet had been thoroughly cleaned, she turned off the machine and opened the canister. There was less dirt than she'd hoped for. Perhaps the carpet wasn't as old as it looked.

"As you can see, the dirt is collected in this cloth bag for easy disposal."

Mr. Stanley mopped his forehead with a handkerchief and straightened his bow tie. He no longer looked startled, but neither did he look impressed. If only she'd succeeded in gathering up more dirt.

"Every woman will want one of these machines," Kate continued. "It'll be the biggest boon to homemaking since the discovery of fire."

"Yes, yes, yes. I know all that." Mr. Stanley sank down in his chair.

"You know . . ." She felt encouraged. "You must have read about my carpet cleaner in the newspaper."

"Newspaper? Can't say that I did. What I mean is, I just agreed to manufacture a carpet cleaner. The inventor cleaned my carpet less than two weeks ago."

Kate felt sick. No wonder she had found so little dirt in the canister. "I don't understand. I own the patent. How could someone else market my machine?"

"It's not your machine. It's much smaller and easier to use. And quieter. Thank God it's quieter! I'd hate to think that cleaning house could render a nation of deaf housewives."

Kate stared at him, not knowing what to say. All her hard work, everything, was wasted. "I see." Close to tears, she gathered up her machine. "I won't take up any more of your time."

She left the office as quickly as possible. Dragging the carpet cleaner down the long hall, she pushed it outside with such force, it rolled in the dirt on its side. She stood and stared, teary-eyed, at the river rushing by and was tempted to throw the cleaner into the murky depths. She was even more tempted to throw herself in the river after it.

Letting her tears fall unchecked, she dragged herself to the waiting cab. Leaving the driver to haul her machine onto the baggage rack, she pulled herself into the dark interior of the carriage. Tears blurred her vision so much, she failed to notice another passenger inside the cab until she'd taken her seat.

"Hello, Kate."

"Jonas!" She didn't want him to see her crying, didn't want him to know how very much she hurt. Feeling humiliated and so very, very vulnerable, she lashed out in anger. "What are you doing here?"

"I want to talk to you."

She wiped the tears from her eyes with a swift flick of her hand. "I have nothing to say to you."

"I'm mighty relieved to hear that. That means you'll hold your tongue and read this." He thrust a piece of paper at her.

"What is it?" she asked, unable to read through her teary eyes.

"It's a legal document that says even if you marry me, you maintain sole ownership of the patent."

She threw the document back at him. "Did you really think I'd fall for such a trick?" She'd been willing to accept his offer on good faith when he first made it, but no more. As her husband, he would be entitled to her income, whether or not he owned the patent. It sickened her to think this was just another one of his tricks.

He looked at her in confusion. "What are you talking about, Kate? It's all legal. I dragged a lawyer out of bed this morning to write it up for me."

"You shouldn't have bothered!" She tried to leave the cab, but he grabbed her arm.

"Aren't you going to at least let me explain why I wrote to Mr. Stanley?"

"It doesn't matter anymore, Jonas." She squeezed her eyes shut to hold back the fresh wave of tears that threatened to fall.

"What are you talking about? What doesn't matter?"

"I'm surprised Mr. Stanley didn't tell you in his letter that someone beat me to it. It would have saved you the trouble of coming all the way to New York and seeking out a lawyer." She gave a short mirthless laugh, but only because she had to do something to release the dull pain that threatened to cut her in two. "You won, Jonas."

Jonas's mouth dropped open. "What do you

mean someone beat you to it? How could that be? You hold the patent."

"Someone else . . . another inventor . . . came up with a carpet cleaner better than mine. Didn't Mr. Stanley tell you?"

"No. All he said was that he'd be interested in seeing a demonstration of my fertilizer spreader. I have the letter here." He reached into his pocket. "See for yourself."

She glanced at the letter in his hand. "This new carpet cleaner is lighter in weight and makes far less noise. Don't you see what this means? My machine is worthless."

He took hold of her arm. "I'm sorry, Kate. You'll never know how sorry."

She yanked her arm away. She reached into her reticule for the carefully folded document she'd received from the patent office and thrust it at him. "It's all yours! Market your fertilizer spreader. See if I care!"

He shook his head. "I'm afraid it's not going to work that way, Kate. The very same technology that makes your carpet cleaner obsolete also affects my machine."

She wiped away the fresh flood of tears that ran down her cheeks. "Oh. I . . . never thought of that." The differences between them no longer seemed to matter as she realized their common problem; they were both out of business. "I . . . I'm so sorry, Jonas," she said, forgetting her own misery. "What are you going to do?"

"Exactly what I came to New York to do. I'm going to convince you to marry me."

She stared at him, not knowing what to think. "Haven't you heard a single word I've said? My patent is worthless!"

"I know."

She studied his face for a long while. "There won't be any financial benefits, nothing."

"Kate, if it were money I wanted, I'd have worked out a deal with Mr. Sears."

Kate felt a warm glow begin to flow through her. Lord, how in the world could she have doubted him? "You ... you mean you really do want to marry me, even now?"

He captured her face in his hands and gazed into her eyes with loving softness. "I never wanted anything so much in my life."

She shook her head in disbelief and wonder. "I have nothing ... no patent. No machine. I can't even get my boiler working. And my fuel-driven buggy is a failure!"

"It's you I love, Kate. I don't care about patents and machines. I don't care about anything but proving my love to you."

Unable to speak, she melted into his arms. "I ... I love you, too." She was crying and laughing at the same time.

He sucked in his breath and it caught in his chest for a long while before he could let it out. Showering her with kisses, running his fervent lips up one side of her face and down the other, he told her again and again how much he loved her. "I have no means of support," he whispered at last.

"Nor do I," she purred softly.

"I have no business taking a wife."

"And I have even less business taking a husband."

He held her at arm's length. "How can you say that?"

"My cooking is a horror, and I can't seem to do even the simplest household tasks without mishap. The last time I laundered clothes, I blew them up and Uncle Barney's long underwear landed on the church steeple."

Jonas threw his head back in laughter. "What makes you think those things matter to me? God, I'd much rather have a woman who understands the intricacies of a motor and who can wire a house for electricity than one who can cook and wash clothes."

"Really?" she asked incredulously. "That's not what Thelma said."

"It just shows you what she knows." He pressed his mouth against hers and moaned softly when she pushed her tongue between his teeth, then playfully nipped his lower lip.

He leaned back against the leather seat and sighed a deep happy sigh. There was nothing, absolutely nothing more satisfying than kissing an inventive woman. Unless, of course, it was making love to her, which he intended to do just as soon as he could get her back to her hotel.

Chapter 39

Kate and Jonas spent every minute of every hour that night making passionate and glorious love. Kate turned out to be even more resourceful than he had thought possible. Every time he was convinced his energy level was thoroughly depleted, she found some new and exciting way to revitalize him. Dear sweet heaven! He never thought a woman could be as exciting as Kate.

The next morning, Kate gathered up her few belongings and began stuffing them into her valise. The bed was in terrible disarray; the sheets were rumpled, the pillows lay on the floor, and the thin wool blanket had somehow managed to end up hanging from the cornice above the window.

She smiled to herself, feeling as if she were in heaven. She tried to imagine how Mr. Sears would go about describing such a perfect night in his catalogue. *Oh, what adjectives he would use*, she thought. "Stupendous," she called out. "Extraordinary."

Jonas, who was buttoning his shirt, whirled about to face her. "What are you talking about?" He frowned. "You didn't come up with an idea for an invention while we were—"

He looked so offended by the idea, she couldn't help but laugh. "As if I could. I was just trying out some advertisement ideas."

She tossed her linen nightgown into the valise, hating the shadow of worry that spoiled her happiness. They had barely been able to scrape up enough money between the two of them for train fare back to Hogs Head.

Kate tucked the last of her belongings into her valise and stared down at the pitiful scant coins on the bureau. "What are we going to do? I already owe money to Uncle Barney and Aunt Hattie. I can't possibly ask them for more."

"I wouldn't want you to." Jonas sat on the bottom of the bed to put his shoes on. "Don't worry. I'll get a job. I was born and raised on a farm. I know how to handle animals and plant crops. I'll hire myself out as a farm laborer if need be, though I doubt it will come to that."

"You hate farming, Jonas."

"It's not farming I hate so much as the manual labor. Besides, I have other ideas. You know that problem I told you about with tractor wheels? I thought of a way to make a chain of wheels that would glide right over muddy land."

"You what?" she squealed, placing her hands at her waist. "You thought of an idea while we were—"

"Of course not," he assured her. "I thought of this idea at Hogs Head Creek. I missed you so much I couldn't stand it, so I went to the place where we'd had our Fourth of July picnic, and as I sat there feeling sorry for myself, I happened to notice this little caterpillar. Just like that, the idea came to me."

His eyes grew smoky with desire as he slipped his arms around her. "I can't think of anything when you're in my arms except how much I love you and what a lucky man I am."

She softened to his touch. "That's exactly how I feel," she murmured dreamily.

His hands on her waist, he lifted her off the floor. "We'll work out our financial difficulties. I promise you."

"Oh, Jonas." Her feet in midair, she stared down at his handsome and endearing face, afraid she might wake up and find herself dreaming. "Are you sure you want to marry me?"

He looked incredulous. He set her on the floor. "How can you possibly doubt me after the night I spent proving my love to you?"

Something wonderful and warm stirred inside her. "I don't doubt your love, Jonas, and I promise you, I never will again. Just as I hope you never doubt mine. But if you didn't have a wife to support, you could better concentrate on your inventions."

He resisted the idea, even as he loved her for having suggested it. "I'd much rather concentrate on a wife," he said, running his hands down the length of her. "And a child."

Kate shook her head. "I don't know, Jonas. We can't even afford fare home and you're talking about having a baby."

"Not a baby," he said. "At least not yet. I was talking about Jimmy."

"Jimmy?" She looked surprised. "You don't have to worry about Jimmy. Mr. Bexler has offered to adopt him."

Jonas studied her face. "Is that what you want? For Jimmy to go and live with Mr. Bexler?"

"Of course. I mean, I want what's best for Jimmy. What kind of person would I be not to want what's best for him?" Oh, but how she was going to miss him. Already missed him. Chastising herself for putting her own needs before Jimmy's, she swallowed back the lump in her throat. "Letting Jimmy live with the Bexlers would be in his best interests. I know nothing about being a mother. I'd make a terrible mother, Jonas."

Jonas kissed her on the nose. "Why don't we adopt him, Kate? You and me. I know we could be good parents."

The idea was appealing, but not very practical. "Haven't you heard one word I've said? I'd be a terrible mother. Besides, I couldn't ask you to take responsibility for a child. It wouldn't be fair. I mean, it's hard enough that you're going to take on the responsibility of a wife and—"

He touched his finger to her lips. "Nothing would give me more pleasure than to be your husband . . . and Jimmy's father."

Her eyes grew liquid. "Even now? With no means of support?"

"I'll find a way to support my family, Kate. Don't you worry about that."

"But what about me? I don't know the first thing about children. I'm more interested in teaching him about electricity than good manners. What kind of mother is that?"

His hands at her waist, he squeezed her tight. "I have it on good authority that you're the bestest ma in the whole wide world."

"You what?"

"Those were Jimmy's words exactly."

Kate stared at him in disbelief. "Jimmy . . . Jimmy said that?"

Jonas nodded, and thinking she was going to cry again, she pulled out of his arms and turned away. "What . . . what does he know? He's only a child. I mean . . ." She whirled about to face Jonas, her eyes shimmering with tears. "Oh, Jonas. Do you think it's possible to learn to be a good mother?"

"I think you're already a good mother." He ran his lips along her neck. "Now, what was that idea you had earlier about making love on the fire escape?"

They arrived in Hogs Head late the following morning.

"Are you all right?" Kate asked, watching Jonas limp back and forth along the platform at the train station. He had fallen down the fire escape and bruised his leg. The long hours on the train had made his sore muscles stiff. "I can go and fetch the horse and wagon if you like."

"I can walk," he moaned, rubbing his injured thigh. "You and your bright ideas."

Kate gave him a sympathetic look. "I'm sorry, Jonas. But you have to admit, it was rather interesting."

A slow grin inched across his face. *Interesting* was hardly the word for it. He could hardly wait to see what that inventive mind of hers dreamed up next.

The sight that greeted them upon arriving at Aunt Hattie's General Store stopped them in their tracks.

"What the . . ." Jonas exclaimed. He and Kate stared at each other and then turned back to gaze at the bags of mail that were stacked high on the front porch of the store.

A narrow pathway had been left between the canvas mailbags, barely wide enough to allow customers to enter the store sideways. The door stood ajar, propped open with still more mailbags.

Upon spotting Kate, Aunt Hattie almost fell off the ladder where she was busily arranging goods on the top shelf. "Well, Lordy be! Jimmy, look who's here."

Jimmy grinned happily from his perch on a stool behind the counter.

Aunt Hattie hurried down the ladder. "I didn't expect you back so soon. Barney, come quickly. See who's here."

Kate gave Jimmy a hug. "You're looking better. And ... what's this?" She held up a new wooden crutch that had a padded armrest.

"Uncle Barney made those for me. They don't hurt my arms so much when I walk."

"That's wonderful," Kate said. "I guess inventors run in the family, don't they?"

"Aunt Hattie said that since I'm going to be properly adopted, I have to stop hiding in my room."

"You're going to be adopted?" Kate turned to her aunt. "Has Mr. Bexler been back?"

Aunt Hattie adjusted her hearing aid and appeared not to have heard Kate's question. "Does this mean you and Jonas have resolved your problems?"

Kate exchanged a look with Jonas. "Not exactly all our problems, Aunt Hattie. But we are going to get married."

Aunt Hattie folded her arms across her chest. She looked so pleased with herself, Kate suspected something was afoot.

"Aunt Hattie, what have you been up to?"

Aunt Hattie looked the soul of innocence. "Why, Kate, whatever makes you think I've been up to anything?"

"Then suppose you tell me about Mr. Bexler."

Uncle Barney walked from the back of the store and dropped two more bags of mail onto the floor. He grinned at his niece. "So how was your trip to New York?"

Kate and Jonas exchanged smiles. "It was wonderful," Kate said. "Jonas and I are getting married."

"And I'm going to live with them!" Jimmy declared.

Kate turned to Jimmy in surprise. "Wait a minute. I thought you said . . ." She turned to face her aunt. "Aunt Hattie? What did you tell Mr. Bexler?"

"I told him he'd get Jimmy over my dead body."

"You didn't!"

Jimmy beamed. "Aunt Hattie said that you and Jonas . . . eh, Mr. Hunter . . . were going to 'fficially adopt me."

"Oh, she did, did she? I wonder how Aunt Hattie would know that."

Jimmy looked worried. He glanced from Kate to Jonas and then back to Kate. "It's true, isn't it?"

"Absolutely," Kate said, lifting him in her arms. "That is, if you want me to be your mother."

Jimmy let out a yelp of happiness and wrapped his arms around her neck. "You're the bestest ma in the whole wide world."

"What a wedding we're going to have," Aunt Hattie declared, dragging a bolt of Chantilly lace down from a shelf.

Kate stared at the delicate floral design. "It's beautiful. But where did it come from?"

"From France, of course. I ordered it special for your wedding."

"But . . . that would have taken weeks to arrive."

"You're darn tooting it took weeks. It's a good thing I ordered it the very day Jonas first came into my store." Aunt Hattie gave Jonas a mischievous grin. "I figured the real reason you came in was because you were interested in Kate."

Jonas frowned in puzzlement. "How in the world

did you figure that? I never even mentioned Kate's name."

Aunt Hattie shrugged. "No, but I saw you down at the train station watching her. Then when you came into the shop to buy cigars and didn't even sniff them . . . well, it didn't take no genius to guess you didn't smoke . . . I just put two and two together."

Jonas chuckled. "I always knew you were a smart woman, Aunt Hattie."

"Can I be in the wedding?" Jimmy asked.

"Of course," Jonas said. "You can be our best man."

"I'm too young to be a best man," Jimmy said. "Can I be the best boy?"

Kate pressed her cheek against his. "You're already the best boy."

Aunt Hattie was busily checking her pearl button supply. "What did I tell you, Jimmy? Didn't I say this was going to be the best wedding ever?"

"You had no way of knowing for certain there was going to be a wedding," Kate said. "I didn't even know myself until yesterday."

"Some things are just meant to be," Aunt Hattie said stubbornly.

Kate pushed a bag of mail out of the way. "What is all this?"

Aunt Hattie's face beamed. "I decided to give Mr. Sears some competition."

"Mr. Sears?" Kate handed Jimmy over to Jonas, then turned to face her aunt. She never thought she'd hear the day her aunt got his name right. "What do you mean, competition? Aunt Hattie . . . now what have you done?"

Aunt Hattie shoved a small pamphlet into Kate's hands. "I had Quincy over at the newspaper print me up some catalogues and I asked everyone I know to give me a list of their friends and relatives all over the country. I then mailed out my own catalogue."

Aunt Hattie's catalogue was nothing more than a one-page pamphlet featuring Jonas's security hearing facilitator. A picture of the hearing aid was included, along with a glowing description. The generous use of adjectives and exaggerated praises made even the Sears, Roebuck mail-order catalogue seem modest in comparison. The back page was covered with complimentary testimony from some of Jonas's most devoted users.

"I don't understand, Aunt Hattie. You only offer one piece of merchandise."

"I know. I offered the one thing that can't be bought in the Sears, Roebuck catalogue."

"But ... but ..." Kate stared in amazement at the stacks of mailbags. "That means that all these bags contain orders for Jonas's hearing aids."

Aunt Hattie nodded. "Isn't that wonderful? It never occurred to me there were so many people who were hard of hearing."

Jonas slid Jimmy onto a stool and immediately set to work calculating production costs per thousand units. "It never occurred to me, either." He studied the figures he'd jotted down on his writing tablet and shook his head in disbelief. He stood to make a handsome profit. Tucking the tablet into his pocket, he gave Aunt Hattie a big hug. "You're a genius!" He limped to the counter, rolled up his sleeves, and grabbed a mailbag. "Come on, Kate. We've got work to do."

It took the five of them, including Jimmy, nearly two days to open the mail and tally up the count.

By the afternoon of the third day, Jonas and Aunt Hattie had placed the order for supplies needed to make the hearing devices. "I'll have to hire help," Jonas announced, checking his calculations. "And I need to make an application for a patent."

Tucking his writing tablet into his pocket, he grabbed Kate by the waist and whirled her about the store.

"We're going to be rich, Kate! Rich! We'll have enough money to pay your aunt and uncle everything you owe them. You can even build them a new house if you want to and there'll still be enough money left over to hire help for my parents' farm. Then we can build a home of our own—" Aware, suddenly, of the concerned look on Jimmy's face, Jonas picked the boy up and jostled him in his arms. "A home with lots of bedrooms."

"One for me, too?" Jimmy asked.

"Well, I don't know. An inventor like you might need two rooms. One to sleep in and one to work in. What do you say, Kate?"

"And maybe even a room to do your schoolwork in," Kate said.

Jimmy wrinkled his nose. "Do I hafta go to school?"

"You most certainly do," Kate said. She smiled up at Jonas, unable to believe her good fortune. "I'm so happy," she whispered. "I never thought I could be so happy."

"I'm happy too!" Jimmy declared. "Even if I do hafta go to school."

"And well you should be, young man," Aunt Hattie said.

Holding Jimmy in his arm, Jonas lifted his free hand to Kate's cheek and whispered in her ear. "Do you think I can entice you with a proposition?"

The seductive tone of his voice made her heart skip a beat. The love shining from his eyes made her feel faint with happiness. "Anything is possible," she whispered back.

"How would you feel about helping me make nine thousand three hundred and fifty-seven facilitators?"

She squeezed his hand tight, her eyes blurring with tears of love and joy. "Nothing would make me happier."